I0720595

Marian Rizzo

Marian Rizzo gives her readers a realistic look at the life of a young minister and his family in this exciting novel. [Presence in the Pew] is gripping, convincing, and gives a true life account of a packed narrative. "Perceptive, vivid, and engaging" fits into this novel. A truly astonishing survival tale of ministry and marriage will keep you from putting this book down.

Pastor Wayne King
48 years of pastoral ministry and church planting

If you are looking for a spine-tingling novel that touches on the reality of spiritual warfare in the church today pick this up! Great warnings of dabbling in the darkness are arrayed against the faithful preaching of the gospel. Don't miss this one.

Art Ayris
Kingstone Studios

Once again Marian Rizzo shares with us a Suspense/Thriller. *Presence in the Pew* is one that you will say "I'll just read one more chapter tonight."

Dr. B. H. Barrs
Church Planter/Pastor

Truth be told, I am not a novel guy. But I have to admit, Marian Rizzo's *In Search of the Beloved* drew me in from the first page. I love how she weaved her characters in and out of the search for the Apostle John. Great read.

Dr. Woodrow Kroll
Creator of *The HELIOS Project*

(*In Search of Felicity*) gives voice to those of us who find inspiration and insight into our own lives through great works of literature. Rizzo's work will resonate with Rawlings fans and even those who will take up her books for the first time.

Florence M. Turcotte
literary manuscripts archivist
George A. Smathers Libraries
University of Florida, Gainesville

Marian Rizzo explores the parallels a young writer uncovers between her own life and that of Marjorie Kinnan Rawlings, whose own focus on rural Florida cracker life earned her a Pulitzer Prize. As she uncovers layer upon layer of Marjorie's unconventional lifestyle, she discovers those parallels may also hold the key to her own social angst in a satisfying climax that will leave you yearning for more.

Emory R. Schley,
Star-Banner columnist for 30-plus years

The invisible world of the angelic and demonic clearly affects our lives, and Marian Rizzo has woven her wonderful story around these realities. I can say this is my favorite of all she has written.

Jennifer Odom, Author of
The *Black* Series

Once again, Marian Rizzo captures the heart of her readers. In this second book in her, "In Search Of" series, Rizzo beautifully interweaves the life of Pulitzer Prize winning author, Marjorie Kinnan Rawlings, with the continuing tender love story of Julie Peters and Mark Bensen. The result is pure pleasure.

Delores Kight, co-author, *Manny the Lamb*

For the reader interested in a Florida of years gone by and Pulitzer Prize winner Marjorie Kinnan Rawlings specifically, this is a must-read story. Often spiritual but never preaching, Ms. Rizzo deftly handles the juxtapositional narrative from early 20th-century Cracker life to the contemporary lifestyle and the complications her characters encounter. Historically speaking, her book is spot-on and readers will find the story not only a delight to read, but insightful as well.

Fred Mullen
actor/director/artist

Marian Rizzo is a gifted storyteller, whether it be for news reporting or fiction. She has a keen eye and ear for the intricacies of a story, which translates into very powerful narratives. Marian can turn the mundane into the magnificent through the masterful weaving of character, context, and scene-setting.

Susan Smiley-Height
Longtime journalist and editor in the newspaper industry

Also By

Marian Rizzo

Angela's Treasures
Muldovah
In Search of the Beloved
In Search of Felicity
O Holy Night
Silver Springs

Presence in the Pew

Presence in the Pew

a novel of suspence

Marian Rizzo

WordCrafts Press

Ten years. Ten years and Mitch Calloway was ready to move on. From the time he graduated from seminary he'd been youth director at the White Hills Bible megachurch in a suburb of Indianapolis. Although he enjoyed working with the teens, he yearned for a church of his own.

So with his pastor's blessing, Mitch sent out applications to several smaller congregations, most of them located in Massachusetts where he grew up.

"You're smart to start small," Dr. Martin Samuels told him. "You can take a struggling little church and grow it up like we did at White Hills. I'll be happy to give you some pointers along the way." The older man rested a comforting hand on Mitch's shoulder. "I hate to lose you, Mitch, you've done such a good job with our youth. But go for it. I'll even write a letter of recommendation." His eyes crinkled at the corners like he was remembering. "I did the same thing when I was your age. Look at my ministry now. Eight thousand members and adding more every day."

Mitch spent the next two days scanning websites. He filled out applications, most of them online, followed by a few hand-written requests which he sent by snail mail. Almost immediately, rejections poured in. They covered a broad spectrum of kind refusals. He didn't have enough leadership experience. The position was filled. He could hire on as a youth minister, but that would have been a lateral move.

His confidence was at an all-time low when a response came in the mail from Mercy Fellowship, a small, historic church in the village of Shadow Glenn, thirty miles north of Boston. Inside was an airline ticket and an invitation to come for an interview. Mitch read the letter twice to make sure it was for real. Then he scrambled to his computer and pulled up a photo of a wood-framed country church, painted white with sky blue trim. It had a traditional steeple complete with belfry and a glittering cross on top. It reminded him of the little church he'd attended as a child.

"Look at this, Lydia," he called out.

His wife appeared in the doorway, a dish towel in her hand. The backlight from the kitchen created a halo around her slim figure. Though she'd given birth to two sons, she'd shed the extra pounds and had eased back into her size 6 dresses. He gazed at her with admiration, still amazed that she hadn't run off with Barry Andrews more than ten years ago.

Lydia's first boyfriend was about to enter law school. Mitch had plans to go to seminary. The two professions were miles apart financially and in the eyes of society. Not only that but Barry Andrews had a "Joe College" look—blond hair, sharp blue eyes, athletic physique—while Mitch faded into the group of average built guys, with unruly brown hair and hazel eyes. For some reason beyond his understanding, Lydia had chosen him.

Mitch allowed himself a smug little snicker and beckoned his wife close with a sweep of his hand. She stepped toward him, and the overhead light painted streaks of gold on her sable waves. Her dark eyes glistened like she was expecting a surprise.

He pointed at the monitor. "What do you think? It's like taking a step back in time, isn't it?"

She leaned over his shoulder, and he caught the aroma of Dawn dish soap mixed with apple-scented perfume—two scents that characterized his homemaker wife. Nothing fruity or seductive, simply the wholesome ambiance she usually brought into a room.

"It's charming." Even her voice seemed to be smiling. "It makes me think of horse-drawn carriages, women in Victorian dresses, and men in cutaway coats."

He chuckled at how easy it was to draw Lydia into the past. At times he wondered if she'd been born in the wrong century. Though they could afford store-bought furniture, she'd decorated their home with thrift store items she could refinish. She stitched little samplers and hung them on the walls, made curtains for all the rooms, and took classes in decoupage and ceramics, adding more creative touches wherever a dark corner needed brightening.

He slid his hand around her waist. "How do you feel about being the first lady of this little church?" He glanced at her face, youthfully aglow in the bright light of the monitor.

Her eyebrows shot up. "Really? Tell me more."

"Well, there's only one paragraph." He turned back to the screen. "It says here, the church is nearly 150 years old. It has its original framework, plus the same pews, hardwood floors, and wooden altar railings. Otherwise, it's been modernized with electric lights, air conditioning, and a separate wing for a fellowship hall, classrooms, and indoor bathrooms. It has a small congregation—about 200." He looked at her again, fearing the low number might discourage her. "So, what do you think?" he said, cautiously.

She wrinkled her nose. "Hmmm. Sounds small."

"Small is good, for a start."

He held his breath.

She winked at him, then said, "Like Ruth said to Naomi, 'Wherever you go, I'll go.' But tell me, dear leader, exactly where *are* we going?"

Mitch chuckled. "You're gonna love this. It's in a quaint, New England town named Shadow Glenn, population 5,278."

Lydia straightened, and a smile spread across her face. "Did you send an application?" The sparkle returned to her eyes, or perhaps it never left.

"I did." He nodded and held up the letter. "They want me to come for an interview."

Lydia's eyes flashed with excitement. "Terrific!" Her voice rose an octave. "When do they want you there? Will the boys and I go with you? What should I wear? I might need to buy—"

"Hold on, honey. I'll have to go up there alone for the interview."

Disappointment swept away her smile.

"Don't worry. If things go well, you can come with me next time."

She nodded and backed out of his grasp. "If you say so."

"This is the way it's done, my dear. I'm going up there this Friday. I don't want to waste any time. Another candidate might beat me to it. And, Lydia, I don't know what it is, but when I look at this photo, I feel drawn to this little church—like I belong there."

She tilted her head. Skepticism narrowed her eyes. "What makes you so sure?"

"I don't know." He shrugged. "This was my first positive response. None of the other churches expressed an interest in me. Doesn't it sound like it's God's will, like He wants us to go to Shadow Glenn?"

He swiveled his chair away from the desk and pulled Lydia onto his lap. She leaned over his shoulder for another look at the screen. A fluff of her hair tickled his neck and brought a smile to his lips. She was his soul mate, the gentler side of their union, the other half of the puzzle. He couldn't imagine going anywhere without her.

Lydia nodded slowly, thoughtfully. "I can picture us living there. New England has a ton of antique shops and second-hand stores. And you know how much I love rooting around in people's attics." She lurched back. "Maybe the house we move into will have an attic. Or a basement."

He stroked her back. "Yep. You'll be in your element, my dear."

She planted a kiss on his cheek. Here she was, the daughter of a wealthy automobile magnate, and she'd given up a life of ease to be married to an assistant preacher. She could have finished college. Could have been dealing in antiques by now or working in a museum. Could have married Barry Andrews. Instead, she'd walked away from a mansion in a high-class neighborhood and settled for a simple home in the suburbs. An attic or a basement to root around in? To Lydia, it would be heaven.

As for Mitch, he'd already begun to have visions of helping the tiny congregation grow into a huge mega-church, like the one he was about to leave. Two hundred members? By implementing Martin Samuels' expansion techniques, he could draw thousands to the flailing little church. Sure, he'd probably have to take a cut in pay in the beginning. But if he could build up the little church the way he hoped, his salary also would climb and he'd be able to provide well for his family.

He tilted his head and smiled at his wife. "Hopefully, it's not too late for me to prove myself to your father."

She tossed her head and laughed. "You haven't heard me complain, have you?"

"Not once, but your dad—"

"Never mind him." Her brown eyes softened. "I'm ready to move on, if you are."

"What about Matthew and Luke?" he said, locking eyes with her. "Do you think they'll be able to adjust to such a move? I mean, what about their friends?"

She gazed wide-eyed at him. "Are you kidding me? Our boys will *love* New England. There's so much to do up there, close to Boston. It's where our nation was born." She slid off his lap and spun in a circle. "Think about it, Mitch—the aquarium, the museum of science, the Red Sox, the Boston Pops, Cape Cod. What a tremendous opportunity for our boys." She stopped in front of him. "And for us." Her smile held a message of encouragement. "You're 32 years old, Mitch. It's time you led your own church."

Mitch looked again at the photo of the little white church and imagined his sons playing catch with other kids on the front lawn, his wife in her Sunday best chatting with the ladies in the congregation, a potluck dinner on the grounds, and himself, perched on the top step, shaking hands with members of his flock.

"Okay," he said with a satisfied nod. "I'll go to Shadow Glenn on Friday, and we'll see what happens."

2

Friday

A two-hour plane trip and another two hours in a rental car brought Mitch face-to-face with the little church on First Street. A wave of disappointment swept over him. The building looked nothing like the pristine chapel he'd discovered on the internet. The outside had fallen to disrepair. Instead of pure white siding, the boards were weathered to a dull gray. The blue trim had faded too. The front steps and sidewalk were cracked and pitted, and the landscaping brought to mind an unkempt graveyard. Flowers and shrubbery had turned into sticks. He huffed out a sigh. It was like a huge, celestial bait-n-switch.

His hopes deflating like a squeezed balloon, he trudged up the front steps. Two men in dark funeral-style suits greeted him inside the front door. They didn't smile, merely ran their eyes over him from head to toe, leaving him uncomfortably aware of his light blue summer jacket and striped tie, perhaps a little too casual for what already threatened to be a solemn visit.

They offered him a limp handshake and ushered him through a side door into what appeared to be the church office.

He stepped inside, and his frown deepened. The tiny room literally cried out for help. Meager furnishings lay in a blanket of dust and cobwebs. The desktop had disappeared beneath a scattering of notebooks, a broken reading lamp, several tattered Bibles, pens and pencils, and a dinosaur of a computer.

More books and papers lay strewn about the room on side tables, on overstuffed chairs, and even on the floor. At the far end, a wall of shelves sagged under the weight of more Bibles, study guides, research materials, and a ton of magazines. A gray steel file cabinet vomited multiple tattered notebooks and bindings, each one with papers spilling out the tops.

Mitch choked back his revulsion. If this was how the board of deacons let the office go, what kind of nurturing had they given the church? And what about their last pastor? Hadn't he cared enough to straighten things up? For that matter, how long had it been since anyone even held the position?

Fortunately, he didn't have to dirty his suit on the dusty old sofa. Several metal folding chairs were placed in a semi-circle, with one lone chair positioned across from the others. The arrangement looked more like the setting for a police interrogation instead of a friendly interview. His throat tightened.

Three more men, also wearing dark suits, filed in. Their somber expressions sent a chill through him. At the moment, they looked less like a gathering of elders and more like a firing squad, but without the guns.

Doubts surfaced. Perhaps he'd acted too quickly. Maybe he should have waited in case more offers came in. But he'd followed what he thought was God's will. He'd come to Boston, and now he faced a gathering of stone-faced judges.

He took a deep breath and settled into the solitary chair. Without warning, he drifted back to his childhood. Instead of a grown man seeking employment, he'd become a schoolboy in the principal's office. His heart pounded like it did years ago when he faced punishment for shooting spitballs in class.

He shook off the sensation and focused on the five men who were taking the seats in front of him. Four of them appeared to be in their early 40s. They shared the same nondescript appearance—neatly combed brown hair, clean-shaved, pale skin like they hadn't seen sunshine in months—and they were close to the same height and weight—about 5-foot 10-inches and 180 pounds, give or take a few. It was like they'd been cloned by some heavenly eugenics machine.

The fifth guy stood out among the rest. He was old, maybe creeping up on 100. The few tufts of hair on his head were pure white. Deep creases etched his forehead and cheeks, and his neck hung in folds like the typical turkey wattle of the elderly. He was so thin he practically swam inside his oversized suit-coat. He limped to the chair closest to Mitch and settled into it with a grunt.

Mitch's lips had gone dry. Could he be one more candidate in a long line of rejections? He ran his tongue over his lips and tried to swallow. He was about to ask for a drink of water but reconsidered after taking a second look around the moldy little office. There was no telling where it would come from.

After a few uncomfortable seconds passed, one of them spoke. First thing, Mitch learned their names. Pete, Larry, George, and John—like a British rock group. Unlike the others who used only their first names, the elderly fellow gave his full name—Elijah Garby.

Immediately, the four younger gentlemen sprang into action and spent the first half-hour boasting about Shadow Glenn's family-friendly atmosphere. Mitch suppressed a chuckle. So far, he'd seen none of that. These men hadn't even cracked a smile.

They continued to market their town—its proximity to Boston, the Atlantic Ocean, Nova Scotia, and a plethora of ski resorts to the north. As though snapping invisible suspenders, they talked about how the townspeople worked hard to maintain Shadow Glenn's old-world charm, how talented craftsmen used their skills to restore crumbling buildings, including the library, several homes in the historic district, and, of course, the church.

Mitch snickered to himself. Had he missed something? What had they done to enhance this church?

"And by the way," George interjected. "Mercy Fellowship will be celebrating its sesquicentennial in November. Now, that's a big deal." The guy almost smiled.

The four of them mumbled words of praise, mostly to each other. They didn't once mention the pastor's responsibilities, nor did they ask Mitch a single question. Finally, with raised eyebrows, they turned their attention to the old man.

Elijah Garby's chin had been resting on the top button of his shirt. A drop of moisture clung to the corner of his mouth.

John leaned closer to the old guy and prodded his shoulder. "Elijah, it's time."

Garby jerked to attention, stroked the corners of his mouth, and gazed at Mitch with an eye-piercing scrutiny that could bring Dirty Harry to his knees.

"Okay," the old man grunted. "Let's get started."

3

As though on cue, the other deacons faded into the background and dropped into noticeable silence. Like spectators at a tennis match, their eyes darted back and forth between Elijah and Mitch. It became obvious that pretty much every decision made at Mercy Fellowship depended on the whims of this old man.

With a razor sharp tongue, Elijah pelted Mitch with one question after another.

"When did you turn your life over to Jesus?"

Mitch didn't hesitate. "When I was fifteen."

"What were the circumstances?"

"I went forward in my church on the second night of a revival."

Garby's eyes narrowed. "When did you commit to serving in ministry?"

"The same night."

The old man's eyebrows went up with interest. "The same night?"

Mitch nodded.

"Fine," Garby growled. "But what sort of formal education have you had?"

Mitch straightened in his seat. He wasn't about to let the old guy intimidate him. He cleared his throat. "As I noted in my resume, I attended Anderson University, where I majored in hermeneutics and minored in eschatology."

"And then?"

"Well, after graduation, I landed a position as a youth

minister at White Hills Bible Church in the suburbs of Indianapolis. I've been there ever since. Last count, there were 960 students in my youth group, and I also oversee the elementary program." Mitch smugly nodded, mentally noting his youth congregation was five times the size of this pathetic church's entire membership. A surge of confidence flowed through him.

Garby snorted. Mitch hoped it was a sign of approval.

"That's all well and good," Garby said, his steel gray eyes glued to Mitch's face. "But tell us, what makes you think you're fit to serve in this church, *Mister* Calloway?"

Mister? Mitch gulped down the offence. He couldn't let the old crank send him running back home, although at this point he didn't know if he still wanted the job. He took a deep breath.

"Well, *Mister* Garby," Mitch said in return. "I want to assure you, I'm qualified for this position. I'm well-educated—graduated at the top of my class. I have ten years' experience in church work. I didn't only minister to young people. I also interacted with their parents. Whenever my pastor took ill or went on vacation, I filled in at the pulpit. I visited the sick, conducted weddings, and oversaw funerals. I pretty much did everything a pastor does, but without the title." He hesitated, then added, "Or the salary."

"So you're expecting to go from a modern, highfalutin' congregation to a humble, little country church?" Garby didn't wait for an answer. "Mind you, most of our folks are descendants of the original members who first gathered in a barn more than a century ago. Our people take pride in their heritage. Not like those new-fangled churches with their guitars and drums makin' a whole lotta noise on Sunday mornings. These folks are die-hard Puritans. They won't take kindly to some young maverick comin' in here and changin' everything. You need to know that."

A nervous twitching turned Mitch's stomach. He poised for the next attack.

"Tell us, young man, what plans might you have for Mercy Fellowship?" Garby's tone was a little gentler this time, his eyes less piercing.

Mitch sought hard for an answer. *What would Jesus do? What would Jesus say?*

He leaned toward the old man. "To be honest, Mister Garby, I've come here with no prideful expectations. I want to serve, not *be* served. I want to find out what the people need, what I can do to help them maintain their walk with the Lord, and how I can encourage them to live out their faith at home and in the community. I've always said, real church service begins when you go *out* of the building, not when you *enter* it."

Silence.

"I–I hope to fit in quite well," he went on, though he needed to summon a fresh burst of enthusiasm. "I grew up in a small church, and I prefer a homey atmosphere where everyone knows everyone else. Large congregations often miss out on such intimacy. A church like Mercy Fellowship sounds like a breath of fresh air."

He stopped himself. Why was he trying to impress the guy? Then he thought of Lydia and how her face lit up at the prospect of moving to New England. For her sake he couldn't give up. Not yet.

"I welcome the opportunity to live in a historical setting," he continued. "My wife has a strong affinity for our nation's history. Lydia's a collector of sorts, and I know she's going to love it here."

He sat back and waited, tried to collect his thoughts, tried to decide if this interrogation was worth the effort.

Garby eyed him with what appeared to be suspicion. "And how does your wife assist in your ministry?"

Mitch's mind scrambled over the last ten years. He couldn't think of a single time when Lydia *had* assisted him. Not physically. He frowned. She'd sat beside him in the pew. She'd listened to his sermons before he gave them, opened their home to the youth. Served them cookies and hot chocolate. Period. She hadn't taught Sunday school or worked in the nursery. Nor had she gotten involved with the women's programs. She was just... there.

He blinked away his doubts. "Lydia's been supportive from the start." Was he trying to convince himself? "She grew up in a Christian home. She's been in church all of her life. She knows what it takes to lead a ministry like this."

Elijah's steel gray eyes darkened. "Having godly parents doesn't automatically make someone a Christian," he challenged. "Neither does sitting in a pew."

"That's true, Mister Garby. But, I'm confident Lydia will fit in quite well here." He paused and looked at his hands, clenched together on his lap. He released his fingers and searched his brain for something positive. "My wife will want to get together with the other ladies, maybe ask them about their ancestors. She keeps a journal about such things."

"You have kids?" Garby growled.

Mitch nodded. "Yes, Matthew is eight, and Luke recently turned five. They're good little boys, don't give me a minute's trouble."

The old deacon snorted, or it sounded like he had. Perhaps he'd simply cleared the back of his nose. In any case, he didn't smile. His lined face gave Mitch no clue what he might be thinking, no indication whether the guy might vote for him or against him. Mitch wished he'd paid more attention in his psychology classes, particularly the sessions dealing with the elderly. He swallowed hard and waited for the next attack. It came immediately.

Garby leaned toward him so close Mitch caught the minty scent of freshly cleaned dentures. "Other preachers came and went over the years," the old man grumbled. "Some didn't last more than a couple of months. They moved on. And up. We need to know, Mister Calloway, do you see Mercy Fellowship as a stepping stone—a temporary position until something better comes along—or can you make a sincere commitment to this work?"

Garby's mental acuity astounded Mitch. There was no sign of the usual tremor found in the voices of people his age. He didn't hesitate or stammer or pause to search for the right word. He spoke glibly and with a confidence that denied his years.

Mitch needed to come up with an answer to satisfy the guy. He briefly regarded the other four. They sat there like statues.

He put all his attention on Garby. "When I start a project, I see it through to the end. I may procrastinate at times, but I'm not a quitter. Such a position poses a few challenges for a young minister like myself. But I trust you and your board will guide me and check me and help me do the best job I can." He passed his eyes over the other four, looking for some sort of response. Had the lines on their foreheads softened? Were their eyes more trusting? Was that a smile on George's lips?

Garby sat back and exchanged glances with the other board members. Like before, they raised their eyebrows, the first sign of life in them since the old man started speaking. He turned to Mitch, his steel gray eyes aflame.

"Tell me this, young man, how do you feel about demonic activity? Do you think it's a real threat? Or fantasy?"

The question came out of nowhere. Mitch thought it a strange thing to ask a candidate at a job interview. He narrowed his eyes. "What do you mean?"

"I mean, have you ever dealt with the supernatural? Do you believe spiritual warfare is taking place all around us?" Garby waved his hand in the air as if he actually saw angels. "Do you believe in another realm, even though you can't see it?"

Mitch cleared his throat again. "Well, I've never conducted an exorcism, if that's what you're asking. But of course, a spiritual evil exists. The Bible teaches about wickedness in high places—"

"Yes, but what have *you* personally experienced with such things?"

He shook his head nervously. "Well, I *do* believe Satan messes with our lives and sometimes hurts our testimony. Though he can't take away our salvation, he works hard to destroy our witness and sometimes succeeds."

Garby huffed impatiently. "I need to know if you think you have the fortitude to withstand a supernatural attack if one comes. Even if it involves your family."

A feeling of unease slithered down Mitch's spine. "I don't know what you're driving at, Mister Garby."

"Young man, what I'm asking you is, are you prepared to face a battle with the devil himself, if necessary?"

Though Mitch had experienced doubts throughout the

interview, this questioning posed a whole different challenge. He'd been thinking he could salvage this little church, but Garby's last remark left him stunned. He chewed his bottom lip and glanced toward the door.

He thought back to the day when, at 15, he'd walked forward inside his hometown church and committed his life to Christ. Missionaries went off to all parts of the world, never knowing what awaited them, but confident God was going with them and would guide and protect them. He'd often dreamed of being one of those forward-looking servants of God, stepping ahead with confidence.

He lifted his chin and drew on a boldness that surprised even him.

"Mister Garby, I'm in the word of God daily. I pray for His help in my home and in my church and in my community. With God's strength I will be able to face every challenge, spiritual and otherwise. Like I said, I'm not a quitter. I don't run away when the going gets tough. I hope that satisfies you."

He thought he caught the hint of a smile on Garby's lips. Several uncomfortable seconds passed. The other deacons said nothing. Their arms were crossed, and their eyes were on Garby. It was as if they were communicating with him without uttering a single word.

Mitch's discomfort mounted. Maybe God hadn't called him there, after all. Maybe he didn't want this job. He started to rise, when Garby struggled to his feet and hobbled toward him.

"I'm satisfied," the old man said with a nod. "I'm sure I speak for the rest of the board by inviting you to return next weekend and address our people."

Mitch nodded weakly.

The other four closed in on him. For the first time since

they'd met, they each managed a semblance of a smile. They gave him pats on the back and limp handshakes, then they filed out of the office, leaving Mitch and Elijah standing face-to-face—alone.

Garby handed him an envelope. "Bring your family next weekend. We'll want to meet them. And make sure you put together a worthy message. None of those sweet-talking, butter-em-up sermons that turn a person's stomach. Give us something real." The old man poked Mitch's chest. "From the heart," he said.

Mitch stood in a swirl of confusion, unsure of what had happened in that little office. He'd been on the verge of walking out several times, and now he was going to come back with his family and preach to the congregation.

He hesitated for a moment, then he shook the old man's outstretched hand. "Thank you, sir. You won't be disappointed."

The old codger raised one eyebrow. "We'll see." With that, he turned his back on Mitch and shuffled out the door, leaving him standing there amidst a pile of books and debris, dusty furniture, and broken-down office machines.

"**I**t went well," Mitch told Lydia over dinner that night. "I think I impressed them—well, all of them except for maybe Elijah Garby. The old geezer put me through a horrible grilling. In the end, though, he shook my hand and invited me back. I still don't know what to make of him. I guess I'll find out next weekend."

"Next weekend?" Lydia's brown eyes sparked with interest. "You're going back to Boston?" She raised her eyebrows. "Alone?"

Mitch gazed into his wife's hopeful face. Slowly and with dramatic effect, he slid an envelope from his pocket.

"They gave me plane tickets." He grinned. "For all four of us. You and the boys are going with me this time."

Lydia let out a squeal. "Really? Let me see those tickets." She reached across the table and grabbed the envelope out of his hand. She flipped through the contents and let out another squeal. Then she slid from her seat, skipped around the table to Mitch's side, and planted a kiss on his cheek. Mitch breathed deeply of his wife's excitement. If nothing else, the trip to Boston was worth the effect it was having on her.

She wasn't alone in her excitement. Young Matthew nearly fell out of his chair. "Yay! We're going to Boston." He looked at Mitch and frowned. "Where's Boston?" he said, softly.

"It's far away," Mitch explained. "We have to ride in an airplane to get there."

"Airplane!" Luke sprang to his feet, spread his arms, and sailed around the room. "Rrr-mm! Rrr-mm!"

Chuckling, Mitch beamed at his boys' response to his news, removing all doubt about whether they'd be able to adjust to such a move. Maybe a trip to Boston didn't promise the same kind of excitement a visit to Disney World might generate, but the two of them were reacting like it did. His heart throbbed with love for them, and he watched them enjoy the moment.

Though the two boys shared the same appetite for adventure, they were physically different. Matthew had his dad's sandy brown hair and hazel eyes, and a medium build. Luke was the exact image of his mother. Dark hair, eyes like ripe olives, and a small frame that attracted school bullies. *Hopefully, he'll go through a growth spurt one of these days*, Mitch thought.

Mitch turned his attention to Lydia. "It won't bother you to leave behind the friends you've made here, will it?"

She shrugged. "I knew this was temporary." She settled back in her chair and tilted her head, her forehead lined in disbelief. "Really, Mitch. You didn't expect to be here forever, did you?'

He shook his head. "No, not really."

She clutched the travel itinerary to her breast. "This is our ticket out of here."

He didn't want to give her false hope. "We'll find out for sure next weekend."

"Right," she said, but her eyes had glazed over, and he knew she'd already moved east.

"Will we stay in a hotel?" Matthew squeaked with delight. "Will we eat in a restaurant?"

"Yes and yes." Mitch nodded but was distracted by Luke's airplane routine.

The boy was circling the table for what must have been

the fourth or fifth time. As he flew past Lydia's chair, she reached out and gently grabbed his arm. "Okay, Mr. Pilot. Sit down and eat. Your dinner's getting cold."

The two boys squirmed into their chairs and started digging into their meatloaf with renewed enthusiasm. Now and then one of them—sometimes both—let out a little giggle.

Now that everyone had settled down, Mitch laid out the plan. "We'll fly to Boston on Friday, rent a car, and find a place to stay in Shadow Glenn." He looked from one to the other to make sure they were listening. "Then we'll drive back to Boston and do some sightseeing. Saturday's also a free day. We'll make a vacation out of it."

The boys shouted, "Yay!"

"Then," Mitch continued. "Sunday morning, I'll preach to the congregation."

Lydia was about to take a bite of meatloaf but stopped. "Don't you have to check in with the deacons?"

He nodded. "I'll phone them when we arrive, but it looks like they don't do things the traditional way." A flicker of doubt surfaced. He gave a one-shoulder shrug. "I guess we'll find out when we get there."

Lydia set down her fork and gazed out the window. He'd lost her now.

"Let's take it slow," Mitch cautioned. "We don't know anything for certain yet. Don't get your hopes up."

She inhaled deeply and smiled. "Oh, Mitch, this is a dream come true." It was like she hadn't heard a word he'd said. "I can't wait to start packing." Suddenly her smile faded and panic swept across her face. "I need to decide what to wear." She stared at Mitch. "What kind of a church is it? One of those stodgy, conservative types? Or did you find it to be more casual? Should I wear a dress? Or is a nice pants outfit okay? I don't want to offend anyone."

He snickered. "Settle down, woman. It's just a church service. Whatever you choose to wear will be fine. I don't expect they'll be going over you with a magnifying glass. Remember, we haven't been approved yet."

"All the more reason to make a good presentation." She flashed a smile at him. "Oh, Mitch. Have you forgotten what you said when you got their letter? You said it's the right move. You said God is calling us there. I feel it too." She settled back in her seat. "Think about it. Finally. Our own church. We'll make the decisions. We'll set the rules."

Mitch was puzzled by his wife's eagerness to pull up roots and move hundreds of miles away. What made her think Mercy Fellowship might be any different than White Hills? Except for the difference in size, the challenges were the same, but on a smaller scale. Both of them could keep on doing pretty much the same things they did at White Hills. The main difference being, he would be in charge and Lydia would join up with the ladies of the church.

Come to think of it, she hadn't made any lasting friendships at White Hills. She'd kept her distance from the different women's circles, didn't even claim to have a best friend. At least he didn't have to worry about her breaking any ties with people. She'd been somewhat of a loner during their entire ministry. Could he expect anything different when they got to Shadow Glenn?

He looked at her and tried to see inside those glistening brown eyes. "You've obviously made up your mind. Don't you at least want to take a look at the place? The house we'll be living in? The people?"

She smirked at him. "Come on, Mitch. Admit it. The wheels are turning. Didn't you already tell your youth group we'll probably be moving?"

He nodded. "I did. I wanted to prepare them in case something worked out. And I needed them to pray for us to make the right decision."

Without warning, moisture flooded to his eyes, and he remembered his last meeting with those kids.

"The guys rallied around me and said they'd miss me." His throat tightened with a rise of emotion. "Some of the girls cried, but they all wished us well. I'll tell you, Lydia, those kids want the best for us. They want me to succeed. But the truth is, I'm gonna miss them."

He used his napkin to wipe moisture from beneath his eyes. A vague unease stirred in a corner of his mind. It had started with his little chat with Elijah Garby and the old man's comment about spiritual warfare. Sure, spiritual oppression existed. But, in a sweet, little town like Shadow Glenn? The name alone evoked images of apple orchards and community fairs. And Mercy Fellowship hardly sounded like the calling card of a troubled church.

Mitch picked up his fork and toyed with the meatloaf on his plate. His mind shifted to his drive through Shadow Glenn.

"There are four churches, and Mercy Fellowship is the only one that can claim any historical significance." He recalled aloud. He took a bite of meat. "The other churches must have sprouted up over the last three or four decades and were slapped together according to whatever designs each congregation wanted. Mercy Fellowship stands out among the rest. You saw the picture, Lydia. Its steeple towers over every other building in town. I caught sight of it the moment I entered that little burg."

He purposely withheld his first impression. Hopefully, a little paint and a hammer and nails, maybe some nice plants, and the church will once again look like the computer image.

Lydia took a sip of lemonade. "Sounds nice."

His appetite returning, Mitch swallowed a mouthful of potatoes and dug in for another. He gazed at his boys. They were shoveling food in their mouths like two hungry puppies. Their eyes sparkled, and their cheeks had flushed to a rosy pink. They were still young enough to be able to make new friends in another city, and they hadn't yet plunged into any long-term school activities, like baseball or band practice.

Instantly, he did what he always did when he faced a decision that might affect his entire family. He clenched his teeth. The responsibility overwhelmed him. He'd been comfortable these many years at White Hills, often ignoring the inner promptings to move on. Now he'd taken the first step, and he didn't know if he could handle what lay ahead.

He scanned the happy faces around the table, and his mind eased.

"Come next weekend, we're going to Boston," he said, more to himself than to anyone else. But even as he said the words, Elijah Garby's remark about spiritual warfare sent another stab of anxiety into his core.

5

One week later

The following Friday morning brought a surge of activity to the Calloways' household. Lydia changed her outfit three times and paraded each one in front of Mitch. He nodded his approval over all three. In the end she settled on a simple gray dress with a matching jacket.

The boys ran back-and-forth from their bedroom, dumping clothes and toys on the living room sofa. Mitch sorted through the piles and chose several outfits for the trip. They could each bring one toy.

After a smooth flight into Boston's Logan International Airport, Mitch rented a compact car. As they drove away from the airfield, the scenery swept by in an ever-changing landscape of harbors and marinas, skyscrapers and department stores, tunnels and bridges, and finally, to a scattering of small towns with quiet thoroughfares, community parks, and brick sidewalks. From Interstate 93, they picked up a two-lane country road to the northeast.

Shadow Glenn lay off the beaten path, down a meandering lane, at the bottom of a valley, a stone's throw from historic Salem. Mitch guided the rental car along the village's central thoroughfare, appropriately labeled Main Street

"There's the spire," he said, pointing through the windshield. "See it, Lydia? Boys? That's Mercy Fellowship in the distance."

Lydia made a muffled comment and looked out the passenger window. Her head turned from side-to-side as they drove past mom-and-pop stores selling everything from toothbrushes to hardware. They passed an old-fashioned ice cream shop, a beauty salon, a bookstore, city hall, and a sprawling emporium that had Lydia swiveling in her seat.

Mitch chuckled. "Hang on, honey. You'll have plenty of time to root around in those stores. But, remember, we're gonna be living on my last paycheck."

Lydia breathed out her excitement. "I'm going to *love* it here. I can't wait to get settled. And Mitch, you'll make a fine pastor. You did a great job with the kids in your youth group. These people are a little older, that's all. You can handle them. And don't forget, we'll be able to celebrate the church's sesquicentennial—150 years. Now, *that's* historic."

Mitch turned a corner. The church's steeple loomed closer. His momentary elation crumbled under another wave of unease. He set his jaw, determined not to let his visit with the board discourage him. There was a moment when Elijah Garby's steel gray eyes nearly lifted Mitch out of his chair and out the door. Now he was getting ready to enter the lion's den again.

Lydia patted Mitch's knee. "Thank you for bringing us here, darling. I love this place already." A wisp of a smile tugged at her lips, and for a moment she looked like the beaming woman who'd walked down the aisle toward him ten years before. She arched her brows. "So, where will we stay?"

Mitch pondered their options. "When I was here last Friday, I spotted a couple of motels at the edge of town." He wrinkled his nose. "They resembled the usual rundown, boring string of rooms, offering TV and swimming pool, but no ambiance—nothing that would impress my wife." He gave her a sideways glance and a grin.

Lydia fastened her eyes on him and waited. Mitch put on one of his *I've-got-a-surprise-for-you* looks.

She perked up. "Come on, Mitch. What?"

"I also spotted a bed-and-breakfast in the center of town. It's just around the next corner. You'll love the name—Abigail's Attic."

Lydia stared out the window. "Abigail's Attic," she whispered.

They turned the corner and pulled into a parking lot, its stretch of pavement bordered on two sides by six-foot lattice fences with yellow clematis trailing upward through the slats. To their left stood a white Victorian-style home with wicker furniture and pots of greenery at inviting intervals along the wrap-around porch.

Before Mitch was able to set the car in park, Lydia unfastened her seatbelt and placed one hand on the door handle. "Oooh, Mitch. It's fabulous."

He snickered and shook his head. "Looks like I've lost my wife to another era." He turned to look in the back seat. "Come on, kids, before your mother abandons us. Looks like were gonna stay here, no matter what it costs."

Inside the inn, a wave of sweet potpourri struck Mitch's nostrils. As expected, the Victorian atmosphere continued to the inside with flowered wall paper and heavy maple furniture. A side room resembled one of those old-fashioned parlors where men once came a-courtin', and a dining area contained five round tables, each with seating for four. Subdued lighting added to the old-world charm, as did a wall of sepia-toned, antique photos of people in period dress.

Mitch led his family to a chest-high counter in a corner of the lobby where guests could sign a visitors' registry. On the other side of the counter, a tall, big-boned woman hovered with her elbows resting on the top. She looked an awful lot like one of the women in the old photos. Mitch guessed her to be in her mid-fifties. Dark roots peaked out of a tangled mass of blond hair, which she'd arranged in a haphazard bun on top of her head. A few loose tendrils hung on either side of her face, much like the way women styled their hair a couple hundred years ago. She wore tons of jewelry, mostly gold, along with an assortment of colored beads. Every movement of her hands set off a resonant jingle Mitch found irritating. Her long fingernails were painted a cherry red like her lips, and she'd applied a heavy coat of mascara to her lashes and a vibrant blush to her cheeks. Her steady gaze sent a ripple of discomfort through Mitch. If he didn't know better he'd guess she was Elijah Garby in drag.

His attention drifted to a desktop name plate: *Abigail Hoffman, proprietor.*

Proprietor. She not only ran the desk, she owned the place. She was *the* Abigail of Abigail's Attic.

Without speaking one word of welcome, Abigail arched her eyebrows and looked down her nose at the two boys. "How long do you plan to stay?" Her voice was crisp.

Mitch forced a smile. "Till Sunday afternoon."

He introduced himself and his wife, then he patted the boys on their heads. "This is Matthew, and this one's Luke. They're well-behaved," he hurried to add.

Abigail tightened her lips and pulled out a check-in form. Where was that old-fashioned Puritan hospitality? He had a good mind to drive back down the road to one of the seedy motels. But Lydia would never stand for it. Anyway, he liked a challenge. Perhaps Abigail Hoffman simply needed to know Jesus.

"On Sunday I'm going to be auditioning for the pastor's position at Mercy Fellowship," he told her, hoping to create a thread of interest. "Do you attend there?"

The woman met his gaze with an icy stare.

"Well, maybe you'll visit us sometime," he said.

Still no response.

He shook off the discomfort, filled out the form, and stepped away from the desk.

Abigail reached out with her painted fingernails and dropped a key in his hand.

"Your room is at the top of the stairs to the right." She gestured toward a staircase. "You have a queen-size bed and a foldout couch, a private bath, and a balcony overlooking the garden. Continental breakfast is served from seven to nine in the morning." She glanced again at the boys. "No exceptions."

"Sounds perfect." Mitch fought the urge to say what he *really* thought.

Lydia bounced up to the desk, smiling, like she hadn't noticed the stilted exchange between the woman and her husband. "We'd like to do some sightseeing while we're here. Can you recommend any activities?"

The older woman ran her eyes over the boys again and smirked. She opened a drawer, pulled out a handful of brochures and plopped them on the desk. Lydia grabbed them and fanned them in front of Mitch. There was a photo of the Old North Church and a title, *Walking Tour of Freedom Trail.* Another showed a dark and dismal picture of tombstones and the words *Nighttime Graveyard Tour in Salem.*

Matthew craned his neck to get a better look at the brochures in his mother's hands. He grabbed the one with the graveyard tour. "Let's do *that* one."

"We'll decide later." Mitch cut in. He quickly gathered up their luggage and headed for the stairs. Lydia and the boys followed close behind.

He sensed Abigail's eyes were on them during the entire climb to the second floor. One thing was certain. He'd met his first evangelistic challenge in Shadow Glenn, but for now he simply wanted to enjoy the day with his family.

Lydia entered the room first. "Oooh, Mitch. This is magnificent. Look at this padded headboard, and the quilt—it looks homemade, like something out of a great-grandmother's trunk. There are so many antiques in this room. This ewer and bowl, this photo of someone's ancestors, in sepia tones like they used to shoot them a hundred years ago. These are some real treasures."

The boys leaped on the bed and started bouncing, eliciting a harsh squeal from the worn springs. Mitch set down the bags and gently pulled his sons off the bed.

"We don't do that here," he cautioned them. "Remember, I told the owner you guys are well-behaved. Don't make me a liar."

After mouthing a drawn out, "Oookaaay," the two boys bounded toward the far wall, opened the French doors, and stepped out on the balcony.

"No climbing," Mitch called after them.

Lydia had paused before a set of framed oil paintings depicting the area's four seasons—snow-covered hills, pink flowering cherry trees, apple orchards with fruit hanging from the branches, and another of more trees, alive with the vibrant reds, oranges, and golds of autumn.

"I can't believe I'm going to experience all of this in real life." Lydia's voice had taken on a wistful tone.

Mitch furrowed his brow. "What do you mean? We already enjoy the four seasons in Indiana. What's so different here?"

She turned to look at him, a surprised expression on her face. "Really, Mitch? Lots of things are different here. New England has its own mystique. A Puritan heritage. A historical charm unlike any other part of the country."

Mitch gazed lovingly at her. His heart swelled, much the same way it did the day he first caught sight of her at her father's automobile dealership. He went there to buy a second-hand car, and he came away with a date.

He drew close and slid his arm around her. "I've always known you liked old things better than you like me."

She laughed. "Not *better* than you, but almost as much."

"I can't complain. Remember how you decorated our first apartment? You bought those beat-up thrift store chairs and a table doomed for a junk pile, and you brought them to life with a sheet of sandpaper and a can of paint. And what about all those cloth thingamajigs you made?"

She tilted her head and gave him a sardonic smile. "Do you mean my granny-square quilts and my cross-stitched samplers? They'll be heirlooms one day—for somebody."

"All I know is, your talents saved us a bundle of money in the early years of our marriage. I may not know the name of everything you ever made, but I sure do appreciate all of them."

She stepped away from him and ran her fingers over a glass figurine on the bureau. "I can't wait to visit the emporium we passed a few streets back."

In seconds, Mitch had lost her again. He checked his watch.

"We should take advantage of our free time. Let's freshen up and get out of this place."

He stuffed their suitcases in the closet and summoned his

boys from the balcony. Then he started for the bathroom, but Lydia stepped in front of him, blocking his path, her dark eyes sparkling.

"We should plan our day, Mitch. Step-by-step. So we don't miss anything. Are we gonna drive straight into Boston? Maybe take in the Freedom Trail? Look at all these brochures." She fanned them out again. "We could visit the museum of science and the aquarium. The kids will love it. And what do you say we go to the harbor for lunch? The seafood has to be awesome up here. We can even—"

Laughing, Mitch raised his hands. "Slow down. We'll have time to do all of those things and more. We have the rest of today and all day Saturday." He stepped back from her. "First, I need to stop at the library."

"The library?!" Lydia's shoulders sagged, and she moaned like a teenager who'd been grounded. He looked at the boys, their faces turned up at him, their mouths turned down at the corners.

"Listen, Lydia. Boys. I need to find out a few things about Mercy Fellowship. If we're going to serve here, I have to know what we're letting ourselves in for."

Lydia smirked at him. "It's a church. What more do you need to know?"

"A lot. I need to research Mercy Fellowship's past and find out if anything of significance happened there."

"I thought you already did the research on your computer at home."

He shook his head. "The internet didn't have much to offer. Many of the small-town libraries have microfiche machines. I want to take a look at some old newspapers. But don't worry. I'll be quick."

The boys heaved dual sighs and dropped onto the edge of the bed, their heads down.

"So much for a trip to the graveyard," Matthew muttered.

"Come on, Matt. If you behave, I'll hold the graveyard tour for another time."

Lydia let out an exasperated sigh. "All right. Let's do what Daddy says and go to the library first." She smiled at him, but the light in her eyes had dimmed. "I suppose the boys and I can spend some time in the children's section while you're doing whatever it is you need to do."

"Trust me, it won't take long. I have a feeling I may not find much, anyway."

6

Fifteen minutes later, they stepped inside the Shadow Glenn Public Library. As soon as Mitch walked through the door, the musty odor of old books and worn shelving hit him like relics from the past. Immediately, he was back in his grade-school library mulling over books on airplanes and rocket ships.

If he'd stuck with his initial dream, he'd be an airline pilot right now, earning five times what he'd made as a youth minister and going on vacations every weekend. But a single night at a revival altered his course. He rarely looked back or regretted his decision, except for times like this. Those little reminders of what he gave up sometimes tugged at his materialistic side. He'd dealt with those temptations many times in the past and would most likely have to deal with them again. For now he was on a different kind of mission.

As she'd promised, Lydia took the boys to a glassed-in children's section at the back of the library. Beyond the huge window stood tot-sized tables and chairs and three-foot-high bookshelves. The boys rushed through the door and took off in two different directions. The sight brought a contented smile to Mitch's lips. If he had chosen the other fork in the road would he have them now? Would he have married Lydia, or a free-spirited flight attendant? It didn't matter. He wouldn't trade his family or his current life for anything in the world.

Breathing a sigh, Mitch returned to his reason for being there. With the librarian's assistance, he settled in a chair in front of the microfiche reader and began to scroll backward through the pages of the town newspaper, *The Daily Messenger*. Page after page flowed by in an endless chain of black and white, with a flash of color now and then. Mitch traveled farther into the past, stopping whenever a headline caught his eye. He passed over the mundane human interest stories about garden shows, art displays, and tea parties of the elite, and kept watch for any mention of Mercy Fellowship.

The most recent reference appeared in a one-paragraph brief about the church seeking a new pastor after an entire year without success. It was dated June 15, 2019, a little over a month ago. Mitch scratched his head. The board allowed a whole year to pass before putting out a call for a replacement. Most churches didn't let more than a month go by without conducting a search. *So who did the preaching over the last year? Elijah Garby? Hah! He'd either fall asleep in the middle of his own sermons or he'd scare the people away with that hawk-like stare of his.*

Another question arose. Exactly how many other bright young ministers applied over the last six weeks? Was he the only one? Or the only one who'd come back?

Mitch scrolled farther back and stopped on March 2, 2018. He gaped at the headline: *Pastor Steven Blocker found dead from overdose in parsonage basement;* and the subhead: *Mercy Fellowship members devastated by yet another loss.*

With a trembling in the pit of his stomach, Mitch read through the newspaper article. Pastor Blocker's ministry lasted less than a year. Members described him as *an energetic, light-hearted individual who'd brought a touch of humor to the pulpit.* But during his last few months at Mercy Fellowship, Blocker stopped telling jokes. He gave up trying to rally the congregation, neglected his wife and daughter, and spent most of his time in the parsonage basement. One of the deacons found him there, along with an empty bottle of antidepressants and a suicide note. The article did not reveal the contents of the note.

Mitch released a shaky breath. He sat back and shook his head. *What could have driven a man of God to take his own life? Apparently, the guy had a quick wit. So what happened? In the beginning Blocker's ministry flourished. Then something went wrong. He needed support. Where were the people of the church? And his wife? Surely they must have seen the signs. Why didn't they help the poor man?*

Mitch reread the story, nervously ran a hand through his hair, then resumed scrolling back in time, the black-and-white images flashing by in a colorless journey into the past.

Almost a year earlier, May 3, 2017, an article carried yet another shocking headline: *Pastor Adam Wheeler arrested for embezzlement of church funds. Charges pending.*

Mitch frowned in puzzlement. One pastor commits suicide. Another steals money from the church coffers. What other melodramas lurked in Mercy Fellowship's past?

Sure enough, on March 16, 2016, the headline answered his question. *Frank Overstreet abdicates church post after four months in ministry.*

His curiosity on fire, Mitch leaned closer to the machine.

Members are reeling from the loss of a man they hoped would restore an atmosphere of good will in the flailing church.

"It's not like the good ol' days when commitment meant something," said head deacon Elijah Garby, 92. "Some come. Some go. Like always, we simply put out a call for a replacement. Maybe one of these days somebody will stay."

Mitch sat back. Somebody? Like him? He read on…

Several members blamed the dearth of leadership on a series of unexplainable phenomena that have plagued the church since the mid-1990s.

"I grew up in this church," said Mary Pendergrast, 75. "Things started to change around the time Pastor Drummond and his wife came here from Salem. Some of us have seen shadows moving around inside the sanctuary. One of the deacons said they were made by a large elm tree swaying outside the stained-glass window. But we know the truth. They're demons."

Mitch puffed out a chuckle loud enough to catch the librarian's attention.

"Shush." She waved an angry finger at him from her desk in the corner.

Mitch gave her an apologetic nod.

He returned to the screen. If Pastor Overstreet could leave after only four months, Mitch figured so could he. It was still early in the game. He could test the waters, and if things didn't improve he could resign. Of course abdication made more sense than suicide. The point was, if things got unbearable he had a way out.

Except for one troubling truth. He'd never quit anything in his life. Not in sports, like when he messed up as a pitcher, he merely settled for the outfield and blossomed there. Nor with his studies. Sometimes difficult classes had driven him to hire a tutor. Even when he failed his cosmology exam, he took the course over, plunged back in and finished with straight A's. Quitting wasn't an option. He possessed a strong compulsion to finish whatever he started. Now he faced a different kind of challenge, and it involved his wife and kids. The consequences could bring huge regrets.

Though a knot had formed in his stomach, Mitch continued scrolling through the files.

More pastors came and went over the years. Some lasted a few months. Others stuck it out a little longer and ended up leaving under tragic circumstances—illness, infidelity, divorce. Noticeable gaps in the ministry revealed months and even years when the church lacked leadership. Most likely the deacons took over during those times. Mitch snorted. *How much support did that miserable bunch give the previous pastors? Hopefully they'd done more than hand over the keys.* Now he may be facing the same trials his predecessors endured.

Mrs. Pendergrast had mentioned demons. The only demons Mitch could identify were the people who'd been running things over the last several decades. Maybe it was not only time to change pastors but also to enlist a new board of deacons.

Mitch tasted blood. He'd been chewing on his bottom lip. He pulled out a handkerchief and dabbed at the wound. He stared at the dots of red standing out starkly against the white linen. With a sigh, he folded the cloth and tucked it in his pocket. A terrible evil was plaguing this church. Demons? Maybe. Garby thought so. A creeping sensation clambered across Mitch's shoulders and up his neck. He shook it off, pulled a small notebook and pen from his pocket, and returned to the screen.

He scrolled back over the articles and scribbled a few dates. Then he strayed to other news stories citing nearby incidents that happened around the same time. A pattern began to evolve. Many of the tragedies at the church coincided with catastrophic events in other areas. Pastor Overstreet left

Mercy Fellowship on April 15, 2013, the same day of the Boston Marathon bombing.

On December 15, 2012, the story about Pastor Wilbur Hanson's divorce was buried on Page 5-B. Meanwhile, a major portion of the A-section was dedicated to stories about a gunman who'd killed 20 children and six adults at an elementary school in Newtown, Connecticut, only a three-hour drive from Shadow Glenn.

A front-page story about the stock market crash of 2008 overshadowed a two-paragraph brief about Pastor Harrison Gladstone's nervous breakdown. And the fatal illness of Pastor William Sportsman was given a tiny blurb on the inside, while the terrorist attacks of September 11, 2001, covered nearly every page of the newspaper. Things happened at Mercy Fellowship. Bad things. But major catastrophes elsewhere sent the local news reports into near oblivion.

Perhaps Mrs. Pendergrast was right. Maybe some kind of demonic activity *was* at work, not only at Mercy Fellowship, but throughout New England. Either those major events had triggered an eerie backlash on surrounding towns, or perhaps a supernatural presence in Shadow Glenn had spawned traumatic events in other locations. Like the chicken-and-the-egg scenario, it would be difficult to nail down the root of the disasters, that is, if such a relationship existed at all.

Mrs. Pendergrast believed the problems started in the mid-1990s. What other connections existed? Still glued to the screen, Mitch scrolled forward to the 1999 crash of Egypt Air's Flight 990, killing 217 people south of Nantucket. He stared in shock at an article at the bottom of the page. A brief story said strange visions were terrorizing members at Mercy Fellowship driving several families to leave town.

He scrolled farther back but found nothing of significance until he reached March, 1993. Over one week's time, multiple articles focused on *The Snowstorm of the Century* that killed 300 people and did more than $6 billion in damage to the eastern seaboard. Local articles said Shadow Glenn was *buried in snow after a blizzard swept through the valley.* One story said people hunkered down in their homes with no electricity. Like pioneers, they lived on canned goods, cured meat, and melted snow. Members of Mercy Fellowship claimed they could hear the muffled chiming of church bells at odd hours of the day and night. Some said it sounded like a funeral dirge. No one entered the church—not even on Sundays—until the snow melted and Pastor Malcolm Smith was able to make a cursory check inside.

Mitch inched the film ahead to a few days after the clearing of the snow. He froze on the headline. *Pastor Malcom Smith hangs self in parsonage basement.*

Another suicide. Mitch's throat tightened. He sucked in a breath of air that brought with it the taste of moldy books. His energy sapped, Mitch checked his watch—10:30. His boys would be as hyper as grasshoppers by now. He reached up to turn off the machine when another headline jumped out at him. It was dated August 2, 1993, twenty-six years ago, almost to the day. Mitch gaped at the screen. *Millionaire Travis J. Hoffman killed in pew at Mercy Fellowship.* The subhead was equally alarming. *Romantic triangle casts suspicion on real estate mogul's untimely death.*

Mitch's mind raced. *Hoffman. Hoffman?* Yes! *Abigail Hoffman.* The proprietor of Abigail's Attic, the inn where he and his family were staying. Curious, he read the account, but the report only said Travis Hoffman was shot to death inside the church. The police were investigating. Period. He checked for more articles. Nothing more.

Mitch clicked off the microfiche reader, rose to his feet, and staggered away from the desk. He needed to return at another time, without Lydia and the boys, when he could spend a couple of hours in front of that blasted machine.

He made a half-hearted effort to shove the troubling reports to the back of his mind, summoned his family from the children's section, and herded them out of the library for their promised day of fun.

But fun escaped Mitch. The newspaper files had pretty much destroyed his vision of a happy, effective ministry in New England. Norman Rockwell's small town Americana had morphed into something akin to Stephen King's fictional *Castle Rock*. He felt a strong impulse to pack up, go home, and face the puzzled reactions of the youth group he'd left behind.

With Mitch holding Lydia's hand and the boys skipping ahead, they marched down the library steps into the warm New England sunshine. He looked at Lydia's radiant face, and the truth struck his heart like a dagger. *She'll never agree to leave this place.*

7

To the boys' excited cheers, they went straight to the aquarium. Inside the meandering hallways, Matthew and Luke scrambled from one pane of glass to the next, squealing and pointing at the brilliantly colored fish and the variety of unusual sea creatures. They paused before a four-story ocean tank filled with plants, coral, and exotic underwater organisms. Colored lights illuminated the display like a scene from *Finding Nemo*.

Lydia hovered beside the boys. Like a doting schoolteacher on an educational field trip, she pointed at the variety of marine life and read the placards aloud.

Though Mitch tried to get in the mood, he couldn't shake off those old newspaper files. He never should have taken the time to stop at the library. The startling reports had clouded his mind. Now he walked around in a daze, barely hearing a word his wife said and hardly aware of the displays behind the walls of glass surrounding nearly every walkway. Every so often he feigned interest in a particular type of fish, or he commented on the colorful swirl of images created by the underwater lighting. In the end, though, he shut off the real world and remained stuck inside the distressing nightmare he'd encountered in the library.

His thoughts also drifted back to his interview. *How many candidates had withstood a similar grilling? Perhaps Elijah Garby scared them off, one by one. Maybe they were the lucky ones.*

And what about Abigail Hoffman, the woman at the inn?

When he mentioned his connection with Mercy Fellowship her reaction went from icy indifference to utter contempt. The truth was, she had good reason to resent this church. The poor woman lost her husband there. Under embarrassing circumstances. A romantic triangle? The article hadn't been specific. Did Abigail's lover kill Travis? Or did another woman's husband murder him? Maybe Abigail took his life. She sure behaved like someone who could.

"Are you with us?" Lydia's query startled him back to the here-and-now.

"Uh, yeah, I'm good."

"What's wrong, Mitch?"

"Nothing. I have a lot on my mind."

"Obviously."

Frowning, she started to turn away. He grabbed her arm.

"Lydia, how much do you want to move here? I mean, are you dead-set on it?"

Trouble flooded into her eyes, but she managed an innocent smile. "I want it a lot." She hesitated, and her smile faded. "Why, Mitch? What's happened?"

He shrugged in an effort to appear indifferent. "Nothing. I just want to be sure."

"I thought you *were* sure. Only yesterday you seemed excited about this move."

"I was—I mean, I am."

"You read something on that machine at the library, didn't you? What did you see, Mitch? Are the boys in danger?"

"No, it's nothing. But—well, we're taking a huge step, Lydia. What if this isn't where God wants us? What if we misread His call? You might discover this place isn't what you expected. Maybe you'll want to go back to Indiana."

She shook her head, and her brown curls bounced. "Believe me, I won't."

"What if the boys miss their friends back home?"

She kept shaking her head and smiling. "They won't. We already went over this, Mitch."

He started grabbing at straws. "If we wait too long, we won't be able to go back. Pastor Samuels has already started interviewing candidates to fill my position. He won't keep it open for long."

Lydia stood in front of him, the hint of a smile on her lips. "Don't worry, Mitch, I won't miss our old church. White Hills grew so big it became claustrophobic. I like the idea of serving in a small church. We can get to know everyone. And they can get to know us. Like one big, happy family."

Sure, one big, happy family. With Elijah Garby in charge and Abigail Hoffman harboring some kind of vendetta.

Mitch forced a smile. "Look, let's enjoy the day. We can discuss this later. The boys are getting ahead of us. We'd better get a move on before we lose them in the crowd."

That was all it took for Lydia to rush after their two sons. Mitch hurried to catch up and made a sincere effort to enjoy the rest of the day with his family.

After leaving the aquarium, they drove to Boston Harbor, strolled along the pier, and stood on the dock watching the sailboats cruise past, their huge, rippling triangles streaked with gold from the sun.

At dusk, they stopped for dinner on the patio at the Navy Yard Bistro. Mitch gawked at the prices on the menu, then he ordered two roast chicken platters for the four of them to share. After a long day on his feet, he wasn't about to walk around looking for a McDonald's. He settled back in his chair and took in the setting. The departing sun cast bronze daggers across the paved patio, and a sense of peace descended on the courtyard. The restful atmosphere consumed Mitch. He bit into a chicken leg and relaxed for the first time since they left the library.

By the time they crashed back at the inn, he barely got the sofa-bed open before the boys fell on top of it, fully-clothed and sound asleep. Working together, Mitch and Lydia got them into their pajamas and covered them with a large quilt.

Lydia disappeared inside the bathroom. Mitch stood next to the sofa-bed and gazed at his sleeping sons. His heart fluttered with love for them. He ran a shaky hand through his hair. On Sunday morning he'd stand before a church full of people and give his candidacy speech. Afterward they'll gather secretly and vote—the final step toward his approval. He felt like he'd boarded a runaway train with no chance of getting off.

Something wasn't right in this church. Elijah Garby had mentioned spiritual warfare. And there were those depressing newspaper stories, the rapid turnover of pastors, and the murder of Travis Hoffman. Demonic activity? It made more sense now. He bit his lower lip. Was the job really worth putting his family at risk? He had a good mind to pack up and get on the first plane out of there.

Saturday

The following morning dawned with fresh hope. Though doubts still swirled in Mitch's head, he determined to keep marching ahead. For now, he surprised Lydia and the boys with tickets to a walking tour on Freedom Trail. He figured the fresh air and historic sites might keep his mind off his troubles—maybe clear his brain and help him to think more rationally.

They drove to the city and joined a group of about a dozen tourists at Boston Common. Their guide, Amy, was dressed for the occasion in an ankle-length early-American frock and a traditional bonnet. Golden curls poked out from beneath the lacy brim and framed her youthful, rosy-cheeked face. Her dark brown eyes glistened as she addressed the group.

"Our walk into history will take 90 minutes and will include eleven stops along the Freedom Trail." Her voice sounded fairly musical. "As we move along, you'll be able to glimpse the exact locations where our nation's history was born. Churches, meeting houses, burial grounds—"

Matthew perked up. "Yes! Let's go to the burial grounds."

A few people chuckled. Amy smiled at the boy. Then she turned her eyes on Mitch and held his gaze a little longer than was comfortable. As though on cue, Lydia slipped her hand in the crook of his arm. Amy turned away and beckoned the group to follow her down the cobbled street.

The brief flirtation sent mixed emotions through Mitch. Though flattered, he reminded himself he was a married man who was about to become the pastor of a church. He had a wife who loved him and two boys who depended on him for their care and nurturing. He didn't want anything to destroy the blessings God had showered upon him.

Lydia released her hold and moved ahead to be near the children. Mitch lagged behind and moved to the back of the group, as far from Amy as he could get while still being able to hear her spiel.

They paused at several locations, including the Boston State House with its gilded dome, and Park Street Church, where bells in the tower sent a melodic chiming overhead. Mitch gazed up at the steeple, more than 200 feet above the ground. Mercy Fellowship would disappear in its shadow. And what about Shadow Glenn's history compared to *this* awesome place? Of what importance were the church's few minor disturbances over the last twenty years compared to what happened in Boston more than two centuries ago? Mitch moved ahead with a fresh surge of confidence. If those early settlers could handle the British, *he* certainly could take on a little skirmish with the devil. After all, God was on his side.

Their next stop elicited a cheer from the kids in the group. They were standing at the entrance to Granary Burial Ground, smack-dab in the middle of Boston. Its concrete and brick pathways meandered between tombstones, many of them marked with the names of early American heroes.

"Lots of famous people are buried here," Amy told the crowd. Her eyes fell on Matthew and Luke. "You might recognize some of the names, boys. John Hancock, Peter Feneuil, Samuel Adams. What about it?"

The boys shook their heads. She turned to the other children. "How about you? Anybody know those names?" Her query was met with shrugged shoulders and more head-shaking.

"Well, no doubt every one of you kids will read about them in your history books in school. Now you're getting a chance to see where they were buried. You'll know something about them even before your teachers mention their names in class."

Like a third-grade teacher, Amy gave a brief history lesson

on a level the kids could understand. Afterward she led the group into the cemetery. At an occasional gravesite, she talked about the person who was buried there. Matthew pointed at a large granite headstone engraved with the dates, January 1, 1735 to May 10, 1818.

"I already know about this guy," he squealed. "It's Paul Revere. He rode a horse into Boston, and he told people the Red Coats were coming."

Amy stepped up beside him and smiled. "You're absolutely right. What's your name?"

"Matthew." He straightened. "Everyone calls me Matt."

"Okay, Matt. Paul Revere did a lot of other things too. For example, he was a craftsman who worked with silver and copper, and he made a lot of engravings. He also took part in the Boston Tea Party."

"Tea Party? Ain't that for girls?" Matthew wrinkled his freckled nose.

Amy laughed, and her eyes sparkled with amusement. "It was a different kind of tea party. It was a rebellion. The colonists dumped tea into the harbor as a protest against British taxes."

Matthew's eyes grew wide. "Wow. It must have been a really *big* tea party. Did the water turn black?"

Snickers rose up in the crowd. Amy winked at Matthew. "I'm sure it did." Then she turned to the adults. "I have a challenge for all of you to do the same thing this little fellow just did. While we pass through the graveyard, I'd like you to read the headstones and call out names you might recognize. Tell the rest of us what you know about those people."

A thought struck Mitch. Education was the key. Not only here in the graveyard, but in the church. Perhaps he should find out what the people knew about the scriptures and encourage them to dig deeper.

His head swam with new ideas, but he followed the crowd moving ahead of him. Lydia came up beside him. "This is such a thrill for the boys," she murmured. "Thank you, Mitch. For today. For everything. The kids are getting a big dose of history. And don't you just love the atmosphere of these old buildings? I feel like I've gone back in time, like I'm walking in a dream world, and I never want to wake up."

Mitch gave her a one-sided smile. "Lydia—" He wanted to tell her not to get her hopes up, but the elation on her face stopped him. No need to spoil her fun. He'd discuss his apprehensions with her later, after he'd had the time to consider all the options.

The congregation might turn him down. Sometimes he found himself wishing for such an outcome. Then again, if he decided to go back to Indiana he needed Lydia to support his decision. The truth was, he hadn't found a suitable alternative, nothing that might appeal to Lydia. He didn't want to fight with her. In their ten years of marriage and even during their courtship, he couldn't recall the two of them ever arguing over anything except which channel to watch on TV. Even then he usually gave up in order to keep the peace. "Choose your battles," his father had cautioned him. So how could he tell his wife they might have to leave this place when she already had set her heart on staying?

As they left the graveyard, Lydia moved ahead of him and kept close to the boys. Occasionally she paused, bent close to them, and whispered something in their ears. Mitch continued to lag behind, but he kept an eye on his family. His kids had learned a few things, maybe more than they could assimilate in one day. Certainly, they'd retain some of the key points. Mitch had to admit, their guide knew a great deal about the past for someone so young.

Perhaps he'd misjudged the little flirtation. During the walk, she'd hit on several other young men in the group. One of them never left her side. Mitch began to relax.

At the end of the tour, he placed a five-dollar bill in Amy's hand and was taken aback when she slipped a note in his. Perplexed, he tucked it in his pocket. He turned away from the girl, took Lydia's hand, and hurried the boys down the street.

They ate lunch at a downtown cafe and discussed their plans for the afternoon. Luke dug into his macaroni and cheese like a kid who'd spent a year in a refugee camp.

Matthew, on the other hand, scowled at his peanut but-ter-and-jelly sandwich. He took one bite and set it back on his plate.

Mitch leaned toward him. "Aren't you hungry, Matt? Is your sandwich okay?"

"It's fine." But the pout on his face told Mitch otherwise.

Lydia tilted her head. "Do you want something else?"

Matthew's scowl deepened. "Yeah, I want the grave-yard tour."

Mitch huffed. "We already did a graveyard tour. Didn't you see all those tombstones? Didn't you hear Amy talking about all the good things those people did?"

"It wasn't the *nighttime* graveyard tour. Remember? The one in the brochure."

"Yeah," Luke chimed in. "We wanna git scared."

Mitch set down his fork. "Boys, the other tour is in Salem. It's a couple hours away from here. And, like the brochure said, it's at night." He glanced at Lydia. She raised her eyebrows at him, questioning. He shook his head. "I don't think the nighttime tour is a good idea. It's too scary."

Matthew smirked. "Maybe it's too scary for Luke, but not for me. Can't we go alone, Dad, just you and me? Mom and Luke can stay at the inn or find something else to do."

"No way." Luke slammed his fork on the table. "I wanna go too. I'm not a baby. You're not gonna leave me behind."

Lydia nudged Mitch. He straightened his back and set his jaw. "We came here together, and we're gonna do everything together." He kept his tone firm. "Nobody gets left out."

The boys glared at each other.

Mitch breathed a long sigh. "Maybe we can do the nighttime tour some other time, after we get settled. But, we'll go as a family—all four of us." He looked sternly at Luke, then at Matthew. "We're not going tonight, and that's final."

The boys groaned.

"Listen, kids, I have to get up early tomorrow. I'm preaching at ten o'clock and I have to go over my notes. I said we'd go some other time. Now finish your dinner, and we'll stop for ice cream on the way back to the inn."

There were no more arguments, no more angry looks. The boys cleaned their plates and quieted down, temporarily appeased.

Mitch glanced at Lydia. She'd finished her own lunch and was immersed in a pamphlet she'd received from Amy.

Amy. Their tour guide. And the note. He slipped it from his pocket, opened it beneath the lip of the table, and blinked in surprise—she'd written her real name, Deborah Staffle, a phone number, and the words, "Call me."

He crumpled it up and was about to toss it on the table, but stopped. Lydia was still flipping through the pamphlet.

If she happened to see the crumpled note, she'd want to read it. She'd ask questions. Though she'd never shown signs of jealousy in the past, he didn't know how she'd react to such a flirtation. He certainly hadn't encouraged the girl. Or had he? He folded the note and shoved it back in his pocket. He could discard it later, in the privacy of the church office.

On their way back to Shadow Glenn, Mitch took a couple of side roads into the country, passed a few gentlemen's farms, and meandered through a small town where Lydia insisted on stopping at an antique store. She bought a few inexpensive items—a crocheted doily, embroidered dish towels, and a milk glass pitcher.

True to his promise, Mitch hit an old fashioned ice cream shop and ordered a round of hot fudge sundaes. By late afternoon, they picked up the highway to Shadow Glenn. Giggles rose from the backseat. The boys poked and prodded each other in fun. Lydia fell silent in the front beside Mitch. She was busy jotting down the day's events in her journal. He let out a sigh. There was no doubt about it. His family had already settled in. If the congregation approved his message tomorrow morning, they'd be moving to Shadow Glenn. The whole thing had slipped completely out of his hands.

8

Sunday

The next morning came too soon for Mitch. A sliver of light oozed through a slit in the curtain. He squeezed his eyes shut and turned over in bed.

"Mitch." His wife's voice came from somewhere near the window. There was the swish of drapes opening, and sunlight flooded into the room.

He pulled the blanket over his head and scrunched down into darkness.

"Mitch." She repeated, louder. She'd moved closer to the bed.

"Leave me alone."

"We have to get ready for church."

"I'm not going. Let me sl—"

His plea dissolved beneath a sudden thumping on his bed and a ruffling of the blankets. He peered out from under the covers at the exact moment when Luke lunged toward his head. He braced for the attack. Matthew clambered on top of him. Struggling, he wrapped his arms around the two boys and held them fast.

"I've got you now," he shouted over their squeals. "You're not getting away."

The struggle continued in and out of the covers, until all three of them tumbled to the floor in a laughing, gasping tangle of bodies and bed linens.

"All right, you wrestling fools." Lydia's tone carried a hint of impatience. She stood over them with her arms crossed.

Mitch shook his head. "We're gonna stay right here. We'll skip church and just have fun today."

The boys cheered him on with shouts of "Yay," and "Okaaay."

"Sorry, boys, you lose." Lydia swept up Luke and carried him into the bathroom. "You, too, Matthew," she called over her shoulder. "Come on. Let's get washed. We don't want to make your dad late for his big debut."

With a moan, Matthew squirmed out of his father's arms and followed his mother.

"Wait. Come back," Mitch groaned. He reached out for them. "Don't leave me."

"You have thirty minutes to get ready." Lydia's lilting call echoed from inside the bathroom. "Better get moving."

Releasing another groan, Mitch sat upright and struggled to his feet. With doubts still swimming around in his head, he laid out his pin-striped suit, a light blue shirt, and a dark blue tie. After Lydia and the boys emerged from the bathroom, he edged past them and turned on the shower. He was groomed and dressed in twenty minutes.

Lydia looked him over. "You look fantastic. Are you ready?"

Mitch nodded. "I went over my notes last night." He avoided looking her in the eye. In truth, he'd merely skimmed them.

Sometime between his interview and his newspaper search at the library, Mitch had lost his enthusiasm. Lately he'd been going through the motions—following what he thought was the call of God on his life. Now he wasn't sure.

He beckoned weakly to his family. "Okay, let's go."

As Abigail had promised, a continental breakfast greeted them in the lobby. Bagels, fruit, and cheese, plus tiny boxes of assorted cereals. Mitch settled for coffee and a Danish pastry. The rest of the family ate with relish. Thankfully, the proprietress was nowhere to be seen.

Entering the church brought a fresh barrage of concerns. People had settled into the pews, waiting for him, but the sanctuary was deathly silent, a complete antithesis of his former church where Sunday mornings sizzled. At that very moment, the White Hills people would be talking out loud, laughing, hugging, pumping each other's hands. Kids would be shrieking with delight as they ran with their friends to the Sunday school rooms. Even the teenagers, though more reserved than the little guys, would be gathering in little cliques, chatting animatedly about video games, school work, and the trials and tribulations of dating.

But not here. Not in this church. No one greeted Mitch at the door. As he walked down the aisle, no one turned around to acknowledge his arrival. They didn't even blink in his direction. With mounting discomfort, he settled in the front row with his family and waited while one of the deacons gave the opening announcements. There was no music, not even an organ or a piano on the stage. No choir loft. No sign of a guitar or a set of drums. His stomach turned.

He sat with his knee trembling in the front pew. This should have been the chance of a lifetime. His own church. On his right sat Lydia, close to his arm, and on her other side their two boys fidgeted in their little blue suits and ties.

A wave of nausea rose to his throat. With trembling fingers he pulled his notes from his breast pocket and leafed through them.

Funny. When he wrote those words, they had a better feel. He sat through the ritual of announcements and the opening prayer. By the time the head deacon invited him up to the podium, his entire body was on the verge of collapse, and he'd broken out in a cold sweat. He mounted the stairs on legs made of Jell-O.

With shaking hands he spread his notes on the lectern and gazed out at the congregation. Clay statues stared back at him with eyes like glass. No one smiled. No one moved. It was as if the entire church was holding its breath.

He chuckled to himself. He'd prepared a message based on the story of David and Goliath. How appropriate. He felt like a little shepherd boy standing in front of an indomitable giant. His discomfort increased. He strayed from his notes, made a vain attempt at a joke and failed miserably. He caught sight of Elijah Garby in a back row. The man's dour expression mirrored the faces of the rest of the congregation.

He kept talking, unsure of where to go with a message that was far less effective than David's sling. He'd gotten halfway through his speech when a movement drew his attention to the third pew on his left. A dark emanation rose up, hovered briefly, and settled on the wooden bench in a shivering mass of shadows. The pew was empty. An eerie prickle ran along his arms and down his spine. He paused in mid-sentence and looked at his wife and kids. *Dear God, what have I done?*

Suppressing a wave of insecurity, he went back to his notes, discarded a few and held onto a remnant of weak scribbles. He scanned the sour faces and chose to stray from his original message. Perhaps if he mentioned the church's upcoming sesquicentennial celebration. He spoke with enthusiasm about the big event. Not a ripple of interest. No shouts of "Amen." No outbreak of applause. Not even the hint of a nod.

He skipped over several more points and wrapped up his speech far short of the allotted twenty minutes. After the service, he and his family stood in front of the altar. People filed out of the church without a backward glance. No one came up to shake his hand. No one asked to meet Lydia and the boys. He stared at the backs of people's heads as they exited the church.

"What just happened?" Mitch whispered to Lydia.

She shrugged. "I don't know. They weren't very friendly, were they?"

"That's putting it mildly. Maybe this isn't the place for us. Maybe we should just—"

"Give them a chance, Mitch."

"What about the shadow in the pew?"

"What shadow? What pew?"

"The third one over there." He nodded toward the left. "While I was speaking, a shadow started shifting back and forth over there. Don't tell me you didn't notice it."

She shook her head. "I didn't see anything."

"What about my message? Did it make any sense?"

"I'm sure it did. To someone. I was busy keeping the boys still."

Her comment struck a blow. If he couldn't keep his own family's attention, how could he reach a church full of strangers?

As it turned out, there was no post-service potluck dinner, no invitations to lunch, no mention of Mitch returning the following Sunday—nothing at all the way *normal* congregations did things. The only sign of acceptance came from John, one of the younger deacons. After the last of the people had left the church, he walked to the front and handed Mitch a ring of keys.

"Well, it's settled. We voted you in. Take a couple weeks to make the move. See you in August."

Puzzled, Mitch frowned and looked at the clump of keys in his hand. Before he could say anything, John turned and started down the aisle toward the door.

"Wait," Mitch called after the departing figure. "Aren't you even going to take a vote?"

John gave him a half-hearted wave and kept walking.

Mitch took a closer look at the keys. One appeared to be older than the pyramids—a skeleton key like those used to open vintage trunks and gates to secret gardens. It must be for the entrance to the church. The other two keys were newer and most likely opened the doors to the office and the parsonage next door.

Lydia raised her eyebrows. "That's it? You're in?"

He shrugged. "Yeah, I guess I am. They're a strange bunch, aren't they?"

She tossed her head and let out a nervous giggle. "Well, it may take some adjusting, but I'm glad the hard part is over."

Mitch shook his head. "I'm not so sure, Lydia. What do you think? Should we drop the keys in a pew and head for the airport?"

"And go where? I don't want to go back to Indiana." A stubborn sharpness had filtered into her voice. "We've come this far, Mitch. It would be foolish to turn back. Besides, I like a challenge. I thought you did too. Once these people get to know us, they'll come around. You'll see."

Mitch let out a long sigh. "Well, we've got the keys. It seems they're expecting us to fix whatever's wrong with this place."

He took his wife by the arm and ushered her toward the door. The boys followed, uncharacteristically quiet for two rambunctious youngsters. It was as if they, too, were overcome by the distressing atmosphere.

"Let's take it one step at a time," Mitch said. "We'll check out of the inn and grab lunch in town. Afterward, we can stop at the parsonage and make a list of what we should bring from Indiana and what we need to buy. I have to be honest, Lydia, I haven't even begun to start serving yet, and I already have reservations."

"So we're staying?" She flashed a hopeful smile at him.

He nodded with less enthusiasm. "I guess so. We'll fly back to Indiana this afternoon. It's gonna take us a week to clean up the rental property. Then we'll load up our car with a few necessities and give the bulk of our possessions to the movers."

A faraway twinkle settled in Lydia's eyes. No doubt about it. In her mind she'd already set up house in Shadow Glenn. And she was happy. His heart melted, and so did his will.

"I can't promise anything, Lydia, but I'll give it a serious try. Just remember, if it doesn't work out, we'll move on."

As though not even hearing him, she took the boys' hands and walked out of the church ahead of him. He picked up his step. Already, his family was leaving him behind. He'd become a follower instead of a leader; a puppet instead of the one holding the strings. There was nothing more to do but move forward and hope he hadn't made the biggest mistake of his life.

9

They grabbed a quick lunch at a McDonald's on the highway outside of Shadow Glenn. After downing hamburgers and shakes, Mitch and his family headed for the parsonage so they could check out their new home. They parked in the church lot and walked along a bramble-covered path to the dilapidated house next door. Mitch gazed with disappointment at the Cape Cod structure with its peeling paint, dark dormer windows, and rickety front porch—exactly the kind of home His wife loved to tackle.

He wasn't wrong. Lydia's face lit up like a kid's on Christmas morning. "It's so quaint," she gushed. "There's a nice big yard for the boys to play in, and look, Mitch, a porch swing. Can't you just picture us relaxing out there in the evenings?"

He couldn't.

"The siding could use a fresh coat of paint." He pointed out more flaws. "The front steps need some reinforcing. Better be careful going up, Lydia. Watch out for that broken railing. It's unstable. Somebody's bound to take a fall."

With a toss of her head, Lydia rushed ahead. She grabbed the wooden railing, looked back at him, and jiggled it. "Look, Mitch. It only needs a couple of nails. And don't worry about the siding. I'll help paint. We can finish it off in one weekend."

His sense of control waned a little more. Lydia bounced off the bottom step and dashed about the grounds, scrutinizing the overgrowth, yanking weeds, and digging her fingers into the soil.

Then she straightened, brushed the dirt off her hands, and

faced him with a huge smile on her lips. "Give me a couple of weeks and I'll have these flower beds bursting with color." She gestured with one hand. "Maybe some deep purple hydrangea bushes over here, some pink azaleas over there, and a long row of bright yellow forsythia along this rock wall."

Mitch couldn't restrain a smile. "Plenty of curb appeal, right? Like they say in the real estate business?"

Lydia giggled and sprinted up the porch steps without grabbing the rickety handrail. Mitch got the keys ready and followed after her. The boys headed for a big oak tree at the edge of the property where a tire swing dangled invitingly.

As he stepped inside the house, Mitch shrank back from the stale odor of old furniture and rotting wood floors. He moved into the living room and drew back the drapes, letting a dust-laden sunbeam in. At one side of the room a stone fireplace cried out for cleaning. On the other side, a wall of bookshelves offered a library of worn and torn books.

Lydia moved about the living room and tugged bed sheets off the furniture, exposing a worn loveseat, two side tables, and an overstuffed chair. She sighed with pleasure and presented the same familiar smile she wore every time she walked into an antique store or a thrift shop. The truth hit Mitch like a Mack truck. He'd already lost the battle.

Lydia turned toward him, and for a brief moment he didn't have to say a word. He merely frowned. Lydia's smile faded, and she stared at him with concern in her eyes.

"You don't like it, do you?" She placed her hands on her hips. "Come on, Mitch," she pleaded. "Where's your sense of adventure? The house is old—probably close to a hundred. And the furniture looks dilapidated. So what? The place simply needs a good sprucing up."

Mitch shrugged. "I suppose so. It's a really small house. There are only two bedrooms, but I guess the boys can share one."

"Maybe in a couple years we can add a room."

A couple years? He doubted they'd still be there in a couple years. No one else stayed. Why should they? "Maybe," he said with diminishing interest. He started for the door.

Lydia blocked his path. "You don't sound happy about it."

"Me? I can live anywhere. I'm concerned for you and the boys."

She shook her head. "Well, I like it. I'm the one who's going to be home most of the time, while you'll be running off taking care of church business."

He tried to see their future through Lydia's eyes. The image eluded him. Then, surrendering, he planted a kiss on her forehead. "I'm sure you'll have this place looking homey in no time."

She stepped back and placed one hand on her hip and one finger on her cheek like she was figuring a plan.

Mitch headed for the front door, then he paused and looked back. "Why don't you make a list of what we need to bring up here from Indiana? I'll be back in a minute. I'm gonna check out what needs to be done in my office."

He followed an overgrown cobbled path to the church annex. *My office,* he mused. *I guess we're here to stay. For now.*

He stepped through the office door and caught his breath. The ten-by-twelve cubbyhole smelled worse than it did last weekend. Kind of like dirty socks in a gym locker room. The place obviously hadn't been aired out in months. A ray of sunlight streamed through a solitary window and showered particles of dust in a steady beam on the wood floor. Furnishings were sparse—a medium-size desk, a couple of chairs, and an overstuffed sofa set up across from the desk, probably arranged for people who came in for counseling. At the moment he needed therapy more than anyone.

He hit the wall switch. A ceiling globe shed light on the room like the high-intensity security lights outside a prison. *Maybe a lower-watt bulb will make a difference.*

But changing a light bulb was the least of Mitch's worries. Like the house, his office was in dire need of a facelift. Rainwater had left streaks beneath the window sill and had turned the wall a mousy orange-brown. *What did Lydia call that ugly color? Ocher?* Mitch caught himself pouting. Before he could even *think* about sermons and other responsibilities, he faced a major renovation. He'd have to paint, sand, sweep, dust, and disinfect every inch of this room. And it didn't appear he'd be getting any help from the board of deacons or anyone else in the congregation.

Mentally, he ticked off the many hours it would take to get his office in shape. Factor in the packing and cleaning in Indiana and helping Lydia prepare the Shadow Glenn house, and there'd be little time to get a sermon ready, which meant he'd be working in a trashy office for the next few weeks. He took another look around at the piles of debris. *Or maybe months.*

His heart ached with disappointment. He'd pictured a man-cave, something masculine, with heavy pieces of furniture and lots of rich reds, browns, and golds, maybe a couple of wilderness prints on the wall, and a bronze statue of an elk or some other virile animal. Kind of like Pastor Samuel's office at his former church. The image burst like an over-inflated balloon.

To make things worse, Mitch hadn't yet survived the

disappointing reception. He'd done his best to prepare a sermon worthy of an adult audience, but the congregation had responded with disinterested boredom. *If that's how they feel about Mercy Fellowship, why do they keep coming back? For that matter, why should I?*

Still, he reminded himself of his personal mantra. *Don't quit.* He'd already stuck it out in many areas where most men would have walked away in frustration. But sometimes his perseverance—or was it persistence?—turned out to be a curse instead of a blessing. Like last November, on the annual Day of the Bible, Mitch organized a Bible-delivery project with pastors from other churches. He trekked all over downtown Indianapolis in pouring rain until every Bible in his wheeling suitcase was handed out to store owners, shoppers, and homeless people. The other ministers went home when it started to drizzle. He'd stuck it out alone and ended up with a bad cold.

The mere thought of quitting put an invisible noose around his neck. An inner turmoil continued, and he struggled to reignite some semblance of enthusiasm for Mercy Fellowship. He held onto one thought, that God had brought him to Shadow Glenn for a purpose. Like the prophets of old who were selected for a special work, he should expect some opposition. God helped them and they succeeded. So with God's help he could succeed, too. He needed to try, if only to prove his father wrong. If Edward Calloway had gotten his way, by now Mitch would be a lawyer or a doctor or an airline pilot. He only knew he couldn't go back to Indiana a failure.

Sighing, he flicked off the light, turned his back on the mess, and locked the office door. He returned to the parsonage and found his wife standing in the middle of the living room, her lips puckered, her eyes darting from one wall to the other, the way a person does when measuring a space without a tape rule. Matthew and Luke ran from the hall, whooping and tripping over their own feet. They tumbled to a stop in front of him.

Matthew caught his breath. "We picked out our bedroom, Dad."

Luke peered from behind his brother. "There's only one bed in there. I want my own bed."

Mitch chuckled. "Don't worry, boys, we'll bring your beds from Indiana, and your clothes, and your toys, and anything else we can cram into this place. Now, why don't you two go back outside? Mommy and I want to look around and make some decisions."

Giggling, the boys raced each other to the door. Mitch followed them. "Stay in the front yard where I can see you." He returned to the living room and drew close to his wife. "So, what do you think, Lydia?" Like he didn't already know.

She wrinkled her nose. "There's a lot to do in here, but I'm up for it."

"What's the kitchen like?"

"Follow me."

They passed through an adjoining doorway. Straight ahead, a bay window framed a small nook with a table and four chairs. There was a galley kitchen with a gas stove, a small refrigerator, and a four-foot-long Formica counter. On top was a toaster, a Mr. Coffee, and a small microwave oven. Everything was spotless.

Mitch frowned in puzzlement. While the rest of the house and his office looked like a junkyard, someone had taken the time to clean the kitchen and had even placed a bowl of fresh fruit on the table.

He lifted an apple. "Maybe somebody *does* want us here."

Lydia grinned. "Of course they do. That's a good sign, isn't it?"

He gave a shrug. "I guess."

Her smile faded. "What's wrong, Mitch?"

He scowled with disappointment. "Well—the office is a mess. I can't work in there. We'll only have a couple of days when we come back, and I'll have to put together a sermon for the following Sunday. How am I supposed to work in a pig sty of an office?"

Lydia responded with half-open eyelids. "Come on, Mitch, how many times have you been called on at the last minute to fill in for Pastor Samuels? I've seen you whip together a sermon in a single afternoon—without an office—sometimes lying in a hammock, or relaxing in your easy chair while watching a ballgame on TV. You simply muted the commercials and jotted down a few notes."

"Okay, but this is different. Back there I was speaking to a receptive audience. I could wing it, and they'd still love me. This group didn't seem impressed with this morning's message. To be honest, I'm a little nervous about getting up to the pulpit again."

She giggled. "Think of them as another youth group. You didn't have to work very hard to prepare a message for those teenagers every Wednesday night."

"They were kids, Lydia. These people are adults and they're obviously set in their way."

She patted his arm. "You'll be fine."

Despite her patronizing tone, she was right. He'd faced

challenges before, and everything had worked out. He needed to trust God. Needed to put aside his insecurities and step out in faith.

Dejected but not destroyed, he checked his watch. "We need to get on the road if we're gonna make our flight."

They turned off the lights and started out the door. Lydia stopped and took one last look around the living room. She released a long, contented sigh. Mitch gazed at his wife's beaming face. For now he was going to have to go along for the ride.

"Come on, honey," he said. "When we get back, you'll have plenty of time to turn this heap into a cozy little cottage."

They stepped out on the front porch. Mitch pulled the door shut. It let out a disheartening groan. He turned the lock and stared with disgust at the chipped doorframe and the peeling paint. More repairs to take him away from his ministerial duties. He let out a sigh. *At least we got the place rent-free.*

10

The trip home was uneventful. Upon their arrival, everyone fell into bed, exhausted. Monday morning, Mitch got the boys sorting through their belongings. They needed to decide what to take to Shadow Glenn and what to leave behind. Thankfully, Lydia created a list to help expedite the process. Matthew and Luke set up their own organized piles and figured out which toys to take and which ones to pass to their friends.

Mitch showed them their mother's list. "We're moving into a smaller place, kids. We need to scale down."

After getting past their initial crinkle-faced whining and fussing, the two boys conceded. Matthew gave his collection of baseball cards and his box of toy trucks to his friend, Adam. Luke shed a few tears over his stuffed animal collection, but in the end he agreed to donate them to a local shelter.

After a quick lunch of sandwiches and fruit, Mitch took a break from the packing to check in with his former pastor, Martin Samuels. They sat on plush, overstuffed chairs in the church office. Mitch gazed with a twinge of envy at the bulky furnishings, the oiled ebony desk, the organized bookshelf. There wasn't a speck of dust anywhere.

Martin leaned back and propped one ankle over the other knee. "Okay. So fill me in. How'd it go?"

Mitch swallowed hard, but the lump remained in his throat. "Fine."

"Fine?" His pastor eyed him with incredulity. "Doesn't sound fine."

Mitch's mind scrambled over the last couple of days. He tried to conjure up a positive memory, needed to prove to Martin—and to himself—that he'd made the right decision. He came up blank.

"Um—there's not much to tell yet. The deacons gave their approval, and I assume the congregation supported their decision."

"You *assume*?" Martin frowned. "Didn't they come right out and *say* they wanted you?"

Mitch shrugged. "Not in so many words. They handed me the keys to the church and walked out."

Pastor Samuels' frown deepened. "What's going on, Mitch?" He narrowed his eyes. "You know, your job's still open, if you want it."

Mitch shrugged with discomfort. "It's just well, the change is gonna be harder than I expected. Plus, I'm gonna miss the youth group. Those kids mean a lot to me."

Martin nodded with understanding. "I went through the same struggle when *I* switched churches. It ain't easy." He paused and stared holes into Mitch. "But I think there's something else going on." His eyes were like double-edged swords cutting through Mitch's facade. "Be honest with me, son. What happened up there?"

Mitch released a long, shaky sigh. "Okay, Martin. You know me too well. It looks like they have a hard time keeping a pastor. I did a little research while I was there. The turnover was unreal. Several left under eerie circumstances. And there were some long stretches when the position remained unfilled."

Martin shrugged. "Lots of churches run through dry periods. Sometimes they hire a whole string of pastors before one sticks. You could be the man they've been waiting for."

Mitch shook his head. "There's more."

Martin stroked his chin and eyed Mitch with interest.

"Weird things have happened in that church. Unexplainable shadows. Several pastors left under terrible circumstances. Divorce, embezzlement, serious illness, even death. Two committed suicide. And there was a murder in the sanctuary."

Martin puffed out a big breath. He didn't speak for a moment, like he was soaking up what Mitch had told him. Creases gathered on his forehead. "Didn't you tell me it's an old church? Lots of things can happen in 150 years."

Mitch nodded. "True, but for decades everything appeared to be normal. It looks like the bad stuff started twenty years ago after a guy was shot to death inside the church. Things began to change. There's an obvious lack of fellowship among the members. They break off in little cliques and don't talk to the others." With embarrassment he shook his head. "My sermon fell completely flat. Nobody listened, or if they did they didn't seem impressed. I'll tell you, Martin, Mercy Fellowship fits John's description of Pergamos in the Book of Revelation. I'm beginning to think Satan himself has set up his throne there."

Martin settled back and chuckled. "I'm afraid you've had it too easy working with young people. They're impressionable and easy to mold. Adult audiences are different. You've stepped up for me in the past, Mitch. You took the pulpit without hesitation. But I have to admit, the temperament of an audience can make all the difference."

Mitch shook his head. "I've lost my self-confidence," he admitted.

"You can do it, Mitch. Satan works overtime to destroy a Christian's confidence, especially in the church. It's naive to think he wreaks havoc only in the outside world."

Mitch stared at his pastor, pleading with his eyes for an answer. "I don't know. I just don't know."

"Have you committed yet? Have you started packing?"

Mitch grunted. "Lydia's running around the house like a white tornado. She can't wait to get up there."

"And you?"

"Well, I *did* call the movers."

"Then it looks to me like you've made up your mind." Martin lowered his leg and leaned toward him. "Listen carefully. I have two pieces of advice. Stay in the Word, and pray without ceasing. You have access to a far greater power than anything you might encounter up there. Tap into it, Mitch. No problem is too big for the Lord."

"So you're telling me to keep pressing ahead, no matter what happens?"

"Only if you're certain God has called you there. Don't forget, missionaries have gone into worse situations in the jungles where they encounter pagan worship and difficult living conditions. They go there despite knowing what's waiting for them. Sometimes it takes them decades to make one convert. They don't quit."

There was that mantra again. *Don't quit.* Mitch chuckled. "Speaking of difficult living conditions, before I even get started I have to spruce up the parsonage *and* my church office. From the looks of things, nobody's gonna rush over there to help."

"As I said, your job's still open. Do you need more time to decide?"

Mitch grunted with resolve. "I'm afraid time is not an option. They have me scheduled to speak a week from Sunday. I'm on a high-speed train, and it's already left the station."

~

That weekend, Mitch's imaginary train picked up speed. Several church members from White Hills came to help clean the house. The men brought their tools and fixed whatever needed repairing—loose door moldings, broken light switches, worn floorboards. The women walked in with casseroles to keep the workers fed, then they tackled the kitchen, swept it free of crumbs, polished the appliances, and wiped out the cupboards and the refrigerator.

A few days later, the movers showed up and loaded their truck with furniture and other items Lydia had set aside. And so, Mitch's train kept on rolling, faster and faster, taking him from the security of his position in Indiana and closer to an unpredictable and frightening future in Shadow Glenn.

On the Calloways' last evening in town, the youth group held a going-away party for them. Hundreds of people showed up in the fellowship hall. They dined on a potluck dinner, followed by a huge sheet cake and homemade ice cream. There were a lot of tears, hugs, pats on the back, and handshakes. The congregation took up a collection to help them get settled in their new location. People donated cash and gift cards, and the Sewing Circle ladies presented them with three hand-stitched quilts.

After the hall cleared and the last of the well-wishers departed, Mitch stepped outside and grabbed a moment alone. He stared at the massive sanctuary, its granite walls glistening in the light of the street lamps. Beyond all the marble and stone beat a living, breathing heart. On Wednesday nights, it pulsed with youth activities. On Sunday mornings, it came alive with songs of worship and messages of hope. Even during weekdays, people filed in and out of those doors, seeking counsel, financial help, or simply to learn more about God.

Without shame, he released a stream of tears and choked out a quiet good-bye. He'd reached a crossroads. It was time to walk away from the life he once knew, time to step out in faith, and face the challenge he'd been handed. The runaway train would keep on going. He'd climbed aboard, and there was no getting off—not until the brakeman pulled the switch.

11

Second week of August, 2019

It took two days for Mitch and his family to drive to Shadow Glenn, this time with their compact Honda loaded with some of their clothes and a few items Lydia had packed for the kitchen and bath. They spent one night in a roadside motel and got back on the road early the next morning. With each passing mile, Mitch felt a little more of his former life slipping away. No more youth group. No more mega-church. No more comfortable home in the suburbs.

He'd called his parents last night to let them know about the change in his career. Like always, his mom bathed him in flowery support. He'd fulfilled her dream. His dad was another story. Still disappointed in Mitch's career choice, he grunted and wished him well.

Now he had to keep his mind on what lay ahead, his new responsibilities, including sermon ideas for reaching his odd congregation. In three months they'll be celebrating Mercy Fellowship's sesquicentennial. To most church members such an occasion was a big deal. *Perhaps the celebration will bring those hardnosed people together,* he thought. *By the time the big day arrives I need to break through the group's tough shell and make some relationships.*

As it turned out, the long hours on the road gave Mitch and Lydia time to talk over the last few days' events. Mitch opened up about what he'd discovered in the library. He didn't want to frighten his wife, so he touched on a few incidentals.

But he wanted to at least keep her informed. If he decided to pack up and leave Shadow Glenn, she'd know why.

Lydia shrugged it all off. "Those things happened in the past, Mitch. People die. People leave. People fall away. The past shouldn't affect our future."

He shook his head, unable—or unwilling—to argue with her about it. Most of the time he took a non-confrontational stance. It was safer. Nobody got hurt. When conversations started to get heated, he simply walked away.

But Lydia didn't let it go. "You're not like those other pastors," she boasted. "You're a sensible guy, Mitch. You've faced tougher challenges, and you've always come out ahead." She turned to look out her side window. "Stop worrying. If you don't, it's going to affect every decision you make."

His wife had a point. He didn't know those other ministers or their past experiences. Perhaps their problems started long before they came to Shadow Glenn.

"I just wanted you to know what I'd discovered, Lydia, in case we—"

"Isn't it wonderful how the leaves are already changing in the north? I *love* the bright colors."

Mitch let out a sigh and fixed his eyes on the road ahead. If things didn't change for the better, he could bring up the subject later. For now he needed to settle down in the driver's seat and keep moving forward.

Upon their arrival, they started unloading the car. Mitch handed a couple of light-weight bags to the boys. He grabbed the heavy stuff. Lydia rushed ahead of everyone with a box for the kitchen. Mitch made several trips back to the car and dutifully placed the boxes and bags Lydia had marked in their appropriate rooms.

They slept on lumpy mattresses that night with only the Sewing Circle ladies' quilts to keep them warm. The next morning, Mitch ran out for donuts, coffee, and orange juice.

While Lydia started tearing open boxes, Mitch went to the church office. He turned on the blinding overhead light and stared blurry-eyed at the task before him. He soon forgot about the newspaper articles, the uncanny turnover of pastors, and the stone-faced congregation he would face on Sunday.

Mitch rolled up his sleeves and started going through the pile of boxes the former pastors left behind. Most of them contained outdated correspondence, tax forms, and old, unpaid bills. He cleared the top of his desk, placed the most current documents in a separate pile, and dumped the rest in one of the empty boxes to burn in the wire trash bin outside.

Next he went in search of cleaning supplies. He found a utility closet in the hallway and came back with a broom, a bucket, a handful of rags, and several bottles of cleaning liquids. With furniture polish in one hand and a tattered T-shirt in the other, he brought the desk to a suitable shine. The lemony scent wafted in the air. It wasn't Martin Samuels' desk, but it would do.

Mitch rolled up the floor rug and dragged it outside along with the odor of dirty socks. He surveyed the wooden floor. It was in dire need of a good sanding and a coat of varnish. For now he only had time to sweep it clean. He could restore the finish later.

He eyed the overloaded bookshelves and the folders spewing out of the file cabinet. Perhaps one of the deacons could help sort through the mess. Then he reconsidered. They might think he couldn't handle the job. Anyway, he didn't want important church records to end up in the garbage until he could go through them.

He went directly to the file cabinet. Methodically, he flipped through the papers in each of the four drawers, discarded whatever he didn't need and retained those he might. In the back of the bottom drawer, he discovered a leather-bound log with a ragged cover. His jaw dropped in amazement. The thing was old. Really old.

He carried it to the desk and settled into the rolling chair. He opened the cover and carefully turned each leaf, one by one. The earliest pages were frayed and time-yellowed, a few of them crumbled at his touch. Smudged and faded ink covered the pages with scrawled notations. The book was a real treasure, went back 150 years to the earliest days of Mercy Fellowship.

Nearly every entry was in a different handwriting—some meticulously printed, some in fine script, others like indiscernible hen scratches. Slowly, he worked his way through the chronology.

November 20, 1869—Five families established Mercy Fellowship. They included: Jim and Mary Barton and their two children, Richard and Lisa; Harold and Sylvia Hedgerow; Matthew and Jane Garrett and their son, William; Sam and Patricia Kent and her Aunt Henrietta; and Elijah and Margaret Garby and their son, Ezra.

Mitch sat back and grinned. *Garby. So the old codger's ancestors really did start Mercy Fellowship. The guy's great-grandfather was among the first. No wonder he cares so much about who's going to lead it. He's got a lot invested here.*

Mitch read on.

Members gathered at the Hedgerow farm in the barn, which

had been converted into a meeting hall, complete with benches and a small stage. At the first meeting, Jim Hedgerow played "Amazing Grace" on his fiddle, and Jonas Rich gave a message about sharing of crops, based on Acts 4:32, "They had all things in common."

Several pages of incidentals noted weddings, funerals, community fairs, and the sale of hogs, followed by more details.

Jonas served for twenty years until he became ill. During his ministry, membership grew to two dozen families. He passed the pulpit to Felix Parks in December, 1889.

Over the next year, under Parks' leadership, the roll doubled, and the congregation drew up plans for a church building. Members held hands and prayed over a piece of land on the corner of Main Street and Second Avenue. Within two weeks, the owner of the property donated the plot and joined the church. The men built a wood-frame structure for a place of meeting over the next fourteen years. After the first service, the members gathered on the grounds for a potluck dinner. The Reverend Parks said a special blessing and dedicated the church to the service of God.

Mitch frowned in puzzlement. The early group held hands? They prayed over the land? Shared a potluck dinner? What had become of that kind of unity?

He scanned the next section with a growing respect for the early congregation. *The Reverend Parks left in 1891 to start a new church somewhere in Connecticut. David Mason came on as pastor, and by 1900, the congregation had doubled again. Members pooled their money and purchased a larger plot of land on First Street, where they built a beautiful church with a steeple and belfry.*

The current location. Mitch leaned back in amazement. Intrigued, he read on. *The city purchased the former church building and turned it into a public library.*

The library. Of course. Mercy Fellowship's first church. After purchasing the box-like structure, the city leaders made lots of changes. They added the glass-enclosed children's section and another wing to accommodate more books. Overall, the building was old—maybe one of the oldest in Shadow Glenn.

The next pages focused on the new church building on First Street.

As was their nature, the members got together for a huge celebration on the grounds. Numerous guests came from the community, and the membership grew. Pastor Mason died of pneumonia in 1913.

Mitch gingerly turned the tattered pages, brushed over more incidentals, and occasionally stopped to absorb an interesting detail or the mention of a new pastor. He read the next passage twice.

During the 25 years of Henry Waters' leadership, the roll grew to 235 members. In 1922, fire destroyed the left side of the building. Members organized a bucket brigade and saved the rest of the church. A month later, the men came out on weekends and rebuilt the damaged portion. Cause of the fire was unknown. In 1923, the church was rededicated. Members also purchased the house and property next door to be used as a parsonage. Henry Waters and his wife, Virginia, and son, Norman, were the first to reside there. He retired in 1938, when he and Virginia moved to Florida. Norman Waters took over the pulpit for the next twelve years.

Mitch tilted his head and mulled over what he'd just read. The church suffered a devastating fire. The people rebuilt the damaged portion, laboring with their own blood, sweat, and tears. Then they acquired the lot next door and the parsonage.

Now the Calloways were moving in. Lydia was right. The

house dated back almost a hundred years—96 to be exact. He suddenly felt a deep respect for the tattered old building.

He checked his watch. Almost noon and he hadn't made a dent in the work he'd planned to do. He'd been distracted by the ancient record book. But now that he'd gotten into it, he was finding it hard to put it down. Chewing his bottom lip, he moved ahead and brushed over the scrawled ramblings, mentally filing the important stuff.

Jesse Hamilton led the church from 1950 to 1971. In 1969 Mercy Fellowship turned 100. The congregation celebrated their centennial with a huge carnival on the grounds. The planning committee brought in midway rides, food vendors, and entertainment. By this time, membership numbered six hundred men, women, and children. Way more than the current roll. Perplexed, Mitch scratched his head. Was there any hope the number could grow like that again?

He read on, stunned by the commitment the people displayed a mere 50 years ago. *New believers were baptized in the river at the edge of town. During the week, members broke into small groups and met in individual homes. Committees formed to take care of the different needs of the church. The staff organized a program to reach out to the needy. They opened a soup kitchen and a clothing pantry. With attendance exceeding the sanctuary's capacity, Pastor Hamilton added an extra service on Sunday mornings. The men got together, built an annex with indoor bathrooms, plus Sunday school rooms, a fellowship hall, and an office.*

Mitch tapped the desk. *This office, where I'm sitting right now. My office.* He looked around the room. My *mess.*

He ignored the disarray and turned the page. *Pastor Hamilton died of a heart attack in 1971. Malcolm Smith filled the pulpit and served for 22 years.* Mitch frowned. Twenty-two years. Back then, the terms of service remained strong. Nobody ran away. There were no scandals, no suicides. The next two pages impressed him even more. *During Smith's time, the church added a heating and air-conditioning system. The members continued to celebrate holidays together—Thanksgiving dinners, Christmas pageants, Easter egg hunts, and harvest festivals. Services included the traditional hymns played on a piano or an organ, and a choir of robed men and women led the congregation in song.*

There was a whole page of photos, most of them in black-and-white. Mitch gazed at the faces. Happy faces. Smiling faces. Nothing like what he'd encountered during his candidacy trial.

He shook his head in disbelief. In the beginning Mercy Fellowship grew like millions of other churches. So what became of the large, enthusiastic crowds? What became of the fellowship? The music? The celebrations? The pastors who stayed for ten to twenty years?

The next section carried a hint.

From 1993 to 1995, the pastor was Phineas Drummond. He'd moved to Shadow Glenn from Salem, Massachusetts, with his wife, Cornelia, who, unlike the pastors' wives before her, spent little time with the congregation. Instead, she often disappeared inside the basement of the parsonage and spent long hours there, alone.

Mitch paused. That was the turning point. That was when a dark cloud settled on the church. He continued on, his heart breaking with every notation. *Home groups disbanded. Church picnics and other celebrations ceased. When something broke, instead of joining together to make repairs the way the men did in the past, they hired workmen from town or left the item in disrepair. People lost interest. They moved away or transferred their membership to other churches across town. The numbers dwindled until only the descendants of the original founders remained. Among them, Elijah Garby was called as head deacon.*

Mitch smirked. His new best friend.

The Drummonds spent two years at Mercy Fellowship. The board asked them to leave in January 1995. No specific reason was given.

After more than a hundred years of progressive growth and activities, it took the Drummonds only two years to tear down everything the former pastors had accomplished. Mitch shook his head. The next ten pages chilled his bones to the core.

From January 1995 until June 2018, ten different pastors came and went. None of them held the post longer than two years, and in most cases they stayed for merely a few months, then they left for a variety of reasons. Some packed up and moved without saying a word. A few became ill. One suffered a nervous breakdown. Another was arrested for embezzling church funds, like the newspaper account stated. In fact, the church records over the last twenty years pretty much paralleled everything Mitch read on the microfiche machine, leaving out most of the gory details. The record book briefly mentioned the couple who divorced and the two pastors who committed suicide.

After Sam Greshman hung himself in the basement of the parsonage a few days before Christmas in 1996, there were seven stretches of time when the church had no pastor, once for four years when the deacons filled in at the pulpit. Then, in March 2018, Pastor Steven Blocker died from a drug overdose. Afterward, the pastor's position remained open for more than a year.

"Then I applied," Mitch mumbled and sank back in his chair.

The record ended there. It gave no reason for the church's abrupt decline and no solution for turning things around. Mitch let out a sardonic chuckle. The responsibility now had fallen to him. He shivered. *How strange to get a chill in the middle of summer*, he thought. *It must be close to ninety degrees outside.*

12

Lydia took the boys to their bedroom and dumped a bag of Hot Wheels on the floor. *That should keep them busy for a while.*

She went in the kitchen and sat at the table with a note-pad and pencil. She'd have to stay within their budget, of course, at least until Mitch's first paycheck came in. He'd be making $200 less a month at this new position, but they would live in the parsonage with no rent to pay. She scratched her temple and came up with a reasonable list of purchases: room-darkening blinds for the two bedrooms, fabric to make cushions and curtains for the living room, and—a definite must—some decorative items from one of the curio shops they passed in town.

It would take at least a month to get the house in order, on top of taking care of the kids, doing laundry, and cooking meals. *Hopefully, Mitch will refrain from asking me to take on any church duties for a while.* Aside from sitting in a pew on Sunday mornings, she wasn't about to plunge right in and start organizing women's meetings or whatever else might be expected of her. During their one Sunday there, she hadn't connected with any of the female members. They didn't say one word to her. Nor did they show up at the house to help clean and unpack boxes. They didn't even bring a welcoming casserole or a pie. *If they didn't make the first move, so be it. I'll be busy enough for a while. But poor Mitch.*

There was no assistant pastor, not even a church secretary. Besides preaching every Sunday, he'd have to visit the sick, comfort the troubled, and evangelize the neighborhood. And, of course, there were the usual baptisms, weddings, and funerals. To Lydia, such rituals added burden upon burden. She shrugged it all off. *It's Mitch's problem, not mine.* Instead, she set her mind on visiting the local antique stores and thrift shops. If she was going to live in a 100-year-old house, she wanted to decorate it like one.

She thought back to the first day they walked over to the parsonage. The attic's dormer windows had beckoned to her, like two big cat's eyes drawing her to the upper level. She hadn't stopped wondering what kind of treasures might be lying around up there. Moved with curiosity, she set aside the pencil and headed for the stairwell in the center of the house. She opened the door. A set of stairs shot upward and disappeared overhead into near darkness. She hit the wall switch, illuminating the stairwell in a soft yellow glow. Grasping the handrail, she began her ascent. Upon reaching the top she breathed in a swell of heat. Of course. The middle of August and the upper room hadn't been aired out in months or maybe years.

"Well," she scoffed. "This place can use a breath of fresh air."

She went to one of the dormers and turned the tiny crank. It squealed from years of neglect. Then she did the same at the other window. A soft breeze wafted in and dispelled the stifling heat. Filtered sunlight painted spatters of white on a jumble of artifacts. Lydia gasped with delight. It was a virtual treasure trove.

She poked around the piles and unearthed several useful items—a china tea service, a large bowl trimmed with gold leaf, and a full set of tarnished silverware. To one side of the room, beneath the slanted ceiling, she spotted a stack of linens, a couple of pillows, two heavy quilts, and some cloth dinner napkins embroidered with the letter B. She collected a few of the items and set them on the floor near the top of the stairwell.

Then she moved farther into the crawl space. There was an old trunk with leather straps and a huge padlock. Lydia's heart raced. *Who knows? The antiquated chest may have belonged to someone's great-great-grandmother.*

"Now let's see what you have in here." She tugged on the lock. It didn't give.

"C'mon," she grunted, and tried again. Still, it wouldn't budge.

"Okay," she mumbled. "There must be a key somewhere."

She straightened, looked around the attic, and spotted a small chest of drawers against the far wall. She nudged aside a stack of boxes and created a path for herself. She opened every drawer and found a few buttons, some hairpins, and an old comb.

Discouraged, she returned to the pile by the stairwell. The chest would have to wait. She gathered up as much as she could carry and carefully maneuvered down the narrow stairwell, clutching her treasures in one arm and gripping the rail with her free hand. She made three trips up and down the steps, moving faster with every climb. In the end she piled her collection in a corner of the kitchen.

She eyed the items with satisfaction, but the locked trunk in the attic continued to press upon her thoughts. With fresh passion, she searched the kitchen cupboards for a key. Nothing. She continued to open drawers hoping to find a tool, anything that might pry the lock open. A screwdriver beckoned to her at the back of the silverware drawer. She grasped it, slammed the drawer shut, and sprinted up the stairwell.

She spent several minutes prying and twisting the lock. At last, the rusted metal gave a loud snap and broke free. Her heart pounding, she knelt before the trunk and lifted the lid. Inside were layers of clothing—vintage dresses in soft cottons, and fancy gowns in shimmering silks and satins. Several dresses had lace collars and appliquéd flowers on the bodice. She ran her hand over the delicate fabrics, fingered the piles of colorful ribbons and sashes. Smiling, she closed her eyes and drifted back to another era.

She pulled out a dress and stood to her feet. A full-length mirror stood propped against the wall. She walked over to it and held the dress in front of her. The turn-of-the-century image brought a huge smile to her lips.

Now on fire, she raced back to the trunk and pulled out several long skirts and dresses. Most of them merely needed a good washing. A few were torn, but nothing she couldn't fix once her sewing machine arrived with the movers.

She smiled with satisfaction. "I have a whole new wardrobe, and I didn't have to go to one store or spend a single dime. Mitch should be proud of me."

She carried several pieces of clothing to the kitchen and spent the next hour sorting through her treasures, leaving once to check on the boys who were racing miniature cars on invisible roads on the floor in their bedroom.

At one o'clock, Mitch walked in. "Got any food?"

She gestured toward the fruit bowl on the table. "There are a couple of apples, but the bananas have turned brown. There's nothing in the house except for a jar of peanut butter and a loaf of bread. Can we go out and eat?"

Mitch frowned. "I'm in the middle of something."

"Okay then, peanut butter sandwiches and coffee."

Mitch wrinkled his nose. "Not peanut butter. Let me wrap things up in the office and we'll go out. I feel like a Philly cheesesteak. Just give me ten minutes."

"Okay," she agreed. "You go do whatever it is you need to do in there, and I'll finish up here."

He planted a kiss on her cheek, then turned away. She scowled at the back of his head. He hadn't even *mentioned* her pile of treasures.

"Mitch..."

He turned and raised his eyebrows.

"I went up in the attic this morning. Don't you want to know what I found up there?"

His eyes glazed over. "Sure, honey. What did you find?"

"All of this—" Smiling, she gestured toward the corner. "And there's lots more."

He glanced at the pile. His eyes flickered with amusement. "Good job." His tone carried a hint of disinterest.

Lydia pinched her lips together and turned away from him. He came closer and wrapped his arms around her. She flinched.

"I'm sorry, honey." His tone was soft, apologetic. "You can tell me all about what you found, later, on the way to the restaurant, okay? I'll give you my full attention. I promise."

She turned to face him and stared into his eyes. Clearly, his mind was elsewhere.

He headed for the door. "By the way, did you remember to pack some laundry soap?" he called over his shoulder.

"I did."

"Why don't you put a load in?"

A sharp bitterness ate into Lydia's heart. Mitch expected her to get the house in order, do the laundry, take care of the kids, and be available at his beck-and-call. And what was *he* doing? Escaping inside his office. He hadn't unpacked a single box or bag. She was about to charge after him, when her mother's pre-wedding lecture wriggled its way into her head. Most of what she'd said eluded her now, but there was something about wives submitting to their husband.

She tore herself away from her collection and trudged into the bedroom. She opened their suitcases and sorted the clothes into piles of colors and whites. Some of her personal items ended up in their own special pile. She wasn't about to use harsh laundry soap on her delicates. For that purpose she'd brought along a mild soap. It was expensive, but she used it sparingly and washed those items by hand.

Next, she checked the boys' pockets. Marbles. Dirty tissues. A penny. A couple of Hot Wheels cars. Last of all she started on Mitch's clothes. He rarely wore anything more than once. She tossed his shirts in one pile, his underwear in another, then she dug into the pockets of the jeans he wore during the historic Boston tour. She came up with a slip of paper. She unfolded it. Written in cursive was the name Deborah Staffle and a phone number along with the words, "Call me."

Lydia's heart sank. She stared at the note. What was going on? Confusion swirled around in her head. Mitch's ministry meant a lot to him. So did his family. So who was Deborah? Did she belong to the church? Did she need counseling? Or was this something else?

She folded the note, went into the kitchen and slipped it in her purse. She'd ask him about it later, but the thought of Mitch with someone else sent daggers into her heart.

She moved about the house in a daze, put a load of laundry in the washer, and got the boys freshened up for the trip to the restaurant, the mysterious note still pressing on the back of her mind.

Mitch returned from the office, and they got in the car. She slid in beside him, still teeming with curiosity. She peered in the back seat. She couldn't bring up the note in front of the boys. What if they got into an argument over it? What if she didn't like Mitch's explanation? She eyed him with suspicion. His expression looked far too innocent.

They drove in silence to a small eatery in the middle of town, chose a booth, and ordered sandwiches and Cokes. Lydia forced down a few bites but left half of the sandwich on her plate. She kept glancing at Mitch, voraciously tackling his Philly cheesesteak like he hadn't eaten in a week. The boys shared a melted ham-and-cheese sandwich. They scraped up every last French fry. She kept watching the three of them eat as if nothing else mattered but the food on their plates. At some point she would have to get Mitch alone and ask him about that blasted note.

Before heading home, they stopped at a grocery store and stocked up on cereal, milk, and orange juice, plus a frozen pepperoni pizza for supper, and a two-liter bottle of orange soda.

Mitch loaded the bags in the trunk. "You and the boys can do the bulk of the shopping tomorrow," he told her. "I've got to get back to the office and start working on my sermon for Sunday."

Lydia seethed in silence. On the way back to the house, Mitch yammered about Sunday's upcoming meeting and his search for the perfect topic.

"I could use your help, Lydia. Got any ideas?"

She shook her head and pressed her lips together.

He shot a glance at her. "Is something wrong?"

"No. Nothing's wrong." Her tone was short, but she didn't care.

"You look upset. Are you mad at me?"

"Stop it, Mitch. I've got a lot on my mind."

"Sorry."

She turned her head and looked out the side window. *Something wrong? There certainly is something wrong. You're keeping a secret that involves another woman. I'll corner him later, after the boys are in bed. He can't lie to me. Not when I look him straight in the eye.*

But, later came and went. When Mitch finished in the office, he ate a few bites of the pizza, took a hot shower, and stumbled into bed. By the time Lydia got the boys settled under their covers, her husband was out cold.

13

The following morning, Mitch grabbed a bowl of cereal and hurried to his office. Lydia hadn't spoken to him since supper last night. *Best to leave her to her household duties,* he thought. *The poor girl is overwhelmed by all the work ahead of her.* He should be pitching in but he needed to get moving with a sermon. Plus he had more to fix in his office, and the entire church stood like a broken vessel crying out for attention. He hadn't even begun to lift a paint brush or a hammer to its crumbling exterior.

He cleared his desk of everything except his Bible, a Matthew Henry commentary, and his laptop. He pulled a yellow pad out of his briefcase, leaned back in his chair, and jotted down several topics. None of them resonated. Neither did any of the ideas he'd considered over the last several days. He scratched his head, twirled the pencil between his fingers, and flipped through his Bible in an aimless search for something—anything. He was a complete blank. If writers got writer's block, then he must be having preacher's block— if such a thing existed.

What about one of the messages I gave to the youth group? He opened his briefcase again and pulled out a battered notebook, searched through the pages, and paused over a few possibilities. Nothing fit the kind of audience he was facing here. The folks at Mercy Fellowship didn't have the wide-eyed, eager looks of the White Hills teenagers. His poignant yet lighthearted talks wouldn't work in this forsaken place.

He stuffed the old notebook back in his briefcase and

turned to the topical index at the back of his Bible. He needed to strike at the core of their stubborn hearts, wake them up, get a rise out of them, even if they pelted him with tomatoes and eggs. At least that would be something.

The office was stuffy. And hot. He adjusted the thermostat to bring in more cool air. He pulled out a handkerchief and mopped his brow. He hadn't gotten a good night's sleep since the night they spent at the inn. Last night he woke up several times with a hundred images swirling around in his head. The stone-faced congregation. The shadow in the pew. The myriad of pastors who had come and left. The newspaper reports. Abigail Hoffman. Her husband—murdered in the same church Mitch had come to lead. A ton of unanswered questions rolled around in his head.

His office door squeaked open, and Matthew poke his head in. "Mom's takin' us grocery shopping. Want anything?"

"Whatever your mother buys is okay with me." He licked his lips and glanced at Matthew. "How about some chocolate chip cookies?"

"Yum. Wanna go with us?"

He shook his head. "No thanks, Matt. I need to work on my sermon."

The boy gave him a wave and shut the door.

Mitch stared at the items on his desk. His mind was still on the murder. He sprang from his chair and opened the door. His wife and sons were getting into the car.

"Wait, Lydia. Will you drop me off at the library?"

She raised an eyebrow. "I thought you were working on your sermon."

"I need to do some research."

She paused and glared at him for an instant, then her frown

disappeared. "Come on," she said with an air of impatience. "We're ready to go."

Once again, they rode in silence. Lydia stared ahead at the road. She didn't look happy, but he wasn't about to ask. He'd been walking on eggshells since yesterday. He blinked back his discomfort. Lydia had never behaved so unreachable before. Perhaps the change of scene was stressing her out. He shrugged inwardly. *She'll open up when she's ready.*

When they pulled up to the curb in front of the library, Mitch mouthed a quick good-bye, stepped out of the car, and bounded up the steps. Once again he settled in front of the microfiche reader. This time he focused on stories from 1992 to 1994, when things started to change at the church, and Travis Hoffman ended up dead in a pew.

He brought up the article he'd read during his last visit to the library. It included a color photo of an attractive, well-groomed, middle-aged man with a full head of hair, graying at the temples, and sharp blue eyes staring directly into the camera lens. For his portrait, Travis Hoffman wore a tailored gray suit and a striped blue-and-white tie with a diamond-studded clip. On his wrist was a fancy gold watch, and he had a large diamond ring on his third finger. The image literally screamed money.

Mitch read the entire piece.

Travis J. Hoffman, a local real estate broker, was shot and killed during the 10 a.m. church service, Sunday, at Mercy Fellowship. Shadow Glenn Police Sergeant Andrew Wallace apprehended the suspect, Milton Meadows, at his home an hour later. Meadows owned a semi-automatic handgun. He did not deny killing his best friend.

According to eye witnesses, Meadows and Hoffman were seen

arguing at a local club the night before. Several patrons said Meadows accused Hoffman of having an affair with his wife, Marilee Meadows.

The shooting incident took place while dozens of people, including children, were seated in the sanctuary. No one else was injured.

"There were two popping sounds and Travis slumped over in the third pew next to his wife," said longtime member, Elsie Filbert, 79. "Abigail started screaming, and Milton ran out the door," Filbert added.

Second-degree murder charges are pending.

Mitch sat back. He ran his hand through his hair and collected a few beads of sweat from his forehead. He'd solved one piece of the puzzle. The Hoffmans were sitting in the third pew, precisely where he'd seen the strange shadow.

He scrolled in reverse and found a follow-up article. Milton Meadows admitted guilt. His lawyer pushed for temporary insanity, and the district attorney lowered the charge to voluntary man-slaughter. Mitch drew back. *Voluntary man-slaughter? The guy came to the church with a gun. If that wasn't pre-meditated...*

Mitch reversed again. Meadows stuck with his plea of temporary insanity and received a ten-year sentence in the county jail to be followed by five years of probation with psychiatric counseling. *Twenty years ago. By this time, the guy had to be released. Did he stay in Shadow Glenn or did he run off to some other town? It might help to know that little detail.*

Mitch did another search for Travis Hoffman's name and came up with the obituary. It mentioned Hoffman's numerous accomplishments, listed his surviving family members, and ended with the time and place for the service, with the Reverend Phineas Drummond officiating.

He let out a long breath and switched off the machine. Puzzle piece number two. The murder occurred during the time the Drummonds were in ministry at Mercy Fellowship. Shortly after, Phineas was asked to leave, and he and Cornelia went back to Salem.

Mitch pulled out his cell phone and started to call Lydia for a ride home, but he changed his mind and tucked the phone back in his pocket. The church was a few blocks from the library. He could jog back.

He went straight to his office, turned on his computer, and typed the words "Salem witch trials" in the Google search box. The idea had surfaced in the library and had stuck with him. Fortunately, the deacons had had enough sense to keep the office connected to the internet. That was something anyway.

A long list of resources came up. He chose the one headed, *True and False Claims about Salem's Witch Hunt.*

From the text he derived several bits of interest: *Salem's witch trials took place during the 17th century. More than two hundred people were accused of practicing witchcraft. Thirty were found guilty. Nineteen—fourteen women and five men—were executed by hanging. At least five people died in jail, and one man, Giles Corey, was pressed to death for refusing to plead. These men and women were accused of both good deeds and bad deeds. Sometimes they cursed people with an illness or a calamity. At other times they claimed to have miraculously healed someone. Personal feuds often ended with people accusing their enemies of witchcraft, even though they could provide no proof. Those who were charged with witchcraft were hung to death.*

The web site offered numerous examples of people—men, women, and even children—who'd been charged with acts of witchcraft. Three-hundred years later, largely due to the efforts of their descendents, they were exonerated by government order, and accusations of witchcraft ceased in Salem.

What if there is a relationship between the Salem witch trials and what was happening at Mercy Fellowship? Mitch pondered. *A man died under Drummond's watch. After the Drummonds left, several pastors fled for their lives. Those who stayed ended up in a scandal or stole money from the church or took their own lives.* Mitch mopped his brow, now wet with perspiration.

He thought about Abigail Hoffman. The woman lost her husband during a Sunday service. She stopped attending church. When Mitch told her he was the new pastor, she responded with obvious disdain. The church went through other drastic changes. Membership began to decline. The former sense of camaraderie vanished. People came to services but didn't get involved. Several families left the church.

He went to the metal cabinet and dug through the files until he found what he was looking for—the hiring and termination of pastors who'd taken the pulpit after the Drummonds left.

He opened the folder and clenched his jaw. *Great. Whoever filed the data didn't bother to put it in chronological order.* It was going to take the rest of the day to organize the pile of applications and resignations. At that moment, he wished he had the funds to hire a secretary. Now he'd have to do the job himself. Privately. He couldn't even tell Lydia what he was looking for. She was already in some sort of snit.

He carried the folder to his desk, shoved his Bible aside, and spent the next two hours arranging the documents according to dates. The tedious job was taking him away from writing a sermon, but he'd responded to a stronger compulsion, and he couldn't stop until he was finished.

He'd barely made a dent when Luke's squeaky little voice came from the doorway. "Dad, supper." He looked out the window. The sun had tipped beneath the treetops. He'd been so intent on sorting through the files he hadn't noticed when his family pulled into the driveway.

"Be right there," he called out. He continued to stare out the window, his heart melting as he watched his little boy run back to the house.

A stab of guilt gripped him. In all the furor, he'd forgotten his main job, the protection and care of his wife and sons. Yet here he sat, a few yards away from them, engrossed in something he never should have gotten involved in. Somewhere along the way he'd forgotten what the Bible said about loving his wife the way Christ loved the church. Something was bothering Lydia, but he hadn't bothered to make time for her. And what about bringing up his children in the nurture and admonition of the Lord? He'd gone off in his own little world and left the job to their mother.

He clenched his teeth, angry at himself for allowing this search to interfere with both his work and his role of husband and father. What happened to sticking to the plan and not quitting? Scowling, he gathered up the files and crammed them back inside the cabinet. With a snap of his wrist, he slammed the drawer shut. *Tonight I'll have dinner with my wife and sons and then take them to a movie. After a good night's rest, I'll tackle the sermon in the morning.*

A sense of peace swept over Mitch as he joined the others at the supper table. A nostril-tingling aroma of fried chicken wafted from the platter in the center. Beside it, a glob of butter melted over a pile of mashed potatoes. There was also a salad of mixed greens and tomatoes, plus a basket of steamy dinner rolls. Lydia was pouring orange soda in four glasses.

His stomach screaming to be fed, he mumbled a quick blessing and dug in. Their conversation turned light. This time he listened with genuine interest to Lydia's animated description of her glorious find in the attic.

"How many cups are in the tea service?"

Like he really wants to know.

"Eleven. One cup is missing."

"Fine. You can invite ten of your best friends for afternoon tea."

She gave a girlish shrug. "I suppose it could happen if the women of the church ever open up to me." She sent him a coy smile. "Or I think I'll get you and the boys to put on some of my vintage clothes and join me for a tea party." She laughed.

"Think again," he said and shoved a forkful of potatoes in his mouth.

Luke giggled. "A tea party? Like the one at Boston Harbor?"

Lydia shook her head. "No, silly boy. Like the kind women and girls attend, all dressed up in fancy clothes."

"No way," Matthew burst out. "I ain't wearin' no dress."

"Me neither," Luke added. "I ain't no sissy."

"Don't say ain't," Lydia chided them.

Mitch chuckled. "I'm afraid I have to side with the boys. You won't catch *me* wearing a long dress with ruffles and lace." He tilted his head and winked at her. "But I can picture *you* in them, my lovely wife."

She stared at him, her brown eyes darkening. "I'm planning to fix up the dresses I found in the attic. And, except for a few notions, it won't cost you a penny." There was a slight edge to her voice.

"Well, your sewing machine will be here in another day or so. You can go to town with it." Best to keep their conversation light. He still had no idea what she was thinking. Sometimes the fire in her eyes disagreed with the sweetness from her lips.

She raised her chin. "I'm looking forward to it. You know how much I love to create something from nothing."

"Like God did?" Luke popped up. "We learned in Sunday school last year how God made everything from nothing."

Lydia smiled. "Well, God didn't need any materials. But I do. I could use a couple yards of fabric and some needles and thread." She gave Mitch a sideways glance.

"You can have anything you need," he said with a nod. Then he reached for another piece of chicken. "Now, eat up, boys. After dinner, we're going to a movie."

They responded with a cheer and a friendly jabbing at each other's arm. Most of the time Matthew and Luke got along fine—a doting older brother and a little guy who tried to emulate everything Matthew did. Now they were giggling and elbowing each other. Mitch enjoyed the moment. He had a loving wife who could cook up a storm and two kids who nearly made the buttons pop off his shirt. What man could ask for more?

After supper, still working on being a changed man, Mitch helped Lydia with the dishes. Then they all piled into the car and drove to town. To the boys' delight, *Finding Dory* was playing at the Bijou. They arrived in time to get an extra-large popcorn and four Cokes. The boys led the way to an open row of seats, and the four of them escaped within the colors and music of the animated film. Mitch sat back and relaxed. There were no threats or shadows or otherworld phenomena in this place. He needed to forget about the weird stuff and start fresh in the morning.

He looked at Lydia. A rainbow of movie lights lapped at her smiling face. Mitch's heart pounded with love for her. He took her hand. "We're gonna be fine."

She stared at him, her eyes wide. "Why did you say that? Did something happen today?"

"No, honey, nothing happened." He swallowed the lump in his throat and smiled.

She eyed him with suspicion.

"Really, Lydia. Everything's okay."

But was it?

14

After spending another agonizing night on a lumpy mattress, Lydia groaned and eased her aching body out of bed.

"I can't wait until those movers get here with our beds." She said more to herself than to Mitch, who was just opening his eyes.

She did a couple of stretches, then pulled on a pair of slacks and a cotton blouse and went to the bathroom to freshen up. Fifteen minutes later, she started putting breakfast on the table.

The boys chose cereal and strawberries. She offered to make Mitch an omelet. He turned it down, grabbed a piece of buttered toast and a cup of coffee and headed out to his office. She scowled at the back of his head as he went out the door.

After breakfast, Matthew and Luke went into their bedroom to play. With school starting in two weeks, Lydia should be signing them up. But, she reasoned, she had all of next week to get them enrolled. For now, she wanted to get the house in order.

She cleaned the kitchen cupboards, discarded items she didn't need, and shoved aside the dishes to make room for her own. Then she grabbed a broom and started sweeping. When she reached the far end of the kitchen she stopped short of a door half-hidden behind a free-standing pantry.

She tried the knob. It didn't move. A key protruded. She turned it with a loud click and opened the door. Before her was a dark, descending stairway. A flurry of excitement ran through her. Feeling a little like Alice descending into Wonderland, she set aside the broom and felt for a light switch inside the opening. She found it, turned it on, and a soft, yellow glow illuminated the stairwell. Smiling with anticipation, she started down. When she reached the bottom, a cloak of mustiness struck her. She found another light switch and flicked it up. A solitary bulb hung on a wire from a rafter and cast a circle of light within the haze. The entire basement measured about half the size of the house above, like an afterthought the builders had added in the midst of construction.

A foundation of weeping rocks and mortar rose on all four sides. To the right was a furnace and a hot water heater. Insulated conduits ran around the perimeter of the ceiling along with a jumble of electrical wires. Scattered about the cement floor were old newspapers, cardboard boxes, broken glass, and pieces of wood. Along one wall dilapidated shelves bore a couple dozen Mason jars filled with the remnants of someone's canning projects. The discolored jars held what looked to be peaches, tomatoes, and peppers.

Lydia brushed cobwebs from the jars, eyed the contents, and backed away in disgust. She wouldn't be able to salvage any of it.

There was a loud thump. She flinched. The thumping continued and sent the light bulb bobbing and swaying. Its movement cast eerie shadows on the walls. She froze and held her breath. Another thump. She exhaled and smiled. The cellar was directly beneath the boys' bedroom.

"Okay," she shouted through the ceiling. "You kids settle down up there. And stay out of trouble. I'll be checking on you."

The thumping ceased, and the light bulb stopped swaying.

Next thing, she spotted a pile of tools on the floor in the corner. She sorted through them and came away with a small garden spade, a metal watering can, and a rake with a broken handle.

"A little white vinegar and some masking tape and these things will be good as new," she declared with confidence. She carried the items up the stairs and lay them near the front door where Mitch would be sure to notice them when he came home.

She poked her head in the boys' room and found them lying on the floor, coloring. Satisfied, she made another trip downstairs. She squinted against the semi-darkness, but perked up with excitement at the sight of a cozy little area in the far corner away from the limited glow of the solitary bulb. The cluster of furnishings included a rocking chair with a red-and-black quilt slung over its back, a wooden crate, and a small table bearing an old-fashioned lamp with a fringed shade. Lydia nearly tripped over her own feet in her hurry to get there.

As she drew close, the air changed from a damp coldness to a pleasant warmth. It was as if a blanket of hospitality had settled there.

She ran her hand over the quilt, then she turned on the lamp. It cast a comforting orange glow on her surroundings. She stooped beside the crate and lifted the top. Inside she found a pile of candles, peacock feathers, a brass bell, and a pewter chalice. She lifted the bell and the chalice, held them up and admired them in the light of the lamp. Setting them on the chair, she returned to the crate where she found a tangle of beaded jewelry, a five-pointed star, and a three-legged incense burner. Near the bottom was a pile of stones in different sizes, dried cattails, pine cones, and multiple pieces of colored glass.

During college, she'd read about some of those items in a book on religious history. The five-pointed star had something to do with witchcraft, but it also had a spiritual significance. So did the chalice and the incense burner. She stared in astonishment. Did someone practice witchcraft a mere ten yards away from the church?

A creaking sound drew her attention to the stairs. She held her breath and a chill ran through her.

"Is someone there?"

No one answered.

"Matthew? Luke?"

Silence.

The dangling bulb jiggled and threw out a shifting of shadows. Lydia darted her eyes about the basement. She was alone, yet she didn't *feel* alone. She closed up the box, picked up the bell and the chalice, and walked with halting steps to the stairs. She glanced over her shoulder, thought she saw a shadow in the far corner. Shivering, she turned off the light, and fled up the steps.

After locking the cellar door, she hid the bell and the chalice behind the sugar bowl at the back of a cupboard. Then she went to the boys' room and stood watching them from their doorway.

Matthew looked up from his coloring book. "Hi, Mom."

Luke put down his crayon, sprang to his feet and rushed over to give her a hug.

"Can we do something fun, Mama?"

"Sure." Then, on impulse, "We'll go back to the library."

Matthew sidled up beside her. "We didn't get to use the computers last time. Too many other kids were there."

"Well, let's see if we can get to use at least one computer," she assured them.

As it turned out, when they arrived at the library, the children's area was empty. Lydia got Matthew and Luke settled in front of two computers, then she hurried to the adult section and searched the shelves. Embarrassed to ask the librarian for assistance, she walked up and down the aisles until she found what she was looking for, an entire section on supernatural phenomena. One large volume in particular stood out from the rest. It had a red cover and raised gold lettering, *Dorcas Redding's Complete Book on Spiritual Energy.*

If the library was good enough for Mitch's research, it was good enough for hers. She took the hefty book to the children's section, squeezed into a tiny chair, and propped the book on the little table in front of her. Matthew was deep into a math challenge, and Luke was involved in a wildlife game. She checked her wristwatch—11:15, almost lunchtime. She opened the book, leafed through the pages, and went to the alphabetical glossary in the back. With increasing fascination, she searched for each of the items she'd found in the basement.

Bell: Used for Christmas carols, hymn singing, calls to order, and other church rituals. The soft chiming can create a relaxed atmosphere. Rung louder, a bell can stir up a passionate fervor. Bells also can be used to ward off negative spirits and to summon positive energy. It's a good idea to ring a bell to begin a sacred meeting and to bring it to a close.

The description sounded innocent enough. Lydia nodded with confidence and turned the page to the letter *C*.

Chalice: A tool of hospitality. When filled with wine, the chalice can be passed around a circle to be shared with guests. Not only does this unite the group, it also carries a promise that they will not thirst.

Despite the warmth in the children's section, a shiver traveled down Lydia's spine. She started to close the book, but shook off the discomfort and flipped to the letter *I*.

Incense burner: A small version of the larger three-legged cauldron used during incantations. The burning of incense can help with the placement and removal of spells.

Lydia swallowed and looked at her two boys. They were still engrossed in their games. She glanced through the window at the librarian. The woman was reading a book. Lydia turned to the letter *S* and searched for the word *Star*. The reference sent her to *P* for Pentagram.

In the middle of a full page of text was a pen-and-ink sketch of a five-pointed star, similar to the one she'd found in the box. She read the first paragraph.

Pentagram: A religious symbol with Chinese and Japanese roots. It should be drawn with one continuous line. Pentagrams protect against negative spiritual energy. Used in a variety of rituals, the five points relate to the five elements of nature—space, air, fire, water, and earth. Inverted, the pentagram is a tool for black magic.

Her throat tightened. She took a deep breath and flipped through the main section of the book. One chapter focused on rituals, incantations, and spiritual sessions—unholy practices she'd heard about while attending youth group when she was a teenager.

"When you let something into your mind it will stay there forever," Pastor Jimmy told the gathering. "Whether it be pornography, cursing, violence, or the lies of Satan, once you've allowed it to penetrate your mind, you'll never be rid of it. Whatever you pour into your brain will affect everything you say and everything you do for the rest of your life. So be careful what you feed your brain."

She looked at the boys. With a heavy heart, she closed the book and returned it to the shelf. She went back to the children's section, knelt between her sons, and tried to get interested in their interactive games.

Pastor Jimmy was right. Though her eyes were focused on the boys' computer screens, her mind was on the items she'd found in the basement. Against her better judgment, she found herself longing to know more.

15

Mitch spent the entire morning reading through passages of scripture, checking commentaries, mulling over different topics, pacing, sitting, scratching his head, and staring out the window. In the end, he was no better off than when he'd started.

Perhaps a change of scene. But where could he go? Lydia had taken the car and was out with the boys. No telling when they'd be home.

He could walk somewhere. Maybe go down to the river. The tranquility of nature might bring him closer to God. Perhaps an idea will surface there.

Or he could talk to somebody. He could call Martin. He looked at his watch. His former pastor was probably doing the same thing Mitch should be doing right then—working on Sunday's sermon.

Okay. Perhaps he could call on someone right there in Shadow Glenn. Someone who knew a lot about Mercy Fellowship's history, someone who could clear up a few questions and set his mind at ease. If he could get some answers, there'd be no need to go through the files, and he'd be able to concentrate on more pressing things, like a fire-breathing message.

He pulled out the business cards the deacons had handed him during his interview. He tossed them one-by-one onto the desk. *Not him. Not him. Definitely not him. He barely looked at me.* Mitch stared at the last card in his hand. *Elijah Garby, head deacon.*

If anyone could tell him about the church's history, Elijah

Garby could. He'd been there longer than anyone else. Plus, the man's ancestors helped start Mercy Fellowship. Hopefully, he'd be able to dig beneath Elijah's rough exterior and find something of substance, sort of like a patient does when he goes to a doctor with rotten bedside manner. It doesn't matter if the doctor isn't a nice guy. The patient merely needs to get the facts and find healing.

He pulled out his cell phone and hesitated for only a moment. The old coot *had* invited him back.

He punched in the number and waited through three rings before Garby's voice grunted over the airwaves.

"It's your dime."

"Mister Garby?"

"You got-im."

"This is Mitch—your new pastor."

"I know it. Your name came up on the screen. Whacha want?"

Mitch started to hang up. Maybe this was a mistake.

"Calloway?" Garby growled.

"Yes, sir, it's me."

"Well?"

"I—um…"

Mitch berated himself. *Come on, you little wimp. Pull it together. You're the pastor. Now act like it.*

"What is it, son? Speak up."

"I was wondering if you and I could meet, maybe get a cup of coffee? I have some things I'd like to ask you."

"Coffee, huh?" Garby's voice had softened.

"Sure, you name the place. I'll buy. Um, I don't have a car right now. Lydia's out with the boys. I'll have to walk over."

More silence.

"Mister Garby?"

"There's a little cafe around the corner from the church on Second Avenue. Meet me there in a half-hour."

There was a loud click, and the phone went dead. *Strange. The old geezer actually sounded friendly.*

He hurried to the house to freshen up, then left for the cafe.

He found Garby already settled in a booth. Two cups of coffee sat on the table along with a bowl of creamers and a plate of jellied scones.

Mitch slid into the booth across from Garby. "Thanks for ordering." He proceeded to doctor his coffee with cream and sugar.

While Garby noisily slurped his java, Mitch took a moment to look him over. Garby's sparse gray hair brought out the steel gray in his eyes. Like most people in their 90s, the skin at his jaw sagged until it blended with the creases in his neck. To say he had wrinkles was an understatement. His face was riddled with them. But they added an air of sagacity to the man's demeanor and definitely made him the most likely vehicle for a trip into the past.

Mitch took a sip, set down his cup, and faced his aged companion.

"Mister Garby, I'm trying to get settled in my position here. I've been thrown in at the deep end of the pool. I sure could use a little guidance—or information, at least—to help me get things going in the right direction."

Garby nodded but said nothing. A flicker of his eyelids told Mitch he was still listening.

"Anyway, I was poking around in the church office, and I stumbled on some old records."

He'd purposely said, "stumbled on." He didn't want Garby to think he'd been prying. His actions might seem distrustful, or nosy. The thing was, those records meant a lot to his position. He had every right to read them.

He bit into a scone and savored the burst of jelly.

"I found a long list of pastors' names. They went back to the beginning. One of your ancestors helped found Mercy Fellowship. The man's name was Elijah Garby, like yours. And there was his son, Ezra, your grandfather, I assume."

Garby took a bite of a scone, brushed the powdered sugar off his shirt, and followed with a swallow of coffee. He looked straight into Mitch's eyes and nodded.

"It ain't nothin' special. Every one of our members has ties to the start of the church. One thing, though—" He straightened his back and puffed out his chest. "My ancestors all held positions in leadership. Deacons mostly. They kept the church going, even during the tough times. They kept people coming back."

Mitch slumped back against the booth. "So, was Elijah your great-grandfather?"

"Yep. I was named after him."

"From the records it seems Mercy Fellowship went through several periods of growth. The people worked together, sometimes doing hard labor. When a part of the building was destroyed by fire, they pitched in and rebuilt it. They also added the annex. And they purchased the adjoining property along with the house."

Garby kept nodding and tore apart another scone. He stuffed a piece in his mouth and chewed slowly.

"I have one concern—" Mitch paused and allowed the remark to sink in.

Garby stopped eating and gave him his full attention. Encouraged, Mitch plunged ahead.

"It appears something changed at Mercy Fellowship during the two years Phineas Drummond served there."

Garby appeared unmoved. "You say something changed? Like what?"

"Well sir, the membership started to decline. People stopped getting together for holidays and church functions. Even more troubling, after the Drummonds left, ten different men filled the pastor's position and none of them stayed. Most of them left after a few months, often under distressing circumstances." Mitch leaned across the table. "Can you tell me what happened, Mister Garby? Why did they leave so abruptly? And why did several months, and even years, pass when there was no pastor at all?"

Garby took a bite of his scone and closed his eyes, like he'd just gone to heaven. When he opened them again, he was staring at Mitch. If the man had a supply of arrows hidden inside those gray orbs, Mitch doubted he'd be able to survive an attack. He gazed back, unflinching, determined to get some answers, even if Garby let those arrows fly.

"They left." Garby's tone was firm, as if those two words should satisfy Mitch's curiosity.

They didn't. "But why? *Why* did they leave?" Mitch persisted.

Garby gave a one-shouldered shrug. "Who knows?" He finished off the scone. "Most of them offered no explanation at all. A few gave feeble excuses—a sick relative, family problems, financial issues. A couple told us they'd been offered a better position."

"What about the suicides?"

"What about 'em? People take their own lives every day. Pastors are people. They have problems, like everybody else."

"But all the trouble happened in the last twenty years. Did

it ever occur to the board the problem could be traced back to Phineas Drummond? Or maybe the man's wife? They came from Salem, for Pete's sake."

For several minutes, Garby stared off at another part of the cafe. He ignored the remaining scone, even let his coffee go cold. He merely sat and stared, like a person does when stumbling through answers.

"Mister Garby?"

The old man looked into his eyes and lowered his voice. "Do you remember at your interview, I asked if you'd ever dealt with spiritual attacks? You told me you believed Satan was at work trying to destroy people's testimony. But you didn't say if you'd ever faced spiritual warfare."

Mitch tilted his head to one side. "I thought you meant the ongoing struggle we have with evil in the world, not an actual demonic encounter. Like I said at my interview, I'm not an exorcist. I'm a simple preacher. Apparently, you hired me to bring life back into a dying church. I'm not sure I can do it."

Garby sat back against the booth. He dabbed his mouth with a paper napkin.

"The only information I can give you, Mitch, is Drummond's wife Cornelia was descended from one of those people who were accused of witchcraft back in the 1600s. There was something unsettling about her. We liked Phineas. He was a solid preacher who spoke straight from the word of God. He backed everything with scripture, applied the verses to modern life, and laced his talks with humorous anecdotes. But after a while, strange things started happening."

"Strange things? What do you mean? What sort of strange things?"

Garby frowned like he was trying to decide if he should say more.

"You've seen the shadows?" the old man said at last.

Mitch shifted in his seat. "Didn't someone say they were caused by an elm tree shifting outside the window?"

"Poppycock."

Mitch smiled inwardly at the time-worn aphorism. "Okay, what *did* cause it?"

"For one thing, there was that dad-blamed murder."

Mitch nodded. "Travis Hoffman."

Garby raised his eyebrows. "You know about that?"

Mitch shrugged. "I read a newspaper story at the library."

"That's when the shadows started," Garby acknowledged, nodding. "A few folks insisted Hoffman's widow and Cornelia Drummond had something to do with them. People stayed away from the pew where Travis was killed. They claimed they couldn't get the blood out of the wood. Other strange things started happening in the church and in the parsonage."

Mitch perked up. "Like what?"

Garby shrugged his bony shoulders. "Like cold bedrooms, flies on the window, strange noises."

Mitch felt a little shiver. He sipped his coffee, hoping to break the sudden chill.

"That's not all," Garby said, almost in a whisper. "About the same time the members started getting into little feuds over trivial matters, like who deserved which parking spot and what the Bible said about certain topics. Our fellowship went downhill. Finally, the board met and voted to ask the Drummonds to leave. They went back to Salem, and we figured things should go back to normal."

Mitch coddled his coffee cup and eyed the old man over the

rim. "But, they didn't, did they?" Now he was whispering too.

"Nope. Even after the Drummonds left things kept going downhill."

Mitch took a deep breath. "Go on."

"All I can say is, some sort of evil presence descended on our church. The members sensed it too. People started leaving. The only members who remained were the descendents of those who founded Mercy Fellowship. We couldn't build up the membership, except for maybe kids being born. The thing is, when they're old enough to go their own way, they leave town as fast as their young legs can carry them. Outsiders visit but they don't come back." Garby grunted. "Mercy Fellowship has become a misnomer. The word fellowship doesn't exist for us anymore. Neither does mercy. People stopped reaching out to one another. Holiday functions ceased. And potluck dinners? We haven't enjoyed one in years."

The poor guy sounded extremely sad about the whole situation. He really cared.

A trickle of unease ran through Mitch. Aware that his hands were shaking, he set the cup down without taking another sip. One question still taunted him.

"I have to know, Mr. Garby, did Cornelia practice witchcraft?"

"We assumed she'd been dabbling in some kind of evil in the basement of the parsonage. Deacon John took a quick look down there, claimed he didn't see anything suspicious, and gave it up."

"It must have been difficult to ask Pastor Drummond to leave."

"We didn't want to fire him. We all liked him. But the church had started coming apart. And so, with much sadness, we let him go."

Elijah swept a hand over the table like he wanted to end the discussion.

"If I were you, Mitch Calloway, I'd concentrate on Sunday's sermon and stop fretting over the church's history. Focus instead on its future."

"That's what I'm trying to do, but I need to know what I'm dealing with here. Do you honestly think I can do any better than all those other preachers who came before me?"

Garby tilted his head and stared at him, like he was evaluating him all over again. The lines on his face softened as did the color of his eyes. "You're not like them. I could tell the day we interviewed you. If you're the kind of preacher I think you are, you'll bathe your family in prayer and you'll set things right in the church. The main thing is, stay in the word, Mitch. There ain't an evil on earth that can stand up to the power of the Holy Scriptures and a man dedicated to following them."

"What about Phineas Drummond? You said *he* was a righteous man."

"Phineas had one flaw, one weakness."

Mitch nodded. "Cornelia."

"Don't fret yourself over them. Just do the job we hired you to do. And keep your kids out of the parsonage basement. It's dank and it's dirty, and there's nothing but junk down there. If you're smart, you'll lock the door and hide the key."

16

Sunday came faster than Mitch was ready for it. Somehow he got through a semblance of a sermon. At one point he thought he caught a flicker of interest, but he wasn't sure. Like before, the gathering sat there looking like prototypes for Mount Rushmore. At the conclusion, he stood with his wife and sons on the front steps. No one stopped to shake his hand. There were no words of encouragement.

At home, he worked hard to shed the morning's disappointment. He needed a distraction, so he made an honest effort to examine the collection of junk Lydia had pulled from the attic.

"Nice bowl," he said, lifting a piece of chipped pottery from the pile. "What do you plan to use it for?"

She shrugged. "Whatever." At least he'd gotten her to smile.

He pointed at the tarnished silverware, couldn't picture himself putting one of those rusty forks in his mouth. "You gonna polish all those?"

She nodded. "Yes, and we're going to use it. Every last fork and spoon."

He swallowed his revulsion and went through the rest of the pile, all the while admitting the truth. Lydia could turn junk into treasure, tattered clothing into tasteful attire, and yes, old flatware into a sparkling dinner setting fit for a queen.

She answered his questions, enthusiastically at first, then her spirit seemed to wane, like she'd figured out he'd lost interest.

In the end he left her to her collection. He drove to the hardware store and bought two cans of white paint, some brushes, and a roller. Time to spruce up the office. If nothing else, a coat of fresh paint would smell a whole lot better than the musty, suffocating odor that welcomed him every morning.

He didn't return to the house until suppertime. Then he discarded his cares amidst crusted roast beef and cheddar-topped scalloped potatoes. One thing was certain, he'd married a super cook. Even the boys were shoveling food into their mouths.

Mitch looked at his wife sitting across from him. She was more than a good cook. She was his soul mate, the love of his life, and she was the prettiest woman on earth—in *his* mind anyway. She'd swept her hair back in a thick bun, and her eyes reflected the overhead light like two onyx stones, dark and exotic.

But she'd changed since coming to Shadow Glenn. He stared at his plate and tried to think back over their conversations. He must have done or said something to upset her. But what? He'd been so busy settling into his job he hadn't made time to corner her for some answers.

He raised his head and locked eyes with her. Their former warmth hadn't returned. Instead, two cold marbles stared back at him.

"Is anything wrong, Lydia?"

She glanced at the boys. "Not now." Then she picked up her knife and fork and vigorously slashed her roast beef.

Monday morning began in a rush. After breakfast, Mitch disappeared in his office. Lydia put the boys in the car and drove to the elementary school. The inside of the car smelled like bubble gum bath oil and minty hair gel. She glanced in the rear-view mirror at two little strangers in freshly ironed shirts, their gelled hair combed flat with a part on the side. Matthew was going into second grade and Luke was starting kindergarten. They were growing up way too fast.

The enrollment process took longer than Lydia expected. The forms contained a lot of questions about the boy's abilities, their likes and dislikes, their allergies, and their home life situation. *Was it a single parent home? Sometimes it felt like it was,* Lydia admitted to herself. *Especially lately with Mitch plunging head first into his new post and spending little time with the family.* Except for dinners—and their one trip to the movies—they rarely saw him anymore.

She still hung onto the note, but her anxiety had settled down. *Surely there is a good explanation. Mitch isn't behaving like the a guy who keeps a girlfriend on the side. No secret phone calls, no sneaking out of the house in the middle of the night. Most of the time he just falls into bed, exhausted and complaining about the lack of interest his congregation showed.*

She completed the paperwork and looked over a separate sheet listing the required vaccinations, the school's dress code, and the academic supplies the boys needed.

"Is there a Walmart in this town?" Lydia asked.

"Closest one's in North Reading. But you can find pretty much everything you need at the drugstore right here in Shadow Glenn." The lady behind the desk smiled with encouragement.

Before leaving the school, Lydia met the children's teachers. Matthew was sent to Miss Kilbourne, a young blonde with what looked to be a permanent pout on her lips. Poor, sensitive Matthew. It had taken two school years to bring him out of his shell. The wrong person could drive him right back into it.

"Here's a list of rules for my classroom." Miss Kilbourne's clipped voice sent a shiver of unease through Lydia. "Make sure your son is aware of every one of these rules, and we'll get along just fine."

Lydia glanced at the list, shut her eyes—and her mouth—and tucked the papers in her purse.

Out in the hall, she bent close to Matthew and lowered her voice. "You let me know if she gives you a hard time."

Luke fared much better with Mrs. Tarbell, the kindergarten teacher. A gray-haired little woman, she greeted him with a smile and a sparkle in her eyes.

"Come give me a big hug." She spread her arms, and Luke melted inside them.

Though Mrs. Tarbell looked old enough to retire, she immediately came down to Luke's level. Lydia smiled with contentment. She wouldn't have to worry about her youngest son adjusting to his first day of school in another week.

When they left the building, Lydia looked at her watch—11:30. In a half-hour or so, Mitch would be rooting around in the kitchen, hungry but absolutely helpless. She should head straight for home, but instead of turning the car left toward the church, she turned right and drove through Main Street's shopping district. They stopped at the drugstore where Lydia purchased the items the boys needed for school. She was still thinking about the book she'd read at the library. She wanted her own copy.

The first day they came into town, she'd spotted a tiny bookstore squashed between two larger shops with a sign in the window that said, *Millicent's Cozy Corner.*

She located the shop, parked the car at the curb, and with both children in tow, hurried through the door to the tinkle of a bell that brought a smile to her lips. The room felt cozy. A hint of musk incense filled the air. And there were books. Lots of them, and multiple shelves with narrow walkways between them.

A young girl wearing the name tag, *Millicent,* surfaced from around a corner. "May I help you?" She had the deepest blue eyes Lydia had ever seen. *Or are they purple?*

"Are you looking for something in particular?" Millicent looked at the boys. "A children's book, perhaps?"

"No, I–uh. Do you happen to have *Dorcas Redding's* book, the one on spiritual energy?" Lydia blushed and quickly explained, "I'm doing some research."

Millicent's face brightened. "It's my favorite book in the whole store. Hold on..."

She ducked around a corner and returned with the familiar volume in her hand. "You're going to love Ms. Redding's approach. She really knows her craft."

"I read a little of it at the library a few days ago. I didn't have time to read the whole book. I thought I should have my own copy."

"I can relate. Once you get past the first few pages it's hard to put down." An uncomfortable moment passed. Millicent raised her eyebrows. "Do you want to take a minute to look it over?"

"No, I don't need to. I want to buy it."

"Will there be anything else?" The girl glanced again at the boys.

They'd been standing there like little angels.

Matthew turned his face up toward Lydia. "I'm hungry, Mom."

Lydia shook her head at Millicent. "No. Nothing else."

She paid the $29.95, plus tax. With cash. *Best not to have the purchase show up on Mitch's next credit card bill.*

With the bag tucked under her arm, she left the store. The tinkle of the little bell gave her a sense of comfort. *I haven't done anything wrong. I bought a book. So what?*

By the time she arrived home, Mitch was doing exactly what she'd expected, opening and closing cupboard doors and pacing from one end of the kitchen to the other.

Lydia scooted down the hall to their bedroom. She slid the book under her side of the bed, shed her coat, and casually strode into the kitchen.

She found Mitch with his head inside the refrigerator and one hand on the door handle.

"Find anything in there you can't live without?"

Mitch straightened. "I'm starving." He shut the refrigerator door and stepped aside. "It's all yours," he said with a gallant sweep of his hand.

"Sorry we're so late. It took longer to get the boys signed up than I expected. Lots of paperwork. Met their teachers. Here, check this out..." she handed him the school's requirement list. "And this," she snarled and thrust Miss Kilbourne's list of rules toward him. "Then we stopped to buy school supplies. My goodness, the morning just flew by."

Mitch grabbed a chair and spread the documents on the table. "Hmm. It looks like things haven't changed much since I went to school. Except for the haircut thing. They made us guys keep ours trimmed above the collar. And if I remember correctly, you girls wore dresses back then, no matter how cold it got."

"I remember all too well," Lydia said, glad to be talking about something other than where she'd been all morning.

She moved quickly about the kitchen and assembled a lunch of cold chicken salad, baloney sandwiches, and a bowl of fresh fruit. She made coffee for Mitch and poured milk for the boys. All the while, her mind was on the book she'd picked up at Millicent's shop. Now she needed two things—time and privacy.

Mitch helped her clear the table but stopped short of washing the dishes. He planted a kiss on her cheek and left the kitchen. She held her breath and listened for the direction of his footsteps. What if he went into the bedroom to take a nap? Her book was under the bed.

"Movers are here," he called from the living room.

Lydia released a long, exasperated sigh. "Great," she mumbled. "There goes my free time."

Over the next hour, Mitch and Lydia instructed the movers where to put the various boxes. The two strong men replaced the beds while Mitch and Lydia arranged the living room furniture to her liking.

One of the movers came out of the bedroom holding Lydia's book. "Found this underneath the—"

She grabbed it before Mitch turned around. "Thanks," she said, and hurried back to the bedroom. Shooting a quick glance at the door to make sure Mitch hadn't followed, she hid the book in the closet and returned to the living room.

"We can take all the old stuff off your hands," one of the truckers said. "Our company donates used furniture to the needy."

Mitch nodded. "Take it with my compliments." Then, he handed them a couple of twenties and let them out the front door.

Lydia stood by the living room window and watched the

movers load the dollies and pads into the van. After they drove away she went to the kitchen, collapsed in a chair, and scowled at the pile of boxes. *Might as well forget about getting in a little reading.*

Mitch came into the kitchen, the car keys in his hand. "I've gotta run to the hardware store again," he said. "Can you handle this stuff alone for a while?"

Lydia raised her head and eyed him with disbelief. He was already halfway out the door when she muttered a disgusted, "Sure."

Releasing a heavy sigh, she slunk over to the pile and began opening boxes. Since she'd already cleaned out a place for her dishes and pans, she filled the cupboards in no time. She broke down the empty boxes and placed them in a stack by the front door. Now on a roll, she headed into the living room and tackled the boxes marked *Linens and Towels.*

She was still opening boxes when Mitch walked in.

She nodded toward the pile of smashed cardboard. "Will you get rid of these empties?"

"No problem. You're doing a great job, Lydia."

As he turned away, she shot invisible darts at his back and opened another box. It was full of books. She jammed them on the bookshelf without taking time to organize them. *Mitch can arrange them to his liking later,* she seethed. *After all, he's the one who has time to read.*

Mitch made three trips outside and got rid of the flattened boxes. When he finished, he brushed his hands together and grinned. "All done. I'll run them out to the dump tomorrow with the rest of the trash."

"We still need to open all of these." Lydia scowled at him and waved her hand toward a stack of boxes in the corner.

Mitch scrunched up his lips. "Oooh, yeah... Can you handle it, Lydia? I need to take care of something, and then I have to get back to the office."

Her shoulders sagged, and she breathed a long sigh. "I guess so." The pout on her lips didn't seem to affect him.

"Good girl," he said, his voice light. Then he hurried off to the kitchen and left her standing there, fuming. Seconds later, the sound of metal scraping against metal rose from the kitchen, followed by a clicking noise, then silence. She shrugged. She could care less what he was doing.

Mitch returned to the living room with a can of orange soda in his hand. He started for the front door, then hesitated, turned around and walked toward her, his eyebrows slanted with concern.

"Sorry to leave you with all the unboxing, honey. I'm done painting, and I need to get another sermon written. This is my third message. I have to try to reach these people. You do understand—don't you?"

She nodded despondently. "It's all right, Mitch. I can finish up. You'd only get in my way."

He kissed her on the cheek, turned, and fled from the room. Her eyes followed him, and her heart iced over a little more. She should have known what to expect when she married a minister. Her mother had spent many hours lecturing her about commitment and standing by her man. She'd even sung a few bars of Tammy Wynette's hit song.

Then, before they left White Hills, Pastor Samuel's wife cornered her at the back of the church, affirming everything her mother had said.

"You're entering a new ministry," Andrea had said, her eyes misting over. "Just remember, a pastor's position is a full-time job. It's not like when Mitch served as youth minister. He'll have more responsibilities now. Get ready to spend a lot of days—and some nights—alone. No longer is Mitch married only to you, my dear. He'll be married to the church."

The truth was, Lydia never doubted she could handle Mitch's new position. She loved her husband and wanted to support him. *He has a lot more responsibilities, now,* she admitted to herself. *He's certainly getting no help from the deacons or anyone else at Mercy Fellowship. The success—or failure—of his work depends solely on him.*

She wanted to help, but she didn't know how. Perhaps Redding's book might hold some answers. Maybe Lydia could tap into her hidden powers, like the TV special said about people using a small portion of their brains. Perhaps she possessed some special gift and needed to learn how to use it.

She headed for the master bedroom and started to open the closet, when she spotted more boxes in the corner. Mitch would want to know why she hadn't tackled them too. Reluctantly, she released the door handle and tore into the boxes. They held more clothes, shoes, grooming supplies, and extra towels. Huffing, she stuffed the towels into a tiny cupboard in the one bathroom they shared with the boys, and she placed the other items in the medicine cabinet, on the sink and toilet tank, and anywhere else she could find a little space. She eyed the disorder with anxiety. They'd moved from an ample, three-bedroom, two-bath home into a little cubbyhole. She hated clutter, but the good thing was, the house was almost a hundred years old and already had given her more pleasure than she could have hoped for. She determined to make it work, even if she had to stash some of their belongings in the attic with everybody else's remnants.

She faced the next few boxes with renewed energy. One of them was labeled *Living Room*. She frowned with disgust. Why had the movers stuck it in the bedroom? Didn't they see those big black letters marked on the side? She dragged the box down the hall to the living room and started unpacking her knickknacks. She tossed out a couple of chipped and broken pieces and placed the rest on shelves and tables and windowsills. Then she broke down the box and added it to the new pile by the front door.

With her hands on her hips, she surveyed the living room. If she didn't know any better, she would have thought they'd moved their Indiana rental to Shadow Glenn. With all the familiar furnishings in place—including the wall hangings and samplers she'd made—the place had begun to resemble what they'd left behind, minus a good facelift.

By mid-morning, the house sank into an eerie quiet. Earlier in the day the boys' shouts and giggles carried down the hall. Now, nothing. She hurried to their room and found them asleep on the floor in the middle of a proliferation of toys.

A wave of guilt passed over her. With all the excitement of the move she'd spent little time with her kids. Over the last two weeks, she'd fed them, bathed them, and put them to bed. She was no better than Mitch. At some point, she'd have to pay more attention to the boys, play with them like she used to, sit on the sofa and read to them, maybe take them to the park.

But she also needed to do some things for herself. With a quiver of excitement, she hurried down the hall to her bedroom and pulled Dorcas' book from the closet. Tucking it under her arm, she went into the kitchen and headed straight for the cellar door. Now she'd have the time to check the items in the crate with the information in the book. She tried to turn the knob, but it jammed. She looked closer. A new lock glared back at her. She bit her lower lip and silently cursed Mitch. So that was the reason for all the banging and clicking. Fuming, she began to look for a key—on the counter, inside the nearest cupboard, in the silverware drawer. She ran her hand across the top of the refrigerator. Nothing.

A surge of heat rose to her cheeks. Trembling, she backed away from the door. Angry tears welled up in her eyes. Her mind raced. She was like a prisoner in her own home. She could storm into his office and demand the key. But, he'd want to know why she needed it.

Breathing a sigh of resignation, she returned to the bedroom and slid the book under the bed. She went back to the kitchen, plopped in a chair at the table, and waited. She'd sit right there until Mitch came home. She'd ask about the lock, of course, but it wasn't the only thing troubling her. She reached for her purse, dug around inside for the note, and spread it open on the table. The message glared back at her and stirred a spark of jealousy, which soon erupted into a roaring blaze of anger.

She crossed her arms and kept her eyes on the front door. And waited.

17

A shadow fell across Mitch's desk. The sun was setting. He shut everything down and headed for the door, with the sermon in his hand. This time he based his sermon on Hebrews 10:25—*Do not forsake the assembling of ourselves together, as the manner of some is; but exhorting one another; and so much the more, as ye see the day approaching.*

He felt good about the this message. It included biblical examples of men and women who accomplished great things because of their unity. Old Testament leaders who rallied for a common cause, like Moses and Joshua leading their people through the wilderness. New Testament heroes of the faith at a time when the survival of the early church depended on loyalty and fellowship. Peter and John continued the work of Jesus in Jerusalem, and Paul hooked up with Barnabas and later with Silas, taking the gospel to the rest of the known world.

Of course, he'd have to bring the issue closer to home. He could use the example of the Puritans who settled New England. He'd talk about how they shared a common religious goal and a strength of purpose, how their laws and customs prevailed through the centuries right up to today. Because of their spiritual bond they were able to help each other through difficult times. He wanted his flock to realize how such unity could make their own lives better.

Perhaps this message will light a fire under those blocks of ice, he mused. *They need to see what's missing in this church. The name alone—Mercy Fellowship—conveys a deep sense of camaraderie.*

This message was only the beginning. Through follow-up sermons over the next month he planned to draw the people closer together, like the members used to be, and then perhaps, closer to him as well. From what he'd read in the church's historic records, a wonderful sense of fellowship existed in the early days. He wanted to restore things to a similar atmosphere. He wanted this Sunday's sermon to be the first of many on the subject, climaxing with the sesquicentennial in November, less than three months away.

With his sermon notes in hand, Mitch rushed to the house to share his message with Lydia. She'd been his sounding board for years. His self-confidence was at an all-time low. He needed his wife's support more than ever now.

He found her sitting at the kitchen table, her arms crossed, her lips pinched together. She stared back at him, her brown eyes darker than he'd ever seen them. Surely the job of unpacking hadn't been too much of a burden. If anything, she should be happy to have all her possessions in place.

He froze, his sermon notes still in his hand. "What's wrong, Lydia?"

She uncrossed her arms, rose to her feet, and stomped past him toward the cellar door.

"What's wrong?" She shot one hand toward the knob. "*That's* what's wrong."

"What?" he said with sincere innocence. "The lock?"

"Yes, Mitch, the lock. What's the big idea?"

"I–uh–I wanted to keep the boys out of the basement. It's not safe. It's no place for kids to be playing."

"The boys? *The boys?* And what about your *wife?* Is she to be locked out too? Doesn't your wife have the right to go where she wants to in her own house?"

He stared at her, aghast. Why was she coming unglued over a stupid lock?

"Lydia, I—"

"Is there a key?" She put her hands on her hips and stared daggers at him.

"Sure, there's a key." He kept his tone soft, yet inside he was ready to blow. There was no rational reason for Lydia to lash out at him.

He slid his hand in his pants pocket and pulled out his key-ring, yanked off one from the pair, and held it out. She grabbed it out of his hand and stalked back to the kitchen table.

With a sigh, Mitch crumpled up the paper and stuffed it in his pocket. This wasn't the time to share a message about unity.

"And what's this?" Lydia snarled.

He looked at her, confused by her behavior. Then he spotted the note in her hand. He'd forgotten about the tour guide.

"I was going to tell you about it, honey. It slipped my mind."

She stepped closer, her eyes fastened to his face, demanding an explanation. He shook his head. "The girl at the Freedom Trail handed it to me." He stumbled over the details. "It's nothing, Lydia. I meant to throw it away." He shrugged and raised his hands. "I forgot."

He stared into Lydia's eyes, certain there were flames there.

"I'm telling you the truth, Lydia. Don't you know by now I love *you*. I never called the girl's number. You have to believe me, I have no interest in her or anyone else."

"Prove it," she snapped, and tossed the slip of paper on the table.

He grabbed the note, tore it in shreds and dropped it in the waste basket.

She lifted her chin. Her dark eyes darkened even more,

sending him one final message of mistrust. Then she turned her back on him and stalked into the hall. His first impulse was to rush after her, take her in his arms, and reaffirm his love for her. But her reaction puzzled him. In the past, they'd always discussed their issues rationally and in calm tones. How was he to handle this unexpected flare-up? Quietly? Not this time. He went to the doorway of the kitchen and stared after his wife. She disappeared inside their bedroom. The click of the lock told him all he needed to know.

He went to the boy's room. They were squatting on the floor, building houses out of Legos. They looked up, their eyebrows arched in boyish puzzlement.

"What's the matter with Mom?" Matthew said.

"Why? What happened?"

His oldest son crinkled his freckled nose. "She's been actin' cranky."

Mitch shrugged. "It's nothing, son. Maybe it's just that time of the month."

Luke tilted his head to one side. "What's time o' the month? Is she sick?"

Mitch released a heavy sigh. "Kinda."

"When we got up from our nap we went lookin' for her." Matthew was whispering now. "She was in the kitchen, just sittin' there—staring. It was weird."

"Don't worry about it, Matt. She'll be fine. Moving into a new home can be hard on a woman. She's probably feeling overwhelmed." He checked his watch. It was past suppertime. "C'mon, boys. Wash up, and we'll go out for pizza."

The rest of the evening went poorly for Mitch. The boys gobbled up most of the pizza. He ate one slice and left the restaurant still hungry. They came home to a dark house.

Lydia remained barricaded in the bedroom. It was deathly quiet in there, but a sliver of light at the bottom of the door proved she wasn't asleep.

Mitch got the boys ready for bed and read them a story until they drifted off. When their breathing came in steady rhythms, he tiptoed from their room. He went straight to the kitchen and made himself a ham sandwich. That night he slept on the loveseat with his neck propped against one of its arms and his legs flung over the other.

He awoke the next morning to the aroma of coffee, bacon, and toast. He struggled to sit upright. His neck hurt, his back hurt, and his legs hurt. With a groan, he pushed off the sofa and staggered into the kitchen.

The boys were already seated at the table. Lydia stood by the stove. She turned toward him, her face aglow.

"Well, well." There was a lilt in her voice. "Good morning, sleepyhead."

Mitch blinked several times, frowned, and flopped into a chair. Lydia set a cup of coffee in front of him, planted a kiss on his forehead, and danced back to the stove. She was humming an unfamiliar but hypnotic melody.

He stared in astonishment at her. Last night she nearly bit his head off. Now she was flitting around the kitchen—singing. His wife's erratic behavior reminded him of a teenager he once counseled. The kid was so heavy into drugs, he was up one day and down the next. But Lydia didn't drink or take drugs, not even over-the-counter meds, not even aspirin. She tried to heal everything the natural way, with herbs and vitamins and chicken soup.

Last night she'd blasted him. Now she was scrambling eggs in a bowl and bouncing from foot to foot while singing. She paused for a couple seconds to drizzle the eggs into a pan, then she picked up the beat again. He might have enjoyed her performance if his head didn't feel like somebody had clubbed it with a mallet.

"Got any Tylenol?" he moaned.

"Most definitely," she sang out. "Let me put these eggs on the table, and I'll get you a couple."

Breakfast, the Tylenol, the daily newspaper—all of it came and went like he'd dreamed it. Thankfully, he'd already put together a sermon for Sunday. He was in no shape to work on it today.

He dragged himself into the bedroom and fell on the bed. When he awoke again, the sun was pouring through the window, its blinding rays bouncing off the dresser mirror. It had to be noon.

He freshened up in the bathroom and put on his jogging clothes. *Maybe some fresh air will help loosen up my brain.*

Just as he reached the front door, Lydia came into the living room.

"Going for a run?" she sang. He eyed her with puzzlement. The Cheshire cat had pasted its silly grin on her face.

"Yeah. I need to regroup, maybe get some endorphins going. I didn't sleep well last night."

She blushed. "Sorry. I won't lock you out again."

He wanted to say, "Well, I'm glad to see you're over your little snit," but he thought better of it.

"By the way," she said, her eyes glistening with interest. "Did you put together a sermon?"

"Huh?"

"You know—your message for Sunday morning."

"Oh, yeah. I feel really good about this one."

She tilted her head and blinked at him. "Want to share it with me?"

He shook his head. "Tell ya what. Why don't you wait until Sunday, and you can be surprised along with everyone else?"

Lydia's smile faded. She blinked a couple of times like she was trying to hold back tears. "Oh, okay."

"See ya later." He hurried out the door. Maybe by the time he got home everything would be back to normal.

When he returned, Lydia was darting about the kitchen, and the boys had already grabbed their seats at the table. Mitch sat down to a dinner of baked tilapia, mixed vegetables, and chocolate cake for dessert. For the time being Lydia was her old self. He could only hope she'd stay that way.

But his moment of comfort was short-lived. Over the next two days, more strange things started happening. Lydia's personality continued to switch from happy-go-lucky to angry silence. He never knew what to expect when he walked in the door.

To make things worse, though the rest of the house remained pleasantly warm, the boys' bedroom had turned bitterly cold. Mitch tried to adjust the flow of heat by opening their air vent all the way and shutting the vents in other parts of the house. It didn't make any difference. At night, Lydia piled extra quilts on their sons' beds. Mitch stacked logs in the fireplace and went out to gather more from a pile out back. The added blaze should have generated enough heat to reach the boys' bedroom. It didn't.

The furnace was in the basement. Maybe some of the conduits were blocked. He waited until Lydia left the house on an errand, then he pulled out the extra key, unlocked the cellar door, and went down to take a look. He reached the bottom step, sniffed the musty air, then walked over to the furnace. He ran his hand along the conduits and found them intact. He took one glance around the room. It looked like a pig sty. He scratched his head. What had drawn Lydia to this den of filth? He noticed a shelf of Mason jars and looked closer. A green mold covered the preserves. Swallowing a wave of nausea, Mitch turned away and went back upstairs. *One of these days I'll have to clean the place—that is if I ever finish all the other chores that are screaming for my attention.* Aside from his office, he'd done nothing to the grounds or the dilapidated church building. It remained the sorriest looking church in town.

With Lydia out of the house and the boys playing in their room, Mitch grabbed a few minutes to kick back. He went to the bookshelf and pulled out one his favorite novels, *The Way West,* by A.B. Guthrie. He dragged an overstuffed chair next to the bay window where the light was better, and for the moment, he escaped within the frontier adventure.

The boys' squeaky voices poured through their open door. They let out a burst of laughter. Mitch glanced in their direction, smiled, and went back to his novel.

He'd gotten lost in the story when the door to the kids' bedroom slammed shut. Mitch sprang from his chair and rushed down the hall. He opened the door and found the boys sitting on the floor in the exact spot where he'd last seen them. They hadn't budged, didn't even appear startled by the slamming of their door.

Matthew looked up. "Hi, Dad." He went back to his game.

Luke waved his hand and gave him a half-hearted, "Hi."

"Did one of you guys slam this door?"

"Huh?" Matthew blinked at him. "What door?"

"Just leave it open. I need to keep an eye on you two."

He stood there watching them play for a couple minutes, then he went back to his chair in the living room. Once in a while, he raised his head and craned his neck toward the hall. He thought about how violently the boys' bedroom door had slammed shut. A draft could have caused it, but from where? All of the windows were painted shut. Not a single part of the house could stir up such a sudden blast of air.

Over the next few days, other disturbing things began to occur. Matthew woke up in the middle of the night, screaming. It took Mitch a good half-hour to calm his son. Luke fluttered his eyelashes, turned over, and went back to sleep. Lydia slept through the entire incident.

One morning, Luke disappeared. The rest of the family searched everywhere. Lydia even went down to the basement.

"You won't find him down there," Mitch called after her. "Remember, we've kept the cellar door locked." She ignored him and descended the dark stairwell. She remained there for a long time.

Mitch found Luke, scrunched in a trembling ball in the corner of his closet. None of Mitch's coaxing could get him to come out, so he crawled in there with him, held his son close, and waited for him to calm down.

"Do you want to tell me anything, Luke?"

The boy shook his head and wept into his father's shirt. Mitch chose to drop it for the time being. Perhaps his son had had a bad dream. No sense in reviving such a traumatic memory.

Sunday morning brought more disappointment. Again, the third pew remained empty—except for a shimmering darkness in the center. Nevertheless, Mitch gave his best sermon to date. His boys sat reasonably still, like well-trained little soldiers. But from the blank expression on Lydia's face he suspected she hadn't heard a word he'd said. The same was true of the rest of the audience. They appeared to be bored to tears. Except for Elijah Garby. The old guy surprised him when he made eye contact and gave him a nod of approval.

He thought about pillars of the faith. Paul the apostle was a good example of someone who faced persecution. Though Mitch could never compare his situation to what Paul endured, he could learn from the apostle's writings. They instilled in him the motivation to continue on, despite repeated rejections. He vowed to do better next week, and the week after, and the week after that. Reaching those ingrates had become a major challenge for him.

No one can call me a quitter, he thought. *I'll just have to dig deeper into the scriptures, find more verses about loving your neighbor and helping one another. I'll pound the same message into their stubborn skulls until they either come to life or run me out of town.*

18

Mid-September

Days flew by. Weeks did too. Autumn sideswiped Lydia like a car running a red light. The change of seasons left her feeling alone and burdened with responsibilities. Mitch was gone more than he was home, holed up in his office, or out jogging, or who knows where else? They'd drifted apart over the last month. He hardly spoke to her, and he tiptoed around the house like he was walking on broken glass. Didn't even mention his sermons anymore, stopped asking if she'd like to hear them. She couldn't remember the last time he asked how her day went. Yet she could feel his eyes on her, certain he was watching her every move.

She loved her husband, but she'd never seen this side of him before. He must be buckling under the pressure of the job. Certainly it wasn't because of anything *she* did. The ministry brought new responsibilities, new pressures. And the people—they posed challenges he'd never experienced in his work with the teens.

Okay, maybe I could *give him more support.* A needle of guilt pierced her heart. She rooted through her drawers until she located the New Testament her mother gave her on her wedding day. Several verses were highlighted in bright yellow—*Wives, submit yourselves unto your own husbands, as unto the Lord,* and *As the church is subject unto Christ, so let the wives be to their own husbands in everything.*

In everything. Hadn't she done that? Hadn't she given up

her own career to stand beside him? In everything? Hadn't she walked away from her daddy's wealth to be a minister's wife?

And what has Mitch given up for me? Not a thing.

So far, the move to New England seemed to be her only reward. For the first few days, she'd walked on clouds, enthralled by the mix of the old and the new. History wrapped up in modern conveniences. And the town. Shadow Glenn. It seemed to have come straight out of a Washington Irving novel.

Each morning she arose to the same old grind. Take the kids to school. Come home to an empty house. Cook, clean, do laundry. Aside from the box in the basement she didn't have much to look forward to. And Dorcas' book had drawn her into its pages like a magnet. She'd been reading it in secret, learning from the writer and imagining how she might implement some of the practices.

Although she'd planned a major renovation of the little house when they first moved in, the truth be told, many of her projects still lay dormant. Walls needed a coat of fresh paint. Carpets needed cleaning. And instead of making new drapes for the windows, she'd simply transferred the 10-year-old curtains from the house in White Hills, though they didn't quite fit. She tiptoed past piles of unwashed vintage clothing, neglected the tarnished silverware, and set aside many more remnants from the attic. Dorcas' book on spiritual energy took precedence, these days.

She hadn't been back to Millicent's shop in a couple weeks. Maybe it was time. After dropping the boys off at school, she sprinted to the parking lot and drove straight to the bookstore.

The tinkle of the bell above the door welcomed her into the cozy warmth of simmering incense and lit candles. Why had she stayed away so long? She inhaled the aroma of burnt jasmine, ran her hand over rows of books on the shelf. Millicent stood behind the counter chatting with a customer. She looked up, flashed a blue-eyed smile at Lydia, and returned to the sale.

Lydia strolled up and down the aisles and examined the tiny curios. Each step took her farther from her troubles at home and deeper into a magical place. At the end of the last aisle, she paused before a glass-fronted cabinet, its shelves laden with tiny statues of Jesus and Mary amidst oxen, cherubs, dragons, and miniature Buddhas. She frowned at the mix of cultures and religious icons. They brought to mind Pastor Samuels' sermon on the evils of idol worship. *Idol worship? Did such a thing even exist today?* She shrugged and moved on.

Fascinated, she scanned the books on the shelf. They dealt with different topics—natural healing, horoscopes, spiritual enlightenment, and astrology. There were a few boxed sets of Tarot cards, a Ouija board, and several versions of the Bible mixed together on one shelf. She reached for a leather bound book with the words, *King James Version,* etched in gold on the spine.

"My favorite version." Millicent's voice came over her shoulder.

Lydia withdrew her hand. "My mother kept this version on her nightstand. Hers was pretty worn. I tried to read it once. I stumbled over all the *thees* and *thous*." She chuckled over her own innocence.

"Yes, the language is archaic," Millicent agreed. "But some of the passages can sound musical, even poetic, especially the Psalms. For that reason I prefer the King James for memorization."

Lydia turned to face the girl. She stared into a pair of captivating eyes. She'd noticed them before, when they looked blue. Now they were more of a blue-green, reflecting the color Millicent's blouse. Did her eyes change with whatever she had on, or did they match her fluctuating moods?

"Why do you have Bibles mixed in with all these other items?" She waved a hand toward the shelf.

"Other items?" Quizzical lines trailed across Millicent's forehead. Then she smiled. "Everything goes together in one way or another. I have my spirit literature and I read the Bible—when I have time."

"You're a Christian?"

"Of sorts."

Lydia flinched. From out of nowhere a verse came to mind. James 2:19 ...*the demons also believe, and tremble.* She shrugged it off. "Where do you go to church?"

She hoped the girl would say Mercy Fellowship.

"Nowhere." Millicent's tone carried an air of nonchalance. "A person doesn't have to go to church to call herself a Christian. Religious institutions have too many rules. Too much pressure to conform to some preacher's idea of what's right and what's wrong." She raised her chin. "I'm a firm believer in individual experience, especially when it comes to spiritual issues."

Lydia frowned. Her mother wouldn't have approved. But her mother wasn't there at the moment.

"Dorcas says pretty much the same thing in her book," Lydia offered. "In fact, after reading it I've changed my mind about a lot of things my parents drummed into my head while I was growing up."

"Like what?"

"You know, the church's view of incantations and lucky

charms, that sort of thing. My pastor back home warned us kids to beware of people who claimed to have supernatural powers. He said they were Satan's servants. But since I've gotten to know you—and after reading Dorcas' book—I've begun to think maybe God created lots of people who believe different things."

Millicent's giggle resembled the tinkle of the bell over the shop door. "The truth is, there are good witches and bad witches. The bad ones cast evil spells. But good witches use their powers to help people. And to protect them, if necessary."

Lydia straightened. "Really? Certain spells can help my family, maybe protect my boys and even heal my marriage?"

Millicent's face glowed. "Sure they can."

Lydia took a step back. "I don't know. I already pray for my family."

"Praying's fine, but you can do more."

She shrugged. "I'll try anything if it'll keep my boys safe."

A shadow moved across Millicent's eyes, turning them from blue-green to almost black. She stepped closer.

"Are you having problems at home?'

Lydia's heart began to pound. She didn't like sharing her private life with strangers.

The girl stroked her arm. "Don't be afraid. You can trust me." She'd lowered her voice to almost a whisper.

Lydia struggled to keep calm, but tears came unexpectedly and she began to crumble.

"My husband's been pulling away from me. We never talk anymore, not like we used to. We're like two ships passing in the night. I'm lucky if he says hello, lucky if he sleeps in the same bed with me."

Millicent's mouth dropped open. "Wow, Lydia. How are you coping?"

She shook her head, and tears streamed down her face. "I feel like I'm losing my mind. Dorcas' book says I have powers I haven't used yet. I'd like to find out what they are. I need to hang onto *some* control in my house."

"If you want, I can teach you some simple incantations." The concerned lines on Millicent's face eased, and her eyes morphed back to a cool blue-green. "You already own the most complete book on the subject."

Lydia felt comforted, even stronger in Millicent's presence, like she'd stumbled on more than a friend, but a shelter from the turmoil in her life.

"What do you suggest?"

Millicent pressed a finger to her cheek, like she was considering ideas. "Let's start you off easy. You might want to keep a journal." She nodded with enthusiasm. "Get yourself a notebook and write down everything—your experiences, your pain, your husband's words and actions, and any questions you might have."

"I already have a journal. I keep a log of all our experiences—the places we've been, our move to Shadow Glenn, my boys—"

"That's fine, but you need to record your feelings, your problems, your answers."

Lydia never poured her feelings on the page. For her, it was always details about life, no heartfelt desires. "I don't know if I can spill all my secrets on a piece of paper for everyone to read."

Millicent shook her head. "No one else has to read what you write. It's only for you. Give it a try. You'll find it extremely liberating."

She hesitated for a second. "Okay, maybe tonight I'll start."

"You also need to get in sync with the universe." Millicent came alive with more suggestions. "Take a walk outdoors and collect rocks and twigs and pine cones. Those remnants of nature will inspire your spiritual senses, if you let them. The fall leaves are a good place to start. They can bring a touch of the outdoors into your home."

Lydia nodded. "I love fall's changing colors. I can take my boys to the park and start collecting some of those items. They can help."

"Yes, and you can include some good luck pieces to keep your family safe."

"Good luck pieces?"

Millicent took Lydia's hand and led her to another part of the store, toward the back where few people shopped. The girl's fingers were icy cold, like they belonged to someone who'd just pulled ice cubes out of a freezer.

"I have everything you need, and you won't have to spend much money." She let go of Lydia's hand and began to fill a bag with an assortment of items from a bin. "You'll want candles, of course, lots of them. Maybe a few crystals. And this set of wind chimes with different phases of the moon dangling." She pulled the wind chimes from a rack. They emitted a muffled tinkle as she lowered them on top of the other items in the bag.

Lydia bit her lower lip. "I—I don't know..."

"It's okay. In time you'll choose more amulets and charms. Today is your first step." She walked around and gathered more tokens. "You'll also need these incense cones. They're an inexpensive way to create an aura of peace and tranquility in the bedrooms. And don't forget the kitchen." She glanced at Lydia. "Hang some dried herbs in the window or place them in a small vase. They not only add color and a pleasant aroma, they also carry protective qualities. Every part of your house should emit some sort of spiritual essence."

She handed the bag to Lydia. "No charge."

"Really?"

"I want to help you get started. You need to trust me, Lydia. I'm your friend."

Lydia clutched the bag to her chest and smiled. "I already think of you as a friend, my *only* friend. I don't know anyone yet. Not in my church. Nor in my neighborhood."

"Oh, one more thing..."

"Yes?"

"You might want to set aside one room—or part of a room—as your own private retreat, someplace where you can meditate, undisturbed. Do you have such a place in your house?"

Lydia nodded. "There's a little corner in the basement. Nobody ever goes down there. We keep the door locked. To anyone else it looks like a damp, old root cellar. She smiled pensively. "It's a private place, all my own. There's a table and a rocking chair, an old lamp, and a crate full of things similar to what you have in your store. It's cold and dark down there, but that one corner has possibilities."

"Sounds perfect. You need to clean it up. You don't want any dirt or mold to spoil your sessions."

Lydia blinked. "My sessions?"

"Trust me," Millicent said, nodding. "With the book and this bag full of items, you're already on your way to protecting your home and your family."

Lydia breathed deeply of the scented aura in the shop. It was like she'd been holding her breath until now.

"Just take it slow," Millicent cautioned. "And don't get discouraged. People will start to notice a change in you. Ignore their comments and keep pressing ahead. If you need to talk to someone who understands, come back and see me."

Lydia checked her watch. It was 11:30. She could start cleaning the basement before it was time to pick up the boys. She thanked Millicent for the bag of items and left the shop.

When she arrived home, she stashed the bag in her lingerie drawer, then she ran a sandwich and coffee to Mitch in his office, removing his one reason to come to the house. Her husband didn't look up when she breezed in and out. He mumbled a "Thank you," and turned back to his computer and the scramble of papers on his desk.

Back at the house, she grabbed a broom, a box of trash bags, and some cleaning supplies, and hurried down the cellar stairs. She donned rubber gloves and tackled the filthiest chores first. Gagging, she gathered up the moldy Mason jars, rusted tools, and bits of paper and wood, and dropped them in trash bags. She made several trips to the garbage receptacle by the side of the road. Working diligently, she brushed cobwebs from the walls and swept the entire basement, stirring the dust into a sneeze-inducing haze. With a clean, dry cloth, she wiped the dampness from the rock walls. Finally, she mopped the cement floor with a scented detergent that left the basement smelling like lemons.

When she finished, she put her hands on her hips and surveyed the transformation. She'd turned a damp, dark, dirty hole in the ground into a private little retreat. Sure, it lacked a certain ambiance, but it would have to do for now. Maybe later she might be able to convince Mitch to panel the walls and put down a tile floor.

She checked her watch. Time to pick up the boys. She'd have to wait until tomorrow to fix up her private little corner. She could polish the furniture, wash the quilt, and toss a throw rug on the floor. Then she could go through the crate so she could decide what to keep and what to ditch. *In the end Dorcas' book will rest on the little table, hidden beneath a stack of novels but within easy reach of the rocking chair,* she murmured to herself.

She sighed with satisfaction. Even if Mitch came down and saw her little area, it wouldn't matter. She'd tell him she needed a quiet place to read and pray. He'd buy that.

"You know how men need their man caves?" she'd tell him. "Well, this is my woman-cave. When I'm down here, I don't have to answer the phone or cook or clean or iron or sew. I can escape for a while."

No whining or pouting or stomping of her foot. She would respond in a calm, determined manner. After all, she hadn't asked for much. A simple retreat is all. She could give it up anytime she wanted to.

19

Early October

Lydia returned to Millicent's shop every morning after dropping off the kids at school. The tiny store had become a second home to her. A retreat where she found comfort and tranquility. Plus she'd made a friend she could trust, someone who spoke with honesty about life and spirituality. Millicent wasn't a hypocrite. She didn't claim to be holier than thou, didn't fall back on all the trite religious jargon Lydia had heard all her life.

She rarely bought anything—couldn't with the budget Mitch had given her. But one day, before leaving the store, Lydia weeded some cash out of her grocery money and purchased a crystal candle holder, a jar of potpourri, and a suncatcher with a pentagram in the center. She left the store smiling. She'd just pulled one over on Mitch, and it felt good.

When she arrived home, she placed the candle holder on the bookshelf, set the jar of potpourri on a window ledge over the kitchen sink, and pressed the suncatcher to the bay window in the living room. Surely none of those items would arouse Mitch's curiosity. They were decorative pieces, nothing more.

Like most days, Mitch sat in his office and stared at his notes, his head a blank as far as sermon ideas went. He'd experienced too many distractions lately. There was tension at home. Lydia rarely spoke to Mitch anymore, except to ask what he wanted for dinner or to show him the boys' school work. Matthew and Luke seemed different too. They avoided each other, played on opposite sides of their bedroom, didn't laugh together anymore. Their interaction involved an occasional battle over a toy or a picture book, trivial things that never came between them before.

The responsibility fell on Mitch to settle things between them. Lydia didn't do anything to quiet their little spats. She drifted about the house in her own world, or she completely disappeared. If she wasn't out "shopping" she spent an uncanny amount of time in the basement. Mitch assumed she used it for storage. What else was that dark hole good for?

Curious, he looked out the window and checked the driveway for the car. It was gone. With Lydia out of the house, he could search the basement and find out just what was going on down there.

He hurried over to the house and opened the cellar door, expecting the dank, moldy odor to consume him. Instead, the scent of lemons wafted up the stairs. For some reason Lydia had cleaned up the place while ignoring the rest of the house. Perhaps she'd started canning fruit and vegetables. Maybe she'd replaced the jars on the shelf with something edible. He could only hope.

He went down the steps, and turned on the light, then stood transfixed with his mouth open and his eyes darting from one end of the basement to the other. It looked like a janitorial crew had come through and had swept the place clean. Overall, it was still a basement, but the walls and floor had been stripped of mold, and all the junk was gone. The shelves were dust-free and totally bare. No canning projects.

But the atmosphere was a far cry from the gag-inducing stench he first encountered down there.

Why has Lydia wasted time cleaning up a damp, dark basement, while ignoring the rest of the house? he pondered. *Didn't she say she wanted to turn the old parsonage into a cozy home for me and the boys? Cans of paint are still sitting in the living room. And what about all the material she'd purchased? Where were the new curtains? Why are there piles of laundry and dirty dishes in the sink? What, in God's name, is the attraction in the basement?*

He stepped to the center of the room. His eyes drifted to the far corner. There was a rocking chair, a table, and an old-fashioned lamp. In any other situation it would look like a nice little retreat. But here? In the cellar of their house?

He walked over and turned on the lamp. Its orange glow fell on a stack of novels. He lifted the top book—*Love Comes Softly* by Janette Oke. Women's fiction. He'd never read it, of course, but a Christian magazine ran a favorable article about the book and the Hallmark TV movie of the same name. His heart lifted. The same novelist wrote the second book in the pile, and the third.

Nothing strange here.

He looked again. The corner of a large book protruded at the bottom of the pile. It didn't look like a novel. He slid it out far enough to read the spine. *Dorcas Redding's Complete Book on Spiritual Energy.*

A cold chill ran down Mitch's arms. He couldn't breathe. He yanked the book from the pile and flipped through the pages, his heart pounding in his throat.

Dear Lord. Where did Lydia get this? And why? More importantly, what do I do about it?

He needed to speak to Lydia, but he'd have to do it in a

non-threatening way. Things were already shaky between them. He had to settle down and pray about it. Until he received a definite answer from God, he couldn't trust himself to handle this right.

Taking care not to disturb the rest of the pile, he eased the large book back in place. He started to turn away when a red-and-black quilt caught his eye. He lifted a corner and found a large crate beneath it. Holding his breath, he pulled the quilt off and lifted the lid. Inside he found pretty much what he'd feared—tools of witchcraft—candles and assorted amulets and talismans.

"Oh, Lydia," he murmured. "What have you been doing?"

His first impulse was to haul everything out to the trash and burn it. But such a move wouldn't solve the real problem. He needed Lydia to get on the same team. *She's* the one who needs to destroy the evil. Reluctantly, he sealed up the box and spread the quilt back in place.

With his stomach churning, Mitch stood for a long time and surveyed the scene. He thought about his boys. Their bedroom was icy cold. It was situated directly overhead. A dozen images swirled through his mind—his sons' aggressive behavior, the slamming of their door when no one was near it, the atmosphere of hostility in his home, and, most of all, Lydia's mood swings.

How had he allowed this to happen? He'd come to this place with a wife who loved the Lord—or so he'd thought— and two sons who played well together—or used to. Somehow, between the day they arrived and the last couple of weeks, Lydia had fallen prey to some sort of supernatural influence, and the boys were drifting apart. He ran his fingers through his hair.

Oh, God, the boys. Please, Lord, keep them safe. Help me rid our home of this evil. And, please, make Lydia aware of what she's doing.

An intense foreboding roiled around inside Mitch. Something evil had taken hold of his wife, and now it was hitting him square in the face. What he'd found in the basement conflicted with everything he knew to be right and good. If he didn't handle this properly, he could drive Lydia away from him, and the devil could destroy everything he cared about—his family *and* his ministry.

He turned off the light and started for the steps. Then he paused and looked back at the far corner, now immersed in darkness. One thing was certain, he couldn't stand alone. He needed spiritual counsel. He could telephone his former pastor. But he didn't want to admit he couldn't handle a spiritual attack. It would prove he wasn't ready to take on the leadership of a church. The Bible said a minister must keep his home in good order first. Sadly, he'd already failed.

If he spoke to the deacons about it, they might send him packing. It seemed they wouldn't need much of an excuse. Left to him, he had two choices. He could stay and fight. Or he could gather up his wife and kids and leave this place. Isn't that what the other preachers had done? Their brief periods of ministry started to make sense now. Like the others, he could leave and there'd be no shame in it. Above everything else, he needed to protect his family.

But he already knew how Lydia would respond. The mere suggestion of leaving Shadow Glenn would provoke a fight. She was determined to stay in New England, and he'd never be able to change her mind.

Anyway, where would we go? Back to Indiana?

By now Martin would have hired another youth director. Lydia closed their bank account weeks ago. She also notified the school the boys wouldn't be coming back. They said good-bye to friends and neighbors, even enjoyed a huge party held in their honor, and came away with gifts for their new home and financial contributions to help them get started.

Okay, so they couldn't go back. He shivered, not so much from the cold dampness of the basement as from the nightmare he'd found himself in. He was required to preach to an icy congregation with no hope of ever thawing them out, and now he'd confronted an evil he didn't know how to fight. He desperately needed an ally.

What was it Elijah Garby said during his interview?

"Do you believe a spiritual warfare is taking place all around us, even though we can't see it?"

At the time, the old man's question didn't make sense. It wasn't the kind of topic people raised at an ordinary job interview. But, nothing about this place was ordinary. Now he understood the importance of Elijah's question, and it frightened him. God brought him to Shadow Glenn and placed him right in the midst of a spiritual warfare. Worse yet, his wife had succumbed to it. God certainly knew in advance that would happen. So why did He allow Mitch and his family to enter this literal lion's den?

Spiritual warfare? How am I supposed to deal with something I've never confronted before?

Well, Elijah Garby had brought it up, so Elijah Garby should be the one to give him some answers. He turned off the overhead light and left the basement. His unwritten sermon would have to wait. *What difference does it make?* he sighed. *Nobody listens anyway.*

Mitch pulled out his cell phone and fell into a kitchen chair, exhausted from his experience in the basement. He dialed Garby's number and waited through six rings. He was about to hang up when a groggy voice answered.

"I'm sorry, Mister Garby. Were you napping?"

"It's okay, Mitch."

Mitch? The old man addressed him like a friend. No more *Mister* Calloway. His throat tightened with emotion, but he managed to ask for a meeting. "Just the two of us—anytime, wherever you say."

"How about tomorrow morning at the coffee shop? Say, nine o'clock?" There was a moment of silence. "Unless it's something urgent."

"No, tomorrow's fine."

Mitch needed to cool down, needed time to think about what he might say to the old sage. Most of all, he needed to pray first. Alone. Just him and God.

He hung up the phone and slowly moved about the house. What else had Lydia brought home? He checked behind every table, behind every chair and dresser, looked inside every closet. He found nothing suspicious. He went to the living room and stared out the front window. An odd sensation crawled over his skin. The scenery began to fade and a suncatcher appeared in front of him. He blinked and looked closer. There was a five-sided star in the middle. A pentagram. He reached out to pull it down, then hesitated. He needed to handle the situation rationally, without making a fuss. If he backed Lydia into a corner, there was no telling how she'd react.

For now, he'd go back to the church office. He'd get started on Sunday's message, and then he'd search the scriptures for verses that addressed demonic influences.

Two hours later, he leaned back in his chair and eyed the scribbled notes scattered about his desk. Some worked together. Some didn't. Defeated, he returned to the house and brewed a fresh pot of coffee. He was sitting at the kitchen table, sipping his second cup, when Lydia walked through the front door. He smiled and was about to comment about the nice weather, when he caught the smug look on her face. She strode toward him, a defiant boldness in her eyes. He didn't recognize the woman.

He thought about the evil he'd found in the basement. And the pentagram in the front window. He pictured his boys, two innocent children, living in a house riddled with evil. A wave of heat rose inside him and rushed to his face.

He lunged from his chair, took Lydia by the arm and pulled her into the living room. She resisted, but he held her fast. He dragged her to the front window and pointed at the monstrosity hanging there.

"What's this?" Mitch choked out the words.

Lydia blinked and tried to pull her arm free. "It's nothing, Mitch. An ornament. Something pretty to brighten up the living room."

"Do you see what's in the middle of it? A pentagram. Do you know what it stands for?"

She shrugged. "It's a five-pointed star—a religious symbol." She looked away. "Please, Mitch, let go of my arm. You're hurting me."

He loosened his grip. "What do you mean, a religious symbol?"

"Well, the five points represent the five wounds Christ endured on the cross."

"Don't be foolish, Lydia. Pentagrams are tools of the devil.

Witches use them to ward off evil spirits and to put curses on people. They—"

"You're wrong, Mitch."

He stepped back, the fury building inside him. "Get that thing out of this house. Now! If *you* don't remove it, *I* will."

He stomped out of the room and left Lydia standing there rubbing her arm. When he returned later, the suncatcher was gone, and so was Lydia.

Mitch could have kicked himself. He hadn't planned to lose his temper, but she'd walked in with a defiant look on her face. Maybe he should have said something about the things in the basement. But she didn't know he'd been down there. She'd think he was checking up on her. Their marriage was supposed to be built on trust. If he handled this wrong, he'd destroy every ounce of whatever trust still existed between them. For now he'd have to be satisfied with the removal of the pentagram. Perhaps his reaction might have planted a seed of doubt in her head. Maybe she'd get rid of the other items, too, without him having to order her to do it.

The rest of the day he walked around like a zombie, unable to speak, unable to think straight. *Okay, maybe I handled the pentagram thing wrong. I grabbed her arm too hard. I've never laid a hand on her before. What's wrong with me? I lost control and let my anger take over. If I want to bring Lydia to the truth, I need to speak calmly, rationally, and convince her to get rid of the evil herself. It's no good unless she agrees.*

A dark foreboding settled on their house. Mitch and Lydia passed each other without saying a word. That evening she made supper, moving around the kitchen like a robot. He picked up his plate and ate alone in the living room. The boys got into another fight, one that turned physical. Mitch pulled them apart and lectured them about brotherly love. He dreaded putting them to bed in a frigid room, but there was nowhere else he could place them. Tomorrow he'll call a heating service.

He needed more than ever to talk to Elijah Garby. Mitch tossed and turned all night. Ghastly images paraded before him while he slept—or tried to. He awoke at midnight in a cold sweat, changed into a clean long-sleeved T-shirt and flopped back into bed. Lydia appeared to be sleeping soundly. He couldn't remember the last time she snuggled up to him.

He lay back and stared at the ceiling. Tears streamed from the corner of his eye onto his pillow. He wanted his wife back. He wanted his kids to get along again. He wanted his old job, his former life, his students. All of it was gone now, so far out of his reach he couldn't retrieve any of it.

At some point he fell asleep. The next morning, the atmosphere at the breakfast table was bleaker than ever. Lydia stared at him, her dark eyes like the barrels of two pistols ready to fire.

He finished eating, then grabbed the car keys off the hook on the wall. "I'll take the boys to school today."

Before Lydia could protest, he stuffed Matthew and Luke into their jackets and swept them out the door. After dropping off the kids, he drove the few blocks to the cafe. He arrived ahead of Garby, ordered coffee for both of them and waited in the same booth they'd sat in before. Fifteen minutes passed. A half-hour. Then an hour.

Mitch pulled out his cell phone and punched in Garby's number. There was no answer and no message machine. He paid the bill and left. Concerned, he drove to the old man's house and knocked on the front door. He peered through the window. The house lay in darkness. He dialed Garby's number again. The phone inside rang nine times. No one picked up.

A footstep scraped along the pavement behind him. He turned to see an elderly woman with one foot poised on the bottom step. Her shabby, unbuttoned coat revealed a flowered nightdress. She wore no makeup, and her hair was done up in pink curlers.

"Are you looking for Elijah?"

"Yes, I am. We were supposed to meet at the cafe this morning, but he never showed up."

"Oh, what a shame." She shook her head, jiggling her rollers. A sadness filled her eyes. "I'm sorry but an ambulance came about an hour ago. They took him to the hospital."

"The hospital? What happened?"

"Don't know. I watched from my kitchen window when they took him away."

Mitch's arms and legs went weak. He dropped onto the top step and caught his breath.

"Are you all right, young man?"

He nodded. "Yes, I'm fine."

He covered his eyes with his palms. A wave of hopelessness flooded through him. His one ally had been taken away.

"Do you want a cup of tea?" the old woman offered.

"No thanks." He raised his head and looked into her sympathetic eyes. "Which hospital?"

"Our only one. Shadow Glenn General—at the north end of Main Street."

"Thanks." Mitch rose to his feet. "I need to go there. I need to see Mister Garby."

"They won't let you in. Not if he's in ICU. I know. I've been turned away in the past, myself."

"Thanks, but I have to try." He stumbled down the steps, got into his car, and dropped against the steering wheel.

God, please let Elijah be all right. Please don't take away my only hope.

20

Mitch circled the lot and grabbed the first parking spot he could find. He jogged up the hill to the hospital emergency entrance, entered the reception area, and headed straight for the admissions desk. The attendant eyed him coldly.

"Can I help you," she said, her eyelids at half-mast.

"I'm here to see Elijah Garby," he said. "I believe he came in by ambulance about an hour ago."

"Sorry, family only."

"He doesn't have any family in Shadow Glenn."

She shuffled some papers. "His son's been notified."

"He has? Where is he?"

She breathed an impatient sigh. "He lives in New Jersey. He's supposed to be coming in this evening. Now if you don't mind, I'm on overload."

"Look, I'm his pastor. Surely, you can admit *me*."

'Sir, I don't care if you're the king of Prussia. They brought him in a little while ago. Like I said, family only." She emphasized the last two words.

He glanced about the waiting room. No wonder the attendant was flustered. About two dozen people were there, some trying to get comfortable in undersized plastic chairs. Others slumped over, looking like they were at death's door. Even with his untrained eye, Mitch could see they all needed immediate medical attention. Meanwhile, Elijah Garby was lying on a gurney somewhere beyond those double doors.

"I just need to know how he is," Mitch persisted.

She heaved an exasperated sigh. "You said you're his pastor. Why don't you pray for him?"

The automatic door opened behind him, letting in a burst of cold air. The receptionist leaned to one side and looked past him. "Next?"

A young woman brushed by him and approached the desk. She looked about ready to deliver.

Shaking his head, Mitch left the emergency department.

Maybe that receptionist should visit Mercy Fellowship. She'd fit right in.

He tucked his hands in his pockets and strode back to his car. If he concentrated on his sermon he could accomplish at least two things. It would get him ready for Sunday. And it would get his mind off of Lydia and Garby and all his other troubles.

Before going to the office, he stopped by the house. There was no sign of Lydia. For all he knew, she'd gone down into the basement and was cooking up a spell. With the boys at school, an unsettling quiet had settled there. He peeked inside the kids' bedroom. It was so cold he could see his breath. He paused in the hall and turned up the thermostat. He pulled out his cell phone and Googled heating and air conditioning services in his area. Then he chose one from a list and set up an appointment for the next day.

Though his sermon was the farthest thing from his mind, he needed to stop stalling and get to work on it. He slapped together a roast beef sandwich, grabbed a can of orange soda, and headed for his office. The instant Mitch walked through the door, the metal file cabinet grabbed his attention. He sat at his desk and tried to come up with a decent sermon, but his eyes kept straying to the files across the room. With

Elijah Garby out of commission, he needed to find someone else to talk to, possibly one of the ten pastors who previously served at Mercy Fellowship.

He took a big bite out of the sandwich and returned the rest to the plate on his desk. Still chewing, he walked over to the cabinet. He searched through the files and pulled out the church's hiring records. Ten pastors had come and gone from 1995 to 2018. He read through the names and jotted down a few phone numbers.

Earl Stevens followed the Drummonds. He was pastor until June 1995. Mitch dialed his phone number. An automated voice said it was out of service.

He skipped over Sam Greshman. The man served for only four months and committed suicide. The poor guy hung himself in the parsonage basement, probably near the exact spot where Lydia set up her private little retreat. Mitch gulped back a sudden reflux.

He bypassed William Sportsman. According to the church file, the man became deathly ill and went home to Colorado.

Mitch paused at the next name—Andrew Stallings. The guy served for one short month. Mitch punched in the phone number. A male voice answered on the second ring.

"Hello, I'm looking for Andrew Stallings."

"Sorry, wrong number." A loud click followed.

Mitch continued through the list, passed over those who'd died, or who'd left because of illness or scandal. He called several of the remaining names to no avail. Either their phone numbers were out of service or they belonged to someone else.

He pressed his fingers against his temples. He was getting nowhere. A couple of pastors had included their email addresses. He focused on Richard Baseman, who served for six months, from June to December 2002, when he left to take a position at a church in Nashua, New Hampshire, just a two-hour drive from Shadow Glenn. Frank Overstreet was pastor from August to November 2012, and left unexpectedly. Mitch sent both of them an email, requesting a meeting.

The familiar sputter of his car's engine starting up drew his attention to the window. Then came the crunch of gravel on the driveway. It was too early for Lydia to go and pick up the boys. He shook his head, a sense of foreboding washing over him. *So, this is the kind of behavior I can expect for a while. Lydia no longer telling me her plans; appearing and vanishing at a whim. She just grabs the car keys and takes off.* He thought about his own behavior. *Haven't I been doing the same thing? We're both at fault, but I should be the one to step up and fix things.* The gap between them had gotten so wide he didn't know how.

He reached for his Bible and checked the topical index in the back. He settled on the word, *forgiveness.* Any plans he made from now on couldn't happen unless he first practiced forgiveness. He needed to forgive his congregation before he could expect to reach them. He needed to forgive Lydia before he could help her escape the evil. And, most of all, he needed to ask for forgiveness for himself. Not only from Lydia but also from God. The truth was, he'd fallen short of his God-given responsibilities to his wife and sons, and his ministry was failing. Perhaps forgiveness was the key to all of it.

In the same respect, the lack of forgiveness may have divided the people in this congregation. If that were true, then he should prepare a message on that very topic. He wrote out a few scripture references, taking most of them from the gospels, and finished with Ephesians 4:32. *And be kind one to another, tenderhearted, forgiving one another, even as God for Christ's sake has forgiven you.*

He could use anecdotes from his own life, how he argued with his father about the path he should take, how they didn't speak during his first year in seminary, and how they came back together at Christmas in an attitude of love and forgiveness. Number one, the congregation would get to know him better, and number two, the message might strike their own hearts, maybe resolve some differences and heal a few wounds. He continued jotting down his thoughts with building enthusiasm.

The time passed quickly. He checked his watch. Two o'clock in the afternoon. He called the hospital to ask about Garby. There was a long pause. He held his breath. Then the receptionist came back to the phone.

"They've called in a cardiologist," she droned, like she could care less. "They may have to change his pacemaker. I can't tell you anything else at this time."

He went back to his sermon. After reviewing his notes, he shook his head, tore them up, and put his face in his hands. Forgiveness? He couldn't even forgive himself. He'd failed miserably. He didn't know his wife anymore, and he didn't know how to protect his sons. He'd also failed to win over this congregation. His messages had fallen flat, so why should a talk on forgiveness make a difference?

The truth was, it didn't matter what kind of sermon he gave. The people either wouldn't hear him or they'd shrug off whatever he said. He looked at the tattered sermon. Piece-by-piece, he taped his notes back together. Another miserable attempt. But he didn't have the time or the energy to come up with something else. He couldn't think straight. The files kept nagging at him. The rapid turnover of pastors. So many unanswered questions. If he couldn't get to Elijah Garby, he'd have to talk to someone else.

He turned on his laptop, hoping an answer may have come in from the two pastors he'd emailed. To his surprise, both of them had responded immediately. He sat up straight and clicked on the message from Frank Overstreet.

Pastor Calloway: I received your email and I have to admit, I was surprised to hear from anyone up there after all this time. I wondered if Mercy Fellowship still existed.

As you already know, I served there for only three months. It turned out to be a troubling time for me and my family. My wife and I nearly divorced, and our teenage daughter gave us a ton of headaches.

After we left our situation changed for the better. My wife and I are still together and are more in love than ever. Our daughter is in college, drawing straight A's, and she's applied to go on a short-term mission trip during her Christmas break.

In your email, you said strange things were happening in the church and in your home. My first thought was you should leave. Pack up your belongings like I did and get out of there. But while I tucked tail and ran, I can't help but hope someone else has come along who can turn things around. Mercy Fellowship is a historic landmark. The church certainly can use a deliverer.

I currently live in La Mesa, California, a little too far for us to meet over coffee. But if you need to talk further, send me your phone number and I'll call in a day or two. I suggest you stay close to the Lord, trust only in Him, and don't give up. Those people need you.

Best wishes, Frank Overstreet

Even though they'd never met, Frank Overstreet appeared to think Mitch might have what it takes to save Mercy Fellowship. Now if he could just measure up to the guy's expectations...

Next, he opened the email from Richard Baseman in New Hampshire.

Dear Mitch,

I received your email and I'm willing to meet with you if you are able to drive up here Saturday morning. Let me know what time works best for you.

Best wishes to you and your family,

Richard Baseman, lead pastor, Grace Bible Church, Nashua, New Hampshire.

Short and sweet, but no words of encouragement. No warnings. No advice. Nothing but a simple invitation to visit.

Mitch wasted no time in responding.

Saturday will work fine and I can be there at ten o'clock.

Mitch walked back to the empty house. The silence emphasized his wife's absence. There was no aroma of a pie in the oven, no rattling of pots and pans, no humming or singing or dancing around the kitchen. He checked his watch. Wherever Lydia was, she'd be picking up the boys in about an hour.

He slipped into a light jacket and his running shoes and jogged back to the hospital, just over two miles away. The fall sky had darkened, and the wind was picking up. Unshackled leaves swirled on the path in front of him. A cold front was coming through, bringing a chill to the autumn climate. He wished he'd grabbed a heavier jacket.

He turned up his collar and picked up his pace. He needed

to talk to Garby. He had lots of questions. A wry grin creased his face as he realized he'd begun to care for the old coot and needed to find out how he was. Their last meeting had opened a door to shared respect, maybe even a friendship of sorts. What's more, Mitch trusted Garby. The old sage wouldn't go running back to the other deacons with juicy gossip dripping from his lips. Mitch could confide in him with confidence.

Again, the hospital lobby was standing room only. This time, Mitch insisted on talking to Garby's attending doctor. A few minutes later a young intern, not much older than Mitch, emerged from a hallway, a stethoscope around his neck and a harried look on his face.

Mitch cornered him. "Please, I need to know how Elijah Garby is doing."

The intern frowned. "Your friend has a serious heart condition. A cardiologist is replacing his pacemaker. I can't tell you anything else at this time. If you want to wait…"

Mitch glanced about the room. There wasn't a single empty seat. "I'll come back, later." He quickly added, "One question—"

The young man's hand went up like a stop sign. "Look, I've got to get back there. We're maxed out."

Mitch backed away. No sense in arguing with the one person who held any kind of authority around there. He left the hospital and buttoned his jacket against the dismal forces of nature. A burst of wind pressed against his back, like it was trying to push him out of town. Mitch snickered. *Must be another part of Mercy Fellowship's welcoming committee.* He'd come to expect the same response every week. Those ingrates showed up on Sunday mornings and sat like stalagmites for an hour, then they dropped a few coins in the tithing box and filed out of the church without uttering a word. Though he stood inches away from them as they departed, not a soul shook his outstretched hand or stopped to say anything about the sermon—good or bad. He didn't care, he'd even accept criticism at this point.

Now the weather was treating him the same way his congregation did, with bitter coldness. The sky continued to darken. A wisp of gray clouds scudded overhead. More leaves trickled from the trees in a steady shower of orange and red. Then it started to rain. Mitch pulled up his collar and kept moving.

He arrived home, shed his jacket, and was about to turn on the coffee maker when his cell phone rang. He looked at the screen but didn't recognize the number. "Hello?"

"Mister Calloway, this is Miss Markum in the school office. It's 3:30. We have your sons here. We need someone to pick them up."

21

Lydia was browsing through books at Millicent's little shop when her phone began to vibrate. She looked at the screen. *Mitch. What does* he *want?* She could ignore his call. He rarely spoke to her these days and never phoned her. Still, maybe it was important. She drew in a deep breath and poked the receiver icon.

"Where are you?" The harsh tone in Mitch's voice came over loud and clear. "The boys are still at school and I have no way to pick them up."

"Oh, my Lord," Lydia blurted out. She checked her watch. She was an hour late.

"I'll get them. Don't worry, Mitch. We'll be home soon."

Lydia's cheeks flushed hot. She fumbled with her coat, jammed her arm in the wrong sleeve, then whipped the garment around and tried again.

Millicent blocked her path. "What is it? Is something wrong?"

"I lost track of the time. My kids—my boys—they're waiting for me at school." She grabbed her purse, groped around for her keys and headed for the door.

"Can I help?" Millicent called after her.

"No, I'll get them," she called over her shoulder. "See you tomorrow."

She rushed out of the store, the tiny bell sounding more like a warning than a greeting. When she arrived at the school, she found the boys sitting in the main office. Luke was sobbing, his face red, the skin under his eyes swollen. Matthew stared at her, the same way his dad did lately, with an angry frown that tied up her stomach in knots. She knelt before the boys and gathered them in her arms. Luke fell against her, blubbering. Matthew remained rigid.

"I'm sorry. Please, forgive me." She glanced at the scowling office worker. "I'm so sorry. It won't happen again."

In ten minutes she'd have to say those same words all over again—to Mitch. While the office worker nodded with acceptance, she expected she'd get a different response from her husband. He didn't trust her anymore. If this little incident didn't prove him right, nothing would.

Lydia and the boys entered the house to stark silence. Mitch stood in the living room, his arms crossed, his feet spread in an immovable stance. The boys took one look at him and headed for their bedroom.

Lydia faced her husband. She felt like a teenager who'd stayed out past curfew. Unable to look into his disapproving eyes, she lowered her gaze. "I—" she began.

"Don't even *think* about taking the car on Saturday," he snapped. "I'm gonna need it."

Without further explanation, he stomped out of the room.

~

For the next two days Lydia kept track of the time. She left after breakfast to take the kids to school, picked them up on time in the afternoon, and came home. It was like she was doing some sort of penance. She felt stifled, like she'd lost her freedom. But for now it would be best to stay away from the bookstore.

Instead, she spent most of the day sorting through the items she'd found in the crate in the basement. She pulled each one out and matched it to its corresponding illustration in Dorcas' book. She took great pains to interrupt whatever she was doing to make sure she arrived at the school on time.

On Thursday she grabbed the car keys off the hook and headed out the door. It was still early, about 12:30. She didn't bother to tell Mitch she was leaving. *Anyway, he'll probably assume I've gone shopping like a good little housewife.*

With a fresh boost of energy flowing through her, she stopped at the cafe, bought two cups of hot chocolate to go, and took them to the bookstore.

Millicent greeted her with a big smile and led her to a little cubby behind a curtain of glass beads at the back of the shop. The tiny space had two floral cushioned chairs and positioned between them a small antique table. Two scented candles emitted a subtle glow that bathed the area in gold. Lydia breathed in the smell of roses and mint.

Millicent waved her inside. "Come on, you look like you can use a break."

Lydia hesitated. "I don't want to keep you from your customers."

Millicent shook her head. "Don't worry. If someone comes in I'll hear the bell."

They sat for a while, carefully sipping their hot drinks. Then Millicent coddled her cup in both hands and lowered it to her lap. "You left in such a frantic hurry earlier this week. Was everything okay?"

Lydia winced with embarrassment. "I was late picking up the boys."

Millicent frowned. "Where was your husband? Couldn't *he* pick them up for a change?"

"I had the car."

The girl nodded like she understood, but how could she? She didn't have a husband or kids.

Time to change the subject. "Millicent is an unusual name these days, isn't it?" Lydia observed.

Millicent smiled coyly, as if she was about to reveal a secret. "Actually, it's not my real name," she admitted, her eyes darkening to a cobalt blue. "My real name is Alice Cohockton." She laughed. "Can you imagine naming this store Alice Cohockton's Cozy Corner? Who'd want to shop here?" She gave a little shrug. "Anyway, I liked the name Millicent. It has a spiritual feel, don't you think?"

Lydia smiled. "I suppose." She gazed at the shopkeeper over the rim of her cup. Then she took a sip and savored the rich smoothness of the chocolate.

They both went silent for a few minutes.

The peaceful, nonthreatening atmosphere gave Lydia a boost of confidence. She pulled out her cell phone and showed Millicent pictures of the boys. For the next ten minutes she talked about the day they went to the aquarium. Then she rambled on about her own infatuation with the area—the thrift shops and antique stores and the historic nature of New England.

She paused a couple of times when Millicent left the room to take care of customers. When the girl returned she gave her full attention to Lydia. For the first time in her life Lydia had a friend who understood her, someone she could confide in. She didn't feel alone anymore.

They chatted for what seemed like an hour when Millicent tilted her head, her eyes flashing to dark blue. "So what's going on with your husband? Is he still giving you a hard time?"

The remark startled Lydia. Her hand shook and she had to set down her cup so she wouldn't spill the cocoa.

"Things aren't going well," she confessed. "I've been trying to follow Dorcas' instructions on family relationships, but nothing has worked. If anything, my situation at home has gotten worse. Mitch and I don't get along like we used to. He's been losing his patience with me, and I've been losing my patience with the boys."

"Have you checked out Chapter Eleven?"

Lydia nodded. "I read it three times. I even prayed for God to help us. Nothing works. I didn't get an answer from the book or from God. What am I doing wrong?"

Millicent smiled. "You're not doing anything wrong. I started out with the same inhibitions. But I didn't have a husband and kids to drag me down." She leaned closer and patted Lydia's hand. "Dorcas' book introduced me to my spiritual powers, but it didn't happen overnight. I spent weeks delving and experimenting before I was able to tap into my inner spirit. You can do the same, Lydia, but you have to be patient. It will come slowly, maybe lots slower for you with a family to think about, but it will come."

Millicent sat back and exhaled, like she was satisfied with the answer she'd given.

Lydia shook her head. "You don't understand. Ever since I started reading Dorcas' book, things have gotten worse. My husband watches me from a distance, like I'm some sort of criminal. He doesn't talk to me anymore, doesn't touch me, doesn't—doesn't *love* me."

Tears spilled from her eyes. She blinked hard to hold them back but they trailed down both sides of her face. She fumbled in her purse for a tissue and blotted the moisture from her cheeks.

Millicent stroked her arm. "You poor dear."

"Did you struggle at first—you know, at the beginning? I know, you're single, but did anyone treat you differently?"

"Well, if a boyfriend counts, when I told Tommy about my chosen lifestyle he said some nasty things about devil worship and God's judgment on me. Then he took off. I haven't seen or heard from him since." She waved her hand in the air. "Who cares? I'm happy."

Millicent pursed her lips in disgust. "Some men just don't understand. Do you remember I said people might criticize what you're doing? You have to stay strong, Lydia. Keep on going, and don't worry about what your husband or anyone else thinks."

"I'm not sure if Mitch has been in the basement yet. He put a lock on the door to keep the kids out. If he ever went down there, I'm pretty sure he'd disapprove of my collection."

"Probably." Millicent tossed her head and her blond hair swayed with the movement. "What he doesn't know won't hurt him."

Lydia chewed her bottom lip. "He got terribly upset when he spotted my suncatcher in the window. There was a pentagram in the middle, remember?"

"Yes, I do remember. It's one of the prettiest suncatchers I carry."

"He ordered me to get rid of it."

Millicent's smile faded, and her brows came together. "*Ordered* you?"

"He said if I didn't throw it out he would."

"What did you do?"

"I took it down, of course. But, I didn't throw it away. I

hid it in the back of my lingerie drawer. Mitch will never look in there."

Millicent chuckled. "Your lingerie drawer?"

"Yes." Lydia giggled. Then she grew serious. "I don't want my husband to be sorry he married me. I want him to love me again, like he used to."

The tinkle of the bell over the front door brought Millicent to her feet. "Be right back," she called over her shoulder. "Why don't you look around the store while I take care of this customer." She trotted off as if she welcomed the interruption.

Lydia released a sigh. Perhaps Millicent didn't want to help her fix her marriage. Maybe she was hoping Lydia would be single again, so they could hang out together more often. The two of them had bonded in a way. But is that what Lydia wanted? To be free, with no restrictions, no one to tell her what to do and when to do it?

She left the little cubby and went to the aisle where different versions of the Bible were wedged between books on witchcraft. She couldn't justify the mix of materials, but Millicent had said there was a purpose. She backed away and went around the corner where a large collection of charms and amulets caught her eye. On one shelf was a stack of pamphlets. She flipped through them. Each one addressed a different topic. She picked up one on relationships and turned the pages.

Suddenly, her cell phone rang. Frowning, she pulled her phone from her purse, switched it to vibrate without looking and ignored the call.

She put the pamphlet back on the stack and strolled to the middle of the store. Customers milled about. She didn't recognize any of them. She stood back and watched with interest as Millicent charmed one customer after another with her sweet smile and animated conversation. *The girl is amazing,* she marveled. *She knows everyone's name and even remembers little details from their last visit.*

Occasionally, Millicent let out a ripple of laughter. She listened closely to whatever they were saying, like she really cared. Sometimes she even gave a little hug. No matter what their mood when they came in, they left with a spring in their step.

A woman caught Lydia's attention near the bin of candles. She was wearing a wool coat with a fur collar, and her fingernails were painted a bright red. Lydia nodded in recognition. *Of course. The owner of the inn. Abigail something.*

Millicent was staring daggers at the woman. Abigail looked up from the bin and locked eyes with the girl. Breathing her disgust, she reached into the bin and grabbed a handful of candles, her eyes never leaving Millicent.

The silent confrontation sent a chill through Lydia. Hoping to dispel a certain argument, she stepped closer to Abigail.

"I know you," she said sweetly. "You're the lady who owns the inn."

Abigail raised her chin and looked down her nose at her. "Do I know you?"

"My husband and I stayed at your inn a couple of months ago."

"So?"

The woman's curt response startled her. "Well, I want to tell you how much I loved your place."

Abigail remained stone-faced.

Lydia took a step back, a mix of anger and embarrassment flooding over her. *Come to think of it, she had the same demeanor at the inn, like angry lines had been permanently etched into her face muscles.*

Millicent moved between them. "You're right, Lydia. Abigail owns the inn." She turned toward the older woman. "Are you gonna buy those candles or melt them in your hands?"

Abigail sniffed loudly. "I'm deciding."

Several more uncomfortable seconds passed. Millicent pressed her lips together and crossed her arms. After the sweet way the shop girl had treated her other customers, it shocked Lydia to see her on the offensive.

Sneering, Abigail dropped the candles in the bin. Two of them broke in half. With a flash of her eyes, she challenged Millicent to make her pay for them. Then she spun away and strode out of the store. The slam of the door nearly brought the little bell down. It rang angrily.

Millicent exhaled and stared at the door. "Good riddance to bad rubbish."

Perplexed, Lydia shook her head. "What happened between the two of you?"

"Don't you know?" Millicent looked at her with amazement. "She's one of those bad witches I told you about, the ones who use their powers to work evil."

"Really? A bad witch? How do you know?"

"Are you familiar with the old church on the other side of town?"

A lump came to Lydia's throat. "Mercy Fellowship?"

"Yeah. Abigail's husband was murdered there—during a service, of all times." Millicent nodded and went on. "It seems Travis—Abigail's husband—had an affair with his best friend's wife. Anyway, the guy found out about it and showed up at church one Sunday morning with a gun in his hand.

He killed Travis right there in the third pew. Shot him in the back of the head. The poor guy never knew what hit him."

Lydia gasped. "How horrible."

"I know, right? Sounds gruesome." Millicent snickered. "In a church, no less. Lots of folks believed Abigail put Milton up to it. He was too much of a wimp to do it on his own. Anyway, he went to jail, and Abigail went free."

"They were members of Mercy Fellowship?" Lydia didn't try to hide her shock.

Millicent nodded, a smug look on her face. "All four of them, can you believe it? After the murder, Milton's wife moved away. Abigail blamed the church for her husband's infidelity. She claimed the fellowship gatherings brought the two of them together."

A wave of sympathy rose within Lydia. "I'm beginning to understand why she acts the way she does. She must have been devastated."

Millicent grunted. "Hurt? Word was, she got a hold of Cornelia Drummond, the pastor's wife, and together they worked their evil. They went into the church and carried out some sort of ceremony in there. They're witches, I tell you. Bad ones. They practice black magic and put curses on people they don't like. I'm guessing they put some sort of curse on the church twenty years ago."

Lydia shook her head. "I don't believe it. The pastor's wife?"

"Don't be naive, dear friend. The Drummonds moved here from Salem. The people liked Phineas. He served them well. But word was Cornelia resented her husband for dragging her away from her friends up there. She connected with Abigail the same week she moved to town."

"You said they were bad witches? Are there any *good* ones?"

"Sure there are. My friend, Penelope." She gazed at Lydia. "And me. We're good witches." Millicent smiled and paused long enough for Lydia to absorb what she'd said. "Don't worry. We only do white magic, never black. Most of the time, we sing and chant, and we even pray together."

Lydia was stunned. "You pray?"

Millicent grimaced. "Of course, we pray. We look up Bible verses and figure out how to fit them into our chanting. We meet every Sunday morning, almost like we're in church. There are just two of us right now." She leaned toward Lydia and lowered her voice. "The magic number is three. Two don't have enough power. Four adds confusion. With three, we could unite our distinct powers and build more strength. We can make things happen."

"Three witches?"

"Yes, like in *Macbeth*, but we work good."

Lydia stared at Millicent and wondered if she should tell her that Mitch was the pastor of Mercy Fellowship. She'd never mentioned it before, never opened up like she had today.

Millicent stepped closer. "You should join us, Lydia. We get together right here in my back room. The shop is closed on Sundays, and we have all these resources at our disposal." She waved her hand toward the shelves.

"Sunday? We're in church."

"Oh, pooh."

Lydia ignored the girl's childish response. She'd love to find out what they did at those meetings. But there was no way she could get out of going to church on Sunday. Maybe it *was* time Millicent knew the truth.

"I need to tell you something." Lydia pursed her lips. "My husband is the pastor at Mercy Fellowship."

Millicent's jaw dropped. "No way..."

Lydia nodded. "I'm afraid so. Now can you understand what I'm going through?"

"You bet I can. How awful."

"You must hate me for not telling you sooner. I feel like such a—"

"Stop it. It's no big deal. We're friends, right? You can tell me anything."

"I don't know why I didn't want to tell you who I was or what my husband did. But now that you know, I feel a lot better. I don't have to hide the fact that I'm a pastor's wife." She'd absentmindedly spit out the last two words. Then, she tried to explain. "You have to know, Millicent, I'm a regular person. I have the same feelings, the same problems other women have. I hate it when people look at me like I'm supposed to be some kind of role model."

"Listen..." Millicent's voice was tender. "You can tell me anything. I won't judge you or make you feel embarrassed. Everything's going to be o—"

Lydia's phone vibrated again. Both of them looked at her purse. With a huff Lydia pulled it out and looked at the screen. *Mitch. Again.*

She punched the receiver icon.

"Well? Where are you?" Even without the speaker on both women could hear him.

"What's the matter, Mitch? I'm—shopping."

"Really? Well, you did it again. I had to spend money we don't have on a cab so I could go and pick up the boys. You'd better have a good excuse."

22

Mitch couldn't believe it. Once again Lydia had left the boys sitting in the school office for almost an hour. She'd neglected her most important responsibility, the care and nurturing of their sons. He was furious. But when she walked in the house he held his tongue for fear he'd say the wrong thing.

For the rest of the day, he couldn't look at Lydia. Like before, he ate his dinner alone in the living room and went to bed early.

During the night, Mitch lay in bed, staring at the speckle of moonlight on the ceiling. A soft sobbing came from Lydia's side of the bed. Her blankets shifted. She was still awake. He reached out to pull her to him, to comfort her and tell her everything was going to be all right. He stopped short of touching her shoulder and drew his hand back. What about the boys? When he picked them up at school they were both crying. He rolled away from her and shut his eyes.

Unanswered questions continued to swirl around in his brain. *What mother in her right mind forgot her children at school?*

He no sooner asked the question when he knew the answer. Lydia *wasn't* in her right mind. Not lately. She'd turned into someone else, a total stranger.

He slept fitfully and woke before sunrise. His concern for his sons continued to fuel his outrage.

Friday passed with everyone going about their day like programmed robots. Lydia drove the kids to school and came straight home. Mitch went to the office, and after struggling with some minor details, he was able to wrap up his message for Sunday. Lydia picked up the kids on time. They ate dinner in silence. Afterward, the boys disappeared in their bedroom, but there was no outburst of laughter, no shrill voices in play, not even a fight over some toy. The house settled into depressing silence.

Early Saturday morning, Mitch left the house before anyone else got up. He stopped at the cafe for a cup of coffee and a bear claw. With time to spare, he sat on a stool at the counter, ate the pastry, then refilled his to-go cup and left the cafe. He drove north out of town and picked up Route 3 to Nashua. He'd already checked the mileage before leaving the house. He expected to arrive in plenty of time for his ten o'clock appointment with Richard Baseman.

With the conflict in his home still roiling around in the back of his mind, he welcomed the opportunity to drive out of town. He could travel farther away from home and into the New England countryside where the last of the gold and red leaves rained their color on the highway ahead. Mitch rolled down the windows and breathed in the fresh autumn air. He sipped his coffee, marveled at the glorious change of colors, and relaxed for the first time in days. With every passing mile his troubles scattered like gravel on the highway behind him. *Hopefully, by the time I leave Baseman's office I'll have put a plan in place,* he thought.

Using his GPS, he easily located the church. With fifteen minutes to spare he pulled into the parking lot, sat back and stared in awe at the huge stone cathedral, with double glass doors in the front and a separate wing on either side. The massive sanctuary stood in the middle of a complex of other buildings. A large lighted sign out front boasted: *Grace Bible Church of Nashua; The Rev. Richard Baseman, pastor. Hours: Saturday, 5 p.m., Sunday, 9 and 11 a.m. Come as you are, but please come.* A smaller sign mentioned *Grace Christian School, grades kindergarten through twelve.*

Three services, Mitch mused. *And a school. And most likely a lot of other ministries and outreach programs. So Richard Baseman left tiny, troubled Mercy Fellowship and within 17 years he'd produced all of this...*

He swallowed, but the lump lodged in his throat. He could only dream about having a church like the one standing before him. A spirit of envy sent him in a downward spiral. His confidence plummeted. He shook off the feeling and tried to concentrate on the issues he wanted to share with Pastor Baseman. Was the man aware of the old newspaper files? Had he seen the church records? What about the shadows? Had he experienced the shunning by the congregation or struggled with family issues?

At exactly 9:55, he exited his car and mounted the stairs to the side entrance with a sign labeled OFFICE. He rapped on the door. A smiling redhead wearing a prim skirt and blouse admitted him to a waiting area. The large room was richly furnished with individual padded chairs, a well-populated fish tank, and a magazine rack filled with a variety of publications—all Christian-themed.

"Pastor Rick will be with you in a moment." The secretary went to her desk and picked up a large stack of cards. Mitch blinked in recognition. Visitor cards. The size of the stack meant only one thing—this church was about to explode with more members. A wave of nostalgia passed through Mitch, and he smiled inwardly. Not long ago he helped with a similar task each weekend, when he was in a normal church, a big church, with three services, multiple outreach programs, and lots of friendly people. Like the visitor cards in the woman's hands, similar responses came tumbling in at White Hills. And the membership grew.

Mitch strolled to the back of the office, bypassed the magazine rack, and peered into the fish tank. He tapped the glass, sending a school of goldfish scattering.

He glanced back at the secretary. She looked up and smiled. "You can feed them if you like. You'll find a container of fish food on the shelf next to the tank."

Mitch located the small plastic jar, popped off the lid, and sprinkled a pinch of flakes on the surface of the water. The fish swarmed together and gobbled up the food. Mitch chuckled, amused by the gluttony of those tiny creatures. If only he could attract his flock as easily.

He was about to add another pinch of fish food when a door opened behind him. Quickly, he recapped the jar and put it back on the shelf. He turned and caught his breath. The man who stood before him was tall and slim. He had neatly groomed hair, with a touch of gray at the temples, and his eyes were sky blue. Beneath a navy vest, he wore a white shirt with starched collar and no tie. His designer jeans brushed the top of his spotless Nikes. He smiled, sending a spray of creases to his temples. The guy could have walked off the cover of *GQ*.

Mitch glanced down at his faded jeans and scuffed sneakers. He tugged at the bottom of his jacket and tried to stretch out the wrinkles. He ran his hand through his mop of unruly hair. Was it too late to cancel?

Richard Baseman smiled warmly as if he hadn't noticed their differences. He extended his right hand. "You must be Mitch Calloway." His deep voice was reminiscent of the announcers on TV game shows. He could have been summoning Mitch down front to pick a door.

Humbled, Mitch took his hand. "Pastor Baseman, thanks for agreeing to see me."

"Please, call me Rick. We're pretty casual around here."

Right off the bat, Mitch could see why the guy's ministry succeeded. Richard Baseman exuded tons of charisma. For an instant, Mitch dreamed of moving his own family to Nashua and joining this church—as members.

Rick admitted Mitch into his office.

"Lisa, will you bring us some coffee, please?" he called before shutting the door. "As usual, we don't want to be disturbed."

Rick began their meeting with his head bowed and uttered a word of prayer. At the conclusion, he belted out a resounding "Amen," and sat up straight, his eyes on Mitch. "So you're the new pastor at Mercy Fellowship. May God have mercy on you. Tell me, what's been happening down there?"

Mitch shifted in his seat. He probably had about an hour. Not enough time to tell the guy everything, but he could hit the important details. He started at the beginning, mentioned his stressful interview with the board, and his first impression of Elijah Garby.

Rick chuckled at Mitch's mention of the old man's name. "Quite a character, isn't he?"

The receptionist whisked quietly in with a tray and placed it on Baseman's desk.

Rick thanked her and slid the tray toward Mitch. "So how is the old grump?"

Mitch leaned toward the tray and added cream and sugar to his coffee.

"He's in the hospital. Something about his pacemaker."

Rick shook his head and let out a boisterous laugh. "Mister Garby keeps on going, doesn't he? Like the Energizer bunny. Just give him a fresh battery, and he's on his way. Is he still as ornery as he was when *I* was there?"

"He is. But I kind of like him."

"Bless you." Rick doctored his own coffee, and, cup in hand, he settled back in his padded chair and propped his feet on the edge of his desk. "Tell me more."

Mitch spoke about the odd behavior of the congregation, how they lacked any sense of fellowship. He mentioned the shadow he'd caught sight of in the third pew, the discomfort he experienced every time he took the pulpit. His throat tightened with emotion when he talked about his wife and kids. Finally, he spoke about Lydia's irrational behavior—the crate he discovered in the parsonage basement, its disturbing contents, the Satanic book, and the pentagram suncatcher Lydia had hung in the front window. He spoke about her lack of interest in their home and how she'd been neglecting their two boys.

"She forgot to pick them up at school," Mitch said. "Twice this week."

Rick listened with interest. He kept nodding and occasionally uttered, "Mm-hmm," otherwise he remained stoic. If the man was moved by anything Mitch said, if he related to any of the trauma, he gave no indication of it. He appeared cool and calm, like a therapist listening to a man spilling his problems during a therapy session.

By the time Mitch finished, his forehead was damp with

perspiration. He slumped forward in the chair and mopped his face with a napkin. It was a relief to finally get everything out, to dump his burden on someone else's shoulders.

Rick hit the intercom and asked his receptionist to bring in some bottled water. Mitch appreciated the temporary reprieve. He could use a drink of water right then. He'd just poured out his heart in front of a complete stranger. Now that he'd dumped the entire mess at Rick's feet, he felt drained.

The whole story was so incredible, Mitch wondered if any of it had happened at all. For weeks, he'd kept the trauma bottled up inside. Now the more he talked about it the more the whole thing sounded preposterous, even to his own ears.

The receptionist reentered with the water. Mitch sat up straight and accepted the bottle, uncapped it, and took several long gulps. He looked at Baseman, cool and calm, a picture of strength.

Then concern filled Rick's eyes. He lowered his feet to the floor and leaned toward Mitch.

"I'm sorry for what you've experienced. I have to warn you, Mitch, this is just the beginning. I stuck it out for six months. I tried with all my might, but I couldn't stop the progression of evil. In the end, I had to think about my family."

Mitch glanced at the family photo on Rick's desk. Seated were Rick and his wife, and leaning over their shoulders were three gorgeous young girls.

"You went through all the weirdness?" Mitch said, incredulous. "Your family too?"

Rick nodded with sadness. "Fortunately, it didn't take over my wife. She stayed strong through the entire experience. We fought this thing together. Which leads me to ask—Mitch, are you certain Lydia is a believer?"

The question punched Mitch in the stomach. He'd been asking himself the same thing lately, yet he'd been making excuses for her.

"All I can say is, I always *believed* she was a Christian. She grew up in the church, and she's lived an admirable life—until now."

"Her behavior has raised a red flag," Rick said. "My wife didn't succumb to any of those influences. We both sensed something wasn't right. We talked it over. We were afraid for our girls, so we both agreed to leave Shadow Glenn." He took a sip of water. "The point is, Mitch, we faced the opposition together, like a man and wife are supposed to. It may be the reason our family survived."

He paused, like he was remembering. "Have you seen the flies yet?"

The question startled Mitch. "Flies?"

"Yes, flies. They covered the entire front window. Couldn't get rid of them."

Mitch shuddered. "No flies. But, my boys' bedroom is icy cold. And once their door slammed shut."

Concerned wrinkles spread across Rick's forehead.

"What should I do, Rick? How do I stop what's happening? Or can I?"

Baseman blew out a breath and shook his head.

"I wish could help you, Mitch. Really, I do. I couldn't stop what was happening when I was there. Neither could a long line of pastors before me. If I could have turned things around I wouldn't be here right now. I'd have stayed in Shadow Glenn and ministered to the folks there, maybe grown the church like I did this one. But the day came when I admitted I couldn't deal with those people. Too many negative energies. Too much friction. I started to feel like a total failure."

Mitch bobbed his head and sighed. "I know the feeling."

"Look here, my friend. You don't have to stay there. When I learned about this opening I jumped on it. It was the best decision of my life. If you're smart, you'll start checking around for other options. Get out of Shadow Glenn. Go someplace else and start fresh."

Mitch stared at the man. How easy it would be to pack up and leave. He'd been wanting to since his first Sunday there. Even if he took a secular job for a while, at least it was a way out. But what about the call? There it was again. The call of God. Or had he imagined it? He'd been certain God wanted him there. It wasn't like he'd had some miraculous epiphany. Somehow, he just knew.

"I don't know," he admitted. "I can't explain it, Rick, but something inside me keeps telling me not to quit. It might be the Spirit of God. I sure hope it is."

"Wow. Maybe you *shouldn't* quit then. There's no doubt those church people need a shepherd. But arm yourself, son. Pray without ceasing. Stay in the word big-time. Rid your house of anything evil. Try to reach your wife. Love her out of whatever is controlling her." Rick smiled. "There's power in love, Mitch. The Bible says so."

"I do love her. I love my family—my wife *and* my kids. Which is why I came here today. If it were only me, I could tough it out. I could face the opposition. But I have other people to think about, people who are trusting me to take care of them. If anyone understands that, you do." He glanced again at the photo on Rick's desk.

Baseman spread his hands on top of his desk, like he was

about to say something profound. "What you said about your wife struck me cold. I suggest you ask her some direct questions about her faith. Find out if she ever received Christ or if she's merely going through the motions. Churches are full of people who show up every Sunday but don't have Christ in their hearts. You've entered a spiritual battle, Mitch. Pray over every room of the house. Walk around the property and pray out there too."

Mitch nodded. "I should have done all of that the first day we moved in."

"Don't worry about it, Mitch. It's never too late." Rick looked at his watch. "Well, I've got to get back to work. I'm expecting a young couple for premarital counseling."

Mitch rose to his feet and shook the man's outstretched hand. "Thanks for your time, Rick. I sure appreciate it. If you don't mind, I'd like to stay in touch, maybe phone you now and then, or at least send an occasional email."

Rick came around his desk and placed a hand on Mitch's shoulder. He uttered a brief prayer requesting God's protection over the Calloway family and over Mitch's ministry. Mitch was moved to tears. Rick gave him a minute to settle down, then he wrapped an arm around his shoulder and guided him out of the building.

"One more thing," Rick called out from the doorway. "Get with Elijah Garby. He may be cantankerous, but he's a faithful man of God. Maybe together you two can beat this thing."

Rick Baseman hadn't solved the problem, but he'd given him a lot to think about on the way home. Mitch envied the guy's huge ministry. He could only imagine what kind of future he'd have if he also left Shadow Glenn. The main thing holding him back was a wife who would freak out if he told her they were leaving—plus there was the nagging thought that God wanted him to restore Mercy Fellowship to its former state, the one he'd read about in the church records... before everything changed.

He mulled again over the progression of former pastors who had come and gone. Like Rick, they'd quit after only a few months. Well, Mitch wasn't a quitter. He was an evaluator, and being an evaluator he started to tick off the points. The problems all started during the Drummonds' time of service. They moved to Shadow Glenn from Salem. Cornelia brought her evil with her. Then she left, but the evil remained.

Mitch needed more answers, and soon. It was a little past eleven, still early in the day. Instead of continuing south to Shadow Glenn, he made a last-second detour onto Interstate 95 and headed east, toward Salem.

23

Lydia remained in bed until long after Mitch left the house. She didn't know where he was going, and frankly, she didn't care. She could lie there until the boys got up if she wanted to. She released a long, calming sigh. Another day of peace and tranquility. Another day to do whatever she wanted, and Mitch wasn't there to give her one of his sideways looks.

The ringing of her cell phone drew her upright. She slid out of bed and headed for the kitchen, grabbed her cell phone, and smiled.

"Hi, Millicent. What's happening?"

"Is everything okay? You ran out of my store in such a hurry yesterday; I almost bit off all my fingernails worrying about you. I tried to call several times, but you didn't pick up."

Lydia chuckled at the thought of Millicent destroying her long, painted fingernails. "I'm sorry. I turned off my phone. I spent the rest of the day tiptoeing around the house trying not to upset Mitch."

"What about your boys?"

"Mitch picked them up. They were fine. He seems to think it's my job. We're both parents, right? Be glad you're not married, Millicent. Women lose a lot of freedom when they walk down the aisle. It gets worse after they have kids."

Millicent laughed. "I think I know what you mean. Compare your life with mine. You're tied down with a husband who doesn't appreciate you and two kids who can't do anything without you. Too many responsibilities in my book."

"I know," Lydia conceded with a sigh. 'But it's my life."

"What life? You're not living, girl. I'm the one who's living. I'm a single, well-adjusted woman who owns a flourishing business—and I don't have to depend on a man to take care of me. I'm financially secure. I can buy what I want, go where I want, and do what I want. I date when I feel like it. Most of the time, it's just me and my cat, Warlock."

Lydia succumbed to a sudden rise of envy. She reflected back to another time, more than ten years ago. "I almost did the single thing myself. At the time, I was working toward a career of my own. I had two years of schooling left. The college counselor even promised to help me get a job with one of the top museums in the country." She lowered her gaze. "I dropped out to get married."

"Oh, how sad." Millicent let out a sympathetic breath.

Egged on, Lydia drummed up more disappointments. "I gave up everything, Millicent, including a study trip to France. As a result, I never did much traveling, never even left home till I came here."

"What a shame." Millicent kept *tsk-tsking*. "Your husband sort of ended your life, didn't he?"

"Mitch swept me off my feet and into a life *he* controls. Since day one, he's made all the decisions for our family. He never asks my opinion anymore. If it weren't for meeting you, Millicent, I'd have no life at all." She was rambling now, but she didn't care. It felt good to unload her problems to a welcoming listener.

"You need to grab onto what you can. It's not too late for you to take a little control over your life." She paused, then added. "My invitation is still open."

"Invitation? What invitation?"

"For you to join Penelope and me at one of our sessions. We're meeting tomorrow at 10:00."

"Sunday. I told you, I can't. Mitch is preaching. I have to be there."

"Oh, pooh."

Millicent's immature response reminded her of their age difference. Lydia had recently turned thirty and the shop owner was in her early 20s at most. She'd wasted the last ten years of her life, and Millicent still had those years ahead of her.

"I can't come on Sunday." She remained firm. "Can't we meet some other time, maybe on a weekday?"

"I don't know when. My store is open six days a week. My friend, Penelope, also works. She's only free on Sunday mornings."

"What about evenings? Mitch will be here with the kids. I can tell him I've joined a book club. It's sort of the truth, isn't it? I mean, we'll be meeting in your bookstore."

"Ummm—let me run it by Penelope. We're exhausted at the end of our workdays. Maybe we can try for a Friday night, if I don't go out and hit a local club. I'd love to help you get more experience with spells and such. You need to tap into your inner spirit, Lydia. You need to start making good things happen."

"I wish I knew how. I have a whole box full of charms, but I don't know how to use them. And every time I try to slip away somebody needs me. I'll tell you, Millicent, these boys are like a noose around my neck. If one doesn't have a problem, the other one does. I'm not my own person anymore. Sometimes I wish I'd stayed single—like you. No domineering husband, no kids, and no stress."

A sniffle drew Lydia's attention to the kitchen doorway.

She turned to see her two boys standing there, eyes wide and cheeks flushed. Puddles had formed in Luke's eyes. Lydia stood in shock.

Matthew pressed his lips together and glared at her. "Problems? Luke and me? We're problems?" Matthew's high-pitched squeal revealed the pain in his heart. "What's wrong, Mom? Don't you love us anymore?"

"Matthew, I—"

He whirled away and ran to his room, slamming the door behind him.

"Sorry, Millicent, gotta go." Lydia ended the call, tossed the phone aside, and rushed toward Luke. He stood very still and began to sob. Tears gushed out of his eyes.

She dropped on one knee and pulled him close. "Oh, Luke, honey, don't cry."

"Don't you love us anymore, Mama?" He echoed his brother's plaintive cry. His little chin quivered, and tears streamed down his face.

"Of course, I love you." She pulled his limp body into her arms. "Oh, my poor baby. I'm so sorry. I do love you so much, Luke. You and Mathew both. I didn't mean what I said on the phone. I was upset about something else, not you kids."

She held him close for several minutes and waited until his sobbing subsided. Then she leaned away from him and brushed the moisture from his cheeks. He stared back at her, his eyes rimmed with red, his lashes moist with tears.

She stroked his arms, pouring a mother's love on him. *How could I have neglected my boys? How could I have said those terrible things on the phone?*

Smiling sweetly, she rose and took his hand. "Let's go check on Matthew."

They went together to the boys' bedroom. Lydia stepped from the warmth of the hallway into the frigid cubicle.

"It's like we just walked into a freezer," she murmured. "When is your father going to do something about this heating system?"

She tiptoed over to Matthew's bed. He was huddled in a ball under a thin blanket. She hurried to the closet and pulled two extra comforters off the shelf. She tossed one on Luke's bed for him to use later and lay the other quilt over Matthew. He turned his head and looked up at her. The pain on his face drove a spear into her heart.

"Oh, Matthew, my darling. I'm so sorry. Please, try to forget what I said on the phone. I didn't mean it, honey. I love you. I really do."

He rolled over and pulled the quilt over his head. "Leave me alone," he mumbled from under the blanket.

Lydia backed away. She silently berated herself. This time she'd really messed up. She needed to make it right. But how? She looked at Luke. He stared up at her, his eyes wide with innocence. He didn't speak, but he clung to her shirt.

She forced a smile. "Let's have some breakfast. Afterward, we'll play a game. What do you think?"

Luke nodded and gave her a sad little smile. Again, her heart broke. She thought about the things in the basement. They were a distraction. They'd led her away from her responsibilities at home—away from her boys.

I should toss out all those items and focus on being a better mother.

So why didn't she? What hold did they have on her?

"Go freshen up in the bathroom," she told Luke. "Then meet me in the kitchen, and we'll make scrambled eggs together."

Luke pulled away from her and went to the bathroom.

She walked in a daze to the kitchen and pulled a tray of eggs out of the refrigerator along with a stick of butter and a bottle of orange juice. Luke walked up beside her. She cracked three eggs in a bowl, added a splash of milk, and handed him the wire whisk.

"Do a good job now. Don't let the eggs splash over the side."

His little hand guided the whisk in circles, then up and down in rhythmic splashes.

"Careful..." Lydia guided his hand and laughed. "We'd like to have something left to eat."

They laughed together. Her heart pounded with love for the little guy. *Perhaps everything will be all right after all.*

While Luke continued to punish the eggs, Lydia went to the kitchen doorway and peered down the hall. There was no sign of Matthew. Fighting off another surge of guilt, she tried to concentrate on getting breakfast on the table. She added dried parsley and cheddar cheese to Luke's bowl. She took a moment to make some toast, then she dropped two pats of butter in the cast iron skillet. She took the bowl from Luke and poured the egg mixture in the pan. All the while she kept one ear trained toward the kids' bedroom.

The frying done, she filled two glasses with orange juice, and she and Luke carried everything to the table.

This is the way things should be in the Calloway household, she mused. *Mother and son making breakfast together. Everybody happy again. How did I lose sight of it all?*

The two of them sat across from each other. Lydia picked up her fork and brought a bite of eggs to her mouth.

Luke sat still and stared at her. "Mama, aren't you gonna say Grace?" He tilted his head and gave her a quizzical look. "Daddy always says Grace."

Reddening, Lydia lowered her fork and mumbled the memorized blessing her father repeated at every meal. *Mitch doesn't use canned prayers. No sir. No memorized blessings from the holier-than-thou pastor.* "Amen." Her brief monologue seemed to satisfy Luke. He plunged his fork into the eggs and made quick work of them, then he gulped down his orange juice.

After they finished eating, Lydia immersed the dishes in a sink of soapy water, left them there, and went into the living room. She selected a board game at random from the bookshelf and took it to the kitchen. Though she looked at the cards she'd drawn and moved her tiny token around the board, her mind kept wandering to the boys' bedroom where Matthew was sleeping away his pain. She cocked her head and listened for sounds of life. When an hour passed and he still hadn't emerged, she thought about what Millicent told her. Could she actually cast a spell and save her family?

She looked at Luke and smiled. He plunged into their third game, his eyes narrowing as he moved his piece ahead of hers.

"Gotcha, Mama," he shouted. "Let's see ya do *that*."

Lydia didn't try to win. She even refrained from moving her piece too far, sort of cheating in reverse. As a result, Luke won every game. Smiling like a good loser, she gave him a high-five and packed up the pieces.

"Time for a nap," she said. "We'll play more games later. Maybe Matthew too."

Groaning, Luke picked up the box and took it back to the shelf with the other games. He returned to the kitchen and gave his mother a kiss on the cheek. "Tuck me in, Mama?" he said. She nodded and followed him to his bedroom. She flung the quilt over his shivering little frame, and stroked his forehead.

"Remember, Luke, Mama loves you more than anything in the world."

"Matthew too?" he said, sweetly.

"Matthew too."

"Daddy too?"

"Yes, Luke, I love Daddy too." The forced admission thrust a knife in her heart.

She stood beside Luke's bed and waited until his eyelashes fluttered shut. Then she tiptoed over to Matthew's bed. He lay motionless, his breath rasping from a stuffy nose, a sure sign he'd cried himself to sleep. She shook her head despondently. Nothing mattered more than those two little boys. She tiptoed out but left their door open, hoping the heat from the rest of the house might add a little warmth to their frigid bedroom.

Moments later, she was in the basement. She'd left the kitchen door slightly ajar so she could listen for any sounds from her boys' room. She flicked on the light, settled into the rocker, and slid Dorcas' book from underneath the pile.

Matthew awoke with hiccups. He slipped out of bed and went to the kitchen for a glass of water. As he stood at the sink drinking, the sound of a woman's humming drew his attention to the open cellar door. He gulped the last of the water, set the glass on the counter, and walked over to the opening. Cocking his head, he listened to the haunting melody wafting up the stairs. He didn't recognize the tune, but he knew the voice.

He placed one foot on the top step, ready to start down, but froze. He chewed his lower lip, drew back, and eased the door shut. He went to his bedroom. Luke was still asleep. Dried tears stained his brother's face. Matthew stared at him and a protective instinct took over. The kid was a pain in the neck sometimes but he was still his little brother. If their mother wasn't gonna look after Luke, maybe *he* should.

He shook his brother's little shoulder and lowered his voice to a whisper. "Luke. Luke, wake up."

"Huh?" Luke rubbed his eyes. "Wha—"

"Shhh. Get up and get dressed. We're gonna go out."

Luke struggled to sit up straight. "Where we goin'?"

"You'll see. Go to the bathroom. Hurry up. And be quiet."

Matthew went back to the kitchen. He slapped together a couple of peanut butter-and-jelly sandwiches, grabbed a banana and two juice boxes, and dropped everything in a plastic grocery bag. He pulled their jackets off their hooks and met Luke in the hall.

"C'mon..." Matthew took his little brother's hand. "Today, we're gonna have a *real* adventure."

"Yes!" Luke punched the air with his little fist.

"Shhh. I told ya to be quiet."

"Don't we need to ask Mama first?"

"Not this time. She's busy. Like always."

They put on their coats, and the two of them slipped out of the house. Matthew pulled the door shut behind them, careful not to make a sound, and they started off down the street—just the two of them, on an adventure.

24

It wasn't long before Mitch spotted the sign. *Entering Salem, Established 1626.*

Within minutes he left behind the modern-day highway with its billboards and brand new subdivisions, and he drove into the past. Centuries-old buildings rose up on either side of the red brick street. For a moment he was struck with a sense of nostalgia and an appreciation for the area's past. But as he got deeper into town, a chill raced through him. Salem's charming antiquity had vanished beneath grotesque decorations for the town's upcoming Halloween festival. Amidst the calming golds and browns of nature, ugly witches and angry black cats hung from branches of trees and lamp posts. Shopkeepers had exchanged their usual window dressings for ghouls, skeletons, and artificial spider webs.

"They just can't let the witch hunt die, can they?" Mitch mumbled.

He didn't want to stay long. He only needed to find out where the Drummonds lived, perhaps meet with them— face-to-face—and then get out of there. If he could talk to Phineas he might be able to learn what happened at Mercy Fellowship.

He stopped at the city government office. None of the clerks could provide any information about the Drummonds. One girl looked through an obsolete telephone book. Another checked a city file on the computer. They came up with nothing.

Since he'd had success with the old newspaper stories in

Shadow Glenn, he figured perhaps the Salem library or one of the local newspapers might provide a few clues.

He drove aimlessly up and down streets, past The Witch House, an intimidating, three-story structure with gray-blue siding, past the Salem Witch Museum that looked more like a cathedral than a place that stored relics of the craft, past the graveyard that Matthew had been begging to visit at night.

He looked for a parking spot, but the town was overrun with tourists, and every lot, meter, and side-street were filled. Automobiles crept along in front of him, like the passengers were out for a leisurely drive. People jaywalked and paid no attention to passing vehicles or traffic signals. Mitch shifted his foot from gas to brake and back again multiple times. He yielded to pedestrians, tour buses, hotel shuttles, and a tourist-laden trolley. *Why should I be surprised?* he mused. *It's two weeks before Halloween, and Salem is the most famous haunted town in the nation.*

He was about to give up and go home when he caught sight of a vehicle pulling out of a spot two blocks from the newspaper office. He grabbed the space and walked back to the entrance.

Inside the lobby, a male receptionist peered at him through thick lenses, raised a pair of bushy eyebrows, and forced a smile.

"Welcome to the Star Journal," he said. "Can I help you?"

The guy was dressed all in black. He had a fake spider on his shoulder, and on his desk stood two Bobblehead dolls—a witch with a broom and a vampire with blood dripping from its fangs.

"I–uh–I'm not sure," Mitch stammered. "I need to look through some old newspaper files. I'm trying to locate someone who may still live here."

The guy frowned like he was considering, then he said, "You'll want our research clerk."

He pressed a button and paged a Mrs. Winters to the lobby. Less than a minute later, a white-haired woman shuffled down the hall, introduced herself as Mrs. Winters, and led Mitch back to her office. He followed her through a door marked "Research," took the chair she pointed out, and waited for her to get settled behind her desk.

He was surprised at how easy this was. He didn't have to show his ID. Nor did he need approval from higher levels of authority. *Mrs. Winters, huh? Hopefully she'll be able to provide what I need, then I can get outta Dodge.*

He gazed at the little woman who'd nearly disappeared behind her massive desk. She had to be at least eighty. It looked like tiny balls of cotton had been piled all over her head, and she had groomed them into an old-lady coif. With her rosy cheeks, pert little nose, and glassy blue eyes she could have come straight out of the North Pole.

Mitch smiled at the image.

Mrs. Winters tilted her head, quizzically. "You're not from Salem, are you?"

He shook his head. "No, never been here before."

She nodded with acceptance, then she stared at him as if waiting for him to say more.

Her steady gaze made him a little nervous. He couldn't just plunge in and ask for her help without breaking the ice a little.

"I was surprised when I drove into town. The traffic out there is horrendous."

She gave a little chuckle. "Wait till we get closer to Halloween, like two or three days before. The streets get so crowded

I leave my car at home and walk to work." She paused and her blue eyes sparkled. "It's not far, just a few blocks."

She folded her hands on top of her desk. "So, how can I help you?"

Mitch took a deep breath. "I live in Shadow Glenn. I came here to find two people who lived here about twenty or thirty years ago. They moved away for a couple of years, came to Shadow Glenn, then they moved back to Salem. They may be living here still."

"And you think the newspaper might have written something about them?"

"I'm not sure. It was a stab in the dark."

She adjusted her computer keyboard and leaned toward the screen. "Their names?"

"Phineas and Cornelia Drummond."

It was like a shock wave had seized the tiny office. The pink on Mrs. Winters' cheeks disappeared. She caught her breath and her eyes puddled over with tears.

The old woman's emotional reaction surprised Mitch. "I'm so sorry." He frowned. "Are you related to them?"

She blinked against the tears, but they spilled onto her cheeks. "No, I'm not." She pulled a tissue from the box on her desk. "I'll be all right." She blotted the moisture from her face. "I haven't thought about Reverend Drummond in a long time."

"You knew him?"

She nodded and blotted her face again. "He was once the pastor of the church I attend here in Salem." She choked out the information.

Mitch was overcome with regret. His heart went out to the little woman. Apparently, the Drummonds meant a lot to her.

"I don't want to upset you, Mrs. Winters."

The tissue still in her hand, she waved away his apology. "Forgive me." She took a deep breath and settled back in her chair. "Now," she said, exhaling. "Tell me what you need to know."

"Well, I was hoping to find them and talk with them. Does your newspaper have any information about where they might be living? Perhaps there's an old news article from when they returned to Salem."

"Oh, I don't have to search for any news articles. I can tell you everything you need to know about Phineas Drummond. It's up here"—she pointed at her forehead—"and in here," she added, pressing her fingers to her heart.

Mitch blinked with curiosity. He'd come here asking about the Drummonds, but Mrs. Winter focused only on Phineas, never once mentioned Cornelia.

She gathered a couple more tissues and held them ready. Mitch settled back in his chair. It looked like she was about to give a long-winded monologue.

"When Reverend Drummond left in 1993, our church nearly broke apart." The far-off look in her eyes hinted that she'd already drifted into the past. "Phineas possessed a rare gift for speaking and a wonderful, strong spirit. People flocked to our church just to hear him preach. Then one Sunday, he climbed up to the pulpit and told us he was going to Shadow Glenn to serve at a little church called Mercy Fellowship."

Mitch nodded. "He did, for a couple years."

"You know of this church?"

"I'm their current pastor."

"I see..."

"At least I am, for now," Mitch shrugged with embarrassment. "I've encountered some problems. Nothing major, but—"

"Problems? What kind of problems?"

The conversation had shifted in his direction. He didn't want to spill everything like he had with Rick Baseman. The poor woman already appeared stressed by the mere mention of Phineas' name.

She stared at him, like she wasn't going to let it drop. If he wanted to find out where the Drummonds lived he was going to have to explain.

He took a breath and proceeded with caution. *Just give her the bare minimum.* "Well, the members seem to have lost their passion." He paused and waited for a reaction. None came. "I thought maybe Phineas Drummond might provide some answers."

Mrs. Winters smiled like she understood. "So, you'd like to reignite a spiritual fire under your flock."

"Exactly."

"That's commendable. I certainly hope you succeed. I know what you're up against. During the two years Phineas was away from us, our people lost their passion too. Then, glory be, the Drummonds came home, and we expected everything would go back to the way it was before." She shook her head, sadly. "It didn't. In fact, things got worse."

She gathered more tissues and wiped both eyes.

Mitch's heart ached for the dear woman. "I'm sorry if I've opened an old wound."

She shrugged her frail little shoulders. "Don't worry yourself about it. I happen to be an emotional woman."

Mitch waited until she finished mopping her face. Then he pressed on. "So set me straight. The trouble started when the Drummonds came back to Salem?"

"Definitely. A terrible darkness fell on our church."

"What kind of darkness?" he pressed.

"Reverend Drummond had aged considerably. He looked drawn, like something had sucked the life right out of him. His sermons fell flat. He didn't interact with the congregation like he used to. Our numbers dropped even lower. People stopped gathering for functions. A few of us who were there from the beginning kept things going, but we began to think our church was dying."

She suddenly became rigid and her blue eyes flamed. "We blamed that wife of his, Cornelia. At one time she stood by Phineas, like other women of faith who support their preacher husbands. But Cornelia had started to change shortly before they left Salem. She stopped coming to services, and she no longer helped with bake sales and other functions."

Mitch perked up. The scenario sounded all too familiar. "What do you think caused the change?"

"Cornelia started hanging out with some unsavory women in an old house on Spruce Street. We never saw her anymore. At first we assumed she was on an evangelistic mission, so we gave her a pass. But then it came out that Phineas had been trying to discourage that association."

"He didn't succeed, did he?" Mitch said, knowingly.

Mrs. Winters shook her head. "Things got worse. I think Cornelia put a curse on our church and maybe on her husband too."

"Wow. Sounds pretty intense. Are you sure someone like her would have that kind of power?" He hoped she'd say no.

"What? You don't believe in witches and curses?"

He shrugged. "There are folks who pretend they can cast spells, but I doubt they have such abilities. Witches are merely part of Salem's folklore, right? They certainly have no place in the 21st century, and most definitely not in the church."

Mrs. Winters' eyes widened with astonishment. "My dear young man. Have you been hiding your head under a rock?"

He chuckled nervously. "Of course not."

Frowning, she leaned toward him. "I have a feeling your church is in deep trouble."

Mitch bit his lower lip. He stared into the woman's crystal blue eyes. They seemed to be looking right into his soul.

"Maybe you're right," he conceded. "Our problem began after the Drummonds arrived, and it remained after they left. The atmosphere in that little church had changed, much like it did at your church. Now I'm just trying to help my members get back to what they were before the difficulties. If I can talk to the Drummonds, find out what happened, maybe I'll be able to—"

Mrs. Winters shook her head and cut him off. "They're gone." Her voice broke. "Gone forever."

He frowned with uncertainty. "What do you mean? Have the Drummonds moved away?"

"Mr. Calloway, don't you know? Phineas Drummond is dead. Burned up in the fire."

Mitch caught his breath. "Dead?"

A terrible sadness flooded into her eyes. "After they returned to Salem, Cornelia started carrying on with who-knows-what in the attic of their house. She wouldn't let her husband go up there, locked the door and wouldn't give him a key. Word was he'd become very distraught over her behavior. He had no power over that woman. He left her alone and stuck with his preaching. But his messages didn't measure up to what he'd given us before. It seemed like a part of him had died."

"You mentioned a fire. What happened?"

"Nobody knows for sure. People think Cornelia was burning candles in the attic, maybe doing some sort of incantation. The flames got out of hand and consumed the entire house. The fire marshal's report said they found Phineas in the stairwell with his face turned toward the attic, like he was trying to reach his wife. In spite of everything he never stopped loving her, not even after she ruined his ministry." The old woman gulped back a surge of emotion. "Phineas died of smoke inhalation, and Cornelia must have burned up in the fire. They never did find her body."

An icy fear gripped Mitch. If Phineas Drummond, a well-respected servant of God, couldn't overcome the forces of evil, how could *he*?

"Where's the house? Do you have an address?"

Mrs. Winters shook her head. "After the fire, the town razed the Drummond manse to the ground. The property has remained vacant ever since. Nobody, and I mean *nobody*, wanted to live on that plot of land after what happened there."

Mitch exhaled. "Wow."

Mrs. Winters tossed the tissues into the waste basket. "So sorry, Mitch. You came here to get answers. I don't know how to save your ministry."

He looked into her eyes and found compassion there. "Right now it seems hopeless. I have a wife and two sons to think about."

"If I were you, young man, I'd leave Mercy Fellowship. If a seasoned pastor like Phineas Drummond couldn't fix it, I doubt anyone can. Cornelia worked her evil there for two years." She smiled sympathetically. "You look like a fine young man. You're probably a wonderful preacher. But you're dealing with something beyond human understanding. My advice—get those people to burn down that church and start over somewhere else."

"They'll never burn it down. Their ancestors started it."

"Then you need to protect your family. Get out of there while you still can."

"Mrs. Winters, I'm a minister of the gospel. I believe God called me to Shadow Glenn with a specific purpose to—"

"That's *exactly* what Reverend Drummond said."

He shook his head. "I can't turn my back on my responsibility."

"So you're willing to lay down your life—*and more*—for an ungrateful group of nobodies?"

He shrugged and gave a half-hearted smile. "I don't think of them as nobodies. They're souls, and they need a rescuer."

"Oh, you poor dear," Mrs. Winters eyes filled with tears again. "I have a feeling you're holding back something. Let me assure you, whatever you say will not go beyond these walls. You can trust me. I'm not a reporter. I'm a historian. There's a big difference."

He stared at the sweet woman. Should he tell her about Lydia's strange behavior? What good would it do? He glanced at his watch. It was past one o'clock.

"I've taken up enough of your time." He started to rise, then settled back in his chair and gazed into her innocent blue eyes.

"What about you, Mrs. Winters? You're obviously a Christian woman. Why do you stay in a place like this?"

"Salem?" She laughed. "It's been my home since I was born. I love the history and the New England ambiance. The church I attend is one of the oldest in the county." She spread her hands. "I have this part-time job at the newspaper. And twice a month I volunteer as a docent at a local museum. My life is full of people and things to do."

"What about all the witch lore and the way these people celebrate Halloween? Don't you find the atmosphere intimidating?"

"Not at all. It's part of the local history. I don't have to believe any of it. Anyway, can you think of a more needy mission field?"

Mrs. Winters had given him a fresh impression of Salem. Aside from the town's fixation on witch hunts and cultic celebrations, she may have been one of many who reveled in the area's historical ambiance.

The world would be a lot better off if there were more people like Mrs. Winters in it, he thought. *In fact, my own church could use a few folks like her.*

With sincere gratitude, Mitch thanked her and left the building. Rick Baseman and Mrs. Winters had given him the same advice. *Leave Mercy Fellowship. Pack up your family and get out of Shadow Glenn.*

He needed to unwind and mull over the morning's events. Plus, he was hungry. He turned off the highway and stopped at a roadside restaurant. When he got back on the road, he couldn't recall what he had eaten, what the person looked like who served him, or even the name of the restaurant. He only knew his hunger pangs had subsided and he was out $15. He'd spent the entire hour sorting through what he'd learned at the two meetings.

There was no doubt he preferred to leave Shadow Glenn. He'd been leaning that way since the beginning. But conflicting thoughts kept telling him he'd been called there for a purpose. And Elijah Garby had expressed confidence in him. If the two of them worked together they could tackle whatever unseen evil prevailed there. The Bible said something about two or more being gathered in God's name. With God's help, perhaps he and Elijah will be able to restore Mercy Fellowship to what it once was.

Mentally, he weighed the facts. He had two responsibilities—the church and his family. Sadly, he'd failed them both. He needed to talk to Elijah more than ever.

Since he'd be entering Shadow Glenn at the north end of town, he'd be driving right past the hospital. *Wouldn't hurt to stop by. This time I'll stand up to the medical staff and insist on seeing Mr. Garby. After all, I'm his pastor. Hospitals always let the pastor in—don't they?*

Even so, he couldn't just barge in and hit the old man with a load of questions. He'd have to evaluate Elijah's condition first. Then, if he felt like the time was right, he'd talk things over with him. Perhaps the old sage will be able to help him decide whether to stay and fight or leave town for good.

25

Matthew tugged his little brother along the sidewalk, taking him farther from home and closer to the forest at the edge of town. He'd spotted it one morning on the way to school. The huge spread of trees, the rise of the land, the dirt path trailing into the brush—they beckoned him into a world of adventure, like the forest where Robin Hood and his Merry Men roamed about doing good deeds.

He imagined going in there and letting the forest protect him and his brother from the outside world. The cluster of trees promised peace and quiet. No arguments, no bad feelings, no ice cold room.

He was only eight, but he was a big brother to Luke. Dad didn't spend much time with them anymore. Mom didn't care. She even complained about them on the phone that morning.

He looked down at his little brother, straightened his shoulders, and stepped closer to the tree line. At the end of the paved sidewalk, he turned onto a dirt path and trudged uphill within the shelter of the trees. The path grew narrower. He grasped Luke's hand and tugged him along behind him. When they reached a level spot, he turned around and peered through the tangle of shrubs at the village far below. It didn't look homey anymore. When they first got there, they went out for ice cream. They ate dinner out and even went to a movie. As a family. Then everything changed. Dad didn't care about anything but church. Mom kept disappearing into the basement and didn't come up until suppertime. He was tired of sleeping in a refrigerator, tired of fighting with Luke for no reason, tired of feeling all alone and helpless.

He stuck out his lower lip and blinked back a sting of tears. "I wish Mom and Dad would hug and kiss each other like they used to," he mumbled aloud. " I wish we could leave Shadow Glenn and go somewhere happy."

"Yeah," Luke sputtered, his own eyes filling with tears.

Matt tightened his grip on his little brother's hand, turned his back on the village, and moved ahead into the thickening forest. Slivers of sunlight filtered through the web of branches overhead. They looked like a giant spider web against the gray of the sky. As they walked on, Matthew swept his eyes from left to right, keeping track of landmarks—a large climbing rock, a bunch of yellow wildflowers, a broken tree trunk that looked like it had been struck by lightening.

"Where are we going?" Luke tried to pull his hand away.

Matthew looked down at a pair of frightened eyes.

"Relax. We're on an adventure in the king's forest. We're on a quest for his magic crown. We might even have to fight enemy soldiers. Or pirates. Or—" he lowered his voice—"or maybe even a *monster*."

Luke giggled. Scary stories didn't seem to bother him anymore. In fact, Luke *wanted* to be scared. He'd made a big stink over being left out of the nighttime graveyard tour. Dad promised to take them there, but they never went. He frowned with disappointment. *I'll probably have to wait until I'm grown up to go there. Okay then. We could make up our own adventure right here in the forest.*

He plodded ahead. The brush closed in around them. The path nearly disappeared. The rumble of city traffic faded to a distant buzz. They'd entered another world where crickets chirped, birds flapped their wings overhead, and twigs snapped beneath their feet.

Luke suddenly stopped walking.

"Look up there." His tiny voice pierced the quiet. "What is that?"

Matthew followed his brother's gaze to a boxlike structure perched on a thick branch overhead. There was a small door and an opening that looked like a window. A big piece of tarp covered the top.

Matthew stared in amazement. "It's a fort! A tree-house fort. It'll keep us safe from the enemy."

"Really?" Luke's eyes grew wide.

"Yeah. A bunch o' pirates must have built it. Looks like they're gone now. We can take it over. C'mon."

He sprinted ahead of his little brother, walked around the tree, and stopped at a place where several boards were nailed to the trunk.

"There's a ladder over here. Hurry up, Luke. Let's check it out."

He started up. But his brother hesitated at the base of the tree and shook his head. "I'm not climbing those sticks."

"It's okay. It's safe. Look. I'm already half-way up."

The sack lunch in one hand, Matthew grabbed onto the boards with the other and scrambled to the top. He leaned over the side and looked down. Luke stood frozen at the bottom, his forehead creased with anxiety.

"Come on, Luke. Remember the rock wall we climbed at the carnival last year? It's like that. Look. *I* made it. You can too."

Luke jammed his hands in his pockets and shook his head. "Look inside first. There might be bats in there. Or snakes or something."

Matthew shook his head with disgust. "Okay, scaredy-cat."

He edged through the opening and looked around the inside. Someone had gone to a lot of trouble to make a bunch of boards look like a real house. They'd nailed a raggedy curtain over the window, and they'd scattered a bunch of pillows on the floor. The small space could hold maybe four kids. Five or six if they squeezed in there together. Juice boxes and empty snack bags were strewn about the floor and there were a few candle stubs and a water-logged box of matches.

Matthew smiled. *This is going to make a great clubhouse.*

He poked his head out the door. "There's no critters up here. Come on up and see for yourself."

His brother shook his head.

"You want some lunch, don't ya'?"

Luke nodded and approached the base of the tree. He slipped his hands out of his pockets and started up the ladder, grabbing each rung as he inched his way up. Matthew leaned across the biggest branch and watched his brother climb.

"Don't look down."

Luke looked down, wavered for a second, then pressed his forehead against the tree trunk.

"Come on, sissy. You're almost here."

Luke moved to the next rung, then the next. Matthew shook his head. "You've gotta climb faster. It's easier if you move fast."

Luke got closer.

"Here." Matthew reached out. "Take my hand."

He helped his brother over the final step and pulled him into the treehouse.

"Whatta ya think, Luke? We can fix up this place. It can be our secret hideout. Whenever we need to get away from

Mom and Dad, this is where we can come. And we can bring our school friends up here and start a club."

Luke looked around and smiled. "Yeah—our own secret hideout."

Together they cleared a spot on the floor, pounded the dust off two pillows and used them as seats. They dug into their lunch bag, devoured the sandwiches, drained the juice boxes, and split the banana between them.

Luke tossed the peel on a pile of wrappings. Matthew grabbed it and dropped it in the empty lunch bag. "No littering in here. We're gonna keep our hideout clean. C'mon. Help me pick up the rest of this garbage."

Crawling around on their hands and knees, the two boys gathered the wrappings, the rotted remnants of food, and the soggy box of matches, and dropped it all in their bag. Matthew tied the top and slung it out the door. It landed with a muffled thump on the grass below.

Beaming, Matthew leaned back against the wall, put his hands behind his head, and grinned at his brother.

"Halloween's comin'. It's only a couple of weeks away. Want me to tell ya a spooky story?"

"Sure." Luke settled back and slid closer to him.

Matthew lowered his voice. "Once there was an ugly old ghoul who lived in a cave at the edge of a quiet village..."

Luke was staring out the window like he was imagining the story. Matthew's heart surged with love for the little guy. With less attention from their folks, he'd grown up a little more in the last few days. His mother said he and Luke were too much trouble. After crying his heart out, he'd come away stronger and wiser. He could take care of his little brother, even if no one else did.

There hadn't been a peep out of the boys' room for several hours. Lydia checked her watch. Where had the time gone? She quickly packed away her candles and Dorcas' book. Then she hurried up the stairs and locked the cellar door behind her. With a smirk she tucked the key in its hiding place behind the sugar bowl.

Thinking the house had gone strangely quiet, she went to the boys' room. "Time to have some lunch, ki—"

She stopped short in the doorway. Their blankets lay in rumpled piles on their beds. Their toys were strewn about the room. There was no sign of the children. She spun back to the hall.

"Matthew. Luke. Where are you guys?"

She moved about the house, from room to room, peeked in closets, looked behind furniture, retraced her steps and looked again.

"Come on, you two. Stop playing games with me. It's way past lunchtime. Don't you want to eat?"

The silence fell on her like a heavy quilt. She took a deep breath. Perhaps she'd missed something. When two little boys play hide-and-seek, they're nearly impossible to find.

She called out their names again. She checked under the beds and behind the drapes. She peered out the living room window. They weren't in the front yard. The tire swing hung lifeless from the old oak. The boys knew better than to leave the house without asking. She raced into the kitchen and looked out the back window. She cocked her head and listened for their voices. Nothing but nerve-wracking silence.

Oh, God, where are my boys?

She went to the front door and found it unlocked. She *never* left it unlocked. They must have gone out. She grabbed her coat and reached for the car keys. They weren't in the usual place. She puffed out a frustrated sigh. She'd forgotten, Mitch had the car today. She picked up her cell phone and started to punch in his number, but stopped. Not a good idea. He'd respond like he usually did these days. He'd patronize her. He'd berate her again for not taking better care of their sons.

Lydia's head swam. Afraid she was about to faint, she dropped into the nearest chair and took several deep breaths. She needed help. But who? On an impulse, she dialed Millicent's number.

When the girl answered, Lydia choked back a sob, then in desperation she blurted, "My boys are missing."

"Oh, Lydia. I want to help but I can't leave the store right now. It's Saturday, and I'm extra busy."

"I need to go out and try to find them. I don't have the car. Mitch went somewhere, and he hasn't come back yet. Oh, Millicent, I need to find my boys."

"I'll call Penelope and see if she's free. She can be at your house in five minutes."

"Um—I don't know. I haven't met her yet."

"It'll be fine. She'll want to help."

"Didn't you say she works during the day?

"Yeah, but she works from home. She makes amulets and charms and sells them in my store and online. It's her own business."

Lydia hesitated. She trusted Millicent, but Penelope? She drew in a deep breath.

"All right. Give her my address."

"She knows it already. We drove by your house the other night and chanted a blessing on you."

Lydia shuddered. The two of them were chanting outside her house? A still small voice urged her to hang up the phone. But she was alone and desperate.

"Tell her to hurry."

Fifteen minutes later a little Honda drove up to the house. Lydia rushed out the door. She left it unlocked, in case the boys should come home while she was out. She hurried down the porch steps, opened the car door and peeked inside. At the wheel sat a brassy redhead wearing a black overcoat and heavy eye makeup.

"Come on." Penelope waved her inside. "I don't bite."

She slid into the front seat and caught a whiff of heavy musk. Penelope peeled out of the driveway. For the next hour, they circled the town, checked side streets, and crept past the elementary school and the playground. Kids were walking in pairs, playing on the jungle gym, sitting on park benches. There was no sign of Matthew or Luke.

Lydia shook her head. "This is useless. Take me home. I need to check the house again."

They pulled into the driveway. As soon as the car stopped, Lydia leaped out and mumbled a quick, "Thank you," to Penelope. Thinking the girl would leave, Lydia hurried up the porch steps. She tore through the house, calling her kids' names. They weren't there. Sobbing, she collapsed on the living room rug and pressed her palms to her eyes.

A hand pressed against her shoulder. Startled, she turned, hoping to see Matthew. Instead, she looked up into Penelope's black-rimmed eyes. The girl bent close and Lydia caught sight of a dragon tattoo on the left side of her neck.

She shuddered. "I need to be alone. Please go."

Penelope shook her head, and the dragon rippled. "I can't leave you like this. Maybe we didn't go far enough. We should drive out to the highway."

"No," Lydia cried out. "They couldn't have gone that far."

The girl helped Lydia to her feet. "It's gonna be okay. Listen, we can hold a little session, light a few candles, and call on the spirit world to bring them home."

Lydia drew back. "I was in the middle of a so-called *session* when my boys disappeared. If I hadn't left them alone—if I'd been doing my job as a mother, I wouldn't have lost them. Oh, God, where are they? Where are my boys?"

Penelope snorted. "You're a novice, Lydia, and you were all alone. With the two of us chanting, we can summon more power. You have to trust me. I have a lot more experience with these things."

A battle raged inside Lydia. The girl insisted she could help. But something wasn't right.

"I don't know—"

"Oh, come on. You prayed right?"

Lydia nodded and wiped away tears.

"Did praying work? I'm sure it didn't. Praying isn't powerful enough. We have to go *beyond* praying."

Helpless to argue, Lydia gave in. She was willing to try anything at this point. She led Penelope into the kitchen, unlocked the cellar door, and took her down the steps. When they reached the bottom, Penelope raised her hands, palms up, and closed her eyes. Then she looked at Lydia and exhaled loudly.

"Good aura," she said, raising her eyebrows. "Get the candles."

Lydia blindly obeyed and lit several candles. The aroma of

sage filled the air. Penelope shut her eyes and began to chant. Lydia grasped the girl's extended hands. Immediately, goose bumps rose along Lydia's arms. Her mouth went dry. She stared at Penelope. The flickering candles painted eerie veins on the girl's upturned face. The dragon on her neck appeared to come alive. Her monotone swelled into a shrill crescendo.

Something wasn't right. Her heart pounding, Lydia slid her hands from Penelope's grasp.

"You have to stop. There's something terribly wrong with this."

Penelope opened her eyes and gaped at her. "I was just getting started."

"No. Stop." Lydia took a step back. "I need to go out again and look for my boys. On foot."

Penelope drew close to Lydia, her distorted face inches away.

"Millicent's gonna hear about this," she snarled. "She insisted you were a willing student. Now I'm not so sure."

She spun away and stomped up the stairs to the main floor, leaving Lydia to blow out the candles and put everything away. By the time Lydia emerged into the kitchen, the girl was gone.

Lydia locked the cellar door and rushed to the front window, relieved to see Penelope peeling out of the driveway, scattering gravel behind the wheels of her car.

Lydia grabbed her coat. Now she could search places she hadn't been able to see from the car window—back alleys and behind people's houses. Again, she left the front door unlocked, hoping the boys would come home, and she started down the street toward the heart of town.

$\sim$

Matthew finished his story and was about to start another when he discovered Luke slumped over, sound asleep.

He drew up his legs and rested his chin on top of his knees. He surveyed the inside of the treehouse. He could invite Billy, his new friend from school. They could play-act their favorite movie scenes, take different roles. He'd play Robin Hood, of course, and his friend would be the Sheriff of Nottingham. They might even camp out there at night, with a sleeping bag and a lantern. Their own private clubhouse. No parents allowed.

After a while, with the setting of the sun, a gray shadow enveloped the little house. Matthew shuddered. Time to start for home. He shook Luke's shoulder.

"Huh?" The little guy unfolded his legs.

"It's gettin' dark. We gotta go. Can you make it down the ladder?"

Luke nodded, but a line of concerned wrinkles returned to his forehead.

"Follow me down. I'll go ahead of you and make sure you don't fall. Stay close to me."

He started down, slowly, with his eyes on his brother a couple of rungs above him. Two of the boards jiggled a little, but they remained stuck to the tree. Together, the boys made it to the bottom. Matthew picked up the sack of garbage, and they started for home.

"Do you know the way?" Luke sounded nervous.

"Sure. I kept track of landmarks on the way up. Look. There's the tree that was struck by lightning. See. We're already on the path. We can follow it straight down the hill."

A few minutes later, the village appeared below. Street lights flickered on, and cars moved along the main roads, their headlights looking like strings of diamonds. The windows of several houses glowed yellow. Matthew thought about their home in Indiana. They were happier there. Warm, yellow windows welcomed them indoors after a day of play, and Mom always had supper on the table. Dad ate with them too, and he always started the meal by saying Grace.

This place doesn't come close to the way things were in White Hills. But it doesn't matter, 'cause now we have a clubhouse. When things get bad we got somewhere else to go. He puffed out his chest and quickened his pace. He'd accomplished a lot of things today. He'd taken his brother on an adventure, and they hadn't gotten lost. They found a treehouse. They ate the lunch he'd made all by himself, and they were getting along again, like brothers, the way they used to.

So what if we live in a strange house with a cold bedroom? So what if our parents argue with each other or don't say nuthin' at all?

His friend Billy told him his parents behaved the same way before they got a divorce. After that Billy started spending the school year with his mom in Shadow Glenn and summers with his dad in California. *They never ask him if he wants to go, just pack his bag and send him off.*

As they mounted the steps to the front porch, Matthew looked at his brother. Luke hadn't left his side for a minute. He opened the door and let Luke go in first. *Maybe our folks will split up like Billy's did. It doesn't matter anymore. Me and Luke will stay together always. I'll make sure of that.*

26

Mitch swung into the hospital parking lot and went straight to the emergency room desk. The same eagle-eyed woman was sitting behind the partition. This time, he stood his ground and insisted on seeing Mr. Garby.

"They moved him to a private room—number 302." The woman responded like a worn-out robot.

In a way he sympathized with her. *How many demanding preachers and family members does she have to deal with every day?* he pondered. *It has to be a tough job.* He expressed his thanks and headed off before she could think of a reason to stop him.

He took the elevator to the third floor and walked a zigzag path up one corridor and down another, checking room numbers until he came to 302. Garby was in a private room all right, but the window overlooked the brick wall of another wing of the hospital.

"Nice view," Mitch quipped from the doorway.

Garby turned away from the flickering TV screen, raised his eyebrows, and gave Mitch a welcoming grin. He hit the button on the remote and turned off the game show he'd been watching.

"These hospital idiots." Elijah's voice sounded more gravelly than ever. "You can't depend on 'em. Ask for a window with a scenic view, and you get a brick wall."

Mitch pulled a chair up to Garby's bedside. He sat down and placed a hand on the bedrail.

"You missed our visit the other day," he chided.

Garby let out a grunt. "Yep. Folks tell me I'm unreliable these days."

Mitch chuckled. "I doubt it. From what I've seen so far, you're not only reliable but you're a downright nuisance at times." He said it with a smile.

A sparkle settled in Garby's eyes and he looked like he was about to laugh. "You ain't seen nothin' yet. I can be more than a nuisance if I have to stay tied to this hospital bed much longer. My cat needs feedin'. My plants need waterin'. And my dirty dishes have been sittin' in the sink for three days."

"What about your son? I thought he was on his way."

Elijah grunted. "He breezed in and out of here, pausing just long enough to make sure I hadn't kicked the bucket yet. I guess he had more important things to take care of back home."

A wave of compassion flowed through Mitch. He thought about his own father and their brief estrangement years ago. Despite their differences, if anything happened to his dad he'd be there in seconds, and he'd hang around until he was sure he was all right.

"Sorry, Mister Garby. I should think your own son would have stayed a while, at least until you got back on your feet."

Garby tilted his head and eyed him with annoyance "When are you gonna start callin' me Elijah? You youngsters make me feel old. *Mister? Sir?* I'm tired of those labels. Listen. I drive a car. I live alone. I walk two miles every morning, and I do crossword puzzles with a pen. Do you think those activities might keep me out of an old age home?"

Humbled, Mitch shook his head and smiled with fresh appreciation for the man. "Okay, Elijah, I get it. But I'd like to help you if I can. Do you want me to go to your house and feed your cat?"

Garby shifted his upper body to get a better look at Mitch. He narrowed his eyes.

"You would do that? For me?"

"Of course. Give me a key. I'll take care of everything."

Garby shook his head in obvious disbelief. "You're a real piece o' work, Mitch. I had a feeling about you the day you sat in the church office, fidgeting like a little school kid who'd gotten in trouble. But you didn't do anything wrong. You showed up for an interview, and the rest of us made you feel like you'd been placed under a microscope."

The reminder left Mitch flushing with embarrassment. Garby's next words surprised him.

"Well, you passed with flying colors. Sad to say, you didn't know what you were gettin' yourself in for. But you took the job, and so far you've stayed. Now you've got questions, and I'm in a position to answer them."

"I was hoping to talk with you the other day, until you ended up in here. Really, Mr. Gar—Elijah, it can wait. I don't want to put any stress on you while you're sick."

"Oh, piffle." Garby spit out the age-old expletive. "I'm fine. I had a little episode is all; nothin' I can't handle."

"We don't have to talk now," Mitch persisted. "We can wait until your doctor releases you. Then we can grab that cup of coffee we put on hold."

Garby stared at him, his usual stony expression melting. He somewhat resembled the grandfather Mitch had never met except through old photos.

"Go ahead. Ask me anything," Garby insisted. "Right now. Ask and you shall receive."

Mitch sat back and appraised Garby's condition. The poor man looked like skeletal remains from a concentration camp.

He'd lost weight over the last couple of days, giving Mitch more concern. Yet the old guy acted like he could jump out of bed at any moment. *They gave him a new pacemaker*, Mitch thought. *Hopefully, it'll keep him going for many years to come.* The color had returned to Elijah's cheeks and a sparkle flashed in his crystal gray eyes. Mitch hesitated to bring up anything that might send him back to the operating room.

"It can wait," he said, a tenderness in his voice. "I stopped by to make sure you're all right. It's no big deal."

"You're lyin', Mitch. You came here because you're in trouble. I know the signs. I've seen them before. Don't be like the ones before you. Don't do like those preachers who stayed a few weeks and left with their tails tucked between their legs. Don't give up on Mercy Fellowship. Our church needs a strong Christian at the helm. I'll help you. When I'm back in action I'll get with you, and we'll face this thing together—with God as our strength, of course."

For the first time in more than two months Mitch felt a sliver of hope. He'd left Nashua and Salem a defeated man. But Garby's positive attitude was sending a boost of energy into him.

"Okay, Elijah, how do we start?"

"We start with prayer. Right now. In front of God and anybody who dares to walk into this hospital room."

Mitch folded his hands and bowed his head. Elijah wrapped his gnarled fingers around Mitch's hands.

"Father, we need your help," Elijah mumbled. "Thank you, Amen."

Then silence.

Mitch didn't know if Elijah expected him to take over or simply say, "Amen." As the man's pastor, he should add something to the prayer. But Elijah had removed his hand. Mitch opened his eyes. The old man had leaned back against his pillow, his eyes on the brick wall.

Mitch scowled. "That's it? Father, we need your help?"

Garby glared at him. "What did you want, the Gettysburg Address?"

"I thought—"

"Listen, young man. We don't always have to say long-winded prayers. Not where God's concerned. He already knows what we need before we ask. Sometimes we can pour our hearts out until we bore everybody to death. At other times, when we're so overwhelmed we're at a loss for words—like you seem to be right now—we have to shut up and let the Holy Spirit speak for us."

Elijah made sense. He realized he had made a habit of almost putting people to sleep during his own prayers that never seemed to end. Like a couple times before dinner when he said a rambling Grace that included a ton of requests and appreciations. When he looked up he found Lydia staring at him glassy-eyed, and the boys appeared to be holding their breath, their hungry eyes on the food growing cold on their plates. He made a mental note to be more considerate before launching out on a lengthy oration at such times.

"Okay, what's next?" he conceded to Garby.

"Now you have a ton of challenges ahead of you. But you have God in your corner. And me. You don't need anything else."

"Mister Garby—Elijah—you seem to think more highly of me than I deserve. The truth is, I don't know what I'm fighting against or how I'm supposed to fight it."

"You lack confidence is all."

Mitch nodded. "I guess I'm not much of a pastor if I allow myself to be intimidated by what's happening in a small church like Mercy Fellowship. I've hardly gotten started, and I already feel like a total failure. Besides, I'm worried about my family."

The old man shut his eyes. "Look. Why don't I lie here, close my mouth, and you tell me what's been happening? Let it all hang out. Don't omit anything." He opened one eye and directed it at Mitch. "And don't worry. You can't shock me." He closed his eye again, snuggled against his pillow, and clamped his mouth shut.

Mitch began with the first day he and his family came to Shadow Glenn. He spilled everything, day-by-day, detail-by-detail. He mentioned the freezing temperature in the boys' room, the slamming door, Lydia's strange behavior, the box of amulets in the basement, even the tour guide's note and his wife's reaction to it.

"I have no interest in that girl. I was planning to throw the note away, but I simply forgot about it. I don't know what's going on, Elijah. It's like somebody—or something—is trying to destroy me."

The old man's expression never changed. He lay there and nodded now and then, the only indication he was still awake and listening. Mitch told him about his visit with Reverend Baseman.

Garby opened his eyes. "Good man. It's too bad he didn't stick it out with us."

"I was impressed by what he's accomplished in New Hampshire."

"Kinda makes a man want to run off and do the same, doesn't it?"

"Sometimes. I have to ask, why didn't you try to work things out with Rick? He seems like the kind of pastor who could have fixed things at Mercy Fellowship."

"I said he was a good man, but he wasn't the right fit for our church. Our situation needs someone who won't get impatient for something more, someone who doesn't quit." He shot a sideways look at Mitch.

The old guy must have listened closely during our interview more than two months back, Mitch mused. *He heard me say I'd never quit anything in my life. For some reason he stored that bit of information away. Impressive.*

"Rick was here for six months," Mitch acknowledged. "I've only been here for two months. How do you know I won't give up too? I nearly packed three times already."

"I just know." Elijah cocked his head. "Anything else troublin' ya?"

He decided to confess his whole day. "Besides visiting Rick Baseman, I took a quick jaunt into Salem."

"Salem? What on earth for?"

"I wanted to speak to the Drummonds. From the sound of things, all the bad stuff started when they came here."

Garby nodded, and he got a faraway look, like he was remembering. "Phineas Drummond, another good man who bit the dust." He was almost whispering. Then he suddenly raised his voice. " So what did you learn from all your diggin'?"

"Some shocking information," he said. He told Garby about his chat with Mrs. Winters. He mentioned the fire and Phineas Drummond's death. Elijah listened intently and at some point he flicked away a tear.

"Such a sad end for Phineas," Garby murmured. "And Cornelia? I can't help but think she deserved what she got."

The two of them fell silent. The minutes ticked by. The sun began to set, and a shadow swallowed up the brick wall outside Garby's window.

A noisy cart came down the hall, its spastic wheels emitting squeals against the slick tile floor. An aide walked in with a tray, set it on Elijah's bed table, and left without saying a word.

"They're like robots," Garby sneered. "Hardly a kind word out of any of 'em."

"There are better hospitals."

"Not in Shadow Glenn."

Mitch snickered. "Maybe they're afraid of you. I know *I* was."

The old man looked at him, and his frown dissolved into a smile. "I'm harmless."

"If you say so." Mitch checked his watch. "It's six o'clock. I need to get home."

Garby pressed a button and raised the upper part of his bed until he was sitting upright. He removed the metal cover from his food dish and scowled at the contents—meat loaf, mashed potatoes with gravy, green beans, and the ubiquitous red Jell-O.

"Same-ol', same-ol'," he grumbled. "Hot or cold, it still tastes like cardboard. And it's too much like what they fed me yesterday."

"Smells good. You'll want to eat a little, get your strength back."

Garby picked up his fork and took a bite of the meat.

"Well, Elijah, I've told you everything. What am I supposed to do with this mess?"

Garby eyed him thoughtfully. "Give me a couple of days to sort through what you've piled on me. Meanwhile, do yourself a favor. Keep an eye on that wife of yours. And if you haven't already done so, commit to memory Ephesians 6:13 through 17 where it talks about the armor of God. You're gonna need it."

Mitch nodded. "I memorized those verses when I was a teenager. I'm ashamed to admit, I'd probably stumble over them now."

"Then rememorize them. Any time you feel oppressed, recite those verses, no matter where you are." The old man set aside his fork. "I'm tired." His voice was fading. "We'll continue our talk some other time. For now, I need to finish eating this bland, salt-less imitation of a meal and get some sleep."

"Do you want me to feed your cat and water your plants?"

"I'd appreciate it. You'll find a key under the mat."

Mitch was aghast. "Under the mat? Why did you put it there? It's the first place a burglar will look."

Garby chuckled. "Burglar? In this town? Nobody's gonna bother to break into my place. I could leave the door wide open. Anyway, you'll be able to come and go with no problem. Just slip the key back under the mat when you're done."

Mitch left the hospital and, for the moment, he also left his troubles behind—in room 302, with Elijah Garby. He went to the old man's house and found the key right where Elijah said it was.

He rooted around in the cupboards and found a bag of dry cat food. He sprinkled some in a little dish and set it on the floor, then he placed a separate bowl of fresh water beside it. From out of nowhere, a tabby cat let out a wail and came running into the kitchen. Mitch backed away and allowed the cat to attack his meal.

"Go to town, little buddy."

He filled a pitcher with tap water and drizzled it over the potted plants lined up along the sill at the front window, then returned to the kitchen to wash Garby's pile of dirty dishes. It took plenty of soapy hot water to remove the caked-on food. He rinsed off the dishes and placed them on a rack to dry. Taking a sponge he wiped crumbs from a Formica tabletop. Last of all, he grabbed a broom from a tiny closet and swept the floor.

An inkling of guilt came over him. Here he was cleaning up after an old man he hardly knew, and he couldn't remember the last time he'd helped Lydia with the dishes or any of the housework. *If she could see me now.*

When they got married, he'd relegated such duties to her. As he'd expected, she'd assumed the household chores without complaint. After all, that was her forte, or so he'd thought. Freed from those mundane duties, he was able to concentrate on his ministry. Now he was doing what he'd always viewed as women's work. He'd messed up again, thinking it was okay to help a stranger while neglecting his own house. Maybe if he helped out a little more at home things might change for the better.

In any case, he'd made up his mind to stay and fight. But at least he won't be fighting alone. A nonagenarian was stepping up beside him. It would have sounded ludicrous if he didn't already know the man. Elijah Garby. A wise old coot with the stamina of a 30-year-old. Somehow the image was beginning to make sense.

The job finished, he passed through the living room on his way to the front door when he spotted an open Bible on a side table. Curious, he walked over to it and took a look at the page. There it was again, the passage of scripture Garby had mentioned in the hospital. He'd circled one of the verses with red ink. Ephesians 6:12, *For we wrestle not against flesh and blood, but against principalities, against powers, against the rulers of the darkness of this world, against spiritual wickedness in high places.*

The passage went on to list the different parts of the armor of God.

Mitch swallowed hard. The old man believed in spiritual wickedness. Apparently, so did the apostle Paul. Otherwise, why did he write those words 2,000 years ago? Perhaps it was time Mitch also acknowledged the evil spoken of in those verses. Perhaps it was time he put on the whole armor of God and got ready to fight back.

27

During the drive home, Mitch thought about the verse Elijah had circled with red ink. Spiritual wickedness? In a church? Anything was possible. Considering all the weird happenings, he couldn't come up with any other answer. Hadn't Mrs. Pendergrast mentioned demons in that newspaper article? And, what about the persistent shadow in the third pew? Someone or some*thing* had tightened its grip on Mercy Fellowship and had affected the people, the parsonage, and now his family.

He pondered his wife's strange behavior. Richard Baseman had spoken the words Mitch had been afraid to address. Had Lydia received Christ as her Savior, or was she merely going through the motions? He'd always assumed she'd made a profession of faith long before he met her. But had she?

Elijah mentioned a similar concern. *"Keep an eye on that wife of yours."*

Mitch's heart was breaking. The girl he'd fallen in love with, the mother of his children, the person he planned to spend the rest of his life with, might have fallen prey to some kind of unearthly influence. Whether demons or the whims of some crazy new friend, he needed to pull her to safety. But how? He wasn't sure what he was fighting against.

As he drove closer to the parsonage, the sky darkened along with the overwhelming blackness of his future. Just as he couldn't see beyond the reach of his car's headlights, so also he failed to envision a light on the horizon of his life. An overwhelming hopelessness settled over him.

His one ally, Elijah, lay helpless in a hospital bed. Nevertheless, the old man showed more courage and spirit than a whole church full of young people. One thing was certain—Mitch needed him.

He sent up a desperate prayer for help.

Please, Father, place Your healing hands on Elijah and help him to get better soon. I can't fight this thing alone. Sure, I know You're with me. But it would be nice to have a walking, talking human being by my side. If You really called me here, if You want me to stay, send Elijah to help me.

He pulled into the driveway and gaped at the front window. It was only seven o'clock but the house lay in total darkness—no lights at all and quiet as a grave.

Mitch entered the house, flicked on a light, and went straight to the boys' room. They weren't there. He checked the kitchen. No Lydia. He unlocked the cellar door. Eerie darkness. Last of all, he walked to his own bedroom, eased the door open, and stared in amazement. The light from the living room fell on three figures. Lydia lay in the middle of the bed with their sons curled up on either side of her. All three of them were sound asleep.

He held his breath and stared at them for several seconds, his heart softening with love for his family. They looked so innocent. Even Lydia.

He tiptoed to the bed, stroked his wife's arm and whispered her name. Her eyelids fluttered open. She blinked a few times, then eased her arms out from under the boys. Mitch offered his hand and helped her out of bed. Quietly, they left the room and went to the kitchen.

Mitch didn't say anything. In the not-too-distant past, their communication hadn't depended on spoken words.

But they'd lost their ability to read each other's minds. With aching heart, he stared at his wife and wished he could see inside her stubborn head.

Lydia ran her fingers through her hair, separated a few tangles, and rearranged the loose strands. She cast an awkward glance at him, went to the refrigerator, and pulled out a casserole. She placed it in the microwave and pressed the buttons. Still no words passed between them. He wanted her to be honest with him. He kept his mouth shut and waited for her to start the conversation. It never happened.

She set the table for two. He took his place at the table. She poured an orange soda and set it before him. The microwave beeped. She put on oven mitts and brought the casserole to the table, then went to get a serving spoon.

She settled across from him and bowed her head. He mumbled a few words of gratitude to God, then listened for Lydia's "Amen." When it didn't come he lifted the ladle and dug into the bubbling macaroni and cheese. A swirl of steam rose from the spoon. He served Lydia first, then he put a spoonful on his own plate, ate every bite, and scooped out another. Neither of them spoke. Nor did Lydia lift her fork. She stared at her plate, like she was avoiding his gaze.

Mitch eyed her with concern. "This is good. Aren't you gonna eat?"

She nodded, took a bite, and set her fork down. She sat back and released a sigh. "I guess you need some answers." Her voice was soft, almost non-existent.

"I do." A trembling started in his chest. He struggled to remain calm. He didn't want to scare her off, like before.

Her chin quivered, and tears spilled from her eyes.

"What's going on, Lydia?"

"I... oh, Mitch." She crumbled forward and sobbed into her hands.

He set down his fork. "You can talk to me, honey. I'm not mad. Just concerned."

She lifted her head and gazed at him. Her dark eyes nearly disappeared behind a veil of tears.

"What's happened, Lydia? Why are the kids asleep? It's only 7:30. And why the group hug in there? Are the boys okay? Are they sick? Did they get hurt?"

"Nothing happened. The boys are okay. They're not hurt." She shrugged one shoulder. "They went on a little adventure today, that's all."

He didn't like the way she was brushing it off. "An adventure? What do you mean, *an adventure?*"

"They must have slipped out of the house when my back was turned, and—and, well, I couldn't find them."

Mitch pushed away from the table. "They left the house? How, Lydia? How did they get out? And where were *you?*"

"I was here, at home."

Probably in the basement, he surmised. He wanted to confront the obvious but thought better of it. He needed to stick with the easier questions. "Did you go out and look for them? Did you call the police?"

She shook her head. "Yes. No. I don't know." Tears spilled unto her cheeks. "I checked everywhere—inside the house and out in the yard. I was frantic, Mitch. You took the car."

You're blaming me?

"I rushed out of here, went up one street and down another—on foot. I went all over town. When I came home I found them here. It was like they'd never left."

Mitch clenched his fists under the table where she couldn't

see them. He loved this woman. He didn't want to fight with her. Yet he needed better answers. In his work at White Hills he dealt with unpredictable teenagers all the time. He'd counseled enough of them to know how to get answers. *But this is my wife, the mother of my children, my* so-called *help-mate.* He stared at Lydia, unable to speak.

She was shaking her head, her remorse obvious. "I asked them where they'd been. They refused to tell me," she said, her voice breaking. "Matthew said it was a secret. Luke clammed up. I kind of fell apart after that. I was so relieved to see our boys safe at home I collapsed in a crying mess on the floor. Those two little guys wrapped their arms around me and led me into the bedroom. For a long time we lay there, hugging, until we all fell asleep." She looked at him, her tear-stained face pleading for mercy. "That's it, Mitch. That's everything."

He suspected there was more, perhaps something about spending too much time in the basement when she should have been with her children. He chose not to press her. The main thing was, his boys were home, and they were safe.

Lydia mopped away her tears and gazed into his eyes. For an instant, she looked like the shy young woman he'd proposed to many years ago. In recent weeks that woman had vanished, and a stranger had taken her place. He wanted his wife back, the way she used to be—carefree, loving, a responsible parent, a lover of antiques, a solid partner in his ministry. He missed her terribly, would do anything to bring her back. Anything.

He thought again about Richard Baseman's words of caution. It was now or never. He reached across the table and gently took her hand.

"What's happened to you, Lydia?" He kept his voice soft

and nonthreatening. "Ever since we moved here, you turned into—I don't know—someone else. I'm facing a real challenge in this church. You're supposed to stand beside me. You should be calling on the other women. By now you should have started a children's program. Together we should be planning functions in order to bring this congregation to life."

She pulled her hand away. "Call on the other women?" Her eyes grew wide with disbelief. Instantly, at his mention of the church, the other Lydia returned, the one he didn't know.

"Get real, Mitch. Those women walk past me in church and never say one word. If anything, they should have called on *me*, should have invited *me* into their homes, should have asked if they could help *me* with anything. Instead, I had to go outside the church to make friends."

He perked up. "Outside the church? Where?" He hoped she wouldn't say a bar.

"The local bookstore. Millicent's Cozy Corner. I became friends with the owner."

Relieved, Mitch went back to the issue at hand.

"All I know is, I need your help. If nothing else, I need you to keep track of the boys and support me in my ministry. It's a simple request, Lydia. You used to support my work at White Hills. Why can't you do the same in this church? What's changed?"

"I told you. It's different here. These people are different. They're not friendly. They don't even talk to each other."

"Well then, maybe we should pack up our things and leave. We can go back—"

"No!" Lydia sprang to her feet. "I don't *want* to leave. Don't you dare drag me all this way and tell me we're gonna turn around and go back. I'll never forgive you, Mitch." She crossed her arms defiantly. "I'm staying right here. If you want to leave, you can go. But you'll go alone."

Mitch lurched back in shock. In seconds Lydia had gone from helpless sobbing to snarling like a junkyard dog. He shook his head. "What's happened to us, Lydia? We never used to fight like this."

"I don't know. I don't like it either, but I've got a life too, and I'm gonna fight to keep it."

He needed to say something about what he'd found in the basement. Elijah said he should get rid of the evil. Though he'd put it off far too long this wasn't the right time. He'd already backed Lydia into a corner. She was ready to pounce if he said or did the wrong thing. But when *was* the right time? He decided to risk it.

"I went downstairs the other day, and I discovered your little corner in the basement. Tell me, Lydia, what's going on down there?"

"What do you mean?"

He hated it when someone answered his question with a question. "You know. The box of junk. The book of spells. The chair. The table. And all those candles and things."

"Nothing down there should interest you. It's my *woman cave*, remember? I created a cozy little place where I can be alone, to read, and meditate, and pray."

"Really?" He narrowed his eyes and tried to look beyond her feigned innocence. "Where you were when our boys went missing?"

She didn't answer, but the fire in her eyes told him the truth.

He struggled to keep from losing it. "Because of your *cozy little retreat* we almost lost our kids. Well, that stops now. I'm gonna get rid of the whole mess."

Lydia's eyes flamed, and she lunged toward him with her hand raised. He dodged to one side and avoided a slap in the face, or worse from the looks of those long nails. Didn't she clip them anymore?

Lydia's cheeks flushed bright red. "Don't you *dare* touch my things. You have no right."

She raised her arm again. He grabbed her wrist. She flinched, and he let go. Mitch backed away, ashamed at his response. He ran his hand through his hair. They'd come within inches of a physical confrontation. Except for the day he found the pentagram he'd never grabbed his wife before. And she'd never raised a hand to him.

"Lydia, what's going on? I don't know you anymore. Help me out here. What's happened?"

"Nothing." She pinched her lips together and rubbed her wrist.

"Then tell me this, have you fallen away from your faith?"

She stopped rubbing her wrist and glared at him. "That's a dumb question."

Rick Baseman's warning was beginning to make sense. The main question hovered on his tongue.

"Tell me, Lydia, are you a Christian?"

"What? Why on earth would you ask me *that*?"

"You've never mentioned a personal relationship with Jesus. I assumed you were a Christian, but now—"

"I'm as good a Christian as you are." She stuck her chin out. "What have you become, Mitch? Some kind of holier-than-thou preacher?" Her distorted face had turned as ugly as her words.

"It's a simple question, Lydia. Have you ever received Christ as your Savior?"

She tossed her head, and her hair bounced. In the past the gesture always caught his attention in a good way, but now, with a scowl on her face and her claws extended, she frightened him.

"It looks to me like *you're* the one who's changed, Mitch. You've become arrogant and self-serving."

He shook his head and tried to gather his thoughts. They'd already gone way past a little tiff. "Lydia," he said, calming his voice. "I don't doubt you are a good woman. But, something's definitely wrong."

She raised her eyebrows and smiled but her dark eyes dared him to keep on. "Physician, heal thyself," she sneered.

Her words stung, but he managed to keep control.

"Those things in the basement—they're used in devil worship."

"You're mistaken."

"And you're confused." He caught the anger in her eyes. He sweetened his tone. "It's nothing to be ashamed of, Lydia. Lots of people grow up thinking—"

"Oh, please, Mitch. Stop throwing your Christian mumbo-jumbo at me. I've suffered with it long enough. My parents used to—"

"Okay," he conceded. "I'll stop. But, please, Lydia. We have to get the garbage out of this house.

"It's *not* garbage. If you so much as *touch* it, I'll walk out of this house and move somewhere else. I'll get a job. I'll find an apartment, and I'll take the boys with me."

She spun away from him and almost plowed into Matthew and Luke standing in the doorway. "Move," she shouted. They leaped out of her way. She stomped through the living room and went out the front door.

Mitch looked in horror at the alarm on his boys' faces. How much had they heard?

"Where's Mama going?" Luke's eyes were wide and already filling with tears. "It's freezing outside. She forgot her coat."

Matthew stepped close to Mitch. "Mom's totally lost it, Dad. Are we really gonna go somewhere without you? Are you getting a divorce?"

His heart breaking, Mitch dropped to his knees and gathered the two of them in his arms.

"Don't worry, kids. Mama had a bad day. She didn't mean what she said."

A frown trailed across Matthew's forehead. "Mama's had a lot of bad days lately," he said with wisdom beyond his years.

Mitch searched their troubled faces. "How about we pray for her?"

"Okay, Daddy," they responded in unison.

Mitch was still praying when Lydia returned home, shivering. She glanced at them and went straight to her bedroom. The click of the lock resonated in the hallway. Another night on the couch. Worse, it was Saturday night and he'd be preaching in the morning. He needed a good night's sleep, but he also needed to take care of the boys.

He warmed up the macaroni and cheese and sat Matthew and Luke at the table. While they ate, he pulled up a chair and leaned back with one leg crossed over the other, putting on as casual an air as he could muster.

"Mama told me you went on an adventure today. Do you want to talk about it?"

The boys looked at him, then at each other. They dug into their food.

"It's okay, kids. You can tell me."

Luke raised his fork to his mouth. Matthew shrugged and scooped up another forkful of macaroni and cheese. "We didn't go no-place." The tremor in Matthew's voice told him otherwise.

"C'mon, you guys. I used to be a kid once. I liked adventure as much as you do."

"We went outside." Matthew shoved a forkful in his mouth.

Mitch waited. The boys kept eating. They avoided his gaze. He wasn't going to get a straight answer. He released a long sigh. At least they'd come home, unharmed.

"Okay, boys. I'll forget about it this time, but don't ever leave the house without permission again. Understand?"

Matthew nodded. Luke stared at his plate. He took a bite of food and finished his meal without once looking at his father.

After dinner, Mitch got his sons into the bathtub. When Lydia didn't come out, he tucked the kids in their beds and read them a story. After they fell asleep, he went to the church office and looked over his notes. Disgusted, he tore them up and pulled out his Bible. Elijah had pushed him toward the Ephesians' account of *the armor of God.*

Okay then. He spent the next hour building a message around those verses. The people at Mercy Fellowship could stand to hear such a sermon. *And with all that's happening at home,* he conceded, *I need to hear it too.*

28

On Sunday morning, Mitch relived the same nightmare he'd experienced every Sunday over the last few months. Once again he preached a message straight from the heart, and once again, he came away bent under the weight of failure. Like every previous Sunday, the people sat like blocks of ice. They stared back at him, their eyes glazed over, giving him no clue whether he'd reached any of them or if they even cared. *Why did they even come to church?* he wondered. *Was the practice so much a part of their routine they couldn't stay away?* Their response was worlds apart from what he used to see at his former church.

At that very moment, Pastor Samuels would be standing before thousands, his audience responding to his message with shouts of "Amen" and "Say it, brother." When the music started, they'd be singing, and clapping, and waving their hands in the air. Mitch longed for such a following. Rick Baseman had one. So did lots of other preachers. So why not him? Why was he stuck in this horrible graveyard with a bunch of corpses?

He frowned with disappointment. Lydia grabbed the boys and walked out with the crowd. Such was her pattern over the last few weeks. She'd left him to clean up the church, alone. When he finished, he doused the lights and locked up the building.

He didn't feel like going home. Instead, he drove to the hospital at the north end of town. More than ever, he needed to talk to Elijah Garby.

He pulled up a chair next to the bed and sat down with a sigh. "I don't know what happened this morning, Elijah. I based my sermon on that passage in Ephesians—the one you recommended. They stared at me like I had a kangaroo on my head. So much for the armor of God. It made no impression at all on them."

Garby set aside his Bible and his reading glasses and looked at Mitch with tenderness in his eyes.

Mitch leaned closer. "I need some answers. At my interview, the other deacons were friendly. I mean, we weren't buddy-buddy or anything, but they spoke to me, and they didn't run me off. Now they're like everybody else in the church—distant, even apathetic."

"And you feel rejected."

"Well, I certainly don't feel welcome." Mitch thought about the behavior he'd witnessed. "Those ridiculous people have their own little cliques. They sit in church with huge, noticeable gaps between their families. There's no fellowship, no mid-week meetings. Nobody helps anybody else. If a family's in trouble, they have to fend for themselves. It's sick, Elijah."

Garby nodded. "Sick is probably the right word."

"If they're not happy, why don't they leave?"

"Loyalty. They have to protect their claim to the church. Their ancestors founded it, you know. They aren't about to walk away."

Mitch grunted with disgust. "And I'm supposed to fix everything?"

The old man groaned and shifted his upper body to get more comfortable. "It's getting harder for me to move about, even in bed. Old age is the pits." He scrunched up his face, and it looked like he grew a whole new set of wrinkles. "I need to stretch my legs and get some exercise. They walk me up and down the hall. Whoopee! If I don't get out of here soon I'll never be able to walk again. Not like I used to."

Mitch suddenly saw his future. *If I stay in this church long enough I'll turn into another Elijah Garby, a die-hard servant of God without a following.* But the old guy had something he didn't have. He'd stored a bundle of information in his brain, and if Mitch wanted to survive he needed to tap into it.

"Everybody I talked to said the bad stuff started when the Drummonds were here."

Garby nodded. "But it wasn't because of Phineas. Cornelia stirred up a lot of evil in the church. She loved to pit one family against another. A minister's wife shouldn't do such a thing. She's supposed to unite everyone. She's supposed to bring pcacc, not conflict."

"And Phineas?"

"He behaved like a wimp. Turned a blind eye to his wife's shenanigans. We thought we hired a roaring lion, but we ended up with a mouse. It was like she'd cast a spell over him."

Garby's last remark struck him hard. Already Lydia was trying to take control. How long before she turned him into a wimp? Or worse.

He forced his mind back on the issues. "According to the church files, before Phineas and Cornelia came here, pastors stayed for years. They had the support of the congregation. The church held festivals and weekday meetings and pot luck dinners. Then the Drummonds came and everything changed. After they left, none of the new hires stayed for more than a few months, and all those activities ceased. Didn't you older members try to do anything about the quick turnover?"

Garby shrugged his bony shoulders. "We couldn't keep

those preachers from leaving. After a while, we stopped trying. We experienced huge gaps between pastors. Some of us filled in, but we needed a full-time preacher." He turned sparkly eyes on Mitch. "We needed *you*."

A warm embarrassment flooded over Mitch. "I have to admit, Elijah, I almost left a couple of times."

The old man patted his arm. "Well, I'm glad you stayed."

"Why do you think *I* can change this mess?"

"You have something the others didn't have. You have gumption, Mitch. I spotted it the first day we met. I've been watching you all along, and you haven't disappointed me. I believe God called you here in answer to my prayers."

There it was again. God's call. He hadn't just imagined it.

He smiled with appreciation. "You're the only deacon who's been supportive. What makes you so different from the others?"

"For one thing, I've been in this church longer than anyone else. I know first-hand how things used to be. My grandfather told me stories. Good stories. Some of our members were fresh out of college when the Drummonds came. They have no idea what the church was like in the old days. They only remember its trouble."

"And I'm supposed to deliver them?"

"I suppose." With a shaky hand Elijah lifted the glass of water from his bedside tray. He drained it and set the empty glass on the table. "You can't tackle everything at once. I'm a great believer in pruning away problems. Take them one at a time, and before you know it they'll all be fixed." Garby looked at him with penetrating eyes. "One topic we haven't addressed, Mitch. Have you taken control of your situation at home?"

He'd been avoiding the subject. Now he slumped back in

his chair, defeated. "The truth is, my personal life has gone out of control. I don't know how I'm supposed to fix the church if I can't even fix my home."

"Then start there. Start in the home."

"I don't know what to do." He was on the verge of tears. "I'm afraid I'm losing my family. Lydia has gotten downright nasty. And she hasn't gotten rid of the box of junk in the basement."

"I thought I told you to throw it out."

"I was going to, but she went berserk. She threatened to leave me, said she'd take the boys and go."

Garby was scowling now. "Call her bluff."

The scene raced through Mitch's mind. He pictured himself going into the cellar, grabbing whatever he could carry and burning it in the trash bin in the yard, or maybe setting it all out at the curb to be picked up by the garbage men. He could expect repercussions. Lydia screaming at him, packing her bags, herding the boys into the car, and taking off for who-knows-where.

"I can't risk it, Elijah. I don't want to lose my family."

"Things are gonna escalate," the old man warned.

"They already have. We lashed out at each other. Physically. I had to get out of there."

Garby shook his head. "Nothing's gonna change until you get the junk out of your home."

"You know as well as I do that Lydia's the one who has to do it."

The visit ended with Garby surrendering with compassion, and Mitch promising to look for opportunities to reach his wife. He trudged out of the hospital, his shoulders stooped. He wanted to throw the evil out, but Lydia would never stand for it. Someone had been putting those ideas in her head. She'd made one friend in town—the owner of the bookstore. Perhaps a visit to the shop might clear up some of his questions. He needed to know just how much influence the woman wielded over Lydia.

He recalled seeing the bookstore on their first drive through town. He made a couple of turns and pulled up in front of the shop. Except for a glimmer of light at the back of the store, it was dark. From what he could see from the road, it appeared innocent enough. A few best sellers were propped up in the window, along with a vase of artificial flowers and a neon light that said, "Closed." Even the name of the place—*Millicent's Cozy Corner*—seemed welcoming. He needed to get inside and meet the owner. Tomorrow he'll drop the boys at school, grab a cup of coffee at the cafe, and stroll over to the bookstore.

When he arrived home, he found Lydia and the boys playing a board game at the kitchen table. The aroma of sizzling meat wafted from the oven. Something boiled in a pot on the stove, and a bowl of salad waited on the counter. It was as if he'd been walking around in a nightmare over the last few weeks, and now he'd awakened. Though he suspected it was temporary, he didn't care. He needed to enjoy the moment.

The boys sprang from their chairs and, squealing, leaped into his arms. He staggered under their weight but held onto them. Lydia looked up and smiled. How long was she going to have these mood swings? He stared back at her, a nervous suspicion mounting in his mind. At any moment, the out-of-control shrew could return.

He let the boys slip out of his arms and to the floor. He gazed at Lydia and smacked his lips. "Something smells good."

"It's one of your favorites. Roast beef and parsley buttered potatoes. I even made an apple pie."

"Yum. So when do we eat?"

"In a little while." Lydia cocked her head and winked. "Why don't you join our game?"

He pulled up a chair and selected a shaggy-haired boy printed on a tiny cardboard game piece. "This guy looks exactly like me. So, how do we play?"

The boys swept the board clear and placed the four cardboard people in a line behind the word **START.**

Matthew straightened his shoulders and looked Mitch in the eye. "Okay, Dad. Here's what you do. When it's your turn, you spin the spinner, and you want to go up a ladder." He tapped the board with his finger. "That's how you win."

"And stay away from the chutes," Luke interjected with a shake of his head. "You might slide down to the bottom and have to start all over again."

Mitch chuckled. *Climb the ladders to success. Avoid the chutes. Strange. I feel like I've been living this game—climbing up and sliding down for the last three months. Now he wanted to climb to the top, whatever it took, and never slide down again. He needed more than a game piece and a spinner. He needed prayer, of course. And the armor of God. And a wife who supported him. And a church of eager members. And a house free of demonic oppression.*

Elijah wanted him to get rid of the filth in the basement. But he'd been treading softly. Apparently those things meant more to Lydia than he could fathom. Now he was caught between the proverbial rock and hard place. He knew the right thing to do. He should sneak down there and clean it up, but Lydia's threat still hung on his mind.

The truth was, his wife's attachment had gone far beyond what he could handle. It was more powerful than the book she'd purchased and all those ridiculous amulets. This was new territory for Mitch. Like the pioneers, he'd have to proceed with caution. First thing, he'd have to visit the little bookstore and talk to the woman who ran it. Armed with more information he might be able to make some solid decisions.

"I need to use the car in the morning," he told Lydia. "I'll take the boys to school."

A glimmer of hostility flashed in those two brown pools. She didn't say a word, merely stared at him with frightening determination. An army of invisible ants ran across his shoulders. He stared into his wife's granite eyes. Then she blinked, and the venom disappeared.

The next morning, Mitch rushed his sons into their jackets, grabbed their lunches, and hurried them out to the car. He slid into the driver's seat and looked up at the house. Lydia was standing in the doorway with her arms crossed. Ignoring the annoyance on her face, he drove off.

After dropping the boys at school, he hit the coffee shop to wait until the bookstore opened. He downed two cups of coffee and a donut, then at nine o'clock he set off on foot.

He entered the bookstore to the tinkling of a little bell. An attractive blond looked up from behind the counter. Surely this young woman could not be the owner. She nodded a welcome and kept sorting through the store's receipts. Mitch strolled about the shop. At first glance it appeared to have its typical stock of books and curios and gift items. It had a cozy atmosphere, like the sign out front claimed, and the air swirled with incense reminiscent of cinnamon and wood pulp.

He strolled down the aisles, passed by a mix of woman's novels, art books, documentaries, and cookbooks. A children's area contained a tiny table and chairs, a set of building blocks, and plenty of coloring books and crayons to keep the little ones busy while their mothers shopped to their heart's content.

A small men's section caught his eye. It offered a few books on auto mechanics, baseball, golf, and fishing. If he wanted to find something on classic cars or on building a home entertainment system, he'd have to go to one of the larger bookstores outside Shadow Glenn.

He continued to walk up and down the aisles, until he came upon an entire bookshelf dedicated to spiritual resources. He flinched. A few Bibles shared a shelf with an unreal number of books on black magic. Among them was a copy of the one Lydia kept in the basement of their house. He pulled it out and flipped through the pages, shook his head with disgust, and returned it to the shelf.

Such trash didn't belong next to Bibles—not on a bookstore shelf, and most definitely not in my home.

The next shelf was dedicated entirely to the supernatural. There were books on horoscopes, boxes of Tarot cards, Ouiji boards, and star charts. On the bottom were a few cross-over novels by authors who'd made a futile attempt at combining religious principles with worldly philosophies. He recognized the titles and the names of the people who wrote them.

"Can I help you find something?" the soft voice came from behind him.

He turned. The young woman's ready smile disarmed him. Her deep green eyes conveyed a wisdom far beyond her years. She looked like any other twentysomething young lady. She wore a name tag. *Millicent.* So she *was* the owner of the store.

"Just looking." He scanned the shelf and frowned. "I'm curious. Why do you have Bibles mixed in with all this occult material?" He didn't try to keep his repulsion out of his voice.

Millicent's smile faded. "Why do I do it? I do it because there are lots of ways to worship God, not only through the scriptures but with many other resources. My store is different from other shops. I don't force one line of thought on my customers, I offer multiple pathways to spiritual wholeness." She spoke with such arrogance Mitch wanted to slap her.

He crossed his arms. "I'm afraid I don't follow you. I'm a pas—um—a Christian. I read the Bible, and I use extra-biblical works, but I stick with those written by believers in Christ. They're more reliable than filling my head with a lot of nonsense."

"Well, I'm a Christian too, and I believe there are many roads to one god."

"Many roads? Or many gods? It seems to me there's a difference."

"It depends on where you're getting your information."

"The Bible speaks about such things. If you're a Christian you ought to know that."

"Look." Millicent's tone was sharp. "I'm not going to argue spiritual issues with a customer I've never seen before. Either buy something or leave my store."

Heat rose to Mitch's face. So this was the person Lydia had befriended. He'd found out all he needed to know.

"I'll leave your store, all right." He stomped down the aisle and threw a final remark over his shoulder. "You don't have a bookstore. You have a den of iniquity."

He walked out and slammed the door. The little bell clattered to the floor.

29

Lydia couldn't understand Mitch's behavior. He didn't tell her where he was going or how long he'd be away. He grabbed the car keys and off he went. No explanations. No invitations for her to join him. Not one word about what he might want for lunch or dinner, or even if he'd be home in time to eat.

After he left, she ignored the dirty breakfast dishes, turned her back on the laundry and the sewing and the cleaning. Many of the treasures she'd found in the attic still lay in a pile in a corner of the kitchen, collecting more dust. Inhaling her newfound freedom, she went straight to the basement and lifted Dorcas' book from the pile. For a long time she sat in her reading chair, and flipped through the pages.

About halfway through the book, she came again to the section on family members. One paragraph jumped out at her. It spoke about family members who caused problems in the home. Lydia reread the part that suggested using photos and strands of a person's hair. She leaped from the chair, set the book aside, and raced upstairs. She located their wedding album on the bookshelf and removed a photo of Mitch standing at the altar. Then she went to the bathroom and pulled a few strands from Mitch's hairbrush.

Returning to the basement she read the instructions again. The ritual seemed harmless enough. She set her jaw. She needed to concentrate only on Mitch. She didn't want to destroy the man—she merely wished to change his attitude. She missed the old Mitch—considerate, helpful, supportive, loveable Mitch.

She spent several minutes in mindless chanting. It didn't matter if those syllables meant nothing to her. According to Dorcas, the process required complete trust. But even as she mumbled the incantations, her mother appeared before her with arms crossed and stern lines trailing along her forehead. Blinking against the image, she pressed on and tried to concentrate. In the end she slammed the book shut and left the basement with her mother's face still hovering before her.

Nor could she suppress the words of advice her mother had said on her wedding day. Remarks about keeping a nice home for her family, standing by her man, taking good care of her children. Protecting. Guiding. Feeding. Loving.

Propelled by an indescribable guilt, Lydia raced about the house, doing the breakfast dishes, making the beds, starting the laundry, dusting the furniture, and vacuuming the rugs. She wasn't complying with her mother's edicts. She was fleeing from them. If she obeyed all the rules, maybe the woman would leave her alone.

She pulled a chicken from the freezer for the evening meal, baked a tray of brownies, and steamed a pot of rice. Sometime during her frenzied activity her mother's image disappeared.

Mitch walked in at three o'clock with the boys in tow. He gave no explanation about where he'd gone. Nor did he ask about her day. He sniffed the air. "Mmm. Smells like roast chicken."

"I'm gonna need the car tomorrow." She blurted it out before her husband could claim their one vehicle again. "I've got to do some shopping."

Without giving him a chance to object, she turned her back on him and tended to the pot on the stove. She grinned with satisfaction. It was like gaining points in a chess match. *But will I ever be able to call out, checkmate?* she wondered.

Suppertime passed with the boys chattering and Mitch and Lydia escaping into their own worlds of silence. The rest of the evening went like a programmed ritual, with Lydia doing the dishes and Mitch leaving for the church office. Matthew sat at the kitchen table and did his homework, and Luke colored a few pages in a coloring book. Then the boys took their baths and went to bed.

That night Lydia lay next to her sleeping husband, her eyes open, staring at the ceiling. An ache gripped her heart, and she longed for the marriage they once had. After ten years of solidarity, something was tearing them apart. She blamed Mitch.

After all, I've done everything in my power to make a pleasant home for him and the boys. And what do I get in return? Suspicious glances, a cold shoulder when I need to talk, and the back of his head always going somewhere else to take care of things that don't concern me.

There was a time when Mitch had referred to her as his soul mate, and she'd called him her hero. These days, they both retreated into deafening silence. Deafening because unspoken words sometimes shout louder than what is said audibly.

Then there's that sideways look that hurts worse than any physical blow.

A tear leaked down her cheek. Lydia was in desperate need of a shoulder to cry on. She thought about the few friends she'd left behind at White Hills. They already had gotten on with their lives. They didn't phone her much back then, and they certainly wouldn't now.

She could call her mother, but the woman's interrogation

would tear her down even more. She'd accuse Lydia of failing in her duties as a wife and mother. She'd want to know where she'd gone wrong.

At this point in her life she could only think of one person she could talk to without feeling embarrassed or intimidated. Millicent. Her new friend. With that comforting thought she was able to relax enough to fall asleep.

After dropping the boys off at school the next morning, Lydia strolled around town until nine o'clock when the bookstore opened. Customers came and went. Lydia browsed the inspirational section until the traffic subsided and the store settled into a quiet tranquility.

Millicent brewed some herbal tea and beckoned Lydia to her cozy corner at the back of the store. They settled in the two chairs. Lydia grasped her teacup with both hands, breathed in the minty steam, and began to relax.

"Penelope told me about your little disagreement." Millicent's remark caught her off guard.

She stared into her cup. "She did?"

"Yeah. You hurt her feelings. But don't worry about it. Penelope is way too sensitive. She'll get over it."

"Her chanting was getting us nowhere, and I needed to find my boys." She looked into Millicent's eyes, deep purple now, like the blouse she wore. The image broke Lydia's confidence. "Please, apologize to her for me," she mumbled.

"I will." Millicent sipped her tea. "When you didn't return my calls, I assumed you found your kids."

Lydia avoided Millicent's gaze. "They came home on their own."

"Great." She took another sip. "So how's everything else going?"

Like always when Millicent prompted, Lydia succumbed to an overwhelming surge of emotion. She blinked hard against a rise of tears. "It's Mitch. He found my things in the basement and threatened to throw them out if I didn't do it first."

"Wow. What did you say?"

"I told him if he even *touched* my personal stuff, I'd leave him and take the boys with me."

Millicent straightened. She smiled and her eyes grew wide like she'd just won the lottery. "Are you serious?"

Lydia nodded. "If I can find a job."

Millicent's smile widened. "I could use an extra pair of hands in here."

"Really?"

"Sure. I never get a day off, except for Sunday." She raised a shoulder. "I couldn't pay much, of course, but enough so you could rent a little place in town. And don't forget, there's alimony—and child support."

Lydia's heart leaped to her throat. Alimony? Child support? What was she thinking?

She shook her head. "I don't want to get divorced. I just want to be in charge of my own life." She looked at Millicent through the vapor rising from her cup. "I love Mitch," she mumbled.

Millicent looked like she was about to lurch out of her seat. "Are you kidding? Look what he's done to you. He's turned you into a whimpering version of his idea of a wife."

"That may be true, but I could never file for divorce. My parents would disown me. Our church frowns on divorce. Mitch would lose his job. We both would suffer terrible embarrassment, maybe even shunning."

Millicent glared at her. "You told me you attend Mercy Fellowship. That church has been caught up in its own scandal for a long time. All kinds of creepy things have been going on over there for years."

A shiver ran through Lydia. "Creepy things? Like what?"

"I don't know for sure. It started when I was about a year old. It seems some couple turned things upside-down. They stayed for a couple of years, and by the time they left, the atmosphere had changed. I'm not sure what happened, but I think God must have left too."

"Wow." Lydia thought about Mitch's remarks about shadows and unfriendly people and his failed sermons. He walked around hunched over like there was a huge weight on his back.

"What happened there, Millicent?"

The girl shrugged. "I heard things while I was growing up. People left and switched to one of the other churches. My parents did too. They joined a big church on the other side of town. I kept going with them until I was old enough to choose for myself. Three years ago my folks moved to Boston, and I stopped going to church altogether. It's no loss to me."

While speaking about her parents Millicent's eyes took on a shade Lydia had never noticed before. It was as if a cloud had passed over them turning them almost black.

"You didn't want to go to Boston with your folks?"

She made a face. "No way. I wanted to stay right here where I was born and raised. My parents gave me the money to open this store, but when they discovered what I sold here, they told me to either get rid of the magic or they never wanted to see me again." She tilted her head and grinned. "Sound familiar, Lydia?"

She nodded thoughtfully. "Mitch said pretty much the

same thing. Sounds a lot like my mother too. If she knew what I've been doing, she'd never let me rest until I purged our entire house of my collection."

Millicent's eyes faded from black to purple again. "I get all the strength I need from my craft." She raised her eyebrows. "You can too."

Lydia ignored the comment. She was already remembering a sweeter time. "When I met Mitch, I was dating someone else. Ben Marshall." She smiled at the memory. "He was the handsomest guy in town. And generous. On my nineteenth birthday, he gave me a dozen long-stemmed roses. And what did Mitch give me? A Bible with my name engraved on the cover. My mother insisted it was the better gift. She likes Mitch, always did."

"She didn't like Ben?"

Lydia shook her head. "He was a little too wild. But he was smart. And motivated. He went to college to study law. He wanted to go into politics, and he did, too. A few years later, he was elected to the city council."

"But you married Mitch."

"Right. Stable, religious, wholesome Mitch. My mother was thrilled."

"Why on earth did you let Ben slip through your fingers?"

She shrugged. "I can't explain it, but I was drawn to Mitch, like someone else was putting the pieces together, and it wasn't my mother. But, here's the irony..." She smiled coyly. "My kid sister, Jessica, married Ben. Now she's into the high-class social scene—fashionable clothes, new Lexus every year, country club membership, the works. Meanwhile, I'm walking around in homemade outfits and searching the internet for multiple ways to cook chicken."

A sliver of guilt pierced her heart. "I suppose I shouldn't complain. My husband's made sacrifices too. He's a good man."

"But he's made life difficult for you, hasn't he?" Millicent prodded.

She released a sigh. "Ever since we came to Shadow Glenn, he's been finding fault with me. I can't seem to do anything right."

The girl reached out and stroked Lydia's arm. "You poor dear."

"Millicent, what if I used one of your *good* spells on my husband? And one on the church too."

"We can try. Do you have a photo?"

"Of course." She set down her teacup and reached for her purse. She pulled out her cell phone and scrolled to her photo gallery, found a shot showing Mitch's face.

Millicent gawked at the picture. Her hand flew to her mouth. "That's your husband?"

"What's the matter?"

"He came in my store yesterday morning and gave me a hard time about my display."

"He came in here?"

"He complained about the Bibles being mixed with my spirit guides."

"Sounds like Mitch."

"You mentioned the same thing, but you were nicer about it. And you accepted my explanation."

"What did you tell Mitch?"

"Not much. I didn't feel like he deserved an answer. He wasn't very nice. I felt like my spirit was clashing with his. I told him to either buy something or leave. He slammed the door on his way out. And guess what? He broke my bell."

"Really?" Lydia gasped in amazement.

Millicent went on, but softened her tone. "Don't blame *him*, Lydia. He's like all the other college-trained preachers. They follow a set of rules and regulations made up by their professors. They can't think for themselves."

A blast of heat rushed to Lydia's cheeks. She had a sudden impulse to defend Mitch. He'd dedicated his life to serving God. He was quick to help someone in need. And he hardly ever lost his temper. Until lately.

She took a deep breath. "Mitch *does* think for himself, Millicent. He takes care of me and the boys, and he works tirelessly in the church."

Millicent gave her a half-smile. "Come on, Lydia. You can't be serious."

"Well, okay. Lately he's been acting like he doesn't trust me anymore. And when he ordered me to throw out those things in the basement his voice shook, like he was emotionally upset. I actually felt sorry for him."

"Listen, my friend. If you want to keep peace in your home, you're gonna have to take charge. Without Mitch knowing it, of course. Listen to me. Your future depends on how well you handle this situation. You can start by setting aside items from your collection, things you can't replace easily, like Dorcas' book, your pentagrams, maybe a couple of charms, and some candles."

Lydia withheld her objections and nodded. She hadn't been able to come up with a plan of her own. Since Millicent wasn't in the middle of the trouble she could think clearly.

"Do you have a trash bin where you can burn stuff?"

Lydia nodded again.

"If you want to get Mitch off your back, take the rest of your collection—the feathers, the beads, and all those items you gathered in the park—and dump them in the trash. Make sure your husband sees you burn them up. Then hide the items you set aside in different places throughout your house where Mitch won't find them. If he's like other guys, he'll search the place. Let him lock the basement door. Who cares? You don't have to go down there anymore. Choose a different place for your meditations."

Lydia smiled slyly. "I already hid my suncatcher in my lingerie drawer. I can put a few more things in there. Mitch will never search around in there."

The thought of Mitch digging into her underwear drawer brought a ripple of laughter to Lydia's throat. Millicent giggled along with her, and the two of them shared a moment of bonding.

Lydia breathed a sigh of relief. "Well, I suppose I'd better go home and start weeding through my collection."

She handed Millicent her empty cup, slipped into her coat, and grabbed her purse. When she reached the front door, she turned. "I miss your bell, Millicent You need to get another."

With fresh resolve, Lydia hurried home, parked the car in the driveway, and glanced toward Mitch's office. The light was on. The timing was perfect. His window overlooked the wire trash bin. He'd be sure to notice when she started throwing things in it, and when she set the pile ablaze.

Like Millicent suggested, she first hid a few small treasures in her lingerie drawer. She slid the candles behind a stack of linens on the highest shelf in her sons' closet. Then she grabbed a pair of shears and cut a square in the carpet in the master bedroom closet. She made an opening large enough to slip Dorcas' book under the rug, and, for more cover, she arranged several pairs of her shoes on top. She stepped back and surveyed the camouflage, satisfied Mitch would never notice.

Without a flicker of doubt, she gave up her private place in the basement. She moved the chair, the table, and the lamp to a corner of the master bedroom. With a self-satisfied smirk she hauled the box and its remaining contents outside. One by one, she dropped candles, feathers, ribbons, and glass beads in the metal bin. She kept glancing at the office window, even tossed items against the side, hoping the noise might carry to Mitch's ears.

She was almost finished when, from the corner of her eye she caught Mitch emerging from his office. His footsteps scraped along the pavement, closer and closer. She doused the pile with lighter fluid and struck a match.

He rested a hand on her shoulder. "You won't be sorry." His tone carried a tenderness he hadn't displayed in weeks.

"I know." She said with confidence and tossed the match into the bin. A blaze shot up and warmed her face. She and Mitch stood together, their arms linked, watching the fire until only a remnant of smoldering ashes remained at the bottom.

30

Mitch expected everything would change for the better, that the evil would vanish from their home. Lydia didn't resist when he asked for her key to the basement. There was no reason for anyone to go down there now, unless the furnace or plumbing needed repairs.

Still, the boys' room remained freezing cold. In fact the temperature also had plummeted in the master bedroom. He turned the thermostat to 79, then to 80, then to 82. It made no difference. The entire family wore heavy pajamas to bed at night and with extra blankets piled on top. Mentally Mitch thanked the White Hills ladies for their quilting gifts.

The heat-and-air guy had come to the house three times over the last couple of weeks. He made several adjustments but the problem remained. During his last visit he simply shook his head. "You might want to consider getting a whole new system." He put his tools away and left.

Aside from costing thousands of dollars, a new furnace might not make a difference. Mitch suspected the problem didn't involve a faulty heating unit but something else. Both bedrooms had plunged to near freezing temperatures. More doors slammed unexpectedly, though no one was near them. And other strange things had begun to happen.

One night Mitch awoke to thumping noises. He got up to check and found nothing out of the ordinary. Occasionally, even in daytime, he caught a glimpse of a drifting shadow about two feet high. The instant he turned toward it, the manifestation disappeared. He tossed and turned in bed every night. Most mornings he rose exhausted and longing for another few hours of rest.

Lydia, on the other hand, slept peacefully. She scrunched down under a pile of blankets and remained there until dawn. They never cuddled anymore.

Another morning dawned, and Mitch dragged himself to his office, coffee cup in his hand. He looked over the transformation with satisfaction. Despite interruptions, he'd painted the walls and sanded and varnished the wood floor. Bathed in a stream of light from the window the entire room glowed with a golden hue. It smelled better too.

He'd also cleaned out the metal file cabinet, leaving one drawer with a few necessary folders lined up in a neat row. He used the empty drawers for his research notes and sermons. He'd polished the desk to a lemon-scented sheen. Though it didn't measure up to Rick Baseman's massive workspace, the uncluttered surface, now free of debris, served as a broad display area for photos of his wife and children, his personal computer, note pads, a jar of pens and pencils, and, within reach, his favorite Bible and commentary. Since he finished the remodeling project, the office was the one place he could escape from the turmoil at home. It wasn't a man cave. Far from it. But it was the next best thing.

He plunged into another sermon, his head full of ideas. Halloween was approaching. It fell on a Thursday this year. So, for the next two Sundays he planned to address the holiday and its origin.

His audience, especially the children, needed to know Halloween started as a pagan celebration. Mitch's research turned up some interesting facts. The observance fell on the eve of the Celtics' new year, which was November first. Druid priests built bonfires and offered animal sacrifices. Celebrators dressed in costumes, danced, chanted, and told people's fortunes. They believed the domains of the living and the dead merged on that very night.

Mitch was adamant. Such heathen practices didn't belong in Christian gatherings. His new congregation could celebrate the way his former church did, with a harvest festival. The kids could dress up as princesses and pirates, not as witches and ghouls. They'd set out pumpkins and bales of hay, not jack-o-lanterns and skeletons. They could hire a horse and wagon for hay rides, and a choo-choo train to take the children on a jaunt around the church property. Of course they'd give out candy, maybe one of those trunk-or-treat events his former church held every year. He jotted down his ideas and prayed over each one.

An hour passed. The crunch of gravel in the driveway told him Lydia had returned from dropping off the boys at school. He broke away to have breakfast with her. When he got to the house, Lydia was already in the kitchen beating eggs for an omelet. Mitch took care of the toast and set butter and jam on the table. For the moment, it was like it always was. He sat across from her, took a bite of eggs, and hit her with his idea.

"What do you say we organize a harvest party at the church, maybe get the people to come out for a fun celebration? It'd be a good way to get the kids' minds off of Halloween, don't you think?"

Lydia stared at him. She furrowed her brow but said nothing.

"I could give a message about first fruits and sharing the harvest," he continued, though his enthusiasm had begun to fade.

She continued to stare and offered no sign of agreement. "What's the matter? Don't you like the idea?"

She grunted. "I don't think the people will go for it."

"Why not?"

"Have you looked at those faces? They could care less what you tell them from the pulpit. They need something—I don't know—something else."

"I've been trying to give them *something else*. Every week. This is different. A celebration. A chance to come together and enjoy themselves. Aren't you gonna help me with it?"

Lydia toyed with her eggs and smirked. "It won't work, Mitch."

He scratched his head. In the past she'd always supported his ideas, or seemed to.

"Okay," he said with a sigh. "What do you think *will* work?"

She looked up, and her brown eyes took on a darkness beyond their natural mien.

"It's not for me to say," she replied, a coldness in her tone.

A raw chill ran through Mitch, and his heart plummeted. Once again, he was looking into the face of a stranger.

He set down his fork, left the rest of the omelet untouched, and returned to the church office. Immediately, he dropped to his knees.

"Please, Father, help me. I don't know what I'm dealing with here. Something is terribly wrong. Do what you must to fix this, but please, protect my family. If I had known what I was getting into, I never would have come here. But, I'm here now, and I need you, Father. Turn this evil away. You promised if we prayed in the name of Jesus you would do it. I beg you now, in Christ's name, help us."

Mitch struggled to stand. He pulled a handkerchief from

his pocket and mopped the tears from his face. Dragging his feet he took a deep breath and settled behind his desk. Now, more than ever, he needed to put together a message on the evils of Halloween. With renewed fervor, he searched through the Old Testament, jotted down a few verses from Proverbs, shook his head and tore up his notes. Fruitless hours passed. He flipped to the New Testament and was about to make out a whole new list, when his cell phone rang. He looked at the screen and breathed easier.

"Hi, Elijah, what's happening?"

"The warden is finally letting me out. I guess they've poked and prodded me enough to satisfy their need to attack the helpless."

Mitch snickered. "They wanted to make sure they could send you home without a lawsuit coming back to haunt them."

Elijah grunted. "You're probably right. Anyway, I need a ride. Are you available?"

"Of course. I can use your help with Sunday's sermon. I'll be there in twenty minutes."

"I'll be ready. And I'm hungry."

"Do you want to stop and get some *real* food for lunch?"

"By all means. In fact, I'm in the mood for pizza."

Mitch looked at his watch—10:30. It didn't matter. "Pizza it is," he said.

Mitch gathered up his notes, donned his jacket, and stopped by the house for the car keys. Lydia had cleaned up the kitchen and was seated at the table, hand-stitching a sampler. She didn't even look up.

"I'm gonna pick up Mister Garby at the hospital. Don't fix lunch for me. We'll stop somewhere. And I'll pick up the boys from school."

Total silence. Mitch got the feeling she was glad to see him leave. *Funny. I don't recall if I ever told her Garby was in the hospital. Communication lately has consisted of a nod, a frown, and a shrug. It's like we live on two different planets. At least it's better than fighting.*

He found Elijah in good spirits, sitting on the edge of his bed. They waited a half-hour for the paperwork to go through. An aid dropped it off along with a wheelchair. The old man refused to sit in it.

"I have two legs. I can walk."

She smiled condescendingly. "Please, Mister Garby. It's hospital protocol."

"I told you, I can w—"

"I'll take him down." Mitch stepped behind the wheelchair and grabbed the handles.

The lines on Elijah's face softened. He winked at Mitch and slid into the chair.

Mitch wheeled Elijah into the elevator and to the front door of the hospital, left him sitting there, and went for the car. When he pulled up, the old man practically leaped out of the wheelchair, and with a huff he slid into the front seat.

Mitch shut the passenger door and went around to the driver's side. He got in behind the wheel and eyed Elijah with amusement. "I can see you're glad to be out of there."

"Yep, the farther away the better."

Mitch couldn't restrain a chuckle. "What makes you so ornery?"

Garby ignored the question. He pulled out a handkerchief and blew his nose. He tucked the handkerchief back in his pocket and snickered. "Did you know that people who live in the jungles think it's disgusting the way we save our boogers?"

Mitch choked out a laugh. "Really?" He shook his head and pulled the car away from the curb.

Garby looked at him in disbelief. "Think about it, Mitch. Where are they gonna get handkerchiefs in the middle of the jungle? They just snort it out on the ground. To them it's more sanitary than putting it in your pocket. Hah! And we think *we're* the civilized ones."

Mitch let go another round of laughter. "I believe it's a cultural thing."

"So are a lot of spiritual problems. People don't worship the way we're told to in the Bible. They bring in their own rituals and ceremonies and pretty soon we've got a hodge-podge of activities that have nothing to do with worship. Sometimes..." He raised an eyebrow and stared at Mitch, like he wanted to make sure he was still listening. "Sometimes, they even invite unclean spirits into the mix."

Mitch shrugged. "I don't know..."

"Don't think for a minute your wife is innocent. Lots of folks fall for the deception of Satan. Lydia may think there's nothing wrong with her little hobby, but those items you found in the basement are pure evil."

"She dumped it all in the trash and burned it."

Elijah raised an eyebrow. "And...?"

"It didn't change anything. The boys' room is still cold, and now ours is too. And other strange things have been happening. Slamming doors. More shadows. Except these are even more elusive than the one in the church. They move from one room to the other. Sometimes, I catch sight of one out of the corner of my eye. Then it's gone, and I'm left believing I imagined it."

"You said Lydia threw all the junk away."

Mitch pulled the car into the eatery's parking lot. He shut down the motor and turned toward Garby.

"I *assumed* she threw it all away." He reflected back, recalled the determination in his wife's eyes, the pile of strange objects in the trash bin. But had she thrown out *everything*?

They sat in silence for a minute, like both of them were trying to figure things out. Then, without warning, Garby opened his door and flung his feet out.

"What're we doin' sittin' here? I told ya, I'm hungry."

They went inside the restaurant and settled in a booth. Mitch gazed at the artwork on the wall and chuckled. Cleverly Photoshopped locations in Italy hung in a row. One of them showed the Leaning Tower of *Pizza* along with mouth-watering servings of the main course. Another displayed the Trevi Fountain spewing Pepsi into a glass. And a third bore the word, COLLA-SEE-YUM, with an array of Italian pastries protruding from the famed arena's openings.

Mitch caught Garby eying the satires. The two men looked at each other and burst out laughing. Mitch sat back and enjoyed the lighthearted moment. It had been a long time since he was able to relax and laugh at something silly. Garby also looked like he'd been starved for a little levity. His eyes sparkled like those of a teenager who just got his driver's license, but in this case, it was an old man experiencing a different kind of freedom. Garby had been released from the hospital after days of confinement, and it was more than he could handle.

In the midst of their laughter, a server came over, left a couple of menus and took their drink orders.

Mitch opened his menu and scanned the choices. "Do you have a topping preference?" he asked Garby.

"Do you?"

"Anything but plain, ordinary pepperoni. My wife always insists on pepperoni and nothing else. She never wants to experiment."

"Okay then, let's experiment. How about everything?" Elijah grinned mischievously.

"Everything?"

"Everything."

"Even anchovies?"

The old man nodded. "The works."

The girl came back and Mitch placed the order. After she walked away, he turned his attention to Garby.

"You know, Elijah, when I first came to Shadow Glenn, a couple of months ago, you gave me a hard time, but now I think you're my only friend. What happened?"

"Nothing happened. I needed to test you, needed to see if you were the real thing. I suspected you weren't like the others." He nodded with assurance. "I was right about you, Mitch. I've been waiting all these years for the right man to come along—a hero, if you will. So, it may have looked like I changed, but I simply reserved judgment for the appropriate time. You don't have to worry about me abandoning you. If you stay committed to Mercy Fellowship, I'll have your back."

"Thanks, Elijah. That means a lot to me."

Garby shifted in his seat like he was getting ready to change the subject. "Now, let's get down to business."

Mitch cocked his head to one side, eager to hear what the old man had to say.

"Regarding what you said about your wife—maybe she hasn't gotten rid of everything. She lied to you, Mitch."

"Well, she never lied to me, not out loud anyway. I assumed

she'd trashed it all. I mean, I was standing right there when she dumped it in the trash bin. She lit a match, and the fire ate up everything except a small rubble of stones and beads. I stayed right there until the blaze dwindled down to a smolder."

Elijah shook his head. "Something's not right. You need to search the house and see if there's anything she might have hung onto. Do it when she's not home. Find whatever it is and chuck it. And, Mitch, you've got to stay in prayer. This evil may be strong, but it's not stronger than the Lord. Remember what it says in First John. *Greater is He that is in me than he that is in the world.* The devil is in the world. The scriptures say so. If you want to get rid of the evil in your home and in the church, you have to tap into the power of God. It's the only way."

The old man's gnarled fingers took hold of Mitch's hand. "Let's pray." Mitch bowed his head. Elijah asked God for spiritual wisdom and strength in battle. He included a plea for protection over the Calloways, and he finished with gratitude for their meal.

While they waited for the pizza to arrive, Mitch mentioned the Halloween sermon he'd been working on.

"I'm stumped. I wanted to warn people about the evils behind the holiday, but I can't seem to find the right scriptures."

"So you've got an agenda, and you're trying to fit the right verses to it."

Mitch nodded sheepishly. "I guess so."

"You're concerned about the effects the holiday might have on your flock."

"Yes, I am. Shouldn't I be concerned?"

Elijah pursed his lips. "Of course. Your fears are

understandable. With all you've been experiencing, Halloween adds a little more doo-doo to your mess."

"I thought you might be able to suggest a few scriptures. The Old Testament verses don't fit, and the admonishments in Revelation seem too strong. I need to speak to the children while also reaching the adults. How do I address two diverse generations in one message?"

Garby shook his head. "You're going about this all wrong, Mitch."

He frowned, perplexed by the old man's remark. "What do you mean, all wrong?"

Elijah chuckled. "What I mean is, you're getting the cart before the horse. I've been listening to you for weeks. You've flopped around with sermons on about every topic but the right one. You're trying to get people to act the way the Bible says Christians should act. You never stopped to ask yourself if they're believers at all, or if they've fallen away from the truth."

"Are you telling me Mercy Fellowship is full of hypocrites? Those people attend services, week after week. Can you honestly say they've never made a profession of faith?"

"Possibly. Like that female speaker Joyce Meyer says, 'Sittin' in a pew don't make you a Christian anymore than sittin' in a garage makes you a car.'" He gave a little chuckle, then lost his smile and leaned toward Mitch. "Only God knows the heart of a man. I'd venture to say most of our congregation made a commitment of faith years ago. But you'll never know for sure until you test them with what they *really* need to hear."

"Like what?"

"They need Jesus, Mitch. Until they admit they're sinners in need of a Savior, you won't be able to teach them anything else, including the evils of Halloween and all the other things you've been trying to cram down their throats for the last couple of months. Even if they *are* believers, they need to be reminded of the basis for their faith. They may just need to recommit their lives to God."

"Then why haven't *you* told them?"

"I have. Multiple times. So did all the preachers who came before you and didn't stick around. They're discouraged, Mitch. They think God has abandoned them."

He stared past Elijah and weighed what the old man had said. The truth struck him like a bolt of lightning. Garby was expecting him to accomplish what no one before him had been able to overcome.

The pizza arrived, and the server refilled their glasses. Elijah slid a piece of pizza to his plate and sat back while it cooled.

"So I guess I'm gonna have to regroup," Mitch said with a sigh.

Elijah nodded.

Mitch lifted a slice of pizza, savored his first bite, and swallowed. "Oh man, this is the best pizza I've ever had."

"Including the anchovies?"

"*Because* of the anchovies. They add just the right amount of—"

"Salt?" Garby finished.

"Yeah, salt."

"That's what you need to be, Mitch."

"Huh?"

"Salt. You need to flavor your sermons with the right amount of seasoning, starting with the gospel."

Mitch made quick work of the slice and gulped his orange soda.

"No wonder I haven't been able to get through to those people. They sit there and stare at me—Sunday after Sunday—with no indication they've heard a word I said." He took another bite. "Salt, huh?" He grinned at Elijah.

Garby started on his own piece and spoke between bites. "It's not your fault, Mitch. You're doing what you've been trained to do."

"I was trained to lead people to Christ. Somewhere along the way, I jumped ahead of myself. We assume because people are in church they're believers. Kind of like my wife. She's been in church all her life. I assumed she was a Christian when I married her. I figured, she's a nice person, she grew up in church, she must be a believer. Now I'm not so sure. This change in our lives has brought out something else in her."

He slumped back in his seat. "What am I supposed to do, Elijah? If I don't know whether or not my own wife believes. How can I reach a whole church full of people?"

"Just do your job. Instead of preaching about the evils of Halloween, why not preach the gospel? To everyone, including your wife. Give them Jesus, and let the Holy Spirit convict them of everything else. Afterward, there'll be plenty of Sundays for you to disciple your converts."

Mitch started on another slice. The first bite stuck in his throat. He washed it down with a swallow of orange soda.

"Why haven't I seen it before? You can't communicate truth to people who are caught in a lie. If Lydia's caught in a lie, she'll never change her behavior. Same thing with my congregation. If they're not ready for meat I have to give them milk."

The wheels began to spin inside Mitch's head. He couldn't wait to get back to his office and write out the ideas now flooding into his brain.

Garby's eyes were smiling. "Take it slow, Mitch. Take care of your family first. Preach the word. Be faithful. Do the things Paul told Timothy a preacher should do, and above all, trust God. If there's one thing I know for certain, He's always in control."

For the first time in weeks, a sense of peace flowed through Mitch. Thanks to Elijah Garby, he could set a fresh course. All he needed to do was preach the gospel, and let God do the rest. Why hadn't he seen it before?

Elijah eyed the last slice of pizza, then he looked at Mitch. "You gonna eat that?"

31

Mitch took Elijah home and made sure he had everything he needed at his fingertips—a lap blanket, a cup of hot tea, the TV remote control, and his Bible. Promising to look in on him tomorrow, Mitch left for the church office to rewrite Sunday's message. With fresh enthusiasm, he dropped the topic of Halloween and focused on helping his flock realize the love of God through Christ.

From day one Mitch had been trying to incite his people to greater involvement in the church, to renewed fellowship, and to a spirit of giving. Garby's advice resonated with him now. *It's like Jesus said,* he mused, *seek first the kingdom of God and everything else will be added.*

He cleared his desk of the pile of notes he'd written that morning. He also put away the commentaries on Halloween, turned off his computer, and dove into the word of God, specifically searching for passages on sin and salvation. He turned first to the book of Romans. But he couldn't shake the nagging feeling that Lydia had not gotten rid of all her evil paraphernalia.

He kept working until Lydia drove off to pick up the boys at school. Then he set aside his Bible and leaped into action. He jogged to the house and went down in the basement. Lydia's corner was bare. She'd already moved the furniture to their bedroom. She'd burned the wooden crate in the trash bin along with its contents. There wasn't a single book or candle or amulet down there. Still, he wondered if she'd left behind any little treasures.

He hurried upstairs and began a search of the house—cupboards, closets, under beds, behind dressers, in the crevices of seat cushions. He found nothing. He opened suitcases and found them empty. A nagging feeling drew him back to the master bedroom. Aside from the chill that still prevailed in the boys' room, it had become the coldest room in the house. He looked everywhere, retraced his steps and looked again. The closet door opened with a squeal. He rechecked the shelves. Nothing there except pillows and blankets.

Lydia's shoes were lined up in a neat little row on the floor. He started to move them, when the front door opened and the boys' voices poured into the house. He shut the closet door, clenched his teeth at the resounding squeal, and made a dash for the living room just as Lydia walked in.

"How come you're in the house?" Lydia's voice carried a hint of suspicion. "Aren't you supposed to be working on your message?"

He balked. "I was." A lump formed in his throat. "I'm thirsty, need a drink of water." Why was he making excuses? He hadn't done anything wrong. This was his house too.

Lydia stuck out her chin and froze him with her eyes.

Mitch went to the kitchen and poured himself a glass of water. He stood by the sink and gulped the cool liquid, then poured another. Lydia came in and walked past him. He caught her reflection in the window. She was turning her head from left to right, sweeping the room with her eyes. She didn't trust him. *The way I don't trust her,* he admitted to himself.

Without taking off her coat, she went to the bedroom. Drawers opened and shut. The closet door squealed. He knew the truth now. She *hadn't* discarded everything.

The boys came into the kitchen and thrust their school papers in front of him. Forcing a grin, he gave them his full attention, gushed over Matthew's A-plus science paper and praised Luke's scrawled version of the alphabet. All the while, he kept one ear trained on the bedroom. When Lydia didn't emerge, he went into the living room, turned on the TV, found an animated film for the boys, and went back to his office.

He spent the rest of the afternoon and the next day weaving evangelistic verses into a message on faith. On Sunday morning, Lydia claimed she had a headache and was going to stay home. She'd never missed church as long as he could remember, although sometimes the bored look on her face told him she'd mentally left their pew. The sad truth was, she'd begun to blend in with the other stone figures in the congregation.

Discouraged, Mitch left with the boys and got them settled in the front pew where he could keep an eye on them. He gave the two of them a quick lecture on church behavior, then he went up the steps and took the podium.

After Mitch and the boys left the house, Lydia shed her bathrobe and hurriedly dressed in slacks and a blouse. She splashed cold water on her face, ran a comb through her hair, and put on a bright red shade of lipstick.

She'd just finished dressing when the doorbell rang. Smiling, she went to open the door. Millicent stood on the front porch, a mischievous grin on her lips.

Lydia looked past her friend and scanned the property. Except for a few stragglers mounting the church steps, the area was empty.

Millicent squeezed past Lydia into the house. "I waited

around the corner until your husband and kids left. Don't worry, nobody saw me."

Lydia took her coat and looked her over. Millicent was wearing an ankle-length skirt, black with gold threads woven into the fabric, a flowered top, and multi-colored strands of beads around her neck.

Lydia raised her eyebrows. "I thought you said casual."

Millicent shrugged. "This *is* casual." She scanned Lydia's outfit from head to toe. "Don't worry about it. You look fine. Anyway, we don't have time for you to change. Didn't you say the church service lasts for about an hour?"

"Yes. But we'll need to stop in forty-five minutes so you can get out of here without being seen. By the way, where's Penelope? I thought the two of you met on Sunday mornings."

"I came alone this time. Since you're new at this, I may have to do some instruction." She lifted the straw tote she was carrying. "I brought some items from the store. Do we need to go to the basement?"

"No. I already moved everything out of there. We'll use my bedroom. I stashed my pentagram and some other items in there. Do we need candles?"

"No, they'll leave a residue. We don't want to alert your husband."

Lydia nodded and led her friend to the bedroom. Millicent spread a blanket on the floor and scattered a few items on it. They squatted there together. Lydia shut her eyes, and the young girl began to chant.

~

With renewed confidence, Mitch preached the salvation message. He wished Lydia could have been there to hear it.

Not even his youth group back home had heard him deliver such a convincing speech. He looked out at his congregation. Occasionally, a flicker of life appeared in some of those icy eyes. A couple of the men mouthed a silent *amen*, or it looked like it. One woman blew her nose. Was it a flood of emotion, or did she have a cold? He may never know. As always, the younger folks fidgeted in their seats. But then, so did some of the adults.

He'd once heard it said that audiences remember about a tenth of a speaker's message. Hopefully, he'd planted a few seeds of faith though he couldn't be sure from the looks of those blank faces. He'd done his part. He'd stuck to the word of God, assured it wouldn't return void. If he reinforced this message with more sermons over the next couple of weeks, perhaps the truth will sink in. He believed God was working in those cold, insensitive hearts, even though he could see no visible proof of it yet.

Only Elijah Garby appeared moved. The man's eyes shone with respect for his young pastor. He smiled and nodded his approval. Encouraged, Mitch gave an altar call at the conclusion. Not one soul came forward.

As the last of the crowd trickled out the church door, Mitch remained at the pulpit, his head in his hands. Elijah stayed behind. He climbed the stairs and rested his hand on Mitch's shoulder.

"Well done, son."

Mitch raised his head and gave him one of his *you have got to be kidding* looks.

"I'm tellin' ya the truth. You have to be patient. Keep poundin' the same message into their heads. You'll see results one day, if you don't give up."

Mitch stared into Elijah's knowing eyes. "I can only hope."

The old man gave him a hug and left the church, leaving Mitch wallowing in a mix of disappointment and determination. If not for Elijah Garby, he'd be planning a way out of this place.

When Mitch got home, he found Lydia at the stove stirring a pot of spaghetti sauce, her face flushed from the rise of steam.

Mitch narrowed his eyes. "I thought you had a headache."

"I did. I took an aspirin." He caught a flash of defiance in her eyes.

Stifling a retort, he clenched his teeth and went to the bedroom. He sniffed the air. No after-scent of burnt candles or incense or any other concoction.

Footsteps came down the hall. He turned. Lydia stood right behind him so close she could have knocked him over. Her face muscles hardened, and her dark eyes sent imaginary bullets at him. A sudden chill raced through him. Their rocky relationship had gone beyond a simple husband-and-wife tiff. Garby was right—an evil was in his home, and he needed the power of God to fight it.

On Thursday the whole town would be celebrating Halloween. The coming holiday warned of more out-of-control evil if he didn't find a way to stop it. While he didn't want to get weird about it, he suspected something wicked was going on right under his nose. He'd entered a spiritual warfare, and his own wife had become his most threatening adversary.

～

Thursday, October 31, Halloween.

The day passed without incident. Mitch kept eying his wife, but she'd been pleasant enough, fixing lunch and baking cupcakes for the school party that evening. Later in the day, she disappeared with the boys inside their bedroom. Mitch sat in his reading chair with the newspaper, but he had a hard time paying attention to what was printed there.

He was about to turn to the sports section, when the boys bounded out of their bedroom, laughing. Mitch lowered the newspaper and stared in shock at them. The two of them were dressed in black shirts, black pants, and black capes made from scrap material. Artificial fangs covered their teeth and fake blood dripped from the corners of their mouths. Mitch tossed the newspaper to the floor and lunged from his chair. The boys stopped laughing. Their smiles quickly faded.

"You're not wearing those outfits."

Lydia was standing behind them.

"Go to your room," he shouted at the boys. "Take those outfits off. Now!"

Their shoulders down and disappointment on their faces, Matthew and Luke slunk off to their bedroom.

"Really, Mitch," Lydia sneered. "Aren't you overreacting? They're costumes. It's supposed to be fun."

"Just where were they going in those getups?"

"To the school party. All the kids are dressing up. This was the best I could do on our measly budget."

"They'll go as hobos or they won't go at all."

"Hobos? The other kids will make fun of them."

Mitch pushed past her. "We don't the have the time or the materials for anything else."

The boys were sitting on the edge of Matthew's bed, black eye makeup streaking down their faces.

"Stop crying. I'm gonna put together different costumes for you, and you can still go to your party."

He searched through their dresser drawers and came up with flannel shirts and jeans with patches on their knees. "Here." He tossed the clothing on the bed. "Put these on."

With long faces, the boys shed the black outfits and got into the clothes Mitch had chosen. He went to the bathroom, wet a washcloth, and cleaned their faces. Then he rummaged through a drawer in the kitchen and found a cork. After singeing it with a match, he used the burnt end to brush a grizzled beard on the boy's chins. He got two parkas from his own closet and slipped them over their tiny shoulders. Last of all, he popped a couple of his battered, old baseball caps on their heads.

Mitch stood back and eyed them with satisfaction. "You look great, kids. Like you're ready to hop a freight train. And guess what? Without those ugly teeth in your mouths, you'll be able to enjoy all the cookies and candy you want. And you won't scare your friends."

Matthew shrugged and Luke turned to look at his mother. She'd been standing in the doorway the entire time, with her arms crossed and her lips pressed together so tight they looked like they'd been super-glued.

"Are you going with us?" Her tone was icy. Uninviting.

"No. I'm tired. I'm gonna read a little and go to bed early." He grabbed a book from the shelf and headed for the chair by the window.

"Fine." She started toward the door but stopped. "Do we have your *permission* to leave now?" she called over her shoulder.

He ignored her sarcastic tone. He'd won—maybe not the whole war—but a major battle anyway.

He opened his book. "Have fun."

With Lydia out of the house, he'd have two hours to

conduct another search. This time he'd concentrate on the master bedroom. As soon as they pulled out of the driveway he slammed the book shut and sprang from his chair.

Once again, Mitch couldn't find anything of significance. Yet he knew the truth. She had defied him. She could have hidden her so-called treasures in places he'd never think to look. The evil could be right in front of him and he'd never know it.

He gave up the search for the time being. He needed to kick back. He poured himself a glass of milk and went back to the novel, a thriller by John Grisham. He dropped into the chair by the living room window where he'd have a good view of the front walk. He tried to focus on the book, but his concentration faltered. There were sounds he hadn't been aware of before. A dripping faucet in the kitchen. The ticking of the mantel clock. A branch scraping against the house. He read the same paragraph three times, maybe four. He must have drifted off, because the next sound was the slamming of car doors, followed by the pounding of feet on the porch steps.

Matthew burst into the living room ahead of Lydia. "Dad! Dad!"

Mitch rubbed his eyes to get the grit out. He blinked a few times, then, focusing, he stared at his wife and son. Matthew looked like he'd been crying. Lydia appeared agitated.

"Where's Luke?"

"Isn't he here?" She moved into the light. Her eyes were red. She wrung her hands. Trembling, she edged closer to him.

He sat upright. "He isn't here, Lydia. He was with you."

She took a step back.

"What's happened, Lydia? Where's Luke?" His heart was pounding against his chest.

She shook her head, and a fresh batch of tears emerged. "He's missing, Mitch. He disappeared. We looked everywhere inside the school. We couldn't find him."

Mitch tossed the book aside and leaped to his feet.

"What do you mean, you couldn't find him? Weren't you watching him?"

He stepped closer, and she backed away from him.

"Gimme the car keys."

"Huh?"

"The keys. The car keys. Give 'em to me."

With shaking fingers, she handed over the keys. Mitch grabbed his jacket and ran out the front door. He took the steps two at a time, fumbled with the keys while trying to unlock the car. Once inside and with the engine revving, he tore out of the driveway and headed straight for the school.

The building was dark. A few street lights glowed near the playground. Mitch got out of the car and ran around the property. He called out his son's name and listened each time, hoping to hear Luke's tiny voice. There was only the crunch of twigs under his feet and the muffled sound of traffic on the distant highway.

He got back in the car and crept along the side streets, peering out one window and then the other, all the while repeating, *Please, God, help me find my son. Please, God, help me find my son.*

He checked his watch—9:30. The party ended at 8:00. Luke was only five years old. Where could he have wandered off to? Worse yet, what if someone had kidnapped him?

Horrifying scenarios raced through Mitch's mind. He had one goal, to find his son. He wouldn't stop looking, even if it took him all night.

After driving around aimlessly for an hour, he pulled out his cell phone and called home. Lydia's choked response sent his head reeling. Luke hadn't returned.

"I'll find him," he told her. "Take care of Matthew. I'll keep looking for Luke. I *will* find our son. I promise."

He wove up and down every road in Shadow Glenn. A handful of people were in the streets. Mostly young couples. He hollered out the window to them. They shook their heads; hadn't seen a little boy wandering around. Aside from them, there were no children on the street. Why would there be? It was late at night. Most five-year-olds were already in bed.

He kept watching the gas gauge. Half full. Then a quarter. Several hours later, it was almost empty. A sliver of pink trailed across the horizon. Another day was dawning. In a little while, other children would flood into the streets, heading for the playground for another day off from school. But Luke wouldn't be among them.

Mitch's heart sank. He parked the car and began to weep. Silently, at first. Then, his strength sapped, he succumbed to heart-wrenching sobs. He fell against the steering wheel and poured out his grief to God. Things had gone way beyond his control. If the Almighty didn't help him now, he could lose everything he cared about. First Lydia. Now Luke. And who knows what damage had been done to Matthew?

32

After putting Matthew to bed, Lydia had stayed up all night in the chair by the living room window. Nothing moved outside except for a few trees disturbed by the wind, shedding dry leaves on the front lawn. At midnight she struggled to her feet and stepped out on the front porch. She looked up and down the street but didn't see a soul.

She phoned Mitch several times throughout the night. His voice cracked when he answered, and before he could say a word she knew he hadn't found their son. She wept until there were no more tears, wailed until her throat tightened with grief.

At some point she must have drifted off because the next thing she knew the gray light of morning streamed through the window and awakened her. She remained in the chair by the window, watching for Mitch's car, trying to imagine her littlest son sitting in the front seat next to his dad, arriving safe at home.

But the vision shattered the instant Mitch pulled into the driveway. He came into the living room. Alone. She looked into his bloodshot eyes, and for the first time in weeks, her heart melted for him. She wanted to run into his arms and comfort him, but she didn't know if he'd receive her. They'd drifted so far apart an impenetrable wall had risen between them.

His first words almost sounded like an accusation. "Did you call the police?"

Her heart began to race. "No, Mitch. I had hoped you'd find him."

Scowling, he dialed 911 on his cell phone. He explained the situation to the dispatcher, answered a multitude of questions, and hung up, his disapproving eyes never leaving Lydia's face.

"They're sending an officer." He strode to the front window.

Lydia crumbled into the chair. Tears ran down her face. She bowed her head, afraid to look Mitch in the eye.

"I turned my back for only a minute," she murmured. "I felt claustrophobic. All those kids in costumes rushing about, their parents swarming around me, teachers pouring punch and shoving cake and cookies in my face. The music blared. The walls were closing in. I–I thought I'd pass out unless I could escape for a while."

She turned to see Mitch staring at her. A tired sadness had settled on his face.

"I went to the ladies' room," she continued. She gazed into his eyes, pleading for his understanding. "I just needed a couple of minutes alone. When I went back inside the gym, Matthew was running around with his friends, and Luke was nowhere. I–I don't know what happened. One minute he was there, and the next minute he was gone. Please, Mitch. Please, don't hate me."

He knelt beside her and sighed. "I don't hate you, Lydia. I love you."

She would have found his admission of love comforting if not for the pain that seared her heart. "My boy," she sobbed. "My little boy. He's missing, and it's all my fault."

Mitch drew her into his arms. "Don't torture yourself. He's got to be all right." She fell against his chest.

"Let's pray," Mitch offered.

"Yes," she murmured, taking his hands. "Pray, Mitch. Pray with all your might."

Their hands were still locked together when a policeman arrived. Officer Daniels went through all the usual questions. Lydia squirmed with impatience. Why did they need to know so many trivial details? Who cares what Luke liked to do for a hobby? Or who his friends were? They'd been at the party, and they all went home—with their parents.

"Do we have to wait forty-eight hours for a police search?" Mitch asked the officer.

"Not for kids. It's an Amber Alert. We don't waste time when it's a child who's missing." The cop flipped to another page in his notebook, asked a couple more questions, and jotted down the information.

Lydia told him what Luke was wearing when he disappeared, his height and weight, and the color of his hair. She handed him a photo. "Will this help?"

Officer Daniels nodded, mumbled a condolence, and went out the door with Luke's photo in his hand.

Mitch paced the floor. Then he stopped walking and faced Lydia. "I can't just sit here and wait for the police to find our son. I'm going out again, Lydia. You stay here with Matthew. Keep him inside the house today. And don't talk about this to him. It will only upset him."

"He knows Luke went missing."

"Just say I've gone out to find him, and tell him everything is going to be all right. We don't want to traumatize the boy. He might think it was his fault."

He surprised her with a kiss on the forehead. He put on his jacket, grabbed the car keys, and walked out the door.

The minutes ticked slowly by. Lydia sat by the front window, staring out at nothing in particular. The reds and golds of autumn had turned a dull brown. Tree branches looked like gnarled fingers of the dead. The vibrant New England world she'd come to know and love had turned cold and lifeless.

Her cell phone bleeped an Amber Alert. She didn't have to read the text. For the first time the sound was personal, heartbreaking beyond anything she might feel for a stranger.

On a whim, she dialed Millicent's number. As soon as the girl answered, Lydia blurted out the details.

Like a true friend, Millicent responded immediately. "I'll close the shop and be there in fifteen minutes. Hang on, Lydia. We'll get your son back."

Lydia waited by the front window until Millicent drove up. This time the girl didn't come alone. Penelope was following her up the walk. They both wore long skirts and knitted shawls, and Penelope was carrying a large, straw tote. Lydia opened the door and let them in.

Millicent entered the living room and craned her neck toward the kitchen. "He's not home?" she whispered.

"Who?"

"Your husband."

"Mitch has gone out to look for Luke." She didn't try to hide her distress. "He left an hour ago."

"Good. Where can we set up?"

"My bedroom, but we have to be quiet. Matthew's sleeping in the next room."

"Okay, Lydia," Millicent said with a nod. "Don't you worry. We're gonna summon your baby home. By the time we're finished, he'll walk through the front door and right into your arms."

Though a sharp caution probed at the back of her mind, Lydia led the two women to her bedroom. They shut the door behind them and started unloading the items from Penelope's tote. In minutes, six candles were flickering. Lydia looked to the others for direction. Millicent grabbed her hand and pulled her to the floor. The three of them squatted in a semi-circle, holding hands.

Millicent started to chant. Her undulating tones swirled about the room, like dry leaves before a swift breeze. Penelope moaned softly. Lydia stared wide-eyed at them and froze. Though she'd memorized several mantras in Dorcas' book she couldn't utter a single syllable.

Instead, a passage came to her mind from the first epistle of John. Something about trying the spirits to see if they were of God. The exact words eluded her. She pressed her eyes shut, tried to block out the Bible verse and willed herself to concentrate on the sing-song monotones of the two women. Her mind drifted back to her youth and the scripture memorizations she'd been handed in Sunday school. For a long time they'd remained stored in the back of her mind, like the antiques she'd searched out in thrift stores and yard sales. Now they were coming back as though released from a dusty old trunk. And what about those Bible passages that spoke about spiritual warfare and Satan's deceptions? Decades later they were flying off the page to her, like she'd never closed the book at all.

She opened her eyes and looked at the two women. They were strangers. Their chins were raised and their eyes were shut. Their lips were parted in impassioned smiles. The flickering candles cast shimmering fingers on their faces. The tattooed dragon on Penelope's neck appeared to be dancing. Their voices overlapped like two people trying to talk at once but saying different things. They chanted the names of various spirits. A thread of truth broke through—*This is the spirit of antichrist, whereof ye have heard that it should come, and even now it is in the world.* Lydia pulled her hands away.

The two women stopped chanting and gawked at her.

"Shouldn't we be praying to Jesus right now?" Lydia managed, her voice meek.

Penelope broke into a surprised smirk. Her angry glare sent a chill down Lydia's spine.

"You interrupted us at the worst possible time," Penelope said, her tone sharp. "We haven't even gotten started."

Millicent patted Lydia's arm. "Jesus was a good man, maybe even a prophet, but he was just a man. We're calling on a greater power."

Lydia shook her head. "A greater power than *Jesus?* I don't think so."

Penelope snarled her disgust. "You have to trust us. We know what we're doing."

Lydia scooted away from them.

"Okay," Millicent said, a platonic smile on her lips. "You sit there and watch. The two of us will summon your boy home."

Before Lydia could stop them, the two women grabbed each other's hands, shut their eyes, and began to chant again. Millicent's droning grew louder, her words more pronounced. She pled with the *spirit of lost children* to bring Luke home. Lydia's heart began to race. She glanced at her bedroom door, tried to hear beyond it, listened for Luke's tiny footsteps coming into the house. Instead, a suffocating shadow filled the room. A door slammed somewhere down the hall. The hairs stood up on the back of her neck. Her arms and legs were shaking uncontrollably.

She struggled to find her voice. "We need to stop. Now!"

Penelope opened her eyes and glared at her. Something evil flickered inside those black orbs. "You need to be patient, Lydia." She looked at Millicent. "Didn't you tell her it takes time to summon the spirits?"

Lydia lurched to her feet. "I don't *want* to summon the spirits. I want to *pray*. To God. Not to some freakish *spirit of lost children.*"

Scowling, Penelope blew out the candles and stuffed everything back in her tote.

"I'm done here," she snarled.

Millicent stood up, brushed the wrinkles from her skirt, and tossed her head. The movement unleashed a fire in her eyes. They were no longer green or blue, but black and smooth like two beetles.

"All right," Millicent snapped. "Do what you want, Lydia, but don't come crying to me again."

The two women left in a swirl of skirts and shawls and beads. They drove off, spitting up gravel. Lydia sat by the living room window and thought about the session in her bedroom. *Those two were calling on unfamiliar names of what? Spirits? Demons? They didn't bring Luke home.* She took a deep breath and tried to clear her head. She'd been living in a fog for weeks, unable to think clearly, knowing right from wrong but unable to take control. *Has Millicent been confusing me all along? Why didn't I see it before? Why did it take losing my son to see how far away from God I've moved?*

She went to the bookshelf, grabbed a Bible, and took it to Mitch's reading chair. Drawing on lessons from the past, she turned to John's first epistle and searched for the passage on discerning the spirits.

"It's my fault my son is missing," she confessed aloud. "I

bought into a lie. Now I've hurt my family." She set her jaw. "Dear God, show me the way. Give me the wisdom and the strength to do the ;right thing."

She found the passage in chapter four. It spoke of testing the spirits, and it warned about false prophets and antichrists in the world. She read the verses twice. Gradually, the fog began to lift. More scriptures came to mind. Another came from James Chapter 4. *Resist the devil, and he will flee from you.* Her mind reeled with Bible passages she had long ago forgotten or suppressed or ignored. They moved from her mind to her heart, and she knew what she had to do.

Setting aside the Bible, she removed every vestige of evil she'd brought into the house. Dorcas' book under the carpet in her closet. The amulets in her lingerie drawer. The stone crystal on the bookshelf in the living room. The pot of herbs on the window sill in the kitchen. The candles in the boys' closet. She tiptoed in so she wouldn't disturb Matthew. She put everything in a large shopping bag, took them outside and dumped them in the metal trash bin. She doused them all with lighter fluid, and with a flick of a match set the evil on fire. This time she'd held nothing back.

She stood close to the blaze, relished its heat on her face. She blinked away the sting from the rising smoke and gazed at the heinous residue as it spiraled upward and coursed through the tangle of leafless branches overhead.

Then Lydia returned to the house. She went to her bedroom and dropped to her knees. She'd barely begun to pray when her bedroom door squeaked open.

"Mom?" Matthew's voice drew her attention to the doorway. He stood there in his pajamas, rubbing his eyes.

"Mama, am I in trouble?"

"Trouble? No, darling. Why do you think you're in trouble?"

"I didn't watch Luke at the party. I ran off with my friends and left him alone."

"Come here, Matthew."

He stepped closer. She wrapped her arms around him and drew him to her chest. "Oh, Matthew, no. It's not your fault." She backed away and looked into his tear-filled eyes. "It's *my* fault, Matthew. I went to the ladies room, and when I came back I couldn't find your brother. Luke was *my* responsibility. Not yours."

Tears came anyway and trailed in rivulets down her son's young face.

"Mama, I think—"

"Listen, your dad's gonna find him." She stroked his rumpled hair. "Now, stop worrying. Get dressed, and we'll have some breakfast."

"But, Mama—"

Somehow, she needed to get his mind off of Luke, needed to keep him from punishing himself over the incident.

"Not another word about it, Matthew. Come on. You can help me make pancakes, okay? We'll make enough so when Daddy and Luke come home, they can have some too. Now go wash up, and then meet me in the kitchen."

After Matthew left, Lydia remained on her knees and gazed out the bedroom window. A scud of clouds drifted over the trees. She sent up a mother's prayer, certain those clouds could carry her plea to the throne of God. *Perhaps He will hear me now and bring my baby home.*

About an hour later, Mitch dragged himself through the

front door. He shuffled into the kitchen and dropped into a chair at the table. He had dark circles under his eyes, and his unshaven chin quivered. He looked beaten.

She couldn't face him, couldn't look into those troubled eyes. She turned her back to him and busied herself at the stove. She needed to appear strong. For Matthew's sake. And for Mitch.

She placed a stack of pancakes on the table, along with a banana and a bottle of maple syrup. He stared at the food. She poured him a cup of coffee. He accepted it, but pushed his plate aside. With the cup in his hand, he walked out of the kitchen. He'd never turned down pancakes before, nor did he drink his coffee black. She could hear him pacing from one end of the living room to the other.

She tiptoed down the hall to the boys' bedroom and checked on Matthew. He was playing with Legos in the middle of the floor. A warmth had settled on the boys' room. Yes, the entire house was warm for the first time in three months. She went in the hall and turned down the thermostat. From there, she joined Mitch in the living room. She perched on the arm of his reading chair and stared out the window at the empty street. Still no sign of her little boy. In fact, there wasn't any life out there at all. Not a breath of air moved the leafless branches. The unearthly quiet stirred a foreboding in her heart. *What if God didn't hear my prayer? What if it was too late, and Luke never came home?*

Tears blurred her vision. She turned away from the window and approached her husband.

"What else can we do, Mitch? We can't just sit—"

She was interrupted by a knock on the front door. Mitch raced ahead of her to open it.

Elijah Garby walked in. "I came to help."

Mitch broke down, sobbing. "Thanks, Elijah, this means a lot to me. But I'm afraid it's hopeless. I've already driven all over town. Multiple times."

Lydia's heart went out to him. He was in so much pain. Elijah must have seen it too. He stepped closer to Mitch and flung his arms around him.

"Let it out, son." The old man's voice broke. "Let it all out, and when you're done, we'll hit the streets together. This time you don't need to drive. We'll walk."

Mitch took several deep breaths and wiped his face. "Walk? Where? I've gone down every street in Shadow Glenn. I've used up two tanks of gas."

"We don't need your car. We can cover more ground on foot. We can go where cars can't go and check out a few places little boys might find interesting."

Elijah turned his attention to Lydia. "No need to worry, my dear. Your son's gotta be playing some sort of hide-and-seek game. Probably lost track of the time is all."

Lydia shook her head and more tears spilled from her eyes. "Oh, Mitch."

Cautiously, she stepped closer to her husband. He surprised her by putting his arm around her. It was the first time he'd touched her in weeks.

She crumbled into his arms. "I'm so sorry," she murmured. "So sorry."

"Stop blaming yourself, Lydia." His voice was gentle. "Luke knew he was supposed to stay at the party. There must be an explanation, and when we find him we'll get an answer. For now, Elijah and I will take another look around town. Maybe I missed something. I won't stop until I find our boy. I promise."

She gazed with adoration into her husband's face. He hadn't slept all night. A stubborn determination appeared in his bloodshot eyes. He hadn't even taken time to freshen up, just kept moving like a soldier in the midst of a battle. One thing was certain, she could trust Mitch. The man she married would never give up the search.

Suddenly, she knew the truth about why she walked away from Ben Marshall and ran into the arms of Mitch Calloway more than ten years ago. They were both good looking guys, considerate, kind, with all the right qualities for a husband. Ben was on a career path to wealth and notability. But Mitch had something else. He made her feel safe. He was like a rock in a storm. A lighthouse in the dark. A pillar of faith and endurance. Now she knew more than ever before, she'd made the right choice.

Mitch started for the door but turned back and faced her with a fresh spark of courage in his eyes. "Try to be strong, Lydia. You have to think about Matthew. He's your son, too. You've got to stay calm for him."

"But I need to *do* something. Please, give me something to do."

Elijah stepped between them and held her gaze. "You can pray. You can be like those Israelites who stayed by the stuff while their army went out and fought the battle. There's power in prayer."

"I been praying too." The tiny voice came from the hall. Matthew stood there with a bunch of Legos in his hands. "I been praying, and I been building a fort for Luke. He can play with it when he comes home."

Lydia rushed to his side. "Yes, Matthew. Build something really nice for Luke to play with. Build it fast, because he'll be here real soon." She hugged him close. "Your dad and Mister Garby are going out to find him."

The boy slipped out of her arms and approached his father. "Can I go with you?"

"No, son. You have to stay here and take care of your mom."

"But, I think I—"

"Don't worry, Matthew. We won't be long."

"But, Dad—"

"We know. You want to help." Mitch patted his son on the head. "Mister Garby and I need to go now. Keep building your fort, so when Luke comes home you'll have a nice surprise waiting for him."

The two men started off together. Lydia stared after them from the front window. The sight of the old man hobbling along beside her husband broke her heart. Elijah Garby had come out in the bitter cold to help find her son. Fresh tears gushed out of her eyes. She was beginning to see what true Christian friendship looked like. It was nothing like Millicent's books and amulets and senseless incantations. True friendship went deeper. It went to the heart.

After the men disappeared from view, she turned again toward Matthew.

"Put a hold on your Lego fort and let's go to the church and pray. We can ask God to help your dad find Luke. Now go get dressed."

"Mama, I don't want to go to the church. Me and you can go out and find Luke."

"No, Matthew. We need to stay close to home, in case he shows up."

"But I got an idea—"

"Stop arguing, Matthew. And hurry up."

The boy let out a sigh, dropped his shoulders, and slunk off to his room. Lydia stood in his doorway while he rifled through his drawer and came up with a pair of jeans and a sweater. Her heart throbbed with love for him. He'd suffer terribly if he lost his little brother.

She silently berated herself. She'd left Matthew with a huge responsibility simply because she needed a few minutes of solitude. If she'd been doing her job as a mother— *But I haven't been doing my job as a mother, or as a wife, or as... anything. Not for a long time. I don't remember the last time I put my sons' needs, or my husband's, before my own.*

Her mother had taught her by example. She'd spent hours with Lydia, talking, listening, playing, caring, feeding, loving, and teaching. And through it all she'd kept pointing her daughter to her own source of strength—the Holy Scriptures.

That was the kind of mother Lydia wanted to be. If it wasn't too late.

33

Mitch and Elijah headed straight for Main Street. An autumn chill had taken over. They buttoned their jackets against the cold, and Elijah donned a knitted cap and gloves. Mitch eyed the old man with concern.

"Are you sure you can handle all the walking? I mean, you just got out of the hospital."

Elijah gave him one of his sideways looks and raised an eyebrow. "I didn't get a heart transplant, Mitch, I received a new pacemaker. It's working fine. Now, stop yer fussin' and let's go find your son."

Mitch shrugged and turned his attention to the street ahead. He didn't have to slow his pace. Elijah kept up with an agility that defied his years.

They moved up one side street and down the next and occasionally left the main thoroughfare to slip down an alley, peek inside a dumpster, and look in sewer pipes. They ventured onto private properties, circled houses, and peered in basement windows. They went to the elementary school where Luke was last seen.

"I've been here twice already. I don't th—"

"Doesn't matter," Elijah broke in. "You may have missed something. Like that gazebo over there." He nodded toward the center of the playground. In the clearing stood a wooden structure with lattice webbing around its base.

"Wouldn't that thing make a great little hideout for a kid?" Elijah moved ahead of Mitch, reached the gazebo first, and crouched beside the latticework.

Mitch drew close and knelt beside him. He peered through the openings within the strips of wood. It took several seconds for his eyes to adjust to the dark.

"I can't imagine my little boy hiding in such a hole. It's dark and damp and who knows what sort of critters are in there? Luke's a skittish little kid. He wouldn't go near this thing."

He stood up and helped Elijah struggle to his feet. "I'm afraid it's hopeless, my friend." He shook his head. A flood of tears spilled from his eyes and ran down his face.

Elijah pulled a handkerchief from his pocket and thrust it in Mitch's hand.

"I'm sorry," Mitch sobbed. He blew his nose, blotted his eyes, and folded the handkerchief.

"No need to apologize. Come on." Elijah gestured toward a park bench. "Let's sit over there while you pull yourself together."

They walked to the bench at the edge of the playground. Mitch bowed his head and pressed the handkerchief to his eyes.

"This is more than I can handle, Elijah. I was already beaten down before Luke disappeared. I appreciate you're coming out to help me, but you can't possibly understand how defeated I am right now. I'm about ready to give up hope of ever finding my son."

Elijah let out a chuckle. Surprised, Mitch raised his head and stared at him. There was nothing funny about losing a child. But Elijah wasn't smiling. His little laugh, it turned out, was more sarcasm than levity.

"You say I can't possibly understand? You're wrong, son. I understand more than you know."

Mitch leaned against the back of the bench, ready to listen. "What do you mean?"

Elijah stared in the direction of the jungle gym, folded his hands, and shook his head. "From the time we met, you've been interested in my ancestors and the people who started Mercy Fellowship. You've asked me about the building of the church, the addition, and the work my grandfather and my great-grandfather did. But, you never asked me about my own life, whether I ever married or had any children."

A wave of embarrassment flooded through him. "I've been so caught up in my own issues I didn't think about anyone else," he said as a way of apologizing. "But, I know you married. And you have a son. He visited you while you were in the hospital."

"Yes, he did. His name's Jeffrey. But he wasn't my only son."

"You have other children?"

"*Had* other children. There were others."

His interest piqued, Mitch turned his upper body toward Elijah. For the moment, he welcomed the temporary diversion. He flung an arm over the back of the bench and gave the old man his full attention.

"My wife and daughter were killed in a car accident 47 years ago." Elijah's voice thickened with emotion. "Kathy was our youngest child. She was ten years old at the time of the accident."

Mitch reached out and patted Elijah's arm. "I'm so sorry, I didn't—"

Garby cut him off with a shake of his head. "It's okay, Mitch. I survived. Not completely, of course. One never gets over such a loss. But I survived enough to go on with my life."

"You said, 'others,'" Mitch reminded him. "Plural."

Elijah nodded. "We had another son. Noah, our firstborn. He came into the world in 1958, and he died in 1966."

Mitch frowned. "Eight years old—my Matthew's age."

Elijah nodded. "I was absorbed with church business. My wife and the kids spent the afternoon at this same park. She'd brought along her knitting and was sitting right about where you are."

Mitch shifted uncomfortably. The old man kept his eyes on the play area, like he'd gone back several decades.

"Mary—my wife—assumed the kids would stay together. They knew the rules. If the littlest one—Kathy—went to the swings, the two older children had to follow. If Kathy headed for the jungle gym, her brothers had to go there too. They didn't like the rules, but they generally obeyed."

He paused and took a deep, shaky breath. "I have no idea what happened. I wasn't there to see it. My wife told me Noah spotted one of his friends on the other side of the street. Instead of waiting for the young fella to cross, he took it on himself to run over to him. He didn't stop at the curb and look both ways like we'd taught him, didn't slow his pace for a second." Elijah swallowed. "He didn't see the delivery truck barreling down on him until it was too late."

Mitch groaned. "Dear Lord. You lost most of your family in traffic accidents?" He shook his head. "Unbelievable."

"I said the same thing a hundred times." Garby's voice broke with emotion. "First Noah in 1966, then, a little over six years later, Mary and Kathy. I buckled under the losses, even drifted away from my faith for a while."

Mitch couldn't imagine a strong Christian like Elijah Garby straying from his faith, not even for a second. But such a loss can do that to a man. He knew that now. With Luke missing, his own faith was coming dangerously close to shattering. He didn't know if he could preach another sermon or spend another minute in God's word. What if he lost Lydia and Matthew too? Something that would have once seemed impossible had become a stark reality.

He turned his attention back to Garby, bent under the weight of retelling the past. "You still have Jeffrey," he offered.

Elijah nodded sadly. "Yes, but I messed up with him. I was so grief-stricken over what happened to the others, I forgot I had a son who needed me. Jeffrey was grieving too, but the poor kid suffered alone. After he graduated from high school he took off for college, shook the dust off his feet, and never looked back. You can see why he spends so little time with his old dad. Too many bad memories, I guess."

"No wonder he cut his visit short."

"Exactly. In a sense, I lost Jeffrey too. I didn't go to the park with my family that day. I was head deacon. I presumed I was doing God's work, when in reality I had neglected the most important job in my life. I should have been a husband and father first. If I'd done that, my work at the church would have fallen in place. I got things turned around so bad, I lost it all. I didn't deserve to have 'em in the first place."

Mitch rested his hand on Garby's back. "You're wrong, Elijah. Things happen. We don't always have control. But God is in control. No matter how bad things get, He's with us."

He startled himself with the acknowledgement. *God is in control. And if God is in control then whatever happens is the right thing. And even if doesn't seem like it's the right thing, He's with us.*

He looked at the old wrinkled face now streaked with tears. How often did the old man weep over his losses? How deep did the pain go? Deeper, Mitch suspected, than a new pacemaker could cure. He'd been so concerned with his own problems he hadn't realized other people suffered loss too.

Perhaps he had a whole church full of hurting people. Now here he was, sharing his pain with a lonely old man who had endured the greatest losses of all.

"Elijah, I—"

Garby brushed away his tears with the back of his glove. "Don't worry yourself over what happened in my life, Mitch. I told you my story so you can know I understand what you're going through right now. You're afraid you've lost your youngest son. And you have a wife and another son at home. They're depending on you to find Luke, and also to be the husband and father God called you to be."

Mitch looked into Elijah's steel gray eyes, searching for strength to go on. The old man merely smiled.

Then Elijah pushed off the bench. "Let's get moving. We've been behaving like two old women whimpering over the past. Let's not waste anymore time. We've got to find your son."

Lydia poked her head in the boys' bedroom and found Matthew sitting on the floor fiddling with his shoe laces.

"Come on. Let's go. I told you to get dressed a half-hour ago."

He finished tying the laces and stood to his feet. The pathetic wrinkle on his forehead pricked her heart. She rushed over and wrapped her arms around him.

"It's gonna be okay, Matthew. We're gonna pray, you and me. We're going to the church and talk to God. We'll ask him to bring Luke home." She planted a kiss on his cheek. "Now get your coat."

She rushed out in the hall and grabbed the keys to the church. Matthew came up beside her, and together they went out the door and crossed the property to the main entrance.

Lydia unlocked the door to the sanctuary and proceeded down the aisle with Matthew following close behind. She paused beside the first row, then turned and boldly chose the third pew, the very place where Mitch claimed to have seen shadows. Though she'd never seen them herself, she believed him now. She thought about the boys' cold bedroom, the noises in the night, the arguments with Mitch, the persistent fog that enveloped her until she couldn't think clearly. Some evil presence had been troubling their home. Why not the church too? Wasn't that Satan's greatest challenge and the most vulnerable place of all because church-goers weren't ready for his attacks?

She settled on the edge of the wooden bench. It creaked slightly under her weight. Matthew slid in beside her.

Almost immediately, a dark shadow enveloped the row. Lydia's heart began to pound. She couldn't breathe. She put an arm around her son's shoulder and drew him close. Trembling, she lifted her chin and focused on the wooden cross beyond the altar.

Oh, Lord. I don't know what this is, but I do know you are stronger and more powerful than anything that can come against us. I don't deserve your help. I know that now. I've failed as a wife and mother. What's worse, I've been living a lie for years. I never knew you. Not the way I'm supposed to. I never saw my sins, never realized my need until now. I went to church all my life. I read the Bible, even memorized verses of scripture, but I never fully understood. Now my son is missing. Until this happened, I hadn't suspected how far I'd drifted away from you. Please, forgive me for all my failures. Create a new heart within me and change my life. Save me, Lord Jesus. Protect my family. Help my husband restore this chur—

She stopped short. The shadow shimmered and began to lift from the pew. A ray of sunlight pierced the fog and settled on the wooden seat beside her. Startled, she whispered the name of Jesus. Suddenly there was a whoosh, as if someone had turned on a huge vacuum cleaner and was sucking the shadow out of the church, like when an airplane cabin decompresses. All Lydia knew was she'd been consumed by a fog, and now the fog had lifted. The suffocating cloak of evil was gone, and the air had cleared.

She bowed her head. Something miraculous had happened. Something comforting and peaceful, and she knew in her heart Luke was going to be all right. Matthew tucked his little frame against her side. She collapsed against him, sobbing with newfound hope.

At that moment she was alerted to footsteps coming down the aisle. There was the rustle of coats being removed and the sound of whispers. She turned. At least two dozen women and several children were settling into the rows behind her. They started praying, some in groups, some individually.

Lydia's mouth dropped open as she recognized the women who'd been coming to services every Sunday. Not one of them had reached out to her. Not one had called the parsonage or offered a welcoming hand. Now they were gathering together to pray. A couple of them stared back at her with moisture in their eyes. Several smiled and offered nods of encouragement, then they went back to praying.

A woman in the next pew placed a hand on her shoulder. "We got the Amber Alert. We've come to pray with you."

Lydia shook her head in awe. Tears ran down her cheeks. She brushed them away and continued to stare at the rows and rows of women sending up petitions to God on behalf of her son.

The door of the church opened again and a group of men entered. Some removed their hats and held them in front of their chests in an attitude of respect. Curious, Lydia slid into the aisle and walked toward them. Matthew followed.

The four deacons were there with several other men she recognized from their church attendance. John, one of the deacons, stepped away from the group and came toward her.

"We've come to help search for your little boy."

Lydia choked out a sob.

"The women will stay and pray with you," John went on. "We men will break into pairs and we'll comb the streets until we find him."

"I–I don't understand. You never—"

"Never what? Never trusted our new preacher? We were wrong to shun your family. We weren't sure, at first, if Mitch would stay. None of the other ministers did. But Pastor Calloway has remained faithful. In his last two sermons, he's been showing us the way back to God. Some of us met privately. We acknowledged our need to return to our Savior. Last week a few people made their first commitment to Christ. Most of us folks had simply fallen away, but we've come back. It's because your husband didn't give up on us. Even when we made it difficult, he stayed the course. Now we want to help."

Lydia was still crying, unable to speak. John placed a comforting hand on her shoulder.

"Don't you worry. We're heading out now, and we won't quit until we find the little one."

He left her there, crumbling with emotion. The men donned their hats and followed him out the door. Lydia turned around and faced the cross beyond the altar. She mouthed a silent *Thank you.*

Then she leaned toward Matthew. "We have lots of help now," she told him. "Jesus is going to bring your brother home."

He looked up at her shyly. "I know, Mama. I been trying to tell ya. I think I know where he is."

34

Lydia could hardly believe her ears. Was it possible that Matthew knew where Luke was? She gave him her full attention.

"The day we went on our adventure..." he said a bit shyly.

She nodded and encouraged him to go on.

"We found a treehouse, Mama."

"Where? Where's the treehouse?"

He took a step back and looked down at his shoes.

"Matthew, please. Tell me where the treehouse is."

"I can't." His voice was almost indiscernible. "It's a secret."

She took his hand and led him out of the church. They paused on the top step. The men were already splitting up in pairs, like they'd said they would. Several had started off in different directions. The four deacons had stayed behind. They stood on the sidewalk in front of the church and appeared to be discussing a plan.

Lydia pulled out her cell phone and punched in her husband's number.

He answered immediately.

"Mitch," she nearly shouted. "Where are you?"

"Just a couple of blocks away. Are you home?"

"We're in front of the church. Matthew said he knows where his brother is." She choked out the last few words.

"Matthew? He knows?" Mitch's voice went up an octave. "Where's Luke?"

"I don't know. He said something about a treehouse. That's all he would tell me. Please, come to the church. And hurry."

"I'll be there in two minutes. Don't leave without me."

~

Mitch picked up his step. The church was just around the next corner. He turned and looked back. Elijah was shuffling along a few steps behind him.

The old man waved him on. "Don't wait for me," he puffed. "You get goin' and find your little boy."

Mitch jogged the rest of the way. Lydia and Matthew were standing on the bottom step of the church. Four men stood nearby on the sidewalk. He recognized them immediately. George, Pete, Larry, and John.

Frowning nervously, he approached Lydia. "What's going on? Why are the deacons here?"

The four men drew closer and circled around them. John offered his hand. "We've come to help find your little boy. The others have spread out all over town."

"The others?" Mitch eyed him with astonishment. "What others?"

"The men of the church."

Goosebumps traveled down Mitch's arms. "Really? All of them?"

"Yes, Pastor Calloway. All of them." John was grinning now. "The women too. They're inside the church, praying."

Mitch shook his head in awe. "I–I don't know what to say." He turned to Lydia. "Did you tell me Matthew knows where his brother is?"

She nodded, smiling but with tears spilling from her eyes. "He said they found a treehouse."

"Where? Where is it?"

She shook her head. "He wouldn't say."

He turned to his son. "Tell us, Matthew, where's your brother?"

The boy bowed his head and twisted his foot on the pavement. "It was supposed to be a secret."

Mitch bent closer and softened his tone. "You want Luke to come home, don't you?"

Matthew nodded but wouldn't look him in the eye.

"Sometimes secrets are meant to be told if they can help someone. So, please, tell me. I promise you won't be in trouble."

He shrugged his little shoulders. "He musta gone to our secret treehouse."

"Where is it?"

"In the woods." His voice was so soft Mitch almost couldn't hear him.

"In the woods?"

Matthew nodded again.

Lydia gasped in shock. "The woods?" She pointed toward the spread of trees a half-mile away. "Down there?"

"Yes, Mama."

Mitch wrapped an arm around Matthew. "It's okay, son. We need you to take us to him. Do you think you can do that?"

Matthew raised his head. Tears had left streaks on his cheeks.

At that moment Elijah came tottering up to the church. He settled on the third step with a grunt.

Mitch eyed him with concern. "Are you gonna be all right?"

Garby took a couple of deep breaths and nodded. "Tell ya' what, I'll sit here and catch my breath while you go find your boy. Now get moving."

John stepped closer. "If it's okay with you we'd like to tag along and help bring him back."

Mitch agreed with a nod. He gave Matthew a gentle nudge. "Come on, little soldier, lead the way. Let's go find your brother."

They started off down the street with Matthew in front and the four men following. Mitch looked back. The old man's head was bowed and his hands were clasped in prayer.

On an impulse, Mitch took his wife's hand and drew her close to him. "And a little child shall lead them," he whispered.

Lydia smiled at him. He furrowed his brow. Something had changed for the better. The Lydia he'd married had returned.

"You're gonna have to tell me what's been happening."

"Later..." She squeezed his hand. "Let's hurry."

Mitch's heart surged with excitement. He walked faster and hoped with all his heart that God had kept the boy safe.

Matthew marched ahead of them like he was on an important mission. He was already growing into a little man. In ten or twelve years, he'd be on his own. Elijah's story had warned him to be the father he was meant to be, before the opportunity was gone. He determined to make proper changes in his schedule and to include plenty of time to spend with his wife and sons.

They reached the end of the street. Mitch looked beyond his son and quivered at the sight of the dark woods ahead. Could Luke have survived a frigid night in a treehouse in such a dark and dreary place? When the boy left the house, he'd been wearing his dad's hooded parka. Was it enough to ward off the chill after the sun went down?

He followed Matthew into the trees and up a hill. The vegetation grew dense and closed in on the narrow path. There was no longer enough room for the two of them to walk together. Lydia slipped her hand free and dropped behind him. He looked back. The four deacons also had hit the trail single file.

Matthew disappeared behind a clump of bushes. Mitch hurried to catch up with him. The ground leveled off. His son moved into a clearing and looked up into the treetops.

"There it is." He pointed. "Our secret treehouse."

About thirty feet up was a pathetic wooden box with a heavy black tarp nailed to the top like a roof. There was a solitary door and a small window. but no sign of life.

"Luke!" Mitch called out. "Are you up there, son?"

He waited a few seconds, then he shouted louder this time. "Luke! Answer me. It's your dad."

A small round face appeared in the window. Mitch's heart began to race. He couldn't believe he was looking at his son. The boy's nose was red, and puffy bags lay under his eyes, but he looked to be unharmed.

"Daddy." Luke emerged in the doorway. "I can't get down."

Matthew grabbed Mitch's hand and led him around the other side of the tree. "Luke can use our ladder. Over here."

Mitch eyed with concern the loosely nailed wooden boards. A few lay on the ground, leaving huge, unreachable gaps between the others.

Matthew's face dropped and he nudged his foot against the scattering of boards at the base of the tree. "They musta broke off."

Mitch circled the tree and tried to find another way up. He shook his head.

"Luke!" Lydia came up beside Mitch, her face turned toward the treehouse.

"Mama." Luke wailed. "Mama. I wanna come home. I'm cold. I'm hungry."

"Oh, baby," Lydia cried. "Daddy's going to come up and get you. Wait there. Don't try to come down by yourself. We don't want you to fall."

The four men stumbled into the clearing.

George looked up at the treehouse. "I live a block away. I can get a ladder."

John came up beside him. "I'll help ya' carry it."

"And I'll bring a blanket," Larry offered. "The kid's gotta be frozen."

Pete charged after them. "I'll get the boy a bottle of water and some snacks."

The four of them ran off, tripping over stones and roots, and lunging down the hill. Mitch inhaled a huge breath of air and let it out slowly. He didn't feel alone anymore.

He turned his eyes up toward his son. "Hold on, Luke. We're gonna help you get down."

The boy was whimpering. "Am I in trouble, Dad?"

"No. You're not in trouble, son. I did the same thing when I was a kid."

Lydia stared wide-eyed at him. "Really, Mitch?"

He shrugged. "Well, sort of."

"Daddy..." Luke squeaked. "I wanna come down."

Mitch craned his neck and kept his eyes on his son. "Hang on, Luke. We want to take you home, but we have to make sure you can get down safely."

Matthew approached his father and yanked on the hem of his jacket. "Dad?"

Mitch looked down at him.

"Are we gonna git punished?"

"No, son. There won't be any discipline. Not this time. But please don't go anywhere without me or your mom, ever again, at least not until you're ready for college. If you want a treehouse, we can build one in the oak tree on our lot, where the tire swing is. It'll be a sturdy treehouse with a deck and a solid ladder."

Matthew grinned and his freckles spread from ear-to-ear. He wiped his damp cheek with the sleeve of his jacket and left a dirty stain there. He blinked at Mitch. "Thanks, Dad."

His heart melting, Mitch bent over and wrapped his arms around Matthew.

"I never want to lose you guys. Neither one of you. In fact, you're gonna start seeing a lot more of me. And guess what? We're gonna tour the haunted graveyard next weekend. You can count on it."

He straightened and glanced down the hill. There was no sign of the men. He looked up at the treehouse. Luke had disappeared inside. He checked his watch. His boy had been missing for almost twenty-four hours. The poor kid had to be cold, hungry, maybe a little dehydrated. But he was alive. Alive!

About ten minutes later, the four men trudged into the clearing carrying the ladder. They positioned it against the tree, and Mitch climbed up. When he got near the top, he called out to Luke. "Come on, son. Turn around and back up to me. I've got you. We'll go down the ladder together."

The boy's shivering frame settled against his father's chest. Mitch cuddled him close, trusting the warmth of his own body to quench the chill. He took the rungs slowly, so his son could stay with him. When they reached the bottom, Larry rushed up with a woolen blanket and wrapped it around Luke. Peter handed him a bottle of water and a snack pack.

Lydia covered Luke's face with kisses. "My boy. My boy," she wept, her voice muffled by the blanket. "Thank you, Lord."

Matthew also began to cry. "I'm sorry, Luke. I should never have taken you to that nasty old treehouse."

Luke tilted his head and smiled at his brother. "Don't be silly," he snickered. "It was the bestest adventure of my life."

35

Things changed more than Mitch had ever dreamed they could. From that day on, the boys slept in a warm and cozy room. They played together like they used to, laughing, their shrill voices echoing down the hall. Mitch and Lydia were talking again, respectfully considering each other's ideas, conscious of each other's needs.

"I didn't see how far I'd strayed from God," she confessed to him while they lay in bed one night. "Then, when our son went missing, I saw how lost I was. The truth is, I'd been deceived. I was reaching out for—something—I don't know what. Then I found those things in the basement, and that awful book. I liked how it made me feel—free, independent, powerful—or so I thought. But the cost was too high. I almost lost Luke. And if I'd continued on the path I was on, I'm certain I would have lost you and Matthew too."

Mitch gently pulled her toward him. She snuggled under his chin, her soft curls pressed against his neck. He kissed her forehead and breathed a sigh.

"So when did everything change?"

"When it started to get really bad, I recalled bits and pieces of what I'd been taught in church while growing up." She turned her face up toward his and smiled. "See? Kids remember what their youth leaders teach them. Here I am fifteen years later and I still recall Pastor Jimmy's words. I'm certain your teens will remember things you taught them too." She grew quietly serious then. "I began to see how wrong Millicent was. I got rid of all the junk. This time I dumped everything. Then I went to the church to pray. If I wanted things to change, I needed to change first." She gazed lovingly into his eyes.

Mitch swallowed the lump in his throat.

"You know what else?" She said, her dark eyes swimming in tears.

"What else?"

"I sat in the pew where you said you'd seen a shadow. And I prayed. Hard. I reached out to God. I confessed my failures and asked Jesus to save me. Almost at once, the shadow rose in the air and left the church. Then the women came in. They prayed for us, Mitch, like our people back home would have done."

Tears rolled down Lydia's cheeks. Mitch brushed them away.

He shook his head in wonder. "I've been working day and night trying to find a way to get their attention. All my efforts failed. I felt helpless. But you, my little woman, through your humble act of repentance, it was you who saved our church." He chuckled over the irony. "Elijah and I had worked out a plan. We were going to beat this thing. Two men on a mission. But God used *you* to save Mercy Fellowship."

She shook her head and breathed a laugh. "I'd love to take the credit, Mitch, but John said you did it with your preaching and your perseverance. He said he couldn't believe you stayed when so many others gave up and left. Because of you several people made a profession of faith and many others recommitted their lives to Christ."

"The truth is, God did it all," Mitch murmured. "Maybe he used us a little to wake people up, but His plan prevailed in the end. He wasn't about to give up on a failing church, and he wasn't about to give up on us. If not for all the bad stuff, you might never have seen your need. You might have continued on the path you were on, never knowing the love and power of an Almighty God. And I would have kept you and the boys on the back burner while I attended to other, more important things, never realizing what is most important."

The following Sunday the atmosphere had changed in the little church. People crowded together in the pews, shoulder to shoulder, arm in arm. They even filled the third pew. There were no more shadows, no deathly auras. When Mitch stepped up to the pulpit the congregation faced him with anticipation written on their faces. The stony looks were gone. The blocks of ice had melted. People smiled back at him. When he spoke, their faces lit up with interest. They actually listened. Shouts of "Amen" and "Preach it, brother," went up throughout the congregation.

Elijah Garby had moved into the front row beside Lydia and the boys. When Mitch spoke, the old man smiled and nodded his approval. Their relationship had solidified over the last couple of weeks, and Elijah was already treating Mitch like his own son.

After the service, folks approached Mitch and told him how much they liked his message. Women stopped to chat with Lydia and offered to help her start a children's program. John invited Mitch's family for lunch. The other deacons gathered around him and asked if there was anything they could do to help his ministry. They talked about making repairs on the church building and the parsonage. Three men stepped up and offered to take turns mowing the lawn, and several ladies volunteered to spruce up the grounds with plants and flowers. A few of the young people wanted to start a worship team and a small band of instruments. Even Elijah Garby gave them his rarely offered thumbs up.

To Mitch, one of the most satisfying changes happened before the service even started. People milled about, chatting and shaking hands. Laughter echoed off the sanctuary walls. Children chased each other up and down the aisles. Teenagers gathered and planned a party for the following Saturday. Mitch scanned the auditorium with amazement, his heart throbbing with joy. The scene was reminiscent of the atmosphere at White Hills, but this time it was Mitch's church, and these people were his flock. An overwhelming sense of gratitude flowed through him and he mouthed a silent message of praise to God for making it all happen.

Though Mitch was thrilled by the way the church had come together, he reminded himself that he needed to put family first, and in doing so he knew he would be putting God first. The Bible was true. Only after he looked after his own home would he be fit to serve in the church. As Elijah Garby had predicted, God had preserved both areas of Mitch's life. His marriage had been restored. And he was the shepherd of a flock of willing sheep. His head reeled with visions of a growing congregation, midweek fellowship, festivals, and celebrations like those that once graced the grounds of Mercy Fellowship many decades ago. What's more, he hadn't forgotten that the church's sesquicentennial had come upon them.

At the end of the next Sunday's service, he announced his plan for a gathering on the church lawn on Thanksgiving Day. He urged the congregation to form committees to handle the food, the decorations, and the seating and table arrangements. Members responded with enthusiasm and took over the preparations with noticeable delight. He gladly let them.

When the big day arrived, members and their invited guests showed up on the church grounds for a potluck dinner, complete with a dozen turkeys, eight hams, and a vast assortment of side dishes, salads, and desserts. Mitch sat at the head of one of the tables and surveyed the gathering. His heart bursting with joy, he stood to his feet and hushed the conversations.

"I'd like to do something a little different on this occasion. Instead of me saying a long-winded grace and letting all the food get cold, I'm going to say a brief word of gratitude and let you start eating. During our meal, anyone who would like to express their thanks to the Lord can stand up and share."

That said, he turned his face toward the heavens. "Thank you, Father, for this amazing food and for all the fine people who prepared it."

He winked at Elijah who was sitting nearby. "Short and sweet, right?"

Elijah chuckled.

Mitch took his seat and grabbed a drumstick, then he scooped a glob of mashed potatoes onto his plate. As the bowls made their way around the table, he piled on more food. People responded to his request. They popped up here and there at different tables and called out their thanks to God for various needs He'd filled in their lives.

Then Elijah Garby struggled to his feet and spread his arms. "Thank you, Lord." The old man's voice quivered with emotion. "Thanks for bringing Mitch and his family to rescue our dying church. When things got tough, he didn't turn tail and run. And, Lord, thank you for Mercy Fellowship's

150 years, for the faithful few who started it, and for the hundreds and maybe thousands who will keep it going for years to come."

Acknowledgements

Books get published for multiple reasons beyond the work of the author. Just like it takes a village to raise a child, so also, the ultimate product depends on the support and encouragement of readers, proofers, artists, editors, and publishers.

I so appreciate everyone who had a part in bringing this book to completion, and especially my daughter Joanna, for her keen eye in spotting errors and also for creating a cover that captures the essence of the church described in this book.

Most of all I thank my editor/publisher, Mike Parker, of WordCrafts Press. After many struggles and many rejections over the years, I am so grateful someone was willing to take a chance on me. I once sat in a class Mike taught at a writers conference. He asked us the question, "Why do you write?" For me the answer is simple. I write because it's the only way I can connect with lots of people without leaving home. Whether near or far, I can reach them and entertain them and hopefully bless them.

And so, I am thankful for my readers who have remained loyal. And I want to encourage anyone who has an idea for a story to go ahead and write it. You never know what can happen.

God uses us in many ways, and He blesses us in many ways. I thank the Lord of hosts for his longsuffering kindness and for wielding power over the "demons" that trouble us from day to day. To Him be the glory!

Pulitzer Prize nominee in the field of journalism, Marian Rizzo has won numerous awards, including the New York Times Chairman's Award and first place in the 2014 Amy Foundation Writing Awards. She worked for the Ocala Star-Banner newspaper for 30 years. She also has written articles for *Ocala Style Magazine* and Billy Graham's *Decision Magazine*.

Several of Marian's novels have won awards at Florida Christian Writers conferences and Word Weavers retreats. In 2018, her manuscript for *Muldovah*, another suspense novel, was a finalist in the Genesis competition of American Christian Fiction Writers.

Marian earned a bachelor's degree in Bible education from Luther Rice Seminary. She trained for jungle missions with New Tribes (now ETHNOS 360), and she served for two semesters at a Youth With A Mission training center in Southern Spain.

Marian lives in Ocala, Florida, with her daughter, Vicki, who has Down Syndrome. Her other daughter, Joanna, has blessed her with three wonderful grandchildren.

also available from

WordCrafts Press

Stranger with a Black Case
  by Jennifer Odom

The Five Barred Gate
  by Jeff S. Bray

A Pale Horse
  by Michelle A. Sullivan

Ill Gotten Gain
  by Ralph E. Jarrells

The Mirror Lies
  by Sandy Brownlee

www.wordcrafts.net

www.ingramcontent.com/pod-product-compliance
Lightning Source LLC
Chambersburg PA
CBHW061306190726
48288CB00002B/379